REVENGE OF THE
LOBSTER LOVER

Hilary MacLeod

The Acorn Press
Charlottetown
2010

Revenge of the Lobster Lover © 2010 by Hilary MacLeod

P.O. Box 22024
Charlottetown, Prince Edward Island
C1A 9J2
acornpresscanada.com

Printed and Bound in Canada
Cover and interior design by Matt Reid
Editing by Sherie Hodds

The first line of Hy's dream on page 12 is from *The Rime of the Ancient Mariner* by Samuel Taylor Coleridge (1798).

Library and Archives Canada Cataloguing in Publication
  MacLeod, Hilary
  Revenge of the lobster lover / Hilary MacLeod.
  ISBN 978-1-894838-48-1

I. Title.
PS8625.L4555R48 2010   C813'.6   C2010-904871-7

Canada   Canada Council
for the Arts   Conseil des Arts
du Canada

The publisher acknowledges the support of the Government of Canada through the Canada Book Fund of the Department of Canadian Heritage and the Canada Council for the Arts Block Grant Program.

Mixed Sources

Cert no. SW-COC-001271
© 1996 FSC

FSC

To my daughter Kirsten, of course.
And to my parents Saxon and Bruce.

"The weather and love are the two elements about which one can never be sure."

—Alice Hoffman, *Here on Earth*

Prologue

Click, click, click.

A lobster claw was tapping on the dead man's teeth.

In a hand turned blue, the corpse gripped the handle of the lobster stunner that had killed him. The plastic inlay had melted into his flesh, creating a strange exoskeleton in the shape of a lobster claw, with the texture of a partly-skinned mushroom, speckled with decay. The rest of it—a long steel rod, like an oversized curling iron—lay on the ground, tossed aside by the powerful current that had coursed through him.

Executed. The implement was designed to kill the creatures in the pond humanely; instead, it had turned on him. He lay partially submerged in the water, an oversized ingredient in a surf and turf supper, eyes staring unseeing at the ceiling with a look of surprise—or shock. A burnt smell like overdone pork chops rose from his body.

One lobster had survived the electric jolt that had traveled through the man and the other crustaceans. She butted up against her dead pond mates, clambered up the rocks and, unable to see, felt her way onto the corpse's chest. Propelling slowly forward on eight of her ten legs, she delicately tasted as she went. With the other two, she began to claw at his eyes, as sightless as her own, antennae circling the air, smelling this potential new food source. Then her attention turned to his mouth, slack and petulant in death. There was something in there that interested her.

The *click, click, click* became a crunch. The creature had found what she was looking for—a morsel of salmon wedged and rotting under a porcelain dental crown.

Crack. The lobster's big claw, the crusher, broke the spike of decayed tooth holding the crown. With the smaller, the pincher, she threw it off.

Dinner was served.

Chapter One

Hawthorne Parker had paid a great deal to ensure his privacy at The Shores, but he hadn't planned on being quite this isolated. He had to fly in by helicopter because it was the only way. He wasn't going to take that ancient river ferry.

From the air, The Shores looked like a big tadpole that had been joined to the rest of The Island by the Campbell Causeway, about a kilometer long. On one end a large rupture had wiped out the only road that connected The Shores to The Island. It was red clay under a wash of blue water.

It had happened suddenly, in January. A storm surge had shoved tons of ice into the fragile strip of land and rammed it at its weakest point. Driven by a northeast gale, the sea ice had pushed the shore ice across the causeway, ripping it apart and piling up in massive white peaks. Then it had come to a stop. It had crushed and buried five houses, killed nine people, tossed cars into the water and pushed boats up onto what had once been the road.

It was over in thirteen-and-a-half minutes.

The Shores was cut off by land. The Campbell Causeway was flattened at one end. Where once the strip of land had risen above the water, it now dipped into it.

Tourist brochures called it "The Gentle Island," and except for the unsightly rupture in the causeway, it still was. Parker gazed with pleasure on the palette of blue and red and green below him. It had the pleasant quality of an old patchwork quilt. Threads of evergreen defined fields of red clay—some bursting with bright new green, others yellow with the dry stalks of last fall's harvest, not yet plowed in. Today the ever-changing blue water was navy in the cool April air.

The Shores was the communal name for three once-thriving fishing and farming communities, now a random collection of houses and farmland cascading down to the Gulf of St. Lawrence. The houses, mostly painted white cedar shingle, or clapboard with green and black roofs, radiated out from the village centre, dominated by a white community hall with a bright green metal roof. There was no church, no school, no store—not anymore. Smoke curled up from the chimneys, floating over the sleepy village of about two hundred people, just three roads, a handful of clay lanes and one of the most spectacular shorelines on an island famous for them.

Hawthorne Parker was a collector of fine things, and the prized piece of waterfront property in The Shores was his latest acquisition. He stroked his razor-thin mustache with his forefinger and felt the glow of pleasure he always felt when he acquired a new and beautiful thing. It helped loosen the knot of anxiety in his gut, if only briefly. He kept a scrupulous list itemizing treasures locked in storage across two continents—with the exception of one. His lover Guillaume was not on that list, though he'd been in storage too.

For Parker, the charm of The Shores lay in its solitude. He had prepared a stunning aerie on a cape, a place to start again after the night that had shattered their life together. He hoped being here would be healing. They might not find love again, but they could, perhaps, reconcile their differences.

The helicopter hovered over Vanishing Point, so called because it would disappear in a fog or because chunks of it kept falling off, no one could quite remember which. Parker was shocked by what he saw. The house was still there. The real estate agent had assured him of that, but had soft-pedaled the damage to the cape, saying only that there had been some "landscape adjustments."

The storm surge had carved a triangle around the house, so that it was sitting on a pie-shaped "v" pointing inland. The A-frame jutted into the sky at the wide end, close to the edge of the cape. So close that, from this angle, the deck appeared poised over the slim strip of shore and surf below.

Landscape adjustments! Parker should have known that the real estate agent was of dubious integrity when he had said, "Sean Connery lived here." Parker had looked at him in disbelief and the agent back-pedaled. "Well, he stayed here." After a silence: "Or so they say." Parker was neither convinced nor star-struck. He bought the house because he liked it, because he needed the mental space it would provide. Even as the helicopter began its descent, Parker's new acquisition was losing some of its charm. His knot of anxiety tightened around the feeling of emptiness deep within him.

No. It had nothing to do with Sean Connery.

Chapter Two

The wind whistled around the northeast corner of the house and the eavestrough rattled. The woman, all long legs kicking and red curls matted with sweat, tossed in her sleep. Her body was buzzing with an electric energy, her mind frozen on the image of her infant self, bobbing on the water of a remote lake.

Alone. Alone. All all alone. Alone on a wide, wide sea.

Then, suddenly, no longer alone. Pulsing. Life. Lights. Flashing. The noise of a siren pierced the silence—high, ear-splitting, causing her child voice to burst out in short startled wails, become shrill, rise to the pitch of the siren, until the two intertwined in one long keening cry that rang out on the wind.

Her cry. Here in this room, not out on some long-forgotten lake. Here, with the wind whipping around the house, Hy McAllister jolted awake, the vibration of the scream on her lips, so that she knew she had actually screamed herself out of the nightmare. Adrenalin coursed through her blood. She was unable to move, afraid to open her eyes.

The old night terror had come ripping through her, ending, as always, with the scream and waking, sweating but frozen with fear. Fear formed from fragments of memory lodged in her infant brain, where they lurked and seeped poison. The nightmare always found her in a wind storm, or after too much wine and too little sleep. Steady, disciplined living wasn't something she was good at.

The room hummed around her, and she felt the dream pulling her down again. She struggled against it. Her blood tingled, the room hummed, the wind took up the sound like a refrain. A gust slammed into the north wall, and she felt the house shift, accommodating its force. The room swayed and changed shape, moved off its centre, sent vibrations singing through her, tendrils grasping and taking her down, back down into the dream.

No. She forced herself up, like a drowning person coming out of the water into the air in one great motion. Gasping. She pried open her eyes and the terror came unstuck. The buzzing ebbed to a low hum. *Free again.*

She propped herself up and looked around.

Reality slipped sideways.

The door wasn't where it should be.

There wasn't a door.

She felt dizzy. *Am I still in the nightmare?* Then she realized she wasn't in her bedroom. She'd fallen asleep on the couch. *Time? What time was it?* Her clock was flashing twelve. *Damn. The bloody wind has caused another power glitch.*

She ran a hand through unruly curls, untangled long, skinny legs all wound up in a duvet and sat up, shaking and cold. She dragged the comforter around her. There was a half-empty glass of red wine on the coffee table, an old wood steamer trunk. On it, curiously modern, a laptop was pulsing like a heartbeat, its green light glowing against the wall. She reached over and hit the space bar. The screen lit up.

The Lobster Lover's Blog

Lobsters must be great lovers. They have two penises.

Scientists view them as two sperm delivery appendages. What else is a penis?

Odd. She'd never clicked on this site. She'd been working on the Super Saver newsletter, promising ten ways to cook lobster in time for Setting Day, when North Shore fishermen set their traps for the season. She remembered why she'd stopped writing last night after a half bottle of wine. She didn't know ten ways to cook lobster. Not even one.

On the lobster love scene no one asks: your place or mine? It's always his. He doesn't go sand bar hopping to find a willing female. She comes to him. He doesn't have to be rich or handsome. Handsome? A lobster?

If she's really ready—there's no polite way to put this—she pees in his face. It's their version of foreplay. After the golden shower, she disrobes, sheds her hard shell, and becomes as vulnerable as any woman standing naked before a man—perhaps more so.

Will he lay her—or eat her? That is the question. Fortunately for the survival of the species and the lobster industry, he usually decides to jump her. He clutches her around the waist, flips her over and takes her in the missionary position, their beady little eyes staring unseeing at each other. Call it a blind date.

He's a surprisingly tender lover. Hard shell, soft heart? She has a hard heart and pro-choice attitude. She stores his sperm and takes off with it. He never gets to know his children but nature has a way of making sure he doesn't screw them too. He may eat them but he won't bonk them.

This is no joke. Experts in the field, or rather the oceans, have studied the sex life of lobsters extensively. We know almost as much about why and how lobsters do it as we do about human sex.

Why the interest in lobster copulation? It's all about population.

The more there are, the more we can eat.

Can you live with that?

They can't.

The blog popped off the screen just as Hy finished reading. Her computer shut down. She rebooted and keyed in Lobster Lover's Blog. No response. She tried again. *Nothing.*

Where did the blog come from? Where did it go?

She couldn't sleep now. Her agenda lay open beside the laptop, the entries slanted upward, underlined, mocking her in a variety of highlighter colours, peppered with exclamation marks. She had three tasks.

Lobster Supper Invites was in black, underlined once in red; *Institute Speaker* in green, underlined twice, one exclamation mark; *Lobster—Super Saver* in red, underlined three times with two exclamation points.

The Super Saver was The Island's only local grocery chain and Hy's regular client. She ran a home-based company, writing and editing material for websites. She called it, in a play on words, Content. She was content, except about the lobster recipes she'd promised to produce. She didn't have any yet, but emailed the Super Saver PR department that the newsletter was nearly ready to pressure herself into meeting the deadline. Almost instantly, the right hand column of her screen filled with links to keywords in the email. Sites advertising jelly and jam recipes, North Shore cottage rentals, the David Letterman show, and labour organizations holding May Day celebrations.

Hy scanned the list.

Lobster Lover? Catch us first.

The blog again? She clicked on the site.

Cooking lobster? Let our expert speakers fill you in.

No. Not the blog. Better.

She selected: *Find Out More.*

Hy liked what she saw. A well-laid-out website, offering guest speakers free to non-profit groups. That certainly described the Women's Institute at The Shores. As always, any money they made from next month's lobster supper would go toward maintaining the Hall. The W.I. had a guest lecturer every month and it was Hy's turn to book one. The last time she'd chosen the topic: "Friday the Thirteenth—Lucky for Women"—it hadn't been lucky for her. The guest she'd invited had been a disaster, talking about menstruation as a sacred act. There'd been strange looks and awkward silences from the village women ever since. She had to redeem herself.

She clicked on Contact Us, logged a request for a speaker, stood up, stretched and looked out the window. There was a thin streak of orange dawn over the water. The fields, the trees, the houses were black outlines on the sky. There was one light outside the house on Vanishing Point. *The new guy.* His recent arrival by helicopter had all the villagers talking about who he was and why he'd come. No one had seen him yet—except Harold MacLean and he didn't count.

Hy gazed across the fields and down the stretch of lonely road. Three dark and vacant farmhouses stood between her and her nearest neighbour, Jared MacPherson. His house was all lit up like a Christmas tree, as her old friend Gus would say.

Jared was out of jail—again. Last year he'd spent six months at the provincial jail, Sleepy Hollow, for selling illegal cigarettes and liquor from his cookhouse on the shore. This time, the offense had been worse—much worse. But he'd served only two weeks.

Hy smiled, thinking of what Gus would say now:

Murderer.

Chapter Three

Parker made immediate inquiries about moving his house back from the precipice. He was told nothing could be done until the causeway reopened. No contractor would promise it even then. The shape of the land wouldn't allow them to bring in equipment big enough to haul the house.

Only one man seemed willing to do it, and he was suspect at best.

"You won't have to pack away one piece of china, we're that careful." Dwayne "Goody" Gaudet rubbed his snotty nose with a beefy hand, scratched his crotch, and cleaned the hand on his trousers. Parker's face wrinkled in distaste. He was neat, slim and compact, always impeccably groomed and dressed. Today he was wearing light wool slacks and a v-neck cashmere sweater in the same soft neutrals he preferred in his decor.

"We'll just lift 'er up, shift 'er over and put 'er down." Dwayne grinned. A front tooth was missing, others were various shades of yellow, brown and black decay. The effort of speaking seemed to leave him out of breath.

Parker smirked. The man obviously had no idea of the value of his treasures. He would be quite prepared to pack them all away when and if he moved the house. He thanked Goody, declined to shake his hand and went back inside.

He gazed with satisfaction at the Great Room of the A-frame with his ancient treasures artfully displayed. He stroked the black balsam body of an Egyptian statue—Anubis, the jackal. His hand caressed the exquisite porcelain of a Ming dynasty cat, hand-painted with gold leaf, made, as the markings on the back attested, for the Imperial Court. *Not that peasant blue and white stuff that's so popular and ubiquitous—cheap but Ming. It was genuine enough, but not the real thing.* His eye rested with pride on the rare Mayan fertility figurines in the glass shelving.

The decorator had done exactly as instructed, with a few minor exceptions. An *objet* placed just so, a quarter-inch turn to catch the light in such a way, and the total effect was—

He inspected the room through cool grey eyes. He stroked his mustache.

The total effect was perfection.

There was just one jarring note—a square painting of a red blob dominated the rear wall of the Great Room. The artist was perhaps the only person Parker had ever loved who'd loved him back—his grandmother. Even that hadn't lasted.

He sat down on the soft kid leather couch, facing the cathedral windows, cleverly fitted into the A-frame design. They were from an island church forced to close when its congregation dwindled to twenty-four people. The ocean and the shore were framed by the big windows, a work of art no human hand could imitate.

But like all new homeowners, Parker had begun to see flaws. At the peak of the A-frame, where the joints should meet, they didn't quite. It nagged at him, but he tried not to think about it. There was a more immediate concern.

The kitchen—dismally small. Hopelessly inadequate.

What would Guillaume think?

His self-satisfaction melted. *Guillaume will hate it.*

Parker stood up and stared out. Directly in front was the water, steel grey under a gloomy sky. To the east, the sea rock sat solidly just offshore, a hunk of the cape separated from the rest by the action of the waves and the weather. The rock grew smaller every year.

He looked at the strip of reddish sand and the dunes, thick with marram grass. Behind the dunes lay a pond, like The Shores in the shape of a tadpole, fat at the top, where tall grasses and bulrushes embraced it. A muskrat lived under the bridge that crossed "the run," the tadpole's tail. It threaded down to the shore and carved a comma across the beach, spilling fresh water into the salty Gulf.

Tucked in beside the pond was a pine cottage. On the other side was an old, grey cedar shingle building slumped into a high dune.

It came to him in an instant.

He threw on a jacket, and went down to the shore, lifting his collar against the raw April wind. The building was old, the roof and shingles worn. It had settled comfortably into its foundation but looked structurally sound.

He walked around it. *An old cookhouse.*

The idea delighted him: it would be old outside, ultra modern inside.

Perfect symmetry.

He wondered who owned it.

A high screech pierced the night like the cry of a giant blue jay. It woke Hy from a sound sleep—the first she'd had in days. It was only the wind tugging on the clothesline, a bad musician joining the chorus of the storm.

She turned over, clenched her eyes closed, and tried, furiously, to go back to sleep. The old house creaked in new places. Something—*what?*—was going *tac, tac, tac* against the roof. Gusts of wind hit the house and made the walls tremble. It pissed her off. She threw back the covers, got up and stumbled downstairs.

The phone rang. It was well after midnight. *Who the..?*

"Hi Dorothy."

Ian. She could see his lights on Shipwreck Hill.

"The wind getting to you?"

She gritted her teeth as another blast shook the house.

"I hate it."

"Well, Dorothy, you're not going to blow away."

She hated it when he called her Dorothy too. He'd phoned to tease her. He'd been doing more of that since last summer, when she was seeing that wildlife biologist, Stephen Wildman. They had an enjoyable August fling. Ian had sometimes gone silent when Stephen's name came up. Once, she'd caught him staring at Stephen with a cold, unhappy look on his face. He'd been his most friendly—grinning, laughing, shaking hands—when Stephen left at the end of the summer.

Sometimes she thought that Ian had been jealous. Though she wasn't sure if it was her relationship with Stephen that bothered him or just the man himself. Stephen was a research scientist with a full head of hair, Ian a balding former high school teacher with a passion for scientific toys. Maybe he just didn't like having someone smarter than him around. Maybe he didn't like someone taking up so much of her time. Maybe she'd imagined it all. When Ian had teased her about Stephen—there had been lots of references to "wild life," "wild man" and biology of various kinds—it had seemed good-natured, part of an easy friendship they'd had for years.

"I've been up on the walk." The widow's walk was an ornate Victorian structure on the peak of Ian's house. It gave him a panoramic view of the village, the Gulf waters and the long stretch of coast—west to the mouth of Big Bay and east beyond Vanishing Point.

The walk's boards were worn by the pacing of worried wives, mothers, fathers and children. If a boat was late or lost at sea, it had been to this house that the villagers had traditionally come to peer out and pray, as if prayers would bring their loved ones back. Sometimes they did. The footprints and the fears had marked the house with a sombre history of lives lived, communal heritage, and a spiritual essence that Ian, an agnostic and a scientist, nonetheless could appreciate. It's why he bought the place. Hy thought it was his saving grace.

"It was glorious," he said. "The lightning was so bright I swear I saw as far as Charlottetown—and the thunder was straight from Thor's hammer."

Fine for him. He wasn't in the path of the wind as she was, with nothing between her and the ocean, where it found its fury. The house shuddered—and she along with it.

"Listen." She held the phone up to the ceiling. It sounded as if the roof were being pried off.

"That house has stood there for a hundred years. It's not going anywhere tonight." That's what he always said.

"Don't mock the gods." That's what she always said.

"What gods?"

"You brought them up. Thor's hammer?"

Ian laughed. "The gods don't have a damn thing to do with it."

"I don't believe in the gods any more than you do." The Furies, she thought, maybe the Furies. "I do believe anything could happen."

"Well, it's not going to. The wind is a simple force of nature. This wind doesn't have the force to do anything but scare you."

"It scares me that it doesn't take sides. It could blow Mother Teresa away and not think twice."

"The wind doesn't think. You're not Mother Theresa. Neither is she anymore," he said. "So I wouldn't worry."

He was so smug, so sure. What she really wanted was for him to come over and keep her company. *At least offer.*

She rang off and went back to bed. Her sleep was punctuated by the compost cart banging against the oil tank. The tarpaulin covering the woodpile had worked free and was slapping the back window. The wind pulled at the clothesline as it tore around the northeast corner of the house, sending the giant blue jay into a frenzy of shrill screaming.

Chapter Four

Parker had soon found out who owned the building he wanted. He'd left his card in Jared MacPherson's mailbox. It had no door, and yawned up at the sky from a crooked stub of tree trunk. When Jared retrieved the card it was soaking wet. It read:

Hawthorne Parker
Aesthete

Jared read "aesthete" as "athlete." He flipped the card over. On the back, in elegant handwriting, with a real fountain pen, streaked and smudged, it read: *Come any morning after ten. The A-frame on the cape. Hawthorne Parker.* The signature was a nest of scribbles.

The rich guy who bought The A. Jared had always wanted to see the inside of that house, but he didn't go that day—he was out of beer and went to town.

He didn't go the next day. He was too hung-over after a get-together with some buddies from Winterside, the main town on this end of The Island, so-called because it was where summer people went to spend their winters. It was where people like Jared went to find booze, drugs and women.

On the third day, Parker watched from the loft as Jared's twenty-year-old black Ford truck rattled its way along the Shore Lane, down Wild Rose Lane and into the private driveway, where it leaked oil. Parker met Jared on the deck.

"Welcome," he said. His eyes blinked shut and stayed shut just a beat too long.

Jared grunted.

Parker motioned him to take a seat. The day had come as a gift in April, deceiving people into thinking that perhaps spring had arrived. The sun kissed the skin and warmed the bones, the sky burned brilliant blue around fat white marshmallow clouds and, down at the shore, lazy waves lapped up against the sand. From where he sat, Parker had a clear view of the old cookhouse, his next acquisition. Jared was staring at the v-shape around the house, carved out of the cape. It hadn't been like that when he was here last. That was in November. He had come up to see if he could find some liquor, but the house was locked up tight and he found no way in.

"The building on the shore—" Parker gestured towards it. "That's yours?"

Jared grunted. It seemed to be his entire vocabulary. He was chewing on a dirty thumbnail.

Parker averted his eyes. "You're not using it?"

"Nope," said Jared, tossing his long greasy hair. He reached into his shirt pocket for a pack of cigarettes. He pulled out a smoke.

"I'd rather you didn't."

Jeez, thought Jared, *we're outside, for God's sake.* He pulled a lighter from his jeans pocket, stuck the cigarette in his mouth and lit it. He took a long haul, blew the smoke not quite into Parker's face, and said:

"Oi'd rather oi did,"

Parker winced at the distorted sound.

"Do you have plans to use it, or would it be available for rental?"

"Moight be."

Again the ugly vowel. "Might be?"

"At the roight proice."

This boy's speech was painful. "The right price—" Parker took care to enunciate particularly clearly, as if Jared might catch on. "Say, a thousand dollars?"

"Wha, just a thousand? Like, on a regular basis?"

"On a regular basis, of course."

"A thousand a month?"

"A week."

"A week?"

"A week. I believe that's not an uncommon amount to pay for a shorefront property."

But not for this property.

"Yeah, roight. Not uncommon." Except those places were usually furnished and all decked out with the stuff the tourists expected: propane BBQ's on fancy decks, satellite TV, internet hook-up and sometimes pools. Maybe he could put that rent money toward sprucing the place up when this guy was through renting it. Finish the insides, put in a Jacuzzi. The idea died as quickly as it was born. Just thinking about it tired him. *Let this guy rent it for a thousand if he wanted.* It was a lot to pay for what it was, but what did he care?

Parker knew it was pricey but he wanted to be sure to secure the property, now that he'd set his mind on it.

"I will want a few modifications."

"Now wait a minute. I ain't gonna spring for that."

"Of course, I'll pay for everything."

"And the rent—cash money?"

"Of course. A gentleman's agreement." Parker gave a critical look at what sat opposite him—dirty black T-shirt and jeans; long, greasy unkempt hair that he kept flipping back; filthy fingernails; nicotine stains on his fingers; socks and sneakers stained with red clay. Parker was glad he had not let Jared in the house. He was thinking about his cork floors.

"I'll pay you a month in advance."

Parker pulled a brown envelope out of his inside jacket pocket—Armani.

Jared had never seen a thousand dollar bill before. They didn't even make them anymore. Parker counted out four of them. Jared stuffed the money in his shirt pocket before Parker could change his mind. He was going to go home, clean up and head into Winterside to look at that Hummer he'd seen at Eustace's New to You car lot. Eustace was a cousin who would accept promises with the down payment and could be persuaded to register it in Jared's dead father's name until he got his license back. Then he'd grab that little blonde bitch at The Lazy Eh for a night of fun. After two weeks in jail, he could use a good hump.

Parker put the envelope back in his jacket.

"You will allow me to renovate as I wish?"

Jared grunted.

Chapter Five

Gus Mack had counted five trips by three different kitchen appliance trucks this morning alone—names she didn't know. They'd been coming and going all week. The week before that it had been plumbers and carpenters and painters, none of them from here. No way to find out what was going on at the shore.

The southeast wind was howling and rain spitting on the picture window that looked out on the village crossroads. Gus was in her purple chair right next to it. For sixty years, she'd seen everything that went by that window. The most dramatic had been when her husband, Abel, came flying out of the General Store, propelled by the explosion of a propane tank. A pop machine had cleared the shop window out of the way for him. He landed, if not exactly on his feet, unharmed, smack in front of the building, or what was left of it. Abel never rebuilt. Gone was the place where the men would sit around the woodstove, smoking and engaging in manly talk—usually about the weather. It was always too dry, too wet, too hot or too cold for whatever needed doing in the fields or on the shore on any given day.

Like the Macks', all the village houses had big windows aimed at the road. People liked to see what was going on. Summer residents preferred to look at the sea. The communities lived side-by-side but back-to-back, close geographically but far apart socially—except when it came to gossip.

"What's his name?" Gus called out to Abel, when she heard him shuffle through the laundry room. No answer.

"That fella who came the first of Aprile." Gus said "April," with a long "i" sound, straight out of Chaucer. Undaunted by the lack of response, she continued: "Is it Harper? Carter?" The sound of an electric drill didn't stop her. *He must be fixing the back door. Now, what was the name?*

"Parker," she called out, suddenly remembering. The drilling stopped. The back door slammed shut. *Fixed.*

Parker, but not the Big Bay Parkers. No. This one is definitely from away. You can tell from all those trucks heading down the Shore Lane as if gas were water, thought Gus. *The new fella at The A must be made of money.* The A was what the locals called Parker's house on the point. All the village houses had names; they often stuck well past their due dates. Hy's house was still called Harper's twenty years after he had lived there. It would only become McAllister's after she was gone.

Gus shifted in the rocker-recliner. It had too much stuffing in it. That made it look comfortable, but it wasn't. "But I'm keepin' it," she announced frequently. "I'll sit in this chair 'til it kills me. They'll have to carry me out in it."

Gus picked up her quilt block—a pink lobster on a blue background. She wasn't very interested in it. She was much more interested in what she saw next out her window. Jared MacPherson in a brand new truck. *Where'd he get that—and him just out of jail?*

Hy had hardly been out of the house all month. She had walked or cycled almost everywhere since the storm surge to conserve gas. She was terrified of the ferry, so it had become a challenge to see how long she could go on the tank of gas she'd bought a month ago. It was still nearly full. Her freezer and preserve shelves were well-stocked. She grew her own vegetables and the milk truck still delivered locally. She'd been getting Ian to pick up essentials on his frequent trips to town. It had become a running joke in the community that she'd still have the same tank of gas at

Christmas. She thought she just might make it to Fall.

It felt like Fall already—like a cold and dismal day in November, with the worst kind of wind—a nor'easter. Every living thing was bent at a nearly forty-five-degree angle, except the strongest trees. Even they grew permanently in the direction the wind blew them, leaning inland and lopsided—showing foliage to the fields and roads, but their backsides to the ocean burned by the wind and bare of branches.

Hy's love of The Shores had survived twenty years of harsh coastal weather. Her romantic notions about living by the ocean had been blown away with the barbecue covers, the clothing, the roof shingles and gutters that had been ripped from the house and flung across the fields. Still, it felt like the only home she'd ever had. Her grandmother had been kind, but resented bringing up a child alone at her age. She'd provided a home, but it had never felt like one to Hy. She didn't have a home. Even here, after twenty years, the villagers still considered Hy from away. Only Gus and Annabelle embraced her wholeheartedly.

"It's blowin' a gale," said Gus now. The sky was grim, nightfall had come early, and Gus had phoned to see if Hy had power. The lights had been flickering off and on for two hours. They were back on now and Hy was watching the wind work away at a birdhouse nailed less than securely to a post.

Gus had also phoned to report her sighting of Jared. "I seen him in a fancy rig. Bran' new truck," she said. "Headin' down to the shore."

"His house has been lit up every night," Hy volunteered, knowing what Gus would say next:

"My land, what's *he* scared of an' him a murderer an' all?"

"Well, it wasn't exactly murder…"

A roof shingle blew past the front window.

"What do you call it then?" demanded Gus. "He'd been drinkin' and smokin' drugs before he got in his truck and hit that ol' lady just crossin' the road to get her mail."

The old woman had died. In spite of his state of intoxication, and the fact that he was driving fast and his brakes weren't good, Jared had gotten off easy. The woman had been wearing dark clothing at night. A reconstruction expert examined the site and concluded that with the curve in the road and the ice on the asphalt, even a sober driver with good brakes would have hit her. It was never proved that Jared had been drinking, because the cops didn't get to The Shores until the next day. So Jared was charged with reckless driving, but not drinking and driving and not manslaughter. He should never have argued in court that the victim was on her last legs anyway. That did not go down well with the sixty-three-year-old female judge. She had doubled his sentence—from eight to sixteen days. Jared had whined that he never got any breaks.

"Murder is murder, I say," Gus concluded. "And it's not the only one he done."

The birdhouse snapped off the post and smashed to the ground. Hy felt physical anger rise in her, but she managed a weak laugh.

"What do you mean?"

"He kilt his poor old mother."

"She died of liquor and cigarettes."

"Just what I say." Gus sounded smug. "An' him runnin' to town for them. The same with his father. He kilt him too."

"How?"

"Who was bringin' Albert cigarettes when he was on the oxygen and din't have the strenth to light a match by hisself?"

"Well, we don't call that murder. I'd say it's more like euthanasia."

"And there he is now, sittin' pretty, livin' the life of Riley…drivin' that bran' new truck…spendin' the money come from his father workin' hard all his life—"

"That's not what you said about Albert when he was alive."

Gus chuckled. "Well, no, but we can't speak ill of the dead, can we?"

"Anyway, what truck? What kind of truck?" Useless to ask, of course.

"Big yella one. Bran' new."

"Where'd he get the money?"

"Oh, I expect ol' Albert had a bit salted away."

Hy doubted it. Everyone thought everyone around here had a bit salted away.

Some of them did. She was one of them herself. That was old history. She'd always had a nest egg.

"Somethin's going on down at the shore," said Gus. "Trucks comin' and goin'. Plumbers, carpenters, you name it. I thought it was the new fella, but Abel says there's work going on at Jared's cookhouse. Where's he gettin' the money for that?"

"I thought you said Albert had some salted away."

Gus could change her tune as rapidly as an Atlantic wind could change direction.

"I smell a rat," she said knowingly.

Hy had also seen the trucks going up and down the lane to the old cookhouse. Everyone had. They all wondered what was going on.

"I'll go see what I can find out. Soon as this wind dies down."

Out of the corner of her eye, she could see the edge of the tarpaulin that covered the woodpile, ragged and threadbare, long bits of plastic fabric twisted and whipping in the wind. Some of it caught and tugged at the clothesline, calling out its blue jay screech. Hy tried to check her temper. *Futile.*

"Now you be careful. He's a murderer an' all." Gus never tired of saying that. If reckless lack of concern for the life of other humans was the mark of a murderer, then she was right, in her way, Hy thought. Jared should at least have gone down for manslaughter. He always seemed to get the breaks.

"I will. I'll take Ian with me."

Gus smiled. She liked to know what was going on—not just outside her window, but all over the village. She couldn't go snooping herself anymore. Having Hy and Ian as her eyes and legs was the next best thing.

Chapter Six

Ian Simmons was waiting for the first ferry of the day, anxious to cross and pick up his brand new iMac. He was leaning up against his Honda Insight—a two-seater, five-speed manual, designed to appeal to people with an environmental conscience and a bit of money. He had bought the hybrid four years ago and he was smugly self-satisfied when gas prices took off and the effects of the storm surge had made it hard to get. Now, so were parts for the car. The model had been pulled off the market within two years. It was a manual. It was ugly. The parts were too damn expensive—as Ian was finding out to his regret.

The ferry had been running for just a few weeks. The government had put it into service as the cheapest and quickest way to re-establish a link between The Shores and the rest of The Island after the ice ride-up had destroyed the causeway. It was an old river ferry, borrowed from a neighbouring province. If work on the road continued this slowly, Ian thought, the boat might be a permanent fixture.

In the two months since the storm surge, the province had poured in tons of rock to shore up the causeway, but hadn't begun building the roadbed yet. The spring had been the wettest on record. Ian was keeping track of the rainfall total. Eyes glazed over at social occasions when he warmed to his favourite theme—climate change.

"Haven't got very far, have they?" Big Ben Mack, Abel's much younger brother, had just pulled up. Ben was a fisherman and had a load of lobster traps stacked onto his ten-year-old Dodge

Ram pickup.

Ian pointed at them. "Aren't you going in the wrong direction?" Big Bay Harbour was on this side of the causeway.

"Naw. A bunch of us are givin' some traps to Hal Dooley over the road," said Ben, thrusting his chin in the direction of the far shore. "Lost his shed and all his traps in the ice." He said it the way all the locals did: "oice." He got out of his truck. Ben was a big man with black hair and a full beard. Not fat, just big—bigger than anyone else. People were always calling him to help them move their appliances. He could pick up a dishwasher and put it down as if it were a twenty-pound bag of potatoes. Some of that strength was behind his next statement:

"It'll never make a good job."

They stood in silent agreement, Ben and Ian, staring at the causeway as the sun rose up over it.

The Islanders had Ben to thank for the ferry. Normally as easygoing as he was big, he surprised everyone with his angry resistance when the province threatened to evacuate The Shores permanently. The government said it couldn't build a bridge for so few people and that fixing the causeway would be only a bandage solution. Moving a few hundred people made a lot more sense.

Not to Ben Mack. His family had been at The Shores for over two hundred years —ever since a sinking ship had dumped a fifteen-year-old stowaway into Big Bay. Ebenezer Mack had survived the winter with the help of the Mi'kmaq. He had cleared land in the spring, sowed seed, and before long began sowing the other kind. There were now so many Macks on The Island, his descendants often said proudly, "He made a good job of it." Ebenezer's spirit had slumbered inside Ben, until the province's threat had woken it up. His family wasn't going anywhere.

He'd mounted a massive protest by land and by sea. The strong March winds had cleared the ice from the Gulf early. He and the other fishermen had put their boats in the water and set sail for the provincial capital. The rest of the villagers followed on land, joined by sons and daughters, uncles and aunts, cousins, grand-children and great grandchildren from all over The Island. They had marched as one big family on Province House. The flotilla of lobster boats anchored in reproach in the harbour and a crowd of more than a thousand people had gathered outside the govern-ment buildings. The most remarkable were the oldest resident of The Shores, 104-year-old Agnes Cousins in her wheelchair, and beside her in a stroller, her great-great-great granddaughter Maisie, just two days old. Talk about photo opportunities.

The protestors' rallying cry may not have come from Madison Avenue, but it came straight from The Island's heart. "Save our shores! Save *The* Shores!" They chanted it like a mantra for two days in a row in the pouring rain. The powerful television images went national and became an embarrassment, especially the old lady and the newborn. The province caved in. It established ferry service as "a temporary measure" and agreed to fix the causeway and the road. It might have happened even without the protest. One of the province's four official scenic routes, The Island Way, was also in the Premier's riding. That alone should have guaran-teed the road would be fixed.

But the rupture would never be fully repaired.

"Goin' over to the mainland, wha'?" Harold MacLean ambled over with a wide grin at his own remark. Ian smiled back. Refer-ring to the rest of The Island as "the mainland" had begun as a joke when the causeway first washed out. The idea wasn't entirely new. There had always been a feeling of distinctness here. Even its geology, thought Ian, was slightly out of whack.

The three men ambled onto the ferry dock where Nathan Mack, Ben's son, ran a mobile canteen. Nathan was just shy of twenty, impossibly tall and thin with a buzz cut, dancing blue eyes and an infectious grin. He had reason to smile; he was the owner of three thriving businesses created since the ferry service started: the canteen, a grocery pick-up and delivery service and a taxi that ran to and from the ferry. He employed several of his cousins and even one of his uncles. He also gave back to the community. Trained as a paramedic, he had mounted a campaign of his own—for donations of used equipment to put together a rudimentary ambulance for the isolated area. It was just his old van equipped with an oxygen tank, a battered old ECG machine and a dented defibrillator, among other things. He had bought a new eight-passenger van for the taxi service.

"No calls this morning?" Ben stirred four sugars into his coffee.

"Got Gladys Fraser at 7:30. Jason'll pick her up. Off to Winterside to have her corns removed."

It was more than any of them wanted to know about Gladys Fraser, President of the Women's Institute and a bulldog of a woman.

"So Harold," said Ian, quickly changing the subject, "what's up with you?"

"Bin workin' for that new fella," he took a short breath in. "Hyup."

"Parker?" asked Ian, with sudden interest. Hawthorne Parker had hardly been seen in the weeks since he'd arrived. Ian didn't know anyone who'd met him. It didn't seem fair that it should be Harold, out of whom you had to squeeze information like the last drop of toothpaste out of a tube. Harold nodded and looked over at the causeway.

"'Spect they'll get it fixed if the weather ever turns. Don't look like it, though." He pointed a finger in the direction of a bank of clouds on the horizon. Ian always marveled at Harold's hands. Not one finger was the same. Each looked like it belonged to a different person. Yet Harold was a skilled carpenter, in spite of his hands and the fact that he couldn't add or subtract. He had sharp

eyes under an unruly mop of greying hair that made him look a
bit like Einstein, which he was not. He *was* a genius with wood.
His work was always beautiful, level and square. His weather
forecasts were not nearly as accurate—except for this spring.
This spring, when Harold had called for rain, it came. But he was
wrong today.

"Them's rain clouds." Pointing with certainty at Ian, he said,
"Don't think they not." The clouds were soft, white, fluffy, appearing not to have a drop of moisture in them. "Rain before noon,
I should say." The sunrise creeping over the water promised a
glorious spring day. Cool now though, thought Ian, passing a
hand over his thinning hair. He should have worn a hat.

"What are you doing for Parker? What's the place like?" Immediately Ian regretted firing off two questions at once. He'd be lucky
if Harold answered one.

"Nice place," said Harold.

"So what *are* you doing for him?" Ian persisted.

"This 'n' that," he said. "Up the house. Shelves 'n' such. Some
other fellas are workin' on Albert's old buildin'—say it's gonna be
goomay."

"Goomay?" Ian shook his head, puzzled. The ferry was reaching
the landing and his thoughts flew back to the iMac, soon to be his.

It was just a small cable ferry with no official name, but the
locals had been calling it Big Ben. It was a cheeky tribute to both
Ben and the boat—he so large and the ferry so small. It could only
take eight cars at a time.

All six waiting vehicles drove onto the boat. People traveling
later in the day wouldn't be so lucky. If they couldn't get on
because there were too many cars, it would be a half-hour wait
as the valiant little vessel chugged back and forth from six to
midnight, free of charge, a crucial link in the provincial highway.

When they got to the other side, it was a half-hour drive into
town. Ian was still going to arrive well before the stores opened.

As he felt the jolt of the ferry starting off from shore, it suddenly hit him.

Gourmet. Harold meant gourmet.

For Ian, gourmet meant that someone else had cooked it.

Fueled by determination and greased by money, the cookhouse had been transformed in just a few weeks. Now it was complete, and Parker stroked his mustache in satisfaction.

"A miracle," he pronounced it.

Vincent Caron, the designer who was making off with the bulk of the project money, agreed. *It was a miracle. That kind of money spent on this kind of thing. It was all the best that money could buy, or almost.* Of course, he'd trimmed a few corners—skimped on the electric, for one. The stove, fridges and freezer were all propane anyway, so he hadn't updated the electrical. He hadn't fiddled with a thing—except the bill. *The wiring was fully fifty years old and dicky at best, but what did a few small appliances and some lights require? The money's much better off in my pocket.*

It was the strangest job he'd ever done. *A beautiful kitchen, mind, but that business in the back, weird. There's no telling with rich people.* He just bowed and scraped and did as asked, with his thin smile, veneered teeth and face like a ferret.

He thought Parker was throwing away his money and he was just glad he'd been there to catch it. A man of his quality would never be content with living in this backwater long enough to justify such a kitchen—*crazy.* Vincent prided himself on being from the big city—Halifax. He also prided himself on being an astute businessman, who beat as quick a retreat as he could on his bowed legs to the new green Jeep Cherokee Parker's money had helped pay for. It was actually maroon, but Vincent was colour-blind. As a result, his kitchen designs were all black and white with shades of grey. It had earned him a comfortable niche in the high-end kitchen market. It was his trademark, this lack of colour, considered a dash of style rather than an inability to identify colours correctly. What Vincent lacked in colour palette he made up for in spatial aptitude. His appliance and cupboard choice, placement and installation were impeccable. Parker was pleased with the black and white decor.

He wished his life were as well-defined.

On the outside, the cookhouse still looked much the same—a long grey cedar shingle building of a certain vintage in reasonably good shape. Inside—well, Parker could hardly wait for Guillaume to see it.

Chapter Seven

Everyone was waiting for Spring. Everyone was complaining—as they did every year—that it was slow in coming. Memories were short in the village. Each year, people imagined that it would be sunny and warm in April and May, but it rarely was. This was a particularly slow and reluctant spring. There hadn't been so much as a scratch on the land, as Gus put it.

Too wet and too windy. It had been blowing all month long with rain most days. A few dawned fine and clear, and this was one of them, without even the breath of a breeze. Only the strong surf crashing up on the shore hinted at yesterday's brutal nor'wester. The computer hummed and the screen lit up: Hy had an email. It was sparsely worded—like a telegram.

Will be there for date and time requested. Happy to inform WI re: lobsters. Need only slide projector and screen.

It was signed *Camilla Samson.*

Hy wrote the name beside her W.I. agenda entry. *Camilla Samson.* She imagined what a woman with a name like that would look like. *Prim and poised. She'd wear a skirt and a string of pearls with a twin sweater set.* It was stereotyping, but also wishful thinking. Hy was hoping for a dull, informative meeting. She didn't want a repeat of Friday the Thirteenth with that crazed feminist. The things she'd said about menstruation and the church. In front of the minister's wife.

Camilla Samson it would be—safe and settled. Hy felt energized. She hadn't found any lobster recipes yet for the Super Saver site, but she planned to ask the village women for their family recipes to give it some local flavour. First, she had to finish the invitation to the W.I. Lobster Supper. When she thought she had just the right look, she hit Print.

The Lobster Lover's Blog

Some people won't eat lobsters because they look like cockroaches. They do—because they are. Cockroaches of the sea.

Lobsters belong to the spider, scorpion and cockroach family— Anthropodia. If they were smaller and were swarming on your kitchen floor you wouldn't eat them, you'd step on them. You'd call the exterminator. Instead, you call the restaurant and make reservations. You should have some. Reservations, that is.

Unless you like eating large crunchy bugs.

They do in some parts of Asia. They eat tarantulas. Like a lobster, a big fat tarantula has crunchy legs and succulent flesh. They're considered a treat. Some people like to eat their stomachs—the spider version of tomalley—a mush of heart, eggs and poo.

If this grosses you out, think about it. What's the difference between eating a deep-fried spider, sauteed cockroach or a lobster?

Size. That's all.

They call them bugs in Maine.

They know what they're talking about.

That blog again, thought Hy. It froze the computer. Again she had no luck when she rebooted and googled Lobster Lover's Blog.

It came and went at will.

She clicked, hard, on the invitation file and hit Print.

This time it spit the thing out.

Lobster Lovers Unite! the invitation to the Hall supper read. She printed up a stack of them, pulled on a sweater, shoved her red curls under a baseball cap and left the house. Then she came back and grabbed her keys—left again. She got in the truck; an old habit still not broken—got back out. She was halfway down the lane on foot when, suddenly, she turned abruptly and came back again. This time she'd left the invitations inside. She snatched them up and set out one last time. She would pop one into each mailbox in The Shores, except for one, which she planned to hand-deliver. Harold MacLean was the only person who had spoken to Hawthorne Parker since he had arrived on April Fool's Day. She intended to be the second.

Ian had been so anxious to open the box that held his new iMac that his hands had shaken. The rigid foam squeaked as, with great difficulty, he pried it out of the box and gingerly removed the clean, flat, white object—his beautiful new monitor. The cardboard, foam and plastic liners that had housed the computer were strewn all over his living room floor. The mess had been lying there for two days. Ian had barely budged from his seat in front of the computer since then.

Moira Toombs would soon have it all cleaned up. A single woman of a certain age, she often arrived uninvited to cook and clean for Ian. He found no reason to stop her. He was oblivious to her intentions. He was oblivious to her.

Moira carried an armful of debris into the kitchen and religiously separated it into the recycling bins as she had been taught. Her father had been promoted, in politically correct language, from garbage man to garbage collector and finally to waste management supervisor. It was all the same job. Moira wiped the counter and stove, then emptied and filled the dishwasher with the stack that had collected in the sink.

Ian, lost in the iMac, checked the status of his online order for a geo-positioning base unit and receiver, and was satisfied to see it had been shipped yesterday. He was interested in the geological damage at Vanishing Point and wanted to keep track of it. He'd been corresponding by email with a National Research Council geologist in Halifax, who'd been helping him understand the phenomenon created by The Big Ice.

It sounds like a bedding plane, the email read. *It's unusual for The*

Island, but I understand the geology of The Shores is unusual too. From how you describe the base of the cliff with inclined layers, I'd say you've got a potential problem there. Sample photos of bedding planes attached.

Ian wanted to set up a monitoring site to measure cliff erosion at Vanishing Point. He would have to get that fellow Parker's permission. He'd been waiting to bump into him and casually bring it up, but the man was as hard to spot as Sean Connery, he thought with a smile.

The smell of the muffins pulled his attention from the screen. Moira held out the plate. A half-hour earlier there had been six muffins—now only three remained. Absently, he took one and bit into it. *Delicious.* Butter ran down his chin.

Moira pursed her lips, disapproval at his manners fighting pleasure at his enthusiasm. She was personally fastidious, dressed in the best the Sears catalogue had to offer, but cursed with sallow skin and mousey brown hair. It was cut short, permed in tight curls with the texture of a scouring pad. Ian wondered if it was possible to mess it up, but had never been tempted to test his theory. He was not attracted to Moira, whose daily concerns moved in a narrow circle of interests, chief among which was cleanliness. She cleaned a few crumbs off the computer desk. She'd have been delighted to know that Ian was thinking about her, devastated at what he thought.

A squeal of tires startled them both. They looked out the window. Jared's yellow Hummer narrowly took the corner at the Hall.

Moira snorted. "He'll be up to no good."

Ian had seen the vans and trucks going down to the shore. He agreed.

He passed a hand across his head, where a few silky threads of grey hair clung valiantly to his scalp. In spite of his baldness and his age (he told people he was fifty, but his birth certificate said he was a bit more than that) he was the most eligible bachelor in

The Shores for any woman over thirty. He was the only man over eighteen not already spoken for. It made him popular. Women love a confirmed bachelor. It gives them a challenge.

The only woman Ian was even slightly attracted to was, of all people, Hyacinth McAllister. Moira noticed how much time Hy and Ian spent together. They saw each other almost every day. Sometimes he'd put on a tie and jacket and take her to dinner in town or Hyacinth would invite him to her place for a meal. He'd return from these occasions late—or not at all. Moira wasn't sure which. She'd watch from her window, but she couldn't be there all the time and sometimes she fell asleep. Of one thing she was sure—nothing much could have come of the homemade meals. She thought, with some satisfaction, of her own trump card: *Hyacinth McAllister can't cook.*

Chapter Eight

"How do you cook lobster?" Hy had stopped in to see Gus on her way down to Parker's.

"You don't know how to cook a lobster?" Gus's eyebrows shot up, her eyes opened wide. She was teasing. They made an odd pair of friends—Hy was nervous, nearly forty and from away. Gus was calm, eighty-two and only from as far away as "up West" —the western shore of The Island. She'd lived in The Shores for over sixty years, ever since she arrived as Abel's bride at the age of eighteen. There were a series of photographs in the "kitchen," a room furnished with a couch and easy chairs as well as a stove. The fridge, sink and cupboards were in the next-door "pantry." The photos showed Gus, first as a winsome, undernourished eighteen-year-old bride with long honey brown hair, standing somewhat taller than her already balding bridegroom, both in their Sunday best. Later followed the acquisition of big glasses, children and larger hips; she became handsome, with a shock of white hair. The Evolution of Gus, Hy had dubbed the images, as her friend grew in size along with her family.

Now, she was receding again. She still had that great shock of white hair and the glasses. They were smaller now, as were her hips. She always wore a dress, white ankle socks and sensible black leather shoes. She and Abel had had eight children. Three were now dead and none of the rest lived on The Island. Visits from her kids were rare. A few of them were close to becoming senior citizens themselves and had a harder time getting around than their mother did. She took after her namesake, Aunt

Augusta, still lively at one-hundred-and-two. Augusta hated her name, but had thought it rude to say so when they named baby Gus after her. They were born on the same day. There was a picture of the two together on their eightieth and one-hundredth birthdays. They looked like sisters.

"Well, technically I guess I could cook a lobster, but I never have. I could find what I want on the Internet, but I'd like a local feel, some down-home recipes." Hy was sure Gus had plenty of them.

"What I really want to know is the best way."

Gus wrinkled her nose. "There isn't one. I stay clear of them. We used to take lobster sandwiches to school when I was growin' up. Them days, you only ate lobster if you was poor. When I married Abel, he fished lobster. We'd can the meat and crush the shells and spread them on the fields. The stink—" Gus shuddered. She could smell it to this day. "I tell ya, I don't want any part of it now." That was why Gus had refused to volunteer for kitchen duty at the lobster supper. It was a big fundraiser for the Hall, constantly in need of cash for repairs and renovations.

The Hall dominated the view outside the Macks' picture window. It was the last of the community buildings still standing, but the others continued to exist in the minds of the locals, who bewildered tourists when they gave directions like: "Take a left where the post office used to be." The same thing happened with the general store and the school. The two-room schoolhouse had been closed and sold to someone from away for a summer home. The romantic notion seemed to die with the purchase. The new owner didn't bother to visit and the building "went down" until the villagers took a match to it. They were nothing if not tidy.

Sometimes the women talked of selling the Hall. That meant they'd have to find a deed. No one recalled if there was one. The Masons had wisely turned the Hall over to the Women's Institute more than a hundred years ago. The women took their responsibility very seriously and kept it in good shape. They did it with nickels and dimes—lobster suppers, strawberry socials, bake sales, flea markets, crokinole games in the winter, and the main event—the annual Christmas pageant, a show remarkable not so much for theatrical skill as for its high good humour and rollicking fun.

The thing that really bothered Hy was the idea of killing the lobsters.

"I read in *The Joy of Cooking* that you're supposed to put them in head first…"

Gus laughed. "You just throw 'em in the pot, any old way. Don't matter."

"Now, Gus, if I were to boil you alive, which would you prefer, head or feet first?"

That silenced her.

"I think it's supposed to stun them," Hy persisted, "so the meat doesn't get tough."

Gus shrugged. "Shouldn't eat them things, anyroad. They feed off the bottom. Garbage. It's eatin' garbage."

Hy noticed the patchwork on Gus's knee.

"What's that?"

Gus held it up. "I call this half-baked. It's for the Institute in Alberta."

"Oh, I forgot."

"These are the colours they asked for. This here pink used to be red, but it sat out in the sun porch for years. It's pink they wanted and it's all I had."

"So what are we supposed to do?"

"It says here—" Gus reached for the bright yellow pamphlet. "Eight by eight inch blocks, pink and blue, with 'symbolic visual images of natural heritage, wildlife and settings.' So I did the lobster."

"Well, I'll try to produce something. By the way, where's Abel?"

"Oh, you know Abel. He'll be around somewhere, doin' some-thin'."

That was Abel. He was always around somewhere, doing some-thing. But you never saw him, thought Hy. She wouldn't have recognized Abel if she'd seen him. She couldn't remember the last time she had, she thought, as she let herself out.

Moira had a shameful secret: she read *Cosmo*. She didn't want anyone to know, so she never put the magazines in the recycling. Instead, she donated them to the county hospital, key articles clipped out and filed in a box she kept under the single bed in her Spartan bedroom. The linens, bedspread and drapes were all old, drab and serviceable—as were the couch covers, curtains and tea towels downstairs, thin with age and too many washings. They did possess newer towels, ordered from their bible, the Sears catalogue, but they were kept "for good," and the Toombs sisters rarely had any guests. Moira didn't want anyone messing up her house and Madeline was too shy and too scared of her sister to invite anyone in. Their mother's best table linens were produced proudly when it was their turn to host an Institute meeting and otherwise only at Christmas, Thanksgiving and Easter.

Moira never read the sex articles in *Cosmo;* she thought they were disgusting, but she pored over all the articles of the "How to Trap a Man" variety, clipped out the useful ones, and stuffed them in the bulging box under the bed. Useful, perhaps, but they had so far failed to rope Moira a man. The muffins and washed dishes didn't seem to be getting her anywhere with Ian, so she flipped through her arsenal of how-to articles again and found "Make His Interests, Your Interests." Of course, that was Hyacinth's game—a supposed interest in computers—well, she could play it too.

The next day, Moira asked Ian if he could show her how to use the computer. It turned out to be the best idea she'd ever had. His face flushed with pleasure. He was always delighted to give advice, especially about computers. She read his pleased look as meaning something more than it did. She flushed with pleasure herself when she was seated in front of the screen and his body touched her arm as he leaned over to explain the intricacies of the keyboard. She didn't care about the keyboard at all. She fumbled. He took her hand and placed one finger carefully on a key. He took her other hand, and put a finger on another key.

"Shift. Control," he said. Her eyes were glazed, half-shut. She was faint with happiness. She wasn't even listening to what he was saying, wrapped as she was in the warm cocoon of his proximity. Why hadn't she thought of this sooner? As he guided her hand to F1, F2 and F3, she smiled, a small secret smile that spread to her eyes. She raised her head and glowed up at him. He was looking down at her, frowning. She'd been so lost in thoughts of their future life together that she'd missed everything he had said. This might be harder than she thought.

"F-what?" she asked, eyes wide open.

Chapter Nine

Hy was like a cat —a Siamese—thin and long-legged. She jumped at sounds. When trying something new, she took short tentative steps, shrinking back like an accordion if surprised, but always pushing forward again, wary and nervous but, above all, curious. She was always sticking her nose into something. Right now it was pressed up against the big front windows of Hawthorne Parker's A-frame. A small cloud of mist from her breath had formed on the glass. She had knocked at the back door first, the one facing the road, because he was new to the neighbourhood. No one knocked here—you just walked in and said hello. Doors were never locked at The Shores. This one was. What made it even stranger was that the door had been fitted with a peephole. *A peephole!* If people at The Shores wanted to find out anything about their neighbours, they just looked right out the window or sat on the stoop, watching in plain view.

When there was no answer at the door, she went around to the front, onto the deck. She hugged the edge of the house, leery of the deck poised so precariously over the shore. It made her stomach queasy. "Built too close to the edge." That's what everyone said, but they said that about every house built on every cape. "Too close to the edge. Bound to slide off." It had never happened, not at The Shores. That fact didn't stop people from gloomily—and somewhat hopefully—predicting that it would. If someone pointed out that it had never happened, someone else would be sure to add "yet."

Now Hy was peering through the glass. There was a lot more to

see than when she'd last looked in this window. All the villagers
had been up here to snoop more than once. It made a fine purpose
for a Sunday walk. They'd had a look around when it was first built
five years ago. They'd checked it out again when it was vacated
last summer to see what improvements had been made, and then
again in the Fall after Parker bought it and the moving van and
decorators had been in and out. That had been disappointing,
because everything had been covered in protective cloths and they
couldn't see any of the furnishings—except what looked like a big
quilt on the back wall. "A quilt on the wall?" Gus had asked in
disbelief, unable to walk down to see the oddity for herself.

The next thing that had drawn the villagers to the property was
the yawning v-shape the January ice had carved into the cape.
"Like someone took a knife to cut a slice of pie, then pushed it off
to the side to cut another piece," was how Ben described it. They'd
all seen it long before Parker had.

Now Hy realized that what everyone had thought was a quilt
was a big painting of a red blob. In front of it, smack in the centre
of the room, was a three-foot-high black dog.

"May I help you?"

Hy had heard about being so scared you jumped out of your
skin. That's how she felt now as she let out a high-pitched yelp.
The shriek scared the bejeezus out of the man who had come up
behind her.

Parker recovered himself and looked at Hy in distaste.

She felt foolish and grinned to cover her embarrassment.

"Sorry, I…uh…sorry." She shoved a stray tendril of frizzy red
hair back under her baseball cap. She didn't like the way he was
looking at her. A look that dismissed her, made her feel small,
even though she was several inches taller.

A man who liked to study every fine point and exquisite
detail of beautiful objects, Parker's eyes were offended by Hy's
fisherman sweater, well-worn and shapeless; the T-shirt hanging

down from underneath it; jeans, with a tear in one leg from her sharp, knobby knees. Her sneakers were expensive, but they'd run hundreds of miles on clay lanes and showed it.

So much for privacy. Not yet here a month and already the natives were banging at his door. It happened everywhere he went. They could smell money and would come looking for jobs or handouts with some lame excuse or another. Perhaps she was a cleaning woman. He needed one. Still, from the look of her... again he eyed her scruffy wardrobe. She stared right back at him. No one here cared what you wore.

"If you're looking for a job..."

"Well, no...I...uh..." She shoved an invitation at him.

Just as he had thought—some appeal for money. He glanced at the paper briefly. *How quaint—a local supper.* He'd be sure to avoid it. He looked up.

"Well," he said with the finality that ends an encounter. He took a step forward in the direction of the stairs. "A pleasure to meet you—"

The way he said it made it sound like anything but. His eyes snapped shut—and held. It always happened when he was being insincere. "Miss...uh...?"

"McAllister." She stuck out a hand. He took it, but didn't shake, just held it limply and inclined his head.

"McAllister. As I was saying, if you're seeking employment, I could use a cleaner. Someone steady. That is, reliable—and, above all, not clumsy." He continued to move forward, encouraging her off the deck.

"I'm not...I don't...I'm a writer."

Just as he thought—she could probably use a job. Parker reached into his pocket, pulled out a small gold case, and slipped a business card out of it. He gave it to her. She glanced at it quickly, not registering the words, and stuffed it in her pocket.

"I really just came about the supper, you know. Maybe we'll see you there."

He said nothing.

"I'd better be going." On that lame note, she left. On the way, she tried not to stare at the peculiar shape of the landscape around Parker's house. Instead, she saw the yellow Hummer headed down to the cookhouse with Jared at the wheel. There was another truck parked there, one Hy knew well. *Flush Riley*, it read. *Number one in the number two business.* A catchy slogan could take a business a long way. Flush was The Island's self-proclaimed "King of septics." He had a fleet of trucks—"doing my business," as he put it, "all over The Island."

The sand was tramped down around the old building and there were deep ruts in the clay lane leading up to it—made by all those trucks going in and out over the past few weeks. *Everyone had seen them, but what had they been doing? The cookhouse looked the same as always. What was Jared up to? Where had the money come from? Parker?* She smiled. *Hardly likely.*

It was only when she got home that Hy took a proper look at the card in her pocket.

Hawthorne Parker
Aesthete

That was it. No phone number, no cell phone number, no address, no email, no fax.

What kind of business card is this?

Chapter Ten

"They've come." Ian burst through Hy's front door, an open box in his hands.

She looked up with a scowl. She'd finally sat down to write the Super Saver newsletter and was already stuck.

If you're delicious, it doesn't matter how ugly you are. The lobster may not be long on looks, but the beauty of this beast is that he is nearly fat-free. Twenty percent less saturated fat than beef. Thirteen percent less than chicken—until you dip it in clarified butter. You could dip a cockroach in clarified butter and it would taste good.

That's where she'd stopped. *Where did that last sentence come from? That blog is getting to me.* It was popping up more frequently, unbidden. She couldn't access the site. There was no Contact Us link. She'd done a web search with no luck. She couldn't figure out how it had invaded her computer and now, her head.

She deleted the sentence about the cockroach and clicked Save. In spite of the frown, she was glad to see Ian. He hadn't been around for days.

"Where have you been hiding?"

He sat down on the captain's chair he always chose. "I got my new iMac the other day, so that's where I've been."

Of course. She'd known that, but forgotten. Instead, she'd nursed a small hurt that he hadn't called and stubbornly hadn't called him.

He thrust the box forward. "Now this. It arrived this morning." She looked inside. "And this is...?"

"My geo-positioning receivers. This—" he pulled one out—"is

the base unit. This—" he groped in the box again "—is the rover."

They looked exactly the same to Hy, but his eyes were bright with excitement.

"I'm hoping that Hawthorne will let me set up a monitoring station on either side of his property. When he realizes the potential, I expect he'll agree."

"I wouldn't be so sure about that."

"Why?"

"I've met him."

"What…" Ian's eyes shifted from the electronics to her with keen interest and then a slight clouding. So Hy had gotten to him first.

"Yup." Big smile. "I went up there and bearded the lion in his den."

"And?"

"He's weird. Small. Fussy. Pretentious. Here—" Parker's card was pinned to her bulletin board. She pulled it off and handed it to him.

Ian read it, smiled and shook his head. "Aesthete. Good God."

"God's gift, I bet he thinks. He looked at me like I was some kind of slimy bug."

"And?"

"He's very pompous—the way some small men are. Shorter than me. Slim. Thin mustache. A sneer. And he does this odd thing. His eyes close and get stuck there. I don't know if it's just a twitch or what."

"I don't have to ask why you went up there. You were snooping, of course."

"Of course," she said, beaming. She got up from the table and slumped down in a fat old armchair, faded pink and green chintz. "But I had an excuse. I was delivering invitations to the lobster supper."

"Of course. Well, you scooped the rest of us."

"Barely." She pointed at the GPS units. "I see you were poised to attack."

"Purely in the interests of science."

"He asked me to be his cleaning lady."

Ian laughed. "Well, I think I'm going to head on over and make my proposal. Who knows?" He winked. "I might come back as his groundskeeper."

Hawthorne Parker was sitting in his 1960 Mercedes roadster in the parking area at the car ferry. The car was idling and people were staring at him. Not just because it was the first time he'd been seen in public. Nor was it entirely the car—although no one here had ever seen one like it except on TV, with Pierre Trudeau or his son Justin at the wheel—silver metallic exterior, red leather interior. No, it wasn't the car or the peculiar man driving it. It was the idling. Since they now had to take the ferry to town for gas, most people tried to conserve it, walking where they could and definitely not idling. Parker didn't care. The weather had been cold, windy and wet all month. A chill fog off the Gulf shrouded the day. Even with the car heater on he was still shivering. A convertible, even with the roof up, was a bad choice for this place most of the year.

Parker looked in the rear-view mirror at his thin face with its pencil line mustache. He didn't like what he saw—mid-facial degradation creeping back again, hollows in his cheeks. If he'd let himself gain a little weight, but no; he passed a hand across his stomach to verify that it was still flat. He'd just have to visit the surgeon in Boston again and get plumped up. With a hand on either side of his face, he pulled it taut. *Yes.* Another visit and he'd be perfect again. He pinched his cheeks and adjusted the collar of his Burberry trench coat.

The ferry was just starting across the bay. It would be a bit of a wait yet. He turned on the radio.

"...province says as long as the weather cooperates, the Campbell Causeway to The Shores should be up and running by early June. That will be a relief to tourism operators in the area, who've been concerned they might lose their season.

"In a related story, the train tunnel will be fifteen years old this July. A new study claims that because of climate change, the train tunnel was the best choice for the Fixed Link after all. Not all experts agree. We'll have full details of that story on the news at nine."

Parker punched off the radio and selected a CD. The sweet powerful voice of Luciano Pavarotti, his favourite artist, filled the car. *"Ave Maria...Ave Mari-i-a..."* He turned it up, and Luciano's voice rose undistorted at top volume through the car speakers. He had met Pavarotti once—a giant of a man, most attractive.

Now more people were staring at Parker as the operatic tenor's voice swelled over the scrubby little parking area that served the ferry. They didn't seem to find the loud music unpleasant—just strange. They were used to country or Celtic rock blasting out of open truck windows and rattling their own.

The ferry docked. No one hurried. Drivers coming off the boat stopped to chat with drivers getting on. Others, there to pick someone up, got out of their cars and stood in the bleak fog-bound day, craning their necks to see the pedestrians walking off through the smoky exhaust of the cars, thicker even than the fog. Parker remained where he was. He could see Guillaume. There was no mistaking that shape—like a pear, womanly, broad in the beam. Not the shape Parker had fallen in love with, but he'd become accustomed to it.

Guillaume was at the front of the line of pedestrians, pushing his way forward, the only one in a hurry to get off the boat. His face was screwed up as if there were a bad smell under his nose. He was darting quick looks around him in every direction, searching for Parker's familiar face, a look of fright on his own.

He had bushy black hair and eyebrows that stuck out from his forehead in profile. In one hand he was carrying a tan leather bag. In the other a birdcage, covered with insulating material and zipped-up against the cold. From under the cover a bird squawked, "All aboard?" That drew everyone's attention solidly away from Pavarotti, whose voice was fading into the last lingering notes of the hymn.

Guillaume got off the boat, still looking around nervously. Parker waited. He needed a moment to prepare for the encounter. Guillaume was just out of rehab after what Parker referred to as his "nervous collapse." The doctors had used more frightening words: "drug-induced psychosis." Parker scanned Guillaume's face for signs of drug use. His nose was bright red and dripping, but that was from the cold.

Guillaume suddenly announced in a loud, desperate voice:

"I am seeking for Mr. Park-air," his French accent very pronounced from the stress of arriving at an unknown place.

"I am zee chef."

"All aboard?" the parrot screamed from under its cover. The drivers boarding the ferry shot quick glances at Guillaume, but no one spoke. Ben Mack had been on the boat and had parked his truck at the canteen to have a few words with Nathan. He walked over to Guillaume and pointed to the Mercedes. It was the least he could do. He was the one who, on the way over, fascinated by the parrot, had taught her to say: "All aboard?" with that annoying upward inflection.

"Tank you." Guillaume made a show of struggling up the slight incline and over to the car. Parker slid down the window. The parrot was covered and that should have shut her up, but it didn't. "All aboard?" she kept shrieking. Parker winced. Jasmine had come from a good store. Her repertoire, in the beginning, had been extremely pleasant. She sang a creditable bar or two of *Ave Maria* in an uncanny tenor, was able to whistle a few phrases from Chopin and knew some lines of Shakespeare by heart. The problem was she was so intelligent, bored and curious that she picked up every new sound she heard and never let go. Parker expected to hear "All aboard?" ad nauseum for the next several days. Then it would be trotted out every now and then as an intentional irritant, a permanent part of her repertoire.

"Hawtorn!" That was also an irritant. After all their years together, Guillaume could not manage to say his name properly. When coached, he could produce the "th," but he always snapped back like an elastic band in everyday speech to a plain "t."

Parker smiled coolly. He got out to help Guillaume put his bag in the trunk. Guillaume squeezed into the passenger seat, the cage on his knees.

"What kind of welcome eez this," said Guillaume. "No kees?" He was being sarcastic. Parker's lips closed tight in a thin line.

"Not here, Guillaume." He slid in, slammed the door, and backed up the car.

"This is not New York or Montreal." Even if it were, Parker did not like public displays of affection. Besides, his relationship with Guillaume was longstanding—the passion was gone. They were companions of habit. Sometimes Guillaume could still rouse Parker with his arsenal of tricks, which he used like dishes on a banquet table, available to all for tasting. It had been a frenzy of such behaviour—nights out with "dirty boys," alcohol and drug abuse that had culminated in that final night—that had made it clear to Parker that Guillaume needed help—long-term, rehabilitative, incarcerated help—a rehab clinic. Guillaume was in no shape to protest. He was completely out of his mind.

Parker examined Guillaume closely. Were his eyes too bright? Was his speech excessively exuberant? That didn't mean he was high. These were the qualities that had first attracted him to Guillaume. Opposites attract.

"All aboard?" squawked the parrot, as they pulled out of the parking area.

If Parker's attention had not been fixed on Guillaume, he might have noticed the odd vehicle that had come off the ferry, waited until he drove off, and then followed them. It was a jeep, painted in an unusual greenish-blue camouflage, with a red lobster-shaped air freshener dangling from the rear-view mirror.

"Chef? His chef? No one ever had a chef here."

Gus shook her head several times in disbelief, as if the information were a personal affront. It must be true. Ben had seen and heard it for himself on the ride over on the ferry. It was such a juicy piece of news that he'd stopped by his brother's house on his way home. He never did that. He was always eager to get back to his glamorous wife, Annabelle, who in spite of her well-groomed good looks, was a fisherman too.

Abel's house wasn't the first place Ben had stopped. He'd been telling anyone who'd listen about the arrival of Hawthorne Parker's chef—"a chef!"—on the ferry that morning—"with a parrot, no less. A parrot!"

"Well, I never," said Gus several times, to Ben's satisfaction.

He stopped at more houses on the way home. He drank tea at every one and a sherry at the last. He was so late getting home that Annabelle had begun to worry. When she offered him tea and he refused, she thought he must be sickening for something. She was the last one in The Shores to find out about Parker's chef.

After Ben left, Gus returned to her lobster quilt block. She had stuffed the appliqué with batting to raise it from the background, an effect she was experimenting with. She had just pulled through the final thread to secure the appliqué, when a rip appeared right down the middle of the lobster, the white batting poking out. Now, wasn't that the way it always went? Gus had made over two hundred quilts. She wasn't going to let one block get the better of her. She grabbed another piece of material and within minutes was attaching a new appliqué in place of the now discarded, ripped original. She pulled the thread through for the last stitch and cut it. The second lobster appliqué ripped down the middle, the white batting bulging out of the sun-faded pink material. It was old, too old.

"Just like me," mumbled Gus, sinking back in the purple chair. "What would I be doin' buyin' new stuff when I have all sorts back there?" The back porch was stuffed with boxes full of quilt patches and material she'd never get around to. Gus had no idea she had plenty of time left—she would live to be a healthy and active one hundred years old. She closed her eyes and drifted into a light snooze. The lobster square never did get finished that day as she had planned—or the day after that. It lay on the floor in a plastic bag for some time, until it caught her eye at just the right moment.

Chapter Eleven

"But what you are doing bringing me to thees backwater…?"

"You know exactly what I'm doing."

"Well, yes, but this is the worse yet." Guillaume looked around him in disgust.

He can't see the beauty, thought Parker. He can't see past what it means to his lifestyle. Guillaume could not. He looked out the car window at the rolling green and yellow meadows, red earth and blue water, the colours faded and soft in the fog—and scowled. Guillaume liked the city, the smell of exhaust fumes, steel and glass buildings and dramatic modern architecture. He thought of green spaces as beauty marks, something to accent the bricks and mortar that were the heart and soul of the city, but one big green space like this?

He shuddered. "It is 'orrible."

"Just wait 'til you see…"

"See what? I tink I have seen enough."

They were not getting off to a good start. Parker was confident that would change when Guillaume saw his kitchen. Surely the best gift he had ever given him.

"I think you'll be happy with the present I have for you."

A spark of interest lit Guillaume's eyes. Presents were always welcome.

"A geeft? What?"

"It wouldn't be a gift if I told you." Parker put a hand on Guillaume's thigh and patted it. Guillaume used all his control not to pull away. *First, see what this gift was…*

"Gift! Gift!" squawked the parrot in the back seat. It then began to make panting noises and orgasmic sounds. The word gift in her experience was often followed by the sound of passion.

Parker frowned. *Damn bird.*

Ian Simmons was down at the shore, at the base of Vanishing Point. He'd printed up some of the photographs the geologist Kevin Murray had sent him of bedding planes. It sure looked similar. With the cliff in front of him, he could see the inclined layers, the strata of the rock leaning toward the sea, the ice abrasions at the foot of the cape—a recipe for disaster. Nothing to confirm that it would happen, but it could. Nothing to say when either, but the ingredients were all there.

He climbed up to the top of Vanishing Point, where the land was perfectly flat, as if nothing were wrong—except for that thin strip that connected the land to the rest of the cape, on which Parker's house was precariously perched. It was only about two car widths. *Parker is never going to be able to move that house back from the edge. How will they ever get the heavy equipment in?*

Ian passed by the house to the far side of the yawning "v" notch. *Yes, this would be the perfect place to set up the base unit.* Then he could use the rover to take measurements at various points. It was tempting not to tell Parker and just place the equipment where he wanted. Still, it wasn't cheap. *If he found it…*

He heard the sound of a car behind him and turned to see the Mercedes coming up the lane. He walked down toward it.

"Mr. Parker!" He called with a false heartiness, a transparent gesture, waving and smiling as Parker eased out of the car and Guillaume pried himself out, handling the birdcage with difficulty.

"Ian Simmons. Pleased to meet you." He held up the geo-positioning units, an apology for not shaking hands.

Parker inclined his head. He ran his forefinger along his mustache. It was an unwelcome interruption, with Guillaume just back, and no kind words between them—hardly any words at all. That damn parrot was doing all the talking on the way home— shifting back and forth between "All Aboard?" and an even more irritating imitation of seagulls squawking. The one small bird was able to sound like a whole flock.

"Can you not get her to stop?" Parker had demanded through clenched teeth. "The sound of seagulls is only, if at all, pleasurable in the context of seaside ambiance." In a small car, all three squeezed in the front, it had been hell on wheels.

"I cannot do anyting," Guillaume had shrugged. "She ees covered. That is supposed to make 'er for silence, but does not work always, when she ees under stress."

Guillaume was fussing over the parrot now, lifting the cover on her cage and showing Jasmine her new "'ome."

Parker appraised Ian, respectably if not fashionably dressed in wool pants, sturdy leather boots and a merino wool sweater under an LL Bean barn jacket. *Acceptable.* Ian's hybrid car, parked just off the lane leading to the house, told Parker he was an environmentalist. Parker had no particular objection to that—he just didn't like fanaticism.

"Let us go in." His collar was up against the wind, so much worse here on the cape. The house shivered in it. He hadn't considered it when he bought the place. He'd lived by the ocean most of his life, just never so close to such a desolate shore and at such a height.

The odd, camouflaged vehicle had followed the Mercedes all the way from the ferry to the top of Wild Rose Lane. It stopped there, and the driver—also in a kind of camouflage—watched Parker's car weave off the road, bump up the lane to Vanishing Point and snake through the small passage out onto the triangle of land where the house stood.

The jeep stayed a long time. The driver watched as Parker,

Guillaume and the parrot got out, as Ian came down to meet them and continued to stay there, even after they had all gone into the house.

After a while, the jeep started up again, bumped along to the top of the Shore Lane and onto The Way, before dipping down Cottage Lane and weaving along private lanes and drives, keeping as close to the coastline as possible. It moved slowly, as if the driver were reconnoitering, until it disappeared.

Shortly after, a sleek white lobster boat slipped into the waters on the far side of Big Bay. It dropped anchor in a hidden cove nestled in behind the sand spit that sent a sheltering arm around the west side of the bay. It was a poor choice: it appeared serene, sheltered, but it was well-known by the locals for its strong ocean-bound current.

Ian was not the least bit prepared for what he saw inside the house. The room was full of primitives:

Mayan and Aztec fertility gods.

Life.

A black basalt Anubis, the embalmer, as a jackal with long pointy ears.

Death.

An armless Venus. Not de Milo, but authentic.

Love.

Parker was watching Ian examine the collection. He smirked. Parker's smile always came out like a smirk.

Ian touched the couch. *Kid leather.* There was only one discordant note—at the opposite end of the Great Room, a six-foot square oil painting. It was like an ink blot, only brilliant red, splashing out across the white canvas, with just a tiny splotch each of yellow and green in one corner.

"What's that?" asked Ian, his tone not at all polite.

"That—" Parker gestured toward it "—is, like all my treasures, rather ancient. Circa 1960." His tight smile suggested he felt he'd made a rather clever joke. "It is, perhaps, an existentialist cry for help."

"It looks like ketchup to me, with a dash of mustard and relish."

"Precisely. Man's hunger now must move from its primitive impulses. We no longer have the hunger for food. We are sated. Now we must hunger for the banquet of life itself."

This guy's a real phony. Still, there was some good stuff here— much of it of borderline legality, Ian thought.

Guillaume was unzipping the birdcage cover. Ian was eager to see the parrot. From the looks of the things Parker liked to collect, Ian bet it was a rare and endangered species, possibly an illegal acquisition.

"Have you got a license for that bird?"

"Don't be ridiculous." Parker stuck out his chin defensively. "That's a garden-variety African Grey. I would have gone for something more exotic myself, but Guillaume insisted."

"Guillaume?"

Parker had not even bothered to introduce them.

"My chef."

"And partner," said Guillaume.

"Yes, and…uh…partner." Parker had a hard time with that word. It sounded so corporate—hardly a word to describe a loving relationship. But it was hardly a loving relationship anymore. Partner: a useful word, when the passion had ebbed or when you wanted to blur the relationship to the outside world.

Guillaume took the cover off the cage.

"Say *bonjour*, Jasmine."

She wasn't the least bit illegal. Not exotic, not rare, not endangered—but absolutely beautiful. Grey-blue with the characteristic red tail feathers of the African Grey. Ian approached her, stuck out a finger and got sharply pecked.

"Silly bugger," said Jasmine.

It was then that Ian fell in love. He was so entranced, he completely forgot to ask Parker about setting up the GPS—and left without the units. They were lying on the coffee table beside a pottery sculpture. Within minutes he returned, made his apologies, and swept them off the table. He accidentally bumped the sculpture and, hands full, watched as it teetered on its base. Ian noticed now that it looked just like a penis. Parker quickly scooped it up. He gave Ian a look of fury. Ian kept his lips tight together as he hurried out, so as not to laugh at the prim man holding what looked like a massive dildo to his chest.

Chapter Twelve

Gus woke up and scanned the obituary page, a daily ritual. Seeing no one she knew, she dozed off again. Her head fell forward and jerked back up, waking her again. The newspaper was lying open at her feet. She reached for it and the effort of bending sent blood to her head, making her pleasantly dizzy. Gus had played spinning games as a child. She had liked that feeling of disorientation. She was disoriented now, not only by the blood rushing to her head but by what she saw outside her window—the village women filing into the hall for the monthly meeting of the Institute.

My land—it's gone one o'clock!

Gus grimaced as she hauled herself out of the purple chair and smoothed her apron. Rose, the minister's wife, had promised to pick her up, but she must have forgotten. The minister was Mr. Rose. That made his wife Rose Rose. She almost hadn't married him because of that.

Gus took off her apron, and looked down at her housedress. She hurried off to change; never mind that she was late.

Ian's presence had interrupted their reconciliation, but had also helped to dispel some of the distance between them. That wouldn't last long.

"How do you feel?" Parker asked tentatively.

It was the wrong question. Any question would have been the wrong one.

"I am fine. Why should I not be fine? You take me from my 'ome, my friends and put me in 'zat place." He always referred to the clinic that way, refusing to call it by its name, Sunaura Spa, another euphemism, because it was a drug rehabilitation clinic, not a spa. Guillaume didn't call it by its nickname either. Some inmates referred to it as "Snore-a" because of how it "cured" its patients—administering drug cocktails with a calming effect.

"To beat drugs, they treat drugs," was the inmates' slogan. Guillaume had spent most of his time there asleep. It hadn't really cured him, just made him too dozy to desire his drug of choice—cocaine. He'd been off the drug just long enough now to appear cured.

"I put you in *that place*, as you insist on calling it, for your own good. You went off the deep end and you know it."

"I do not know." Guillaume communicated his displeasure by refusing to look at Parker as he moved Jasmine's cage over to the window where she could see out.

"Aaaak," she screamed, seeing the gulls. "Aaaak."

"Oh Lord, shut her up please."

Guillaume still wouldn't look at Parker. He picked up his bag and, with his back to him, said:

"My room?"

"Upstairs. In the loft."

Guillaume grabbed his bag and heaved it up the stairs. He didn't come down all afternoon. He didn't even eat lunch—the ultimate accusation. Parker had to suffer alone through Jasmine's entire new repertoire. Besides the call to come aboard and the seagull's cry, she sang two different versions of *Satisfaction*—as Mick Jagger or Britney Spears, sometimes alternating the two voices and sounding uncannily like a duet—a clever trick that one of the inmates of the "spa" had thought would be amusing to teach her. Parker didn't find it the least bit amusing. He hated the sound of Britney and Jagger. He hated the sound of Guillaume's silence emanating from the loft.

He hoped things would improve when he showed him the

cookhouse.

When Guillaume finally emerged later in the day, he made a cursory inspection of the kitchen.

"I am cooking 'ere? Pah!" Guillaume spat out. "A keetchen? *Non.* An alcove."

"This is a summer home." Parker looked apologetic. "There's a barbecue on the deck."

As if Guillaume would cook outdoors. As if he himself would enjoy eating outside. He was hugging his surprise, nursing Guillaume's displeasure, knowing he had a way to stop his whining.

Guillaume swept an angry hand across a small square of counter by the stove, opened and slammed closed the few cupboards. Jasmine, charmed by the banging of the doors, took up the sound. She made the small kitchen sound like it had many more cabinets than it did. Parker frowned. Guillaume folded his arms across his chest.

"I can do nothing 'ere!" He loaded the last word with contempt.

"Perhaps it's time for your surprise."

"Surprise?" said Guillaume. He uncrossed his arms, thawing just a bit.

"Surprise!" squawked the parrot and slammed another cupboard door shut.

Parker took Guillaume down to the cookhouse. Guillaume did not like walking in the fog or the sand and he didn't like the look of the building either. He eyed it with suspicion and despair as they approached. *Is this the surprise? It doesn't look like much.* He sniffed. The chill spring air made his sinuses run. He could use a snort. In spite of the weeks of rehab, Guillaume was far from cured. He was just good at hiding it.

Parker swung the door open. He hit the light switch. Guillaume gaped.

For a moment, he said nothing. Just stared.

The room shone with stainless steel everywhere: a three-foot-long shallow sink; appliances and shelving that sparkled under the light; a Jenn-Air six-burner stove; a steel grey refrigerator; a walk-in freezer. Countertop gleamed everywhere you looked— brilliant black granite contrasted with the white ceramic tile floor and faux tin walls.

"*Incroyable.*" He took a step forward and then another, until he was in the centre of the room, surrounded by everything a man could possibly want in a kitchen. A thin smile crossed Parker's face.

"But ees perfec'!" said Guillaume. He pirouetted around the island in the centre of the kitchen. It was topped with a massive butcher board and held an industrial dishwasher and two sinks. He gave the countertops, stoves, the fridge, little taps with his hand, taps of delight, as he danced around from one lovely bright shining new appliance to another.

Now this was a kitchen.

"Look at this." Parker was caught up in Guillaume's excitement. He opened the cupboard doors that lined one wall to reveal racks of copper, cast iron and stainless steel pots and pans and small appliances. Filling one set of shelves, specially designed to fit them, were boxes and freezer cartons in a variety of shapes and sizes. Parker pulled one out and handed it to Guillaume. On the top was a graphic of a chef's hat. Angled a certain way, it looked like a lobster. Guillaume moved it back and forth in his hand, delighting at the *trompe d'oeil* effect. *First a hat, then a lobster, then a hat!* At the top was printed, in an elegant script: *Specialties St. Jacques* and along the brim: *Homme aux Homards.* Loosely translated it meant man of the lobsters. It sounded better in French.

"The company will market the line for you."

Guillaume frowned.

"No pressure," said Parker, reassuring. "Treat it as a hobby. Make only what you want, when you want. I certainly don't care if it makes any money. Whatever you create is what is available. The customers will just have to line up and wait for inspiration to strike you."

Guillaume was unable to speak. They were out of the habit of speaking kindly to one another. He didn't know how to say thank you. Thank you didn't seem enough for all—all this.

Parker wasn't finished.

He flicked the switch that illuminated the far recess of the cookhouse. The floor had been removed at the back of the building and a deep pond dug into the ground, rust red sandstone rocks piled up around it, forming a dark grotto. Parker flicked another switch and water began to ripple down the island stone, a waterfall cascading into the murky brine, filled with more rocks of the same sandstone.

"The Lobster Grotto," he announced.

Guillaume moved with unusual speed across the room. He caressed the stone. He splashed water onto the rocks. He examined every detail of the structure, so superior to a tank, designed to replicate lobsters' natural habitat on the ocean floor with crevices where they could hide. A place they would wait to be put to death.

Parker had known what to do because Guillaume had dreamed out loud about all this for years, right down to the name of his specialty line. He still wasn't finished. He pulled out a long black box from one of the cabinets.

"Your invention," he said. "I have had it manufactured."

Guillaume's eyes gleamed. He ripped the box open hungrily. He pulled out a foot-long rod that looked like a giant curling iron—mostly metal, with a clever plastic inlay in the shape of a lobster claw on either side of the handle.

"Ze lobster stunner." He stroked it reverently down its length, eyes shining.

Stimulated, Parker put a hand on Guillaume's shoulder. Guillaume knew he would have to pay for these gifts later. Right now, he was not thinking about that. He was thinking that now he would be able to kill lobsters. He was too squeamish to slice a knife into the creature's head the way other chefs did, or listen to its screams as it died in boiling water. The stunner would do the job quickly, humanely. It would not sicken him nor toughen their meat. Because of the pond and this weapon, the lobsters would be happy and healthy until they were killed, cooked and eaten. He would be able to prepare the finest of lobster dishes, for the truly discriminating palate—like his.

It will be a culinary triumph.

Parker had replicated, in fine detail, everything Guillaume had ever told him he wanted in a kitchen. Except, he thought, its location. He found he could live with that. With all this—he looked around the room again.

His eyes were bright with moisture.

Parker looked into them.

It was going to be a good reunion after all.

He could hardly wait to get back to the house.

Chapter Thirteen

"*Homarus Americanus.*"

The woman pointed at the ugly creature looming over her. She stood centre-stage at The Shores Hall, dwarfed by the screen behind her, with its image of a giant-size red lobster lying on a wooden trap. At the back of the stage on either side, half-hidden by the screen, were portraits of a girlish but regal Queen Elizabeth and a no-longer-boyish and balding Prince Philip. To one side at the front, there was an ancient piano that had been played often but never well. Now, in protest, it refused to be tuned and sounded worse with each new player. There was a graceful arch at the front of the stage, set off by red velvet curtains that opened and closed by a hand pulley.

The thirteen members of the Institute were seated in one row of chairs below the stage, surrounded by pink wainscoting. On one wall was a quilted hanging, made by the women to commemorate the Institute's one-hundredth anniversary. The rest of the wall decor included irregularly placed groupings of awards, photographs of visiting politicians, a dedication to local war heroes and ten consecutive Best Float plaques from the Community Harvest Festival in Winterside.

Hy had arrived late, out of breath, making apologetic gestures with her hands and shoulders as she fluttered in. Gus said Hy was always trying to catch up with herself. It was true. She generally left for a place at the time she was supposed to arrive there. She was greeted by an articulate silence and grim looks that had nothing to do with her lateness. Hy wasn't sure exactly what it meant, but it appeared almost immediately that the problem was the guest. Looks went from Hy to the stage and back to Hy.

She looked up at Camilla Samson. It couldn't be the way the guest looked—almost exactly as Hy had imagined. She wore clothes of good quality, if a bit large—a sweater set, a simple pencil skirt and sensible pumps, along with the predictable strand of pearls with matching earrings. She was slender, average height, with honey-blonde hair worn in a sleek bob, cool grey eyes, a straight nose and good teeth. *She looks perfectly respectable, so why the stony looks?*

"*Homarus Americanus,*" the speaker repeated, as Hy took her seat. "The North American lobster. Not just an item on the menu, a creature with intellect and a social life. Although he is a bit of a loner."

Annabelle Mack, sitting two seats down from Hy, opened her eyes wide in comic shock and mouthed, "a loner?" Hy put a finger to her lips, but judged from Annabelle's cheeky behaviour that the guest had made a poor first impression. It must have been something she'd said before Hy came in. It didn't matter. It couldn't have been any worse than what was to come.

"He also has an emotional life."

The screen image changed.

"And a sex life."

The slide showed a lobster mounted on another lobster in the missionary position.

There was a taut silence.

The stage of the Shores Hall was noted for its ceilidhs and annual Christmas pageant. Last Christmas, after sixty years, Gus had consented to speak one word in a skit. She did so to the most tumultuous applause of the evening. It had made her blush. She was blushing now for a different reason—and she wasn't the only one. Sex was not generally a subject that came up in the Hall.

"Well, yes, and if they didn't mate, where would we be?" Annabelle called out. It was meant as a good-humoured jibe, but in this group it had a deeper resonance. There was hardly a woman in the room who didn't owe her living to the lobster industry. Annabelle fished lobster with her husband Ben. You'd never know it. She wore dresses with plunging necklines, used bright red lipstick and nail polish and wore high heels whenever she could. They looked great on her long, shapely legs. When lobster season began, she shoved her thick blonde hair into a baseball cap and put on jeans. She cut her fingernails, kicked off her heels, and put on rubber boots. She still looked great.

Click. The image changed to a hand holding a blue-green lobster, poised over a kettle of boiling water. Hy relaxed. Now, surely, the woman would start talking about cooking.

"And they feel pain. That high-pitched sound you hear when you drop a lobster in boiling water is a scream of pain. That clunking sound is not just the hard bodies knocking against the side of the pot, it's living creatures clawing desperately to get out. To get out of hell."

Click. To an image of a giant lobster claw holding a housewife in an apron over a pot of steaming water.

"How would you like to be dropped, headfirst, into a vat of boiling water?"

Headfirst. April Dewey had always wondered if that was the right way to do it. She was the best cook in the village. Some people swore that the air of The Shores was scented, not just with the grasses and grains and tang of the ocean, but with the sweet, sweet smell of April Dewey's blueberry muffins. April was always in demand for her wedding and anniversary cakes, which she topped with an all-butter icing that teenagers dubbed "to die for." One elderly villager had done just that—died when he ate a slice, but he had died happy, a smile on his face and the half-eaten piece of cake clutched in his hand. It was no wonder Abel Mack said she cooked like an angel, praise she was too modest to fully accept. She'd go red every time he said it.

"They are living breathing creatures. God's creatures. Like you and I."

Click. A man inside a trap.

Click. Two children struggling to get out of a trap.

Click. A couple of human-sized lobsters standing on their tails, tossing naked humans into a bin in front of a fish shed on a wharf.

Hy had to admit it was well done. It was also beginning to rival the Friday the Thirteenth fiasco.

"Just imagine. You, your husband and your children, tempted into a new restaurant. Suddenly, the door closes on you. You're trapped inside. You can't get out. Your small children escape, but you are left—desperate.

"A large claw comes and yanks you out, wraps your hands in thick elastic bands, drops you in a plastic bin, on ice. Shoves you in a truck and throws you in a tank, where you swim around until someone drops you in boiling water—headfirst, if you're lucky."

So headfirst *was* best, thought April.

Gladys Fraser glared at Hy.

Worse, it was worse than Friday the Thirteenth.

"Ladies, I am not here to tell you how to cook a lobster. You know how."

There were murmurs of assent. Hy was suddenly hopeful. Maybe things were getting back on track.

"I could not begin to tell you how to cook lobster. You have loads more experience than I do. The fact is, I've never cooked a lobster. The reason is, I don't think we should be cooking lobster at all."

"Should we be eating it raw?" Gladys whispered to Moira Toombs. Gladys, President of The Shores chapter of the Institute, was square and solid in build and nature. Some of the women were afraid of her because she always looked pissed off. She usually was. She certainly was right now.

Moira tittered politely, but she hadn't really been listening to what Gladys—or Miss Samson—was saying. She'd been staring at the guest, admiring her outfit. It was better than her own—and she was wearing the best Sears had on offer. She smoothed the wrinkle-free polyester dress. She put a hand to her hair. It was perfectly coiffed. Moira noted with satisfaction that she was, as usual, the best-turned-out woman in the Hall, guest included. The woman's clothes didn't fit right, Moira concluded, and would have looked much better on her.

Moira thought April Dewey was a disgrace. Between her baking and her six children, she had little time for her personal appearance and could often be seen with flour in her hair or on her clothing. Today there was a smudge on her cheek. She couldn't afford to be less than meticulous with her appearance, thought Moira. Neither could Moira, but she tried not to think about that. No matter how she primped, she couldn't escape the misfortune of her looks. It's what made her so critical of other people's appearances—self-defence.

When Camilla Samson said: "We should not be eating it at all," April looked confused. *Then why were they here?*

Gus, usually Hy's staunchest ally, nudged her. "She's right there, you know."

"Just because they're ugly, doesn't mean it's okay to eat them. Don't be fooled into thinking there are humane ways to kill them. It's still killing."

Annabelle frowned at Hy. They were friends, but she wasn't looking friendly now. Annabelle was going to be trapping lobsters herself in just a few days.

This was making Friday the Thirteenth look good.

When Hy had organized the program last February, she'd invited a Professor of Women's Studies from the University of Toronto to convince the women that thirteen was a lucky number.

Many of them thought having thirteen members was a jinx. They were always trying to recruit more, but whenever they signed up a new one, they'd lose one—someone got too old, too ill or died. They were constantly sending out condolence and get-well cards. They couldn't get away from the number thirteen.

The professor, Eleanore Walpole, had had a long Modigliani face and was draped in a black dress and shawl. She was the author of several books, including *The Goddess in You, The Moon and the Matriarch* and *The Menstrual Earth.* She'd told the women that the number thirteen was lucky for them because the thirteen lunar cycles represent women's monthly rhythms, a sacred act. That had made a few of them squirm in their seats. Friday the Thirteenth was especially lucky, she'd told them, because the day's name comes from Freitag, the Goddess of All Creation before male Christianity began burning and looting and killing in the name of God. That had made a few more women shift in their seats, Rose Rose among them.

"So celebrate your womanhood—for you are all goddesses!" She had raised her arms in triumph. Everyone had looked at Rose. She was the one who'd been chosen to thank the day's guest. She had done so with as few words as possible, her expression careful not to betray her real thoughts.

"Interesting," said Annabelle.

"Different," said Estelle Joudry, which is what she usually said.

The neutral comments were the women's way of saying they weren't sure they liked what the professor had to say, but they were always polite to guests who took the time to come to speak to them. When they filled out their Institute booklets that day, under the heading: "What did I learn from the program?" most of the women dutifully wrote: "Thirteen is a lucky number."

Gus wrote: "We're lucky to have thirteen."

It was true. Institute chapters all over the country were closing down as members got old and no young ones joined. The women of The Shores felt they had to keep the Institute going to keep the Hall going, so the village itself didn't disappear.

"Murderers!"

The sound echoed through the hall and snapped Hy back to the awful mess today's meeting had become. Camilla Samson moved from the podium to the front of the stage. She leaned forward.

"If you have ever cooked a lobster, you are a murderer!"

The ladies looked at Hy in varying degrees of shock, dismay, disgust and anger—even Moira's sister, little Madeline Toombs. She barely scraped five feet in shoes, shopped in the children's department, and was usually entirely unsure of what her opinion was or how it might be received. The way she was looking at Hy now was the closest she got to expressing her point of view—it wasn't positive. Hy felt the tips of her ears burning red in embarrassment. This meeting was certainly not going to resurrect her reputation in the village. This woman hadn't turned out one bit like her name or clothes suggested.

"Shame, shame on you—murderers, all. Killers every one. You—" The woman pointed at Gladys.

"And you." Pointing at Madeline.

"A murderer." Her finger aimed at Moira.

"And you. A killer." Estelle.

"And you." Annabelle. "A slayer of innocent creatures."

"And you." The accusing finger swept along the line of ladies.

"Killers every one of you."

Yes. Much worse than Friday the Thirteenth.

It was one thing to be called goddesses, quite another to be called murderers.

The screen went dark and with it the room. Madeline, Estelle and Harold's wife, Olive, scrambled over to the windows to pull up the blinds—anything to avoid that woman. That Woman was how the Institute members would always refer to Camilla Samson in the future. In the end, she turned out to have so many names, they didn't know what else to call her.

She was frozen there, her arm still outstretched, finger pointing at them. Each woman felt it was aimed at her, but Hy felt it most. It was all her fault. Madeline, Estelle and Olive stayed where they were; the rest sat still, looking anywhere but at the stage and the accusing finger. There was silence. Gladys was the one who was supposed to thank the guest. She turned to Hy, slid her forefinger across her neck in a slicing motion, shook her head, crossed her arms and turned back. Hy had to do it. She stood up and spoke—words she didn't remember afterwards. There had been a lot of stuttering. She had not been able to look Miss Samson in the eye.

The meeting broke up quickly. The women didn't stay around longer than it took for the obligatory lunch—a snack of assorted sandwiches, cheese and crackers, homemade cookies, brownies and squares and a cuppa tea. They didn't know what to say to someone who had just called them killers. They had filled out their Institute booklets, and under the section "What I learned today…" wrote:

"Lobsters have feelings too." Madeline Toombs.

"Fishermen have feelings too." Annabelle Mack.

"Guest lecturers shouldn't swear." Rose Rose.

"Guest lecturers should wear clothes that fit." Moira.

"Lobsters like to be thrown headfirst into boiling water." April Dewey.

And Gus: "Don't eat lobster."

It turned out there was canned lobster meat in some of the sandwiches. Their guest bit into one by mistake and spat it out. It didn't take long for the Hall to clear after that.

Hy and Camilla Samson were left alone. Hy felt she should say something, but she didn't know what, after the woman's appalling rudeness. Was it cowardice or politeness that choked her words? Cowardice, she decided, plain cowardice. When she and the woman were back-to-back—Camilla putting away her slides and Hy stuffing her Institute booklet into her purse—she finally managed to speak.

"I thanked you before, but I was just being polite. I take it back."

The woman turned. "I'm sorry—but it had to be done."

Now Hy turned around, still not able to look her in the eye.

"But you lied. I thought—"

"I know what you thought, but I didn't lie, did I? What did I say?"

Hy remembered the email had been abrupt, but she couldn't remember exactly what it said.

"I said I'd be happy to talk to the Institute about lobster. That wasn't a lie. I'm happy every chance I get to promote the cause. That's what I did."

It was true.

"But the link to the website—"

"All the link said was—"

She pulled a piece of paper out of her leather portfolio and handed it to Hy.

Lobster Lover? Catch us first. Cooking Lobster? Let our expert speakers fill you in.

She had to agree—nowhere did it say that Camilla Samson would give cooking tips. That was Hy's assumption. *Even so—*

"You knew what you were doing."

Camilla closed up her portfolio and came down off the stage.

"I'm a member of the Lobster Liberation Legion. We're a militant animal rights group. We're fighting a war, and in wars people get hurt. Worse than you." She looked directly at Hy. Her eyes were intense—oddly so. Hy had never thought of light eyes as anything but cold, but these were burning with purpose. Hy's own were slightly moist with tears of frustration. A series of emotions flickered across Camilla Samson's face. Suddenly she looked younger, softer.

"Look, it's nothing personal," she said. "Just tactics. It was—"

she paused, "a group decision. I can't change that." Camilla didn't usually offer explanations or apologies for her actions. She had become hardened to her purpose, but there was something about this Hy McAllister. Maybe it was the stuttering way she thanked her. Maybe it was the feeling that she and Hy had been alone even when all the other women were there. Camilla had seen the looks the women shot at the two of them. They were both outsiders, a different species.

"These tactics are agreed on by our members. That website has got the word out to more people—"

Hy pursed her lips, looking doubtful. "It's dishonest—and you're so strident. Don't you think you could get your message across some other way?"

"No." Camilla's eyes hardened. "You wouldn't have invited me at all. And if I had just presented the scientific facts, these women would have fallen asleep."

"You could have given them a chance…"

"Look at it this way. There's nothing else those ladies will be talking about for the rest of the day, face it, the rest of the week. By tomorrow morning, it's going to be all over the village. By this time next week, it'll be all over The Island. All I had to do was take half an hour with thirteen people."

"Thirteen decent people whom you've offended."

"Even if I've offended them, I've got them thinking. I've got them thinking in a way that will get the message across much more loudly and much more clearly than if I'd come here and—" she'd seen what the minister's wife had written in her booklet— "spoken politely."

Hy shrugged. She couldn't really argue. People would certainly be talking, talking about Hy's latest disaster. She would never be accepted if she kept pulling stunts like this. It was lucky she didn't have to organize another program until next June. When she did, she swore it would be basket weaving. With her luck, someone would come to argue the rights of ornamental grass and corn leaves.

Camilla was digging into her laptop case. She pulled out a DVD.

"Here, have a look at this when you get the chance. Then maybe you'll understand us better. Why we do what we do."

More propaganda, thought Hy, but she took it with as much grace as she could muster. "How will I get it back to you?"

"Keep it. I have more. Besides, we may bump into each other again."

Hy let out a heavy sigh, fear and frustration bundled up in it. She hoped not.

"What do you mean by that?"

"That would be telling." Camilla smiled like someone hugging a secret, or teasing her.

Hy had every reason to dislike her, but she couldn't help smiling back. Camilla looked like she might be interesting to know in different circumstances, different clothes and on a different mission. She supposed her cause was admirable, if misguided.

Camilla pulled out her cellphone and ordered a cab from Nathan. Hy was relieved. That meant she'd be taking the ferry out of here. So she had been teasing.

There were a few moments of uncomfortable silence, but Nathan arrived quickly and honked his horn. Camilla left the Hall and Hy looked at the DVD. Its title was *Liberating the Lobsters. Yup, definitely propaganda.* More of the same she'd heard today. She threw it in her red leather shoulder bag, and forgot about it by the time she got outside where Gus was waiting for her.

"Thought you might want a few words with her." She smiled softly. Her eyes twinkled. Gus was an odd mix. She was a real old-timer with strong ideas about what was "fittin'" and what wasn't, but she also liked seeing things "shook up a bit." They'd sure been "shook up" today.

"The look on Gladys Fraser's face," she said now. "So help me Hannah, I thought she was going to have a stroke." She slapped her thigh and began to laugh.

Hy grinned. Laughed in relief. Gus was great that way.

"You'll get some hard looks," she warned. "Murderers is worse than goddesses. Much worse."

Hy remembered the real end to that other disastrous meeting. The professor had claimed goddess-given powers of perception. She had pulled Hy aside and said to her, "I see danger for you, in the night. I see water and dark and light."

Annabelle had overheard and given it a lighthearted spin.

"Danger always comes in the night," she said.

But it was like the dream, Hy thought. *Had the professor seen that? About the water and the light? Flashing? Was she seeing the past—or foretelling the future?* Hy had felt faint and had needed to sit down.

Now, she felt suddenly breathless.

"Anything wrong?" Gus put a hand on Hy's shoulder.

"Nothing," Hy shook off the memory. Nothing had happened, had it?

"I guess I'm going to be on my own with 'Ten Ways to Cook Lobster."

Her tone was light, a lightness she didn't feel.

Chapter Fourteen

Nathan was surprised when the good-looking woman who'd called from the Hall asked him to drive in the opposite direction from the ferry. Strictly speaking, he shouldn't have. His cab was subsidized by the government and the contract stated that it was a shuttle exclusive to the boat, tied to its half-hourly schedule. But there were no calls for the next ferry, coming or going, so he didn't mind. He eyed her in the rear-view mirror. He liked older women. Not that she looked it. She was maybe thirty-something, but that pink flush on high cheekbones, the glow of her skin, gave her the fresh look of a nineteen-year-old. Her clothes and air of authority said she was older than that.

"Sure this is where you want?" he asked, concern and curiosity mixed.

She had asked to be dropped at a clay lane that, as far as he knew, led nowhere except to a windy cape and a rough piece of shoreline.

"This is fine." The expression on her face prevented him from asking more.

There had been a homestead back there one time, but he wasn't sure it was there anymore, or who might be living in it. Truth was, he'd never been down that lane and, as small as The Shores was, he didn't know everyone in it—especially those from away who came and went at odd times of the year, some in out-of-the-way places like this. Probably there was a mansion in back, built while they were all busy gossiping about someone or something else.

She got out of the car and didn't move until he wheeled around and drove out of sight. She's an odd one, he thought. Those shoes she was wearing wouldn't take her very far on that lane if that were where she was going. They weren't instruments of torture like his mother's high heels, but still hardly made for walking.

Hy was staring at a photograph of Camilla Samson posing with that other notorious Camilla, standing with Prince Charles on the banks of the River Dee. The prince was pretending to break his fishing rod over his knee. They were all smiling.

Hy had googled Lobster Liberation Legion as soon as she got home and she knew quite a bit about Camilla now. No personal background. Nothing about where she came from. Just that she was the founder and chief spokesperson, the face of the Legion. There were photos of her—and of an unidentified legionnaire who appeared to be her second-in-command, dressed in lobster-like camouflage of blues, greens and touches of red. The legion-naire was photographed emptying traps into the water, standing in the middle of the road, preventing a truck from delivering live lobster to a seafood restaurant, paddling a dory out to confront an entire fishing fleet. The message was clearly one of David and Goliath and the modus operandi seemed to be good cop, bad cop, the refined Camilla and the roughneck legionnaire, of somewhat indeterminate gender.

All the photos of Camilla were with European government and industry leaders, and then there was the one with the two Camil-las and the prince: the duchess—big and horsey, with a gummy smile; the lobster activist—fine, slender, with honey-blonde hair. The only similarities were their names and style of dress: wool sweaters and skirts in shades of heather, strings of pearls and sensible rubber boots.

Camilla could have used those rubber boots now, as she picked her way along the muddy, puddle-filled lane to where she was staying. She was wearing reasonably sensible pumps, but with feet like hers, it hurt to squeeze into them. She'd walked five miles to get to the Hall and stood for over an hour. Her feet were screaming at her and her back was aching. Once inside, she pulled off the shoes and put on her well-worn sheepskin slippers. She took off her pearls and placed them neatly in their black leather case, the gold lobster clasp centered in the box. She removed her clothes and hung them tidily on a hanger, put on silk pyjamas and took out her contacts. She tucked herself in under a comforter, her laptop balanced on her knees. It slipped from her grasp and slid to the floor. *My lifeline.* She picked it up, opened it and clicked it on, hoping there was no damage.

The Lobster Lover's Blog lit up the screen. She scrolled down.

People will eat anything. Just about. Anything that doesn't eat them first. The human race has only one real rule about what you shouldn't eat: don't eat other humans.

Lobsters don't have this rule. They will eat anything they find on the ocean floor—even sons and daughters and potential mates. That's bad news for Junior-to-be, or not to be.

Humans try not to eat each other and rarely stomach their kids. Otherwise, they eat just about anything too. If it moves, eat it. If it doesn't move, eat it. We're omnivores. We eat anything that doesn't eat us first. Which may be why we don't eat lions and tigers.

It does make you wonder why people eat lobsters. You have to fight them to eat them, even though they're already dead: the shell resists you; the claws prick you; the salt burns you. You come out of the experience soaking wet, sometimes with blood—like Lady MacBeth.

Serves you right.

Amen, thought Camilla. She snuggled under the goose down duvet in her cosy berth. The lapping of the waves rolling off the ocean lulled her to sleep.

Chapter Fifteen

Boiled. Steamed. Baked. Barbecued. Cold in a lobster roll.

Did lobster rolls count? Sure. How about Lobster Thermidor? Hy wasn't sure what it was. She googled and found a recipe. She'd abandoned the idea of asking the village women for their recipes for the newsletter. She dare not mention the word lobster to any of them—although she had offered, as penance, to cook as well as serve at the supper after Setting Day. It was the least she could do. She still had three recipes to go and the deadline was tomorrow. She came up with Lobster Newburg, Lobster Chili and Lobster Bisque. The bisque recipe was over a page long with a preparation time of one hour. That ensured that Hy would never make it.

All the recipes referred to *Step One: How to kill a lobster.* There it was in graphic detail and photographs, words and images that kept flashing through her mind:

...rubber bands secure around the creature's claws...flatten the tail...grasp it where it joins the body...take the point of a hefty chef's knife...an inch and a half from the eyes...into the head... blade down between the eyes...all the way through...a clean kill, quick and painless.

No wonder people just threw them in the pot.

Hy now had ten recipes, but she still wasn't satisfied. There was nothing special about them. They could be found anywhere.

Frustrated, she put the laptop to sleep, padded in her sock feet across the room and pulled on her sneakers. She'd been up all night, napped a couple of hours, looked out at the fog and went back to sleep again. It was nearly noon and the fog had cleared off. The wind was brisk, but a welcome sun shone in a crisp blue sky. *Maybe a run would clear my head.* She was curious about what was going on at the cookhouse, even though the activity seemed to have ended. *Perhaps Jared has finished whatever it was he was up to. Maybe some of those trucks had been headed for Parker's house. Could be they were up to something together.*

She smiled and shook her head. *No it couldn't.*

"I want you to provide me with lobster."

"I'm not a fisherman."

Parker waved a hand dismissively. He frowned as Jared reached for a cigarette.

"I know that. I don't want a fisherman. I just want small quantities—on a regular basis. I don't want to have to get a license." Parker had a loathing for forms, licenses, papers—the mundane details needed to get things done. It was why he had Sheldon running the business for him.

"This is not a commercial operation. I will not have Guillaume down to the wharf every day to pick up a few dozen lobsters." He smiled, a small smile, seeming to find the image of Guillaume on the wharf funny, but Jared didn't get the joke. It was a thin one anyway. What Parker didn't want was Guillaume down at the wharf spending money on boys and drugs. He had clearly never been to Big Bay Harbour. It wasn't that kind of wharf at all.

Guillaume came out onto the deck, a white apron stretched across his midsection. The apron was fresh and clean, even though Guillaume was cooking a Szechwan shrimp with a messy but delightful spicy garlic tomato sauce in "zat pat'etic leettle galley."

"Guillaume, this is Jared MacPherson, our lobster man."

Guillaume raised his eyebrows. They matched the thick, bushy black hair escaping from his chef's hat.

"*Enchanté*." He bowed slightly, but kept his hands clasped

behind his back. Guillaume thought that if he were to touch this filthy human, he would have to forget about cooking lunch while he cleaned and sanitized. But he studied Jared with interest. He was unnaturally thin, like someone who lived on cigarettes, booze and dope. Guillaume knew a possible source when he saw one.

"Jared will provide us with lobster."

"Mmmmm." And more, thought Guillaume.

" How many will you need?"

"I can use two dozens a day."

"Except on weekends." Jared had no intention of giving up his Saturday nights in Winterside, especially since he had met that little blonde tart last week. *She was a goer—a real hottie.* She had sat on his lap and made herself quite obvious before they'd said hello.

"I can get that." He'd poach them. He'd done it before. "What'll you pay?"

Parker named a good price and Jared started to do the math, but got lost in the numbers. It was lot of money.

"Two dozen a day, five days a week, an' pay me top price an' all? I don't get it."

"You don't have to get it. Just deliver the lobster daily."

Did Parker know he'd be poaching, Jared wondered? *What do I care? I'm going to be rolling in it. I'm going to be rolling that little tart. Her and her sister, the kind of money I'm going to have.*

"Can we call it a deal?" Parker signaled the interview was over by gesturing Jared towards the stairs that led off the deck.

"Deal." He better go check out that dory behind the cookhouse.

A man and woman in their early sixties were watching Jared from the deck of the cottage by the run. Like the swallows that return to Capistrano in mid-April every year, this human pair migrated to their cottage at about the same time. The woman had big glasses from twenty years ago that covered her face, except for her mouth and a tiny tip of her nose. They were reading glasses, but she wore them all the time so she wouldn't lose them. Everybody said she looked just like an owl.

She sounded like one, too, when she raised an arm and yelled, "Hoy…hoy…hoy…" loud enough to scare the Piping Plovers, the tiny endangered birds she was trying so fiercely to protect. Jared was coming along the beach and about to place a dirty foot on one of their nesting sites, just a tiny scoop in the sand.

She cupped her hands around her mouth.

"The plovers! Mind the plovers!"

He looked up. She waved a hand at the sign she had planted just that morning, warning people away from the nest.

"Bugger off," he called back, and planted his foot firmly in the sand. He missed the nest by a fraction. The mother bird, clearly upset, moved away and limped around, trying to draw the large predator away from her chicks by looking injured herself. Jared kicked her and she went flying across the sand, fell, fluttered and died.

The man on the deck began moving toward the stairs, not making good progress. He walked like a seagull. Even in his haste, the best he could do was to walk a few steps, stop, cock his head, dart a quick glance from side to side and swallow, his Adam's apple rising and descending in his gullet. Then he would repeat the pattern. It was slow-going. His big beak of a nose looked like it could topple him over on his skinny legs at any moment.

The pair of bird-lovers was Noddy and Do Byrd—a happy coincidence of their name fitting their passion—or perhaps predisposing them to their path in life. Noddy and Do had met as science students at Dalhousie University, married and then both pursued advanced degrees in ornithology. Noddy's specialty was the Argentinian swallow, the little bird that drilled its nests along the top of the capes and hastened their erosion. Do was an expert on plovers.

People couldn't help making fun of them. What kind of name is Noddy for a grown man? was a common question. Do was often called Dodo behind her back. Even Noddy did it, affectionately. He never gave a thought to what it really meant.

Jared took one look at Noddy, laughed and kicked sand into his face.

"This is my beach," he said, "I own these dunes and I'll go where I want."

Jared's claim was the subject of some dispute. Tradition had it that islanders whose land backed onto the shore owned that shore, or at least up to the high water mark—the point at which the federal and provincial governments got into a wrangle about who owned what. New laws to protect the dunes from development had changed things, restricted what and where people could build on the shore, challenging traditional ideas of ownership. But most still did whatever they wanted. If Jared or Parker had requested a building permit for the cookhouse, they would never have received permission for the renovation, and certainly not for the ugly addition that stretched across the beach down to the water.

Now that he was going to be poaching from this shore, his shore, named after his family, Jared wanted the Byrds out of the way. He thought they were a pair of nosey parkers, always watching through their binoculars.

He spied the plover nest, raised a foot, and began to bring it down, but Noddy lunged forward and pushed him. They were both surprised when Jared fell backwards into the run. He pulled himself up, took one step toward a terrified Noddy, then stopped. He had too much riding on his latest venture to risk an assault charge.

"You watch it," he said, "or there'll be more than one dead bird on this beach," His eyes under his single eyebrow were menacing.

Noddy, with uncharacteristic speed, retreated to the safety of the deck.

"Bully." Do was outraged, brushing sand off Noddy's face and fluffing a wisp of hair that grew like a faint trail of smoke directly upward from the top of his head. It made him look like some odd chick a long way from his nest.

Hy crested the dune behind the Byrds' house in time to see Jared stalking off and getting into his truck. *A Hummer. And it looks brand new, like Gus said.* She wondered where he got the money for it. She climbed the steps up to the deck. Do was weeping.

"Our fault." She choked out the words. "This is our fault."

"What's going on?"

Noddy told Hy what Jared had done.

"That bastard!" Hy made fun of the Byrds like everyone else in the village, but they were harmless. Jared was a brute. "You should call the police."

"Oh, I don't think we'll do that."

Noddy and Do continued to peer at the run, searching for the father to come back to the nest. Both plover parents take care of their young, Hy knew. Everybody in the village knew. The Byrds were strong advocates for their little charges and had managed to preserve, and even increase, the local plover colony. Their method was unconventional—it mostly involved yelling from their deck at tourists who strayed too close to the nesting site. The plovers—who don't like noise—had somehow grown accustomed to the Byrds' vociferousness, perhaps because it was similar to their own noisy bossing of their fledglings.

The three stood watching until, finally, the father came winging back to the nest.

Noddy tiptoed carefully down onto the sand and retrieved the dead mother bird.

"We'll bury it out back."

Hy watched from the deck as Noddy dug a hole and Do put

the bird in a decorative box from the dollar store kept for just such purposes. They each said a few solemn words and stood in respectful silence for a moment. When they came back, Do still had tears in her eyes.

"We'd better go to the house."

"Yes, Do, dear, we'll go back to town for a while."

Hy was outraged. "You can't let him bully you out of your home."

"Just for a few days." Do blew her nose—it sounded like the honk of a goose. "The weather's supposed to turn nasty anyway. The surf's picking up already."

It was a signal for all to look at the water, and that's when Hy noticed the black cylindrical shape cutting across the beach.

"What the hell is that?"

Noddy pulled out a pair of binoculars.

Do shaded her eyes with a hand and squinted through myopic eyes.

"I don't know. Something to do with Jared's cookhouse. There's been a lot of work going on. They've been taking in kitchen equipment. Restaurant quality."

"Now there's this weird fellow—Frenchman by the look of him—going in and out of there." Noddy had picked up the thread; the Byrds always talked in tandem. "I guess he's got it rented." He raised the binoculars to his eyes.

"Looks like a pipe."

Hy was already off the deck and marching across the beach. It was a pipe. She took off her shoes and socks and followed it into the water. *Jesus!* It was cold. Her feet throbbed with pain. It shot up her legs. She squeezed her eyes tight, as if that might help. The pipe ran well out into the water beyond the sand bar.

Back on the sand, she sat down and rubbed warmth into her feet. She pulled on her socks, wincing as they tugged at her wet skin. She'd lost the feeling in her little toes. She put on her shoes and followed the pipe up the beach and over the dune, where it entered the cookhouse at the back of the building. She could hear a pump rasping inside the wall.

"Hoy…hoy…hoy," Do's plover call rose from the deck. Hy ignored it. She went over to a window, stood on tiptoe and tried to see in.

"Hoy…hoy…hoy…" Do was sounding more frantic. Hy glanced over. Do was waving her arms. Hy strained for more height, grabbed the sill, and hauled herself up.

"Hoy…hoy…hoy…" It was becoming annoying. She jumped down and looked over at Do again. The waving was directed at her, but she couldn't figure out why.

She pulled herself up again. She couldn't see anything.

"Do you make a habit of this?"

She let go in shock, fell on her ass and looked up into the pointedly ironic face of Hawthorne Parker. Do had been trying to warn her that he was coming around the front of the building where Hy couldn't see him.

"Uh…no…I…uh…" She was stuttering again. She pulled herself up as Guillaume appeared behind Parker.

"Guillaume, this is—" Parker paused.

Hy stuck out a hand. "Hy McAllister."

In spite of his disapproval, Parker was eager to show off his latest possession. He hadn't been able to show this one to anyone except Guillaume, and the thrill of that was already gone. One shamefully passionate night—the shame was in how easily Guillaume could play him, how he could awaken and satisfy Parker's otherwise ambivalent sexuality—and then nothing. He opened the door and gestured her in.

"Wow," she said at the sight of the gleaming stainless steel, black granite and white ceramic. She could hear water flowing somewhere.

"Wow," she said again, when Parker worked the dimmer switch

to gradually illuminate the grotto, bathing it in a soft glow.

"The Lobster Grotto," said Parker.

"The Lobster Grotto?" She moved forward and peeked in. The pond was empty.

"When the season starts, we'll fill it with lobster and Guillaume will start cooking…"

She touched Guillaume's arm.

"You know how to cook lobster?"

He looked at her as if she'd asked him if he could cook an egg. "But of course."

"When you boil them, do you throw them in headfirst?"

His eyes popped open, an exaggerated expression of horror on his face.

"*Dieu, non.* I do not boil. I do not throw." He grimaced as if that last were an action that was inconceivable. He brought out the lobster stunner. Hy found it frightening.

She left with a head full of Guillaume's theories on live storage and humane killing—surely an oxymoron? She also had recipes for some unusual dishes to use in the newsletter. She'd promised to credit them to the "Internationally Acclaimed, Award-Winning Chef, Guillaume St. Jacques." Parker had frowned as Guillaume had reeled off his recipes and she'd scribbled them down. They'd included: *Homard St. Jacques, Jambes d'Homard Croquants*, and *Lobster Roly Poly.*

Lobster Roly Poly?

Chapter Sixteen

A comet crashed into Jupiter, fading into ice floes on Mars and the Martian landscape, red like the soil of The Island. Ian was staring at his computer screen, but didn't see any of it—not the exploding star, the Magellanic cloud, nor one of his favourites— the moon with Venus rising. He missed it all because he was over the moon himself. In a few hours, Hy would be coming to spend the night. He was not thinking about her, but about the new female he had met—Jasmine. *What a beautiful bird—smart, too, and cheeky.* He liked that about her.

It was the eve of Setting Day, and it had become a tradition for Hy and Ian to stay up all night, drinking and star-gazing, waiting on his widow's walk to watch the boats go out on the water at dawn. Ian had been trying to hook up his night-vision telescope to a webcam out on the roof and have the images play on his computer screen in the house. The webcam looked down on the village and over the water. It was meant for scientific observa- tion of the skies and seas. But Ian not only loved stargazing, he harboured a secret wish to bust a drug-smuggling operation. Prominently on his desk, right by the computer, were the coast guard guidelines for spotting suspicious activity at sea: vessels with no names on them, operating on no fixed schedule, whose crew appeared not to be fishermen, whose hull might be riding low in the water. The fact that there was no evidence of any drug smuggling at The Shores, and never had been, didn't deter him. He thought the area was ripe for it—especially now that it was so isolated. It was only a matter of time. His chances would be better, he thought, if he could monitor activities day and night.

Even without advanced technology, Ian had seen some interesting stuff through his rooftop telescope. *Nothing illegal—just damn interesting.*

Last August he'd viewed Hy and that American scientist down on the beach, the day after he'd teased her about the guy. She'd laughed and said nothing was going on. If it wasn't, it sure was by the time he spied them—or spied on them. Ian wasn't a peeping Tom. He'd been searching for suspicious boats on the water when the telescope had slipped—to a pair of male hands pushing up a woman's dress. Ian knew that dress—and he was reasonably familiar with the anatomy. Hy wasn't wearing panties. She had a nice ass, with or without clothes, but especially without. He'd felt differently about her after that. Sometimes, when he was with her, he would think about what he'd seen. She'd been so energetic, so joyful. But they were friends. Just friends.

Ian's real obsession with bringing night views inside was the technological challenge of setting up the system. He might never use it. Bent as he was on completing the hook-up, he was still distracted. He kept thinking about Jasmine. Maybe he needed a bird in his life.

Hy was pleased with Guillaume's contribution to her Super Saver newsletter, especially the Lobster Roly Poly recipe. She'd written them up and now she was working on a sidebar. She'd called it "Lobster Lore: Five Things We Bet You Didn't Know."

1) Lobsters can weigh 50 pounds and live one hundred years.

2) Island lobsters that had been tagged and transplanted to B.C. swam home—all the way down the west coast of North America through the Panama Canal and back up the east coast.

3) Lobsters are related to cockroaches and spiders. Deep-fried tarantulas are a delicacy in some parts of Asia.

4) Boiling lobsters alive is illegal in Reggio, Italy. The fine is up to

$600.

Then she ran out.

She needed one more fact.

She googled lobster. And it popped up again.

The Lobster Lover's Blog

Lobsters have two things going against them: they're ugly and delicious. If you're delicious, it doesn't matter how ugly you are. If you're ugly, you're toast…or on toast, in a sauce, over the flames, barbecued, grilled, boiled to death.

Just because lobsters are ugly, doesn't mean they're stupid. Traps are a dumb way to catch them. Scientists found that out when they stuck an underwater camera on a lobster trap. It got over 3,000 "hits"—attempts by lobsters to get into the trap and eat the bait, which was fresh herring. Since lobsters usually eat garbage, this was like a gourmet meal. They lined up to get some, like humans at a popular downtown restaurant or bar. They jockeyed for place, fought each other, lost a few limbs, and fewer than fifty got in. Of those, almost all got out.

When it came time to count the catch, there were only two edible lobsters left.

Even two is too many.

Hy printed the blog to take with her to Ian's. Maybe he could explain why she kept getting them. In the meantime, she now had fact number five—how easily lobsters can escape their traps. She had brief second thoughts about using the bit that linked lobsters with cockroaches and spiders. Customers might not like it. The Super Saver public relations department might not like it either. The head of PR, Eldon Frizzell, was a bit of a tight ass.

To hell with him. It was true, wasn't it? She did a quick edit, a spell-check and posted the newsletter. She was finished—several hours ahead of deadline.

Chapter Seventeen

All the local seagulls were circling over Big Bay Harbour the night before Setting Day, swooping and squawking as the fishermen loaded their boats with baited traps. They were stacked five feet high, with their curved wood and lath tops and flat bottoms, weighted with concrete. Green netting and wire caging enclosed the traps on sides and ends and divided the inside into two rooms. A hooped funnel was the way into the "kitchen," where the bait was, but the only way out was through the second, smaller room, the "parlour," with its small exit to let undersized lobsters escape. Yellow and green trap lines puddled on the wharf below each stack of traps and from the trap lines hung buoys in each fisherman's distinctive colours—bright pinks and oranges, neon greens, sober navies and brilliant blues, stroked with identifying numbers in black.

There were a baker's dozen of lobster boats—blue, green, red and sparkling white, their names painted in script on bows tipped upward: *Bay Runner, Tide's In, The Caper.*

The boats were mostly modern, remaining true to the traditional exterior look. Inside, some were equipped with all the latest GPS technology—and all with a more rudimentary convenience: "the head." It was now politically incorrect to pee in the water, but they still did.

There were dozens of bait bins, filled with fresh dead herring, their glassy eyes staring up blankly. Some seagulls stood on the traps, or on the wharf, motionless, wary, closely watching the humans and the bait, facing straight ahead, able to see every movement peripherally. The odd brave one trotted a few steps closer to its object, stopped, moved a few more steps forward, then stopped again.

Ben and Annabelle's boat had a hundred and sixty traps squeezed and stacked onto every inch of the deck, with just room to get by them to the wheelhouse. Ben was like a big kid on Christmas Eve—he could never go to sleep the night before Setting Day, so he and Annabelle would stay on the boat. Ben had bought it because it had a folding double berth—and because of the way the seller had advertised it: *Lobster Love Boat. Share Work and Play. Dual Steering Systems and a Custom Bunk Built for Two. One heck of a deal and slightly negotiable.* It became *The Annabelle,* but folks had begun calling it by Hy's nickname for the couple, AnnaBen, their own local Brangelina.

Annabelle did not look as glamorous in rubber boots and fishermen's gear as she did in high heels and plunging neckline, but Ben thought she looked great. He abandoned the last bait bin on the dock, jumped onto the boat, and squeezed into the wheelhouse behind her. He wrapped his arms around her, hands clutched under the familiar weight of her breasts, his head nuzzled into her neck. He was a tall man, but her legs were very nearly as long as his. They tucked comfortably into one another.

Neither spoke. They stared out at the setting sun, glancing off the clouds and streaking across the water, beams of red shining on the bay like a good omen, a blessing on the day to come. The thin layer of cloud held the colour as the sun slipped down and the sky became a red-pink canopy.

"Red sky at night, fisherman's delight," Ben chanted softly in Annabelle's ear, breathing in the sweet scent of her hair, like wild roses, burying himself in it, moving his hands up onto her breasts. She turned to him and they held each other, locked together, as the sky behind them darkened.

He kissed her as the last weak rays of golden light gave up the day and they went down below the wheelhouse where Annabelle had made up the double bunk with clean sheets that smelled of fresh Island air. The smell of herring was stronger, but it didn't bother them. This night was their little island of calm.

Visitors would soon invade The Island—ten times the population would arrive wanting food, shelter and fun. They were attracted by the laid-back lifestyle, but no one was busier than Islanders from May to September. These six hours were the last relaxed time Ben and Annabelle would have for months and they always spent it here on the boat, in each other's embrace. Annabelle would manage a few hours' sleep, but not Ben. He would hold her all night, breathe in her scent, and wait for the signal in the morning, the rush out to the water, the thrust into the short, intense season of hard work, here on this boat he loved, on the water he loved, with the woman he loved. They were squeezed into the bunk like sardines, happy in each other's arms.

Ian was skimming *The Lobster Lover's Blog* that Hy had just handed him.

"What is this?" He frowned. "Are you turning into an animal rights activist?"

"No. At least, I don't think so. It popped up on my computer. Appeared out of nowhere."

Hy was sitting on the floor in front of the woodstove. Ian had the same furniture he'd had in university. It had come out of his parents' house—Danish modern. At least it had been modern in the fifties. It was incongruous in this historic home and not suited to the dry heat of the woodstove combined with the damp climate of The Island. It was always collapsing.

The room was lit only by the fire and by Ian's screensaver images, currently flashing the birth of a new star across the room.

"It's not the first time. It's happened a few times."

"You must have accidentally subscribed."

"How do you do that? You always have to answer all those questions...name, address, email address, password, password again. I didn't sign in, log-in or call it up. The first time it popped up, I'd been working on the Super Saver newsletter. I fell asleep on the couch. When I woke up, I hit the space bar and there it was."

"Did you use gmail? Did you press a link?"

"Well, yes, but not until later. Anyway, it doesn't come through email. It comes anytime."

"You must have been doing something wrong. You said you'd been sleeping. Drinking wine?"

"That's right, blame it on me. The human's wrong, never the almighty computer."

"Computer error is always human error. Except that when computers go wrong, they're easier to fix."

"I swear that machine has a mind of its own. Look at all the links that pop up when you post a gmail."

"That's just a technical trick—word recognition." He tapped a finger on the piece of paper. "This has to have an explanation, too. How did this one appear?"

"I was writing the newsletter and needed another fact, so I googled lobster."

"Just lobster?"

She nodded.

"And this came up, straightaway?"

She nodded again.

"No Google page?"

"Nope."

He wrinkled his brow. "Have you *ever* googled the blog?"

"I told you—no." There was an edge to her voice. "Well, I did once, but only after two of them appeared on their own."

"That must be it." He crossed the room and tapped the keyboard. The birth of the star was suddenly aborted. He tapped some more. He stopped and stood back for a moment, looking puzzled. He tried again. Nothing.

She came up behind him. "What are you doing?"

"Googling *The Lobster Lover's Blog.*"

"I told you I'd tried."

"Yes, but—" He wouldn't give up. "There are a ton of blogs about lobsters and lovers and—well, you can imagine—but nothing by that name. Yet it's right here, slugged at the top of your page."

"I know." She looked smug. "Face it. That computer's only human. Made by a human with an imperfect brain."

"It's ridiculous." He was getting frustrated, hammering at the keys with increasing speed. "What's the point of a blog if it's not public?" He scrolled down, his body stiff, his movements abrupt.

"There *has* to be a logical explanation."

"You're just trying to prove I screwed up. I didn't. I know I didn't." She sat on the floor again. "What's bothering you is you can't prove I'm wrong."

"Just give me a minute."

The minute became five.

"Give it up, Ian. Let me tell you about murder at the W.I."

He responded with a grunt.

"Are you sure you didn't just write this yourself?" He punched a few more keys.

"It's not to get back at me for my Christmas gift?"

She shook her head. "Nope."

The "gift" he'd given her had been to secretly install screensaver images on her computer that included satellite photographs of Hurricane Katrina obscuring much of North America in its swirling fury; thunder clouds over the ocean; winds scouring the Sahara and a close-up on the eye of a storm over a small island. He'd done it to torment her, but she actually liked the images. It was only the wind battering at her house and making it sway that she hated—and the way Ian was acting now, all his attention on that damn computer.

"Are you listening? I said there was murder at the W.I."

Finally, he looked up. "What? What murder, where?" He came over, and sat in a chair beside her. The arm fell off when he rested his hand on it.

As he fiddled to put it back in place, Hy told him all about Camilla Samson and her performance at the Hall, the Google pages with the photograph by the river Dee, the Lobster Liberation Legion's activities in Europe and then returned to The Shores and the W.I. meeting.

"She called us murderers. Murderers!" She had to smile, thinking of it now.

Ian laughed. "I don't know why you bother with that bunch of old crows."

She looked offended. "Don't say that. I like crows."

A dark figure moved with quick, nervous steps through the village, along the road and up and down the lanes and driveways, wherever there were houses—scurrying, darting quick looks to all sides, making sure no one was awake or watching. The sleepy little village was completely dark—the only lights were those glowing in Ian's living room. Mailbox to mailbox, the night messenger went, putting a notice in each one.

Chapter Eighteen

Most of the clouds had moved out on a soft wind and the sky was clear when Ian and Hy climbed to the widow's walk. It was clear and bright with the moon nearly full, so that only a few of the brightest stars could be seen. Last year, the sky had been dark and dusted with the light of millions of stars, but Ian had kept his telescope trained on the green blip, blip of a satellite. *Gadgets.* Ian's obsession, thought Hy. *Gadgets.* They were all around as she unfolded a lawn chair and sat down: webcam; night-vision binoculars; telescope; patio heater and flare gun.

"Flare gun?" Hy picked it up and turned it over in her hands.

"You never know."

Hy was warmly dressed in her good jeans, with no holes in them, and the new Irish knit sweater Gus had made her for Christmas, but she was still cold. The temperature was hovering near zero. Ian switched on the patio heater and poured them each a mug of steaming coffee. The hot mug warmed her hands instantly. Ian sat down close to her, not quite touching, a thread of warmth between them.

Ian had the telescope aimed at the shore. He had spotted something on the water, just this side of Big Bay—a boat, but whose? He stood up, flipped on the night-vision goggles, searched for a name. He could find none. It was a boat with no name and one he didn't recognize. He knew all the boats that fished out of Big Bay. What was this strange vessel doing so late, entering the harbour on the eve of Setting Day?

He swivelled the telescope over to Hy. "What do you see?"

"A boat pulling around the cape, toward Big Bay. Big deal," she said. "Name's *The Crustacean*. Ever heard of it?"

"Never." He grabbed the 'scope from her, but the boat had gone around the cape and out of sight. *Damn.*

Ben and Annabelle were still awake when the unfamiliar vessel slipped into Big Bay, anchored at the mouth of the harbour and lowered a Zodiac into the water. The smaller vessel motored into the harbour, cut its engine and floated silently up to the end of the dock. Ben and Annabelle didn't hear it. They never heard the two intruders board their boat and cut their trap lines. They didn't hear them open the bait bin Ben had left on the wharf and spread the herring carcasses on the dock, spelling out the word *Killers*.

But the vandals heard them. When Annabelle screamed they took off, thinking they'd been spotted. Ben's grunts only made them go faster, convinced they were being pursued. The pair fled, in a rhythm with the passionate eruptions, back to their own craft. Assuming they'd been discovered, they fired up the ignition. The sound of the throbbing engine was lost in Ben's low moans rising in volume as he met Annabelle's passion. They couldn't possibly have heard a thing except each other.

"A pond? In the cookhouse?"

"Yup. Right at the back, with an intake pipe that goes all the way across the beach and down into the water."

"That can't be legal."

"No, but who's to stop him? Albert and Jared always did what they wanted with that beach. Always said it belonged to them—all the way to the water."

Hy and Ian had been discussing their separate meetings with Guillaume and Parker. He'd described the rare works of art he'd seen in the house; she had told him about the cookhouse, including Guillaume's theories about healthy and humane trapping and killing. "I think it's creepy," she ended. "That pond's just a high-end death row for lobsters."

"I can't help thinking it all fits together somehow. These people, here, all at once. The blog."

Hy dismissed it with a flutter of her hand.

"I think it's just a coincidence. Parker and Guillaume came because they liked the place and the house. Camilla came because I invited her and brought the legion with her."

"The blog? How do you explain that?"

She shrugged. "I don't know. I just got on the list, I guess. Random."

"I still think something's going on."

Hy raised her eyebrows and groaned. "Not your old drug-smuggling theory?"

"Don't forget the boat."

"*The Crustacean*?"

"I'm glad you saw the name. I wonder if Ben or Annabelle saw it?"

An hour before dawn, clouds moved back in and a soft steady rain began to fall, something more than a Scotch mist, but not much more—a fine spring rain that would green up the grass and set the lawnmowers putting and whirring. A flock of seagulls had descended on the fog-filled dawn to retrieve the herring bait spread along the dock at Big Bay. Ben was cursing and kicking and yelling at them to clear the road. Annabelle took a bucket of water to toss at the birds, but she stopped and wrinkled her brow. Was that a word? *Kill.* It looked like it spelled out *kill.* Dead fish eyes like flat marbles stared up from the word, one of them dotting the *i* nicely. *Teenagers. Just teenagers fooling around.* She tossed the water onto the dock and sent the birds flapping up into the sky in a great cacophony of displeasure. The gulls would soon follow the boats out of the harbour, hoping to steal bait that fell out of the traps. That's what they'd come for. The herring on the dock had been a bonus.

When it was time to move the boats out past the sand bar to wait for the signal to start the season, it had become what Gus called a dirty day. Sheets of rain chased across the water by blasts of wind. The wind, from the North, was blowing off the cold water, enshrouding the bay in fog. Annabelle took the wheel while Ben, his mouth set in a thin angry line, began replacing trap line. He was snarling and shaking the water out of his beard like a wet dog.

The lobster boats sat out beyond the sandbar for some time, their engines throbbing under the crash of the waves on the shore, a long low hum of anticipation. They looked, from a distance, like lobsters themselves, their sterns weighted down by traps, their proud prows sticking up out of the water, their bow lights like beady little eyes, shining with expectation. They waited, hungry to begin the season. A fisheries official, in a boat out on the water with them, gave the signal at precisely six a.m. The low hum turned to steady drumming, as the Big Bay fishing fleet moved out of the harbour into the open Gulf, leaving one huge wake behind it.

The morning mist made it difficult for Hy and Ian to see the flotilla when it came around the cape. They got only one good look at the boats heading into the water and the fog. The fleet disappeared, leaving one old wooden boat in view. Both it and its owner should have been long retired, but retirement meant death to eighty-two-year-old Wyman Matheson. He wasn't ready to go to his grave yet. His old tub, with just a few dozen handmade traps aboard, was dragging along, bobbing behind in the massive wake the others had churned up.

Watching the boats bob and rock on the water suddenly made Hy feel queasy. She shoved the 'scope to the side and sat down, bending her head to her knees.

"Anything wrong?"

Flashing lights. A migraine? No, just the old torment. Get over it. Will I never get over it?

She shook her head.

"No, I'm fine." She managed to produce a smile. "Just felt a bit dizzy for a moment."

When she looked up, even Wyman's boat was gone. As abruptly as it had begun, the start of the lobster season had ended. The boats were hidden, the fishermen laying down their lines in thick fog. The show was over.

"I'm glad we stayed up." Ian said those very same words every Setting Day.

"Yup, not the best year, but still pretty cool." Hy stretched. "Happy New Year."

That's what she always said. It always felt like the real new year at The Shores—a new beginning, fresh hope—the threshold to summer days of warm weather and bountiful harvests from the ocean and the earth.

Camilla, watching the boats disappear into the Gulf, thought of it quite differently. She thought of it as the beginning of the slaughter. It was why she was here. There would be work for the legionnaire tonight, and this was the perfect place to do it. Here— where he lived—his mind might be changed. Here there might be a big victory for the LLL. So far they had saved one lobster at a time, like the Chinese proverb said: *Little drops of water wear down big stones.* This time, the Legion might succeed in knocking down a whole pile of big stones.

After the rest of the boats had left, Scott Bergeron and Tom McFee took theirs out on the water, with not too many traps aboard. They didn't care if the other fishermen got into the season ahead of them; it meant more catch for them to poach, less work, and longer lie-ins on summer mornings. They headed out of the harbour to the high cry of a lone gull—another latecomer, wondering where the boats and bait had gone.

Scott and Tom would be wondering the same thing in the coming days, when they found the traps they tried to poach empty, inside each a small capsule containing a slip of paper spouting lobster rights.

After all the fishermen had returned home late in the morning, two vessels remained on the water—one, a small wooden dory. In it, a lone figure was wearing lobster camouflage and studying a local map of the Gulf bed. The fog made it difficult to see much farther than a few feet, but there was the odd break in the mist, allowing a man in the second, bigger, boat to spy the dory and its lone occupant.

"There!" the short man called to his companion, who grabbed the binoculars, looked through them, and said a rather odd thing.

"Coffin was right."

Chapter Nineteen

Over breakfast, Ian and Hy rehashed the mystery of the blog, the drama of Camilla's performance at the Institute meeting and the appearance of Parker and Guillaume in the neighbourhood. They munched on warm blueberry muffins Moira had produced the day before—not as good as April's but still delicious, with fresh farm butter melted into them. She would have laced them with laxative if she'd known Ian was sharing them with Hy.

They couldn't come to any conclusion—or agreement—about what was going on, but determined to quiz Ben and Annabelle at the lobster supper the following night. Perhaps that would turn up a few answers.

When Hy got home, there was a crumpled piece of paper stuffed between her screen and storm doors. It was a clever copy of her invitation to the lobster supper. Superimposed on it, in red print, it read *Cancelled*.

She knit her brow. *Who could have done it? Worry about that later. Have to undo the damage first.* She got on the phone. Gus had received one just like it. Ian had one stuffed in his mailbox. Call after call went out. Everyone seemed to have received one. It must be Camilla. *More guerrilla tactics.* Hy used the W.I. phone chain and organized the women to call everyone they could think of to make sure no one paid attention to the bogus mail-out. She made over forty calls herself.

"What does it mean?" Wayne Mahew, a very literal individual, asked. "It says cancelled, but still and all, it is an invitation. So which is which?" There was more of the same. Agnes Cousins, one-hundred-and-four and the oldest villager, when told it was a hoax, deemed it "the devil's hand at work in computers, typewriters, even the telephone, but not the warshing machine, no, not the warshing machine, that's a godsend."

The calls took all morning. There were chats with the shut-ins, delighted at receiving a phone call, conversations with people Hy hadn't had a chance to talk to in a while.

"That Woman." Annabelle had called Hy immediately when she got home and pulled the fake invitation out of her mailbox.

"I'm afraid so."

"Look, someone cut our trap lines and spread bait on the wharf. I think it spelled out a word—I think it said *kill*."

Hy bit her lip. "That sounds like her." Except she couldn't imagine Camilla getting her hands dirty with fish bait. The legionnaire must be here as well.

"I tell you, this is bad. Ben's growling. Came in off the water soaking wet, angry as a bear."

It was hard to imagine, but Annabelle knew Ben better than anyone. Other people just saw his easygoing side.

"I had hoped she was gone," Hy said after an awkward silence. "Maybe she is. This might be the other one."

"You mean there's more?"

"Well—" She was reluctant to admit it. "Well, there could be." She told Annabelle about the Lobster Liberation Legion.

"I really thought she was gone. Nathan picked her up after the meeting. I was sure he had taken her to the ferry. Do you know where he took her?"

"No, he never mentioned it. I'm only his mother."

"Can you ask him?"

"No."

"No?" Was she that pissed off?

"He's not here. You know Nathan always disappears for a few days around Setting Day." Hy knew. Nathan had gone fishing with his father since he was old enough to haul a trap, but when he reached puberty, the strangest thing had happened. The Setting Day he turned fourteen he became violently ill. He was so seasick he was rolling around in the bottom of the boat most of the way out and all the way home. Ever since, he'd made sure to be away when the season opened. That's when Annabelle had started fishing with Ben. They liked it so much, they didn't mind if Nathan came or not.

"Won't be back for a day or two. You can ask him then."

"Is the sandwich board sign ready?"

"Yup."

"Let's put it up outside the Hall."

"Already there," said Annabelle.

"Great. Thanks." While she was on the phone with Annabelle, Hy had changed the original invitations. When she got off the phone, she printed up the new copies with a bold headline at top: *Supper Still On*. She got back in her truck—*this was costing her gas!*—and delivered every one of them. In some cases, the bogus flyer was still in the mailbox, so she simply removed it.

Moira smirked when she saw Hy at her mailbox. She'd seen her go up to Ian's house last night and not emerge until morning. It happened every year and every year she watched and the bitter knot inside her tightened. Serves her right, thought Moira, turning her attention from the window to the oven. The muffins would be ready to take to Ian in just fifteen minutes. She went to change into a new dress. She didn't make any of the phone calls Hy had asked her to make.

It was late afternoon when Hy got home and dragged herself up to bed. When she awoke, it was nearly evening. She made tea and checked her email. She had an entire screen full of new messages.

Re: Your newsletter referring to lobsters' kinship to cockroaches, the first one began, *this is to inform you that I shall be making an official complaint...*

She scrolled to the bottom. It was from Clarence Cadogan, President of the The Island Fisherman's Association. It didn't bother her too much. He'd find any excuse to write a letter of complaint. She opened the next one:

How dare you...

Deleted it and opened the next:

I was disgusted...

Delete. Open.

The state of the fishery is bad enough as it is without people from away like you sticking their oar in and stirring the soup...

Interesting mix of metaphors, thought Hy. She deleted and scrolled to the next. They were all like that, email after email, expressing disgust, shock, fury. She steeled herself to keep looking through them. There was one relatively benign but religious email from The Island's most fanatical animal rights advocate, Maisie Alexander:

Were you meaning to cast aspersions on the cockroach? Let us not forget that the cockroach, too, is one of God's creatures...

Finally, Hy got to the last one.

Please be in touch A.S.A.P. regarding monthly newsletter...

It was from the Super Saver's Head of Public Relations, Marketing and Advertising—as his emails always reminded you. Eldon was probably going to give her the can.

Can of worms, she thought.

Chapter Twenty

"Yes?"

Sheldon Coffin held a cell phone in one hand and a ruler in the other. The phone was registered to a numbered company. He used it whenever he didn't want anyone to know what he was up to.

He was crouched on the lawn behind his oceanfront home, measuring the length of the grass. It swept down in one mani-cured swath to the shore of a private cove. What he heard next cleared the idea of daily lawn measurement right out of his head.

"Jesus Christ. Not again…"

Her again. Butting into his business.

"Deal with it." He threw the ruler across the lawn, stood up and brushed some loose clippings off his bare knees. It was a bit early in the year to be wearing shorts, but he warmed easily. He was sweating and dizzy from being crouched over and standing up so suddenly. He pulled a handkerchief from his shirt pocket and wiped it across the glistening round bald patch at the top of his head. It was surrounded by snow-white hair, clipped close like his lawn. The bald patch was turning pink under the warm Maine sun.

"How should I know? You figure it out. I don't want this knock-ing at my door."

He flipped the phone shut and threw it on the ground—end of conversation. Many of his conversations ended that way—always had. Only it wasn't like the old days, when you had the satisfac-tion of hanging up on someone by slamming down the receiver.

By the time he reached the stone patio—and a much-needed

gin and tonic—Sheldon was short of breath. He was a large man, made of solid fat. The circumference of one of his thighs exceeded the waist measurement of his perfectly kept wife, Stella—or so she claimed. It was her duty, part of the job of a wealthy man's wife, to remain reed-thin. It was also part of the unspoken job description that she be significantly younger than he, which she was—forty-something to his sixty-something—and that she should anticipate his every need. She was waiting for him on the flagstone patio in front of the French doors, his gin and tonic in hand. He grabbed it and slumped down in the soft pillows of a wicker chair. It creaked under his weight.

"Troubles, darling?" She instinctively made the word plural. It made it more innocuous. She didn't want to rile him. He riled so easily.

"Nothing." He said curtly. "Nothing at all."

Then what, she allowed herself a traitorous thought, was his cell phone doing in the middle of the lawn? She went over to pick it up. He took a long, slow haul on his drink, leaned back, shut his eyes and tried to calm down.

Stella placed the phone quietly on the table in front of him and slipped into the house. She knew better than to disturb him when his eyes were closed like that.

Sheldon was relaxing by visualizing money: Ben Franklin on the hundred dollar bill, Ulysses S. Grant on the fifty, all the way down to George Washington on the one dollar bill, with its reverse of the eye and the unfinished pyramid and the inscription: "Annuit Coeptis—He has favored our undertakings." In his day-dream, "He" was a god of Sheldon's own making, at his command.

After a few minutes, he opened his eyes and finished his gin and tonic. By then he felt good enough to resume measuring the lawn—except he couldn't find the damn ruler. It was one of those see-through plastic ones, six-inches long. Later in the evening it would get jammed in the lawn grooming equipment and would lose his gardener a half-day in the never-ending battle to keep the grass just the length Mr. Coffin liked it.

It was past midnight, but there was a fisherman on the water off Vanishing Point—a poacher. He was dressed in black, the hood of his sweatshirt pulled up around his face against the chill spring air. The water was calm, lapping up against his dory, where the lobster lines were.

Each time he pulled up a trap, water slopped up against the boat. And then again. *Was that an echo?* The poacher darted quick looks around him in case he was seen or, more likely, heard.

He tried to work quickly, but the traps were weighted with concrete and they were heavy. He grunted as he yanked up the load. When the trap was in the boat, he opened its door and tried to grab the lobster, low down on its back. He fumbled and was pinched by a claw, right through the thick rubber of the fisherman's glove. His thumb pulsed with pain. He tried again. He got the lobster this time, plugged the claws with wooden pegs, and tossed it, with an angry twist, into a bin of ice at the back of the dory. Then he lowered the trap into the water and hauled up the next one.

He had twelve. Another twelve and he'd call it a night.

On the other side of Vanishing Point, someone else was working the lobster lines. Not a fisher. Not a poacher. A member of the Lobster Liberation Legion. Dressed in a peculiar camouflage outfit—not wearing gloves, but it didn't matter. The legionnaire slid the lobster out of the trap with ease, chanting hypnotic sounds, in a thin, high reedy register, supporting the animal's body with tenderness, soothing it with soft strokes on its underside, as if it could feel the gentleness of the touch through its hard shell. The human moved slowly, alternating the whispering and the high-pitched hum, and slipped the creature back into the water.

Out beyond the lobster lines, a tall third figure watched from a vessel shrouded in darkness. *Two on the water. Two. Who was the second? Hauling lobster into the boat. Not releasing them. A poacher. Just a poacher. Not a concern. It was the other. The Legionnaire would have to be stopped. Coffin had made that quite clear. Quite clear.*

Hawthorne Parker saw none of it—not the poacher, the Legionnaire, nor the offshore vessel—as he closed the blinds on the night. He couldn't see beyond the railing of the deck. He thought he heard something. It was a sound he couldn't identify—like the earth groaning.

The sandwich board was propped up outside the Hall. In a variety of cheery colours it announced:

ANNUAL LOBSTER SUPPER
Wednesday 6 p.m.
EVERYONE WELCOME
Fundraiser for Hall

Hy was dragging herself around inside, short on sleep and slightly depressed, setting up tables for the supper the following night. The ladies had been cooking the lobsters a day ahead. It meant they'd be a bit tough and not that tasty. April knew this and had argued the point, but common sense and tradition prevailed. They'd always done it this way and how would they ever handle the number required if they had to cook them fresh, Gladys had stuck out her chin and stared at April with a belligerent face, hands balled into fists as if she might strike her. April gave in. Gladys looked around the table, pugnaciously, at each lady in turn, daring them to protest. No one did.

One reason Hy felt low was the cold looks she was getting from the other ladies. It was too soon for them either to forgive or forget the disastrous Institute speaker. Gladys Fraser never would—forgiving and forgetting was not in her genetic makeup.

Hy was also suffering from low blood sugar because she couldn't eat, not after what had happened in the kitchen when she tried to help April and Annabelle cook the lobsters. Her salivary glands overloaded with nausea every time she thought of it.

It was awful—the wild thrashing about when she dropped them into the boiling water—headfirst didn't make any difference. The lobsters emitted high piercing squeals, clawed the sides of the pots in a frantic attempt to escape and jerked their tails six times—always six times. Hy had counted. She'd wanted to pull them back out, but she knew it was too late. After cooking one pot, she'd traded with Estelle and offered to clean and set up instead.

The clean-up had taken a long time. Cooking even a couple of lobsters makes quite a mess. Cooking dozens—along with pounds of potato salad and coleslaw—had taken the ladies all evening. It was midnight before they'd finished making a mess. It was two in the morning before Hy headed home.

The Legionnaire slipped the dory into the cove, several inlets west of Vanishing Point in the shadow of Big Bay. Dragged up on the sand beside the old ruin of a boat shed, flipped over and covered with busted lobster traps and clumps of eel grass, it looked—if you could tell it was a boat at all—like some old wreck washed up on shore. Sand kicked around concealed the most obvious of the marks made from dragging the boat. Not that anyone would see them—nobody came to this place. It was The Shores' only rocky beach. Masses of seaweed gathered here, pushed in by the current, and it was like a jellyfish Killing Fields in the summer—hundreds of the slimy blood-red creatures, as big as a plate and as small as a quarter, were impaled or stranded on the rocks when the tide came and left without them. The locals called it Bloodsucker Cove. The beach was almost inaccessible except by boat. By land, it was a long climb down steep cliffs from one of the windiest capes on The Island. To get to the cliffs was a hike through a patch of prickly brush, from a lane that was not maintained and treacherously rutty.

The Legionnaire had a knack for finding such secret places and was blessed with a talent no one else possessed—the ability to tickle lobsters into a state of ecstatic insensibility. Sheldon Coffin always said it was a shame that such a talent was so squandered. Who knew the ways in which the fishing industry might benefit if it were only used for the right purposes—his purposes.

When she got home, Hy checked her email. *Just one.* She opened it.

You brought that bitch here. Now get rid of her.

Blood rushed to her head from embarrassment and anger. *Who'd sent it?* It just read *C. From my Blackberry. Couldn't be a fisherman. Or anyone local. No one at The Shores had a Blackberry—except Ian.* She'd figure it out later when her nerves stopped singing. Now she was going to get a decent night's sleep, if she could. It would be another long day tomorrow.

Just how long, Hy had no idea.

Chapter Twenty-One

The villagers began arriving at the hall before 6 p.m. The only person not there was Gus. She couldn't stand to be in the same room with the smell of lobster. Abel was nowhere to be seen either, but that wasn't unusual.

The folding wood tables with metal legs were set up in three rows down the full length of the main room. They were covered with white paper tablecloths and at each seat was a plastic knife, fork and spoon wrapped together in a paper napkin and stuffed into a Styrofoam cup. Baskets of dinner rolls and biscuits Gus had baked were placed down the centre of the table, along with tiny bud vases holding daffodils and crocuses. The tables were filling up quickly, some napkins already tucked under chins and placed on laps, knives eagerly spreading butter on rolls and biscuits.

Ben caught up to Harold going into the hall. "Nice night."

"Yup." Harold paused on the stoop and looked up at the clear sky. "'Spect it'll rain by nightfall."

"Hello there, Ben, Harold," Ian called from behind. "How's tricks?"

"Well, to be honest...here, come sit down."

The Hall was packed. They sat at the end of the last table. Hy came over to take their order.

"Lobster or chicken?"

Ian tucked his napkin into his sweatshirt collar and smiled up at Hy. "Lobster, of course."

Ben grunted. "Not for me. Can't stand the stuff. I'll have the chicken."

He turned to Ian. "Never could abide lobster. Makes a good living, most times, but I don't know how people can eat 'em. Just like big cockroaches to me."

He likely didn't know how right he was, thought Hy, as she headed to the kitchen to get their meals.

"Even a cockroach would be tasty dipped in butter and accompanied by the ladies' potato salad." Ian had a single man's appreciation of home cooking.

Ben was fiddling with his 50/50 ticket, folding and unfolding it.

"So what's on your mind, Ben? You look troubled."

"Well, and I am." Ben leaned his big elbow on the table and cupped his chin with thumb and forefinger, rubbing away at the coarse beard and thinking maybe he'd shave it off. His face was full, round and ruddy, weathered by the Gulf winds and salt spray.

"Someone cut my lines on Setting Day, upended a bin of bait on the wharf—Annabelle swears it spelled out *kill*—and now there's been tampering on my lines."

"Poachers?"

"I'm not sure if they've taken lobster or not—I can't say my catch is down—we're havin' a good season. But I run off my gear to the west and I've found some of 'em the odd time runnin' east."

"We've had strong winds. Couldn't the motion of the water and the currents shift them?"

Ben looked doubtful.

"Never seen it happen before. S'pose there's always a first time."

Hy arrived with their suppers, two heaping platefuls—one lobster, the other chicken, each with potato salad and coleslaw in the shape of an ice cream scoop. She put down the plates just as Ben was saying:

"You know, the other thing is, I run my lines nice and tight. I lower a trap down, then I play out the line all the way before I set the next trap down. I'm finding some of mine all in a bunch."

More trouble, thought Hy. *Cut trap lines, herring bait on the wharf, the cancelled invitations and now Ben saying someone was messing with his trap lines. It had to stop.* She'd have to find some way to stop it. She thought about the email. *Someone else wanted to stop it too. And not, from the sound of it, in a nice way.* She grit her teeth. Her head was starting to ache.

"That's robbery!" A high-pitched voice focused all eyes on the entrance where a white-faced Madeline stood with mouth wide open, unable to utter a sound, her mute stare frozen on Hawthorne Parker. He was dressed in pale olive slacks and a cashmere turtleneck—a perfect fit—his black hair slicked back, his lips so tightly clamped together they were as thin as the razor line of his mustache.

"Twenty dollars!" He patted his pockets, in search of his wallet. "That's far too much. I've seen those lobsters practically leap into your boats." The real problem was that he couldn't find his wallet. He'd left it at home. He had only the neatly folded ten-dollar bill he always kept in his pocket. Embarrassed, he pulled it out and looked at it, as if it might magically turn into a twenty.

"Ten is surely enough for whatever—" he gazed around at the diners and their dinners with eyes half-closed in contempt "—you have cooked up here. That's an awfully strange sign you have outside, I might add."

Annabelle, delivering dinners along with Hy, glared at Parker. She had made the sign. She made all the signs for all the events. She'd even won an Island poster contest several years before. She was used to compliments on her work. Certainly no one had ever complained before.

It wasn't the best way for Hawthorne Parker to introduce himself to the community. Only a very few locals had seen him at all. Now they were getting an eyeful and an earful. Tiny Madeline straightened up to her full height.

"But it's for the Hall," she squeaked.

"Oh, it's for the Hall," said Parker, his voice rising high with irritation. Then, more to himself, but loud enough for Madeline and those nearby to hear, "All for the Hall. All for one and one for all." He brushed his mustache with one finger and smirked, thinking himself terribly clever.

Hy wondered if he was drunk. He wasn't, but he was angry—angry with Guillaume. They'd had a big fight before he came here. He'd caught Guillaume snorting cocaine. He had raged at him, demanded to know where it came from and if there was any more. Guillaume had said not a word, but sat stubbornly on the couch, arms crossed, lips closed tight. If only Jasmine had been as silent, but she chose to echo Parker. She especially liked repeating "bloody hell." Parker had been so furious he had made himself dizzy. It had felt a bit like the floor was moving beneath him, but it couldn't have been. "Bloody hell…bloody hell…bloody hell…" Jasmine's screams had risen to a crescendo, and Parker had gritted his teeth and slammed out of the house. He'd gone for a drive to cool off. He'd forgotten all about the Hall supper until he saw the sign.

When he'd seen it, of course he'd had to come in.

Parker handed Madeline the ten dollars. It was U.S. currency. "This should do, surely." She looked carefully at the American money. The bills all looked the same. When she saw it was not a twenty, she looked around the room like a scared rabbit and caught Ian's eye. He got up and went over, pulling a clump of crushed bills out of his pocket.

"It's okay, Madeline, I'll get it." Ian singled out a reassuringly purple and thoroughly crumpled Canadian ten and stuck it in her hand with Parker's green bill. It was an unusual gesture for Ian, who parted with money reluctantly, except for what he spent on his toys. But he was still hoping to get Parker to agree to his GPS experiment. This might help his case.

Madeline looked at The Shores' only eligible bachelor with adoring eyes. Ian looked at the rest of the crumpled bills in his hand and stuffed them back into his pocket. He turned to Parker. "Why don't you come sit with us?"

Ian introduced him to Ben. "Of course, you know Harold," he said as they sat opposite the two men. Parker was trying hard to remember Ian's name. Hy came up to the table. "Mr. Parker, glad you could come."

He nodded curtly and looked around him with distaste. Why had he come in?

The sign, of course, the sign.

"Came to meet the locals." Parker's eyes shut and held just a moment too long. It struck Hy then what the tic meant. *Insincerity. Discomfort.* She took his order as the three other men turned their attention to their meals. She thought Parker looked odd and lonely sitting there, completely out of place, and she felt a bit sorry for him. She remembered what it was like the first time she had walked into the Hall, a stranger, and all eyes had turned on her.

A few had their eyes on her tonight too. There were some ugly stares, sour looks, from Germain Joudry, Estelle's husband, and some of the other fishermen. Their wives had told them all about the disastrous Institute meeting. Hy was trying to smile her way through it.

Near silence fell on the Hall as the villagers dug into their suppers. The lobsters had big claws and fat tails, a generous contribution from the Big Bay fishermen. Ian split open a claw and the salt water spilled out, stinging his arm. He stuck his fork into the white and pink-tinged flesh. It came out of the shell in one clean, perfect shape, the way he liked it. He dipped it into the pot of melted lemon butter on his plate. As he stuffed it into his mouth, a thin trickle of butter escaped down his chin. The lobster meat was sweet but not as tender as he liked it. It should have melted, like the butter, in his mouth. It would if it were freshly cooked. Still, he made a quite genuine moan of appreciation and slid the next claw out of its shell.

Harold liked to save the best for last. He was sucking on each little leg, drawing out the tiny treasure of flesh inside, slowly building up to the claws and tail.

"What brings you to The Shores?" Ben asked, one cheek chubby with chicken, another forkful already on its way up to his mouth. He was what Annabelle called a good eater.

"Personal reasons," said Parker stiffly, in a way that made Ian look up from his meal. "None of which I care to discuss."

Ben shrugged and turned his attention back to his meal. Hy caught the comment—and Ian's eye—as she delivered Parker's lobster. She had just set the plate down when there was another disturbance at the door.

"Free the Lobsters!"

Startled, Madeline accidentally upended the big jar that held the 50/50 money and tickets. She crawled under the table, chasing the rolling coins, glad to be out of the line of fire.

"Welcome the Lobster Liberation Legion!" A figure, dressed in full lobster camouflage, face covered with a bandana, strode into the hall waving a sheaf of papers.

"It hurts to boil to death!"

Everyone stopped eating.

"Read this and weep!" The Legionnaire slapped down a pamphlet in front of Germain. He was not a nice man and was a militant supporter of the controversial seal hunt that had just ended to the usual round of international protests. Grumpy was as good-natured as he ever got. There was the sound of a sharp intake of breath—a communal anticipation of Germain's reaction, in which Hy joined. Fortunately, his English was not all that good, and he hadn't yet figured out what was going on.

The Institute ladies came out of the kitchen and peeked around the doorway. Moira covered her mouth with her hands. Olive gripped her apron. April bit her lip. Rose Rose sat down on the stairs with a thump. Annabelle, two lobster suppers held aloft, pushed her way past the others, her eyes burning with what Ben called her man overboard expression. That was the look that made him, as he put it, give her a wide berth. Normally easygoing, she was very easy to read when she was riled. She nudged Hy with an elbow. The plate in her hand tipped precariously.

"Is it a man or a woman?"

The voice was deep and powerful, the figure stocky but small. The Legionnaire from the Website photographs.

"I don't know. It's hard to say."

Hy tried to relieve Annabelle of the lopsided plate.

"Liberate a lobster!"

The Legionnaire slapped pamphlets down the full length of one table.

The lobster slid off the plate and dove to the floor.

Hy bent over, picked it up and put it back. Annabelle elbowed her again, almost sending the lobster off the plate a second time.

"Hy, what have you done?"

Hy stiffened. "How could I know?"

Annabelle put the plate down in front of Wally Fraser. He was surprised—he'd seen the lobster fall to the floor. He shrugged and began to eat it anyway, keeping an eye on the action at the same time.

Hy watched numbly as three pamphlets landed in front of Ian, Ben and Harold.

Seeing Parker, the Legionnaire froze.

Parker pressed his lips together.

Their eyes locked.

Neither spoke.

Chapter Twenty-Two

Parker and the Legionnaire just kept staring at each other. Parker broke contact first. His brow furrowed. He looked down at the table. In a defiant gesture, the Legionnaire slapped a leaflet down in front of him, crossed the floor, and delivered one to everyone in the room. No one got in the way—not even Germain. His blood pressure had shot up and he was so red in the face his cheeks were almost purple. Estelle waddled over and made him take one of his heart pills.

Ian looked at Parker, trying to figure out what had just happened, but Parker's face gave away nothing. He was staring down at the pamphlet and stroking his mustache.

Ian read: *Lobsters are like you.*

There followed the Lobster Liberation Legion's entire manifesto, a radical message of the right to life of, not just lobsters, but of all the shellfish in the sea.

The Legionnaire climbed onto the stage. "Free yourself," came the jubilant yell. "Join the LLL—The Lobster Liberation Legion!" arms raised and hands open. The remainder of the pamphlets went flying up into the air. They fluttered and landed, most of them, on the dessert table on top of Olive's cream pie, Annabelle's chocolate squares and Moira's chewy brownies. One wedged itself, upright, into the thick butter icing of April Dewey's heavenly white cake.

Everyone had stopped eating, a few with forks halfway to their mouths. They put them down, staring instead in a mix of shock, horror, amusement and anger. There was some tittering, some muttering, some sounds of outrage. Some were looking everywhere *but* at the Legionnaire, others were pushing the leaflet around on the tables, not knowing quite what to do, and one or two were reading it.

No one said a thing. But they'd have plenty to say afterwards. Gladys later remarked that if this was the kind of purpose the Hall would be used for in future, she wasn't sure she cared to support it anymore. Madeline refused to take on door duty ever again.

There were two men huddled near the stage. They looked like fishermen, but Hy didn't recognize either. One of them was tall and thin, the other short and plump. The tall one vaulted onto the stage, a handful of pamphlets crushed in his fist, and lunged at the Legionnaire, who refused to budge, legs apart and arms akimbo.

"Shut it!" he yelled, bringing his raised fist down. The Legionnaire leaped out of the way.

"Bug-lovah!" yelled his friend, as he hauled himself up to join in the assault. Without stopping to think, Hy dashed to the rescue up the side stairs to the stage and took the Legionnaire's arm, dragging the Legionnaire into the kitchen and out the back door. She paused for a moment to lock the door from the inside, then pelted down the long wooden flight of stairs and into the parking lot over to the lobster-camouflaged jeep, still holding onto the Legionnaire's hand. Roughened red hands, long delicate fingers, an Irish wedding ring.

Man? Boy? Woman?

She looked into the hazel eyes above the bandana.

A woman. Another one.

Now there were two—at least two. Two lobster lovers, breeding like cockroaches. Camilla and her second-in-command.

"Who are you?"

No response.

"Are you with Camilla?'

The eyes blinked, but still no answer.

"Please, go away."

There was banging on the door at the top of the stairs.

"You can't keep doing this. Screwing up the invitations…"

The Legionnaire didn't speak. She looked bewildered.

"…cutting Ben's lines…"

Furrowed brow.

"…poaching for all I know."

Hot anger blazed in her eyes. Her voice was muffled by the bandana.

"That's not the Legion."

How could she lie with such genuine eyes?

"Then who?"

"Not the Legion," she repeated, emphatically, looking Hy straight in the eye. *A sincere look. What did it mean?*

The door burst open.

"Get in. Go. Now." Hy grabbed hold of the door handle and opened it. "You'll only make trouble. For me. For yourself."

She took a quick look back.

The two men were pounding down the stairs.

"You better get out of here. Fast!"

The woman didn't budge.

Hy stamped her foot. "Hurry."

The Legionnaire stepped around her and strode purposefully across the parking lot toward the men. The tall one with the concave stomach raised his fist at her. He sneered, revealing one long, yellow front tooth crossed over the other. His mouth was large, wet and hungry. He licked his lips with a tongue burred with white. His nose looked as if it must have been broken more than once.

The Legionnaire kept walking toward him. She stopped a few feet in front of him and he and his short friend stopped too, unnerved. Hy came up beside her, mouth dry with fear. The Legionnaire said nothing. The men said nothing. They hadn't expected this. Threats they were good at. *More?*

"Just go." Hy said in a tone of disdain.

The tall one pointed a finger within an inch of her face.

"You brought the bitch here. Now you get rid of her."

The words echoed in Hy's head. *You brought the bitch here. Now you get rid of her. The email.*

"Or else," snarled the short one. His eyebrows were thick and wild—stray black hairs so long they looked ready to fly away. He had a pug nose and small teeth, gaps between each one of them. His belly thrust out aggressively. He had almost as much girth as height. He had to look up at Hy to make his threat. She was looking down on him. That helped.

"Or else *what*?" She spat out the last word with contempt.

"Or else don't count on havin' any teeth ta eat bugs or baked goods," said the tall one, looming closer, his skinny chest thrust out in an unconvincing threat.

"Hey! What's going on out here?"

Ian. Standing in the glare of the outside light at the top of the stairs. *Thank God.*

The tall man shot a surly look at Hy, but he backed off. The short one did too, but as he moved back he clenched and unclenched his fist in a muted threat. Mutt and Jeff, thought Hy. The two men cleared off, heading at a run across the parking lot and down Cottage Lane to Mack's Shore.

"Thanks." The Legionnaire turned and went back to the jeep. She grabbed something from a pile on the passenger seat and shoved it at Hy.

"Here. You might find this interesting."

Another DVD. Hy had forgotten about the other—it must still be in her bag. She stuffed this one in her skirt pocket. The Legionnaire got in the jeep, shut the door and rolled down the window. Her hazel eyes smiled above the bandana.

"See ya." She waved and sped off.

Ian came up behind Hy.

"What was that all about?"

She shrugged.

"Are you all right?" He placed a hand on her shoulder. But before she could reply he burst out:

"Jesus Christ! Will you look at that?"

Ian was pointing at the sandwich board. She hadn't noticed it in the drama of the last five minutes.

On the board, in slashes and drips of red and black spray paint, nearly obliterating the original cheerful invitation, it read:

LOBSTER MURDER!
TORTURE IN THE SHORES HALL!!
FREE THE LOBSTERS!!!!
"FUNDRAISER FOR HELL."

"So that was what Parker was talking about." Ian folded the board and stuck it under his arm. They went back up into the kitchen and he set it down. The women crowded around.

Line by line, they read the sign. Ian laughed, but not one of the women even smiled.

"We'll have to be getting a new board," said Olive. "Wood don't come cheap." She was counting the night's take and recording it in her little black book down to the last penny.

"Oh, c'mon, Olive. Harold made this one from scraps. He can do it again. It won't cost anything."

"I suppose…"

"Well, that's not what I wrote," said Annabelle, as if anyone would think it was. "That Parker was right when he said it was strange. It sure is. Ben's going to be as mad as a hornet about that lobster lover."

"You better come home with me," Ian said to Hy. "Just wait here while I get my jacket."

Hy didn't want to be left alone with the ladies, and Annabelle's questions. She had seen truth in the Legionnaire's eyes, genuine bewilderment. *If it wasn't the Legion doing these things, then who?*

"Did you find out anything?" Annabelle.

"Not really. It's another woman. She denied the Legion did any of that stuff—cutting the lines, the invitations, all of it."

"She's lying." Moira.

"I'm not so sure. She looked really sincere."

"Well, look what she *has* done. It's damn obvious to me. Who else could it be?" Annabelle again. "You didn't find out anything else?"

Hy shook her head. She felt the DVD bulging in her pocket.

"Who were those two bullies? They looked like fishermen, but not any of ours."

Hy shrugged. "No idea."

Back in the main room, a group of angry men were picking up the pamphlets. They weren't intentionally cleaning up, they just wanted to get rid of them.

"It's hard enough to earn a living as it is…" Hal Dooley was snatching pamphlets off the desserts and tearing them up.

"*C'est ça.*" Germain, his colour returned to normal, grabbed some off the floor. He reddened from the effort. A few of the younger fishermen, Nathan's friends, were swearing and crushing the papers into balls or ripping them and stuffing them into the garbage. Moira followed them around with a recycling bin, trying to get them to toss the papers in it, without any success.

A few people continued to eat their meals. Parker was one of them. Ian found him sucking on the last tiny lobster leg. Ben was still eating too. He'd polished off a piece of lemon meringue pie, a slice of April's cake, and now he was demolishing a fudge brownie and a couple of peanut butter cookies.

"Mm…delicious." Parker tossed the little leg onto the heap of red shells on his plate.

"Worth your ten dollars?"

Parker gave a thin smile. "Perhaps. Not the lobster. It was tough. Tasted like it was boiled to death. Ha!" He smirked again in appreciation of his own wit, stroking his mustache. "Which of course it was," he added, in case Ian or Ben had missed the humour. "Boiled to death, but—" after a pause, "not to die for."

This time he smiled. It was a surprise, a pleasant smile, genuine for a change—a nostalgic smile.

"That potato salad, on the other hand, with a generous amount of egg, grated as was the onion, with rich homemade mayonnaise, reminds me of the kind my grandmother used to make, down on the coast of Maine."

"Why didn't you buy a cottage in Maine?" Ian risked another rebuff. "Why come here?"

"Nice place." He sounded like Harold MacLean.

There must be more to it, Ian thought. Something to do with what had happened tonight. *That look that had passed between Parker and the Legionnaire. Recognition?*

"Yes, it is a nice place, but as you know…" This might be his last chance to propose taking cliff measurements. "…the ice damage has left your house in a very precarious position, too close to the edge. If you'd let me—"

"Well," Parker pursed his lips. "I think that's my concern, not yours." His eyes narrowed to slits. "And I'll thank you to keep out of my business and off my property." The fact was, he didn't like to think about the precarious position his house, his treasures, his relationship were in. He patted his mouth with his napkin, folded it neatly, twice, into a square, and set it on the table. He stood up and left the Hall.

Ian smiled. Some of these Hall events could be deadly dull. That could not be said of tonight. "Well now, Ben, that was quite an evening, wasn't it?" Ben grinned back, but it was a bit forced. There were worry lines on his usually smooth forehead.

"It don't take much to see this Legion is messin' with my trap lines." Ben was rolling a cup around in his hands. He crushed it.

"You could be right. There are a few strange things going on. Hy and I saw a vessel called *The Crustacean* move into Big Bay on Setting Day eve. Have you seen it?"

"Can't say I have. Don't know about anyone else, but I could ask."

"Don't you stay overnight on the boat? I'm surprised you didn't hear anything."

The colour rose in Ben's already ruddy cheeks. He felt warmth flood through him. It wasn't embarrassment, although he looked sheepish. It was the warmth of desire. Ian could feel the big man's mood lighten, though he didn't know why. Ben was wondering if Annabelle could come home with him soon.

Ian pulled his jacket off the back of the chair.

"Well, if you find out anything, let me know."

"I'm goin' to have to talk to the guys about all of this. See what we're goin' to do if it keeps up." Ben's expression darkened again. He hated confrontations. Ian gave him a pat on the shoulder and went in search of Hy.

"Thank you, ladies, for putting on a magnificent meal as usual," he said when he returned to the kitchen. They smiled or lowered their heads or got back to their chores in response to his compliment.

Hy was helping Annabelle and April shove plastic cutlery, paper cups and plates into garbage bins, while Moira looked on with disapproval. Madeline and Olive were washing dishes. Hy thought Gus would be upset that she'd missed all the fun.

"Can you leave?" Ian asked her.

"Well—" Hy looked around at the other women working.

"Go on." Annabelle grabbed Ian and Hy by the arms, and pushed them in the direction of the door. "Hy—you cooked, set up, served and stood up to a couple of bullies. Leave the cleaning to us."

The gesture was meant as a small apology for the hard thoughts she'd had that evening and it made Hy feel a lot better. But if there were more trouble, the friendship might not survive. She'd have to figure out a way to stop whatever it was she'd begun. Can of worms, she thought again.

"You go and do—" Annabelle winked—"whatever it is you do." She knew Hy sometimes stayed over at Ian's. They made no secret of it. People talked, but no one could really figure out what was going on between them. Hy said that nothing was, and Annabelle believed her...to a point. *Nothing yet, but something was going on beneath the surface. Certainly something.* She doubted if they even knew themselves.

Moira had joined Madeline at the sink. As Hy and Ian left, she slammed a large plastic serving dish into the rack. Ian would not get any muffins—or cleaning services—for a couple of days as Moira fumed over the two of them going off together.

They'd have been surprised to know how carefully she watched them.

Chapter Twenty-Three

The Legionnaire headed down Cottage Lane, the way the two men had gone. She heard the buzzing of a motor, stopped, and squinted into the distance. It was still light and she could see a small boat—a Zodiac?—headed for the far cape, this side of Big Bay.

Sheldon's boys. She hadn't expected them to show up this quickly. She turned around, drove back past the Hall and down Wild Rose Lane.

She looked up at The A as she got out of the jeep. *He wouldn't be there, he was still at the Hall, but that's not why she'd come.* She saw the shadow of movement flit across the big windows. *Guillaume. Her real enemy.* She wondered why he wasn't at the Hall too.

She'd come down because she was interested in the low-slung cedar shingle building. She'd been watching late one night and seen Guillaume go in and out of it. Her keen senses told her there were lobsters in danger in there.

She killed her lights, cut her engine and let the vehicle roll silently down the lane as far as the pond. She made her way to the cookhouse in the twilight, glancing frequently up at the house to see that she wasn't spotted.

The door was unlocked. She peeked in and crept inside. She stared, unblinking, at the stainless steel appliances, smudged with the fingerprints of use; black granite counter, dusted with white powder; white ceramic floor, tracked with red clay footprints.

She followed the sound of the water to the back of the room, moving forward with tentative steps, glancing behind her frequently as if she might be discovered at any moment, with no way out. Like a lobster in a trap, she thought grimly. Ceramic tile gave way to concrete underfoot, rocks and streaming water—an artificial pond. It was empty, but there had been lobsters in there.

She could smell them.

She marched over to the freezer and opened the door. *Lasagne aux Homards, Lobsteroe* and *Tomato Tomalley,* stacked in labelled cartons on one shelf. On another, a plastic bag of cooked lobster claws. She shook her head sadly. *The carnage.*

Her mood shifted. Her eyes blazed. She began pulling the cartons off the shelf and emptying them into the pond, one after the other, shredding the boxes as she tore them open, cutting her hands on their sharp frozen edges, box after box after box, until her hands were red and swollen and dozens of chunks of lobster bobbed on the surface of the water. She cared more than the crustaceans did. Had there been a lobster in the pond, he might gladly have eaten his own.

An object on fire seemed to fly across the room. It was a cloud in a nebula, riddled with young stars, the flickering image dancing with the flames from Ian's wood stove. He had installed the new screensaver images from the Spitzer space telescope just that morning. The dusty leftovers from the birth of a planet, winds swirling around a newborn star, the silk veil of a space cloud: the otherworldly images brought a strange warmth to the room of life unknown.

The images cut out abruptly but a world very nearly as strange unfolded on the wide screen TV when Ian installed the Legionnaire's DVD. The picture was dark, blurry and jarring, but riveting. A pair of hands released a lobster from a trap, bare hands with long, well-formed fingers stroked its underside with slow, sure movements—movements of such delicacy that the creature appeared under the spell of the human, and of the inhuman sounds: a strange whispering followed by an ethereal cooing with a high sustained tone. It was not unpleasant—at least the lobster seemed to like it. It didn't move, not one of its ten legs nor its antennae, until it slipped into the water and suddenly burst back to life, plunging under the surface with a powerful thrust of its tail. Gone—in less than a second. The whole DVD wasn't a minute long. When it ended, neither Hy nor Ian spoke for a moment.

"So was that her—the one at the Hall tonight?" Ian pressed Pause.

"I guess so. You can only see the camouflage sleeve and…run it again."

They watched it again. "Pause it," she commanded. "There." She pointed at the screen. "See that?"

"What?"

"The ring." It was a gold Irish wedding ring. "It is her. I saw it on her hand."

"The things you women notice."

"Well, Mr. Drug Bust." Hy poked him in the side. "You have to have a sharp eye if you want to be a detective." She tossed him the DVD Camilla had given her at the Institute, that she'd found at the bottom of her purse.

Ian put it in the player.

"Exactly the same," she said as they watched the two hands nestle the lobster and release it, accompanied by the whispering and high-pitched sound.

Ian grinned when it ended. "Sounds a bit like Yoko Ono."

"Not as unpleasant. What is it? Not a hum, not a chant…"

"No." He ran the DVD again with the volume turned up. It should have been annoying, especially at that level of loudness, but it wasn't.

"Strangest thing I ever heard." Ian shook his head.

"Strangest thing I've ever seen." Hy flopped back in her chair, released from the images that had kept her sitting forward, a prisoner of the screen. Had it made her understand, as Camilla said it might? *The images and sounds were hypnotic, more powerful than the rhetoric of either woman. The power was in the visible bond between human and creature—such a creature. Lobsters weren't cute and cuddly like baby seals. They couldn't appeal with big limpid eyes. They were trapped and killed well out of sight, not bashed to death by clubs on ice floes crawling with celebrities and photo opportunities. The baby seals appealed to people's protective instincts, but lobsters? What was to love about them, all wrapped up in their hard shells, with legs like insects and creepy antennae? Maybe they did need an advocate. A champion. Maybe they'd found that in Camilla and the Legionnaire.* This much Hy did understand: those two saw something in lobsters that she had yet to see.

When Guillaume saw her, his eyes immediately flew to the lines of white powder threaded across the black granite counter. In his hand he held the silver straw he'd gone back to the house to fetch. He'd been careless.

She had the lobster claws out of the bag and in her hands when he came in. She turned to him and his eyes fixed on her face, the bandana that had covered it looped around her neck.

"You," he said. An accusation.

"Yes."

"Does he know?"

"Oh, yes, I think so."

"Why do you come?"

"To stop the slaughter."

His mouth twisted with bitterness. Disbelief clouded his eyes. He kept darting glances at the cocaine on the counter, licking and biting his lips. He could feel the drug's metallic taste in the back of his throat from the line he'd already done. It was just enough to make him want more—even with her here. *One line. One rush.*

Then he'd get her out. He leaned down, the silver straw poised above the powder, one eye on her.

She held up a lobster claw, dangled it over the pond and dropped it in.

His head jerked up, the straw slipped across the counter, and the cocaine scattered and spilled to the floor.

She held up the second claw, dangled and dropped it.

He charged at her.

She held up the third and let it go.

She backed away as he lunged forward, but he wasn't coming for her. As she dashed behind the island and headed for the door, he went straight for the pond, scooping the claws out of the water, dropping two, clutching the other to his chest as if it contained something very precious. It did—the last of his cocaine stash, obtained while at the Sunaura Spa. Clinics were ideal places to score drugs.

At the door she looked back at him with contempt. He was pathetic—kneeling on the floor, clutching the claws to his chest, a sobbing mess of a man.

Satisfied, she got into the jeep and headed for Bloodsucker Cove.

Chapter Twenty-Four

Hy was frowning, thinking about the trouble she'd brought to The Shores, now spreading through the community and hurting people she loved, like Ben and Annabelle.

Ian was fussing with the fire.

"No one but us has seen *The Crustacean*." He closed the wood-stove doors. "I asked Ben—he hadn't, but said he'd ask around." He poured two brandies. "Who do you think it belongs to—the Legion, or those two thugs who chased you out of the Hall?" He handed Hy a glass.

"Mutt and Jeff?" She swirled the brandy around and took a sip.

Ian looked quizzical. "You know them?"

"Idiot. Mutt and Jeff. Tall and thin. Short and fat."

"Oh, yeah." He said it uncertainly, as if realizing it was something he should know, and trying to act as if he did. He'd never been a comic book or cartoon kid.

Their real names were Bill and Wendell. Bill had a record as long as his thin arm of assaults, all the result of drinking bouts. He had one assault with a weapon—when he took a baseball bat to his buddy at a game one time. Wendell had been up for exposing a part of himself that was as short, stubby and insignificant as he felt. He got away with it for years, in spite of numerous sightings and reports to police—until he flashed a youngster whose mother was the head of a child protection organization. Both men had served time—not for being dangerous exactly, but nasty.

Ian sat down beside Hy.

"That was gutsy of you—and her—standing up to them like

that."

"I didn't think about it. She did. She knew what she was doing. They're bullies—they don't know what to do if you stand your ground."

"Still, I'd watch out, Hy. They're after her—and now they're mad at you too."

"They're not the only ones."

"They're the most dangerous ones."

"Who do you think they are?"

"I never thought I'd say this in all honesty, but they're from away, that much I know."

"I wouldn't be surprised if the Legionnaire and Camilla know them. Old enemies, something like that."

"Well, be careful, because they're your enemies now, too."

She didn't care about them. She cared about what people in the village thought of her—the Institute women, Annabelle and Ben. She flushed at the thought of the ugly looks she'd received that night. She felt dizzy with despair. What Ian said next didn't help.

"Ben's going to get the fishermen together to talk about what they should do. They want to get those Legionnaires out of here."

"It might not be the Legion, you know." Hy had told Ian about the Legionnaire's denials in the parking lot, those honest eyes, but he brushed it off, then and now.

"You're too soft, Hy. It's obviously them."

"I have to try to find Camilla and speak to her."

The sun had set and the moon had not yet risen. When it did, it would be too bright, and she'd have to head for shore. Until then, she was hauling them up, trap after trap, freeing the lobsters one at a time, then sliding them back into the water, carefully laying the lines back in the direction she found them. Jared, over in the next cove, was keeping the lobsters and tossing the lines and the traps back any which way. She became aware of his presence first.

As she let go of a trap the sound started up again, like an echo. Someone else on the water?

She held her breath, all movement frozen, a silent listener in the silent night. A trap splashing into the water—from where? She stayed still. Then—the sound of a trap being hauled into a boat—from beyond the point. A poacher.

She was hot with anger. She hated poachers. Fishermen were one thing, but poachers—scum, vermin, she thought. She hauled up her anchor and began rowing toward the sound.

"I don't know why Parker was slumming it with the locals—and he came without Guillaume. I don't know what that's about either. I do think he's hiding something."

Hy looked up from staring into her glass, swirling the brandy around. "Why?"

"It was the way he and the Legionnaire looked at each other. Like they knew each other."

"Really?"

"It looked like it. A long stare."

"So what do you think the connection might be?"

"Beats me."

"Lobsters?"

"Well, he likes eating them, like the rest of us."

"Speak for yourself. I wonder if I'll ever be able to eat another… after hearing them claw away at the pots."

"Just a natural escape response."

"Exactly. That's what upsets me."

"I mean without thought. There are few creatures with a smaller brain than a lobster. A mosquito maybe. You kill them."

"I do not," she said. Hy had literally not killed a fly until she moved to The Shores. They were thick on the air in summer and fall when the farmers spread manure on the fields. They lived in attics and walls in winter and in the spring came out to travel up and down sun-warmed windowpanes. They were stupid and dozy and died easily, stuck lifeless to curtains or fell dead into your hair. They were disgusting. Oh, yeah, she could kill flies, but they didn't scream when you swatted them.

"You like a burger now and then. You eat steak, I've seen you do it. Don't you think it's worse to kill a cow than a lobster?"

Hy thought of the cow that Gladys Fraser's husband Wally had fattened up one year. He kept it in a pasture smack in front of the house. Every evening when he came home, the cow charged across the pasture to greet him and trotted back alongside the car as it drove up to the house. The cow made eye contact with everyone who went by, gave a toss of its head and a welcoming moo. She became a village pet with a variety of names: Bessie, Bossie, Judy and Liza. Wally just called her The Cow—and one early morning in late Fall, he drove her off to be butchered. Her moos and bellows of distress woke the whole village. Most villagers refused to eat at Gladys and Wally's that winter. He had never fattened up a cow for the kill again. Killing and eating livestock had once been the way of life in The Shores, but the villagers now preferred the aisles of the Super Saver, where their beef came in anonymous packages.

Some organic farmers had begun to put names on the animals they raised as food. Last Thanksgiving Hy had eaten an organic chicken called Eva. Eva was delicious, but Hy hadn't liked eating something with a name. Maybe that's where she should draw the line.

"I know I eat animals. I just don't like to think about it."

"You'll be reduced to eating chips and chocolate bars like Atwood's *Edible Woman*. Then somebody will start campaigning for junk food rights. They'll say it's cruel to trap potato chips in dispensing machines and talk about the pain they feel when they're dropped into the tray."

"Yeah, yeah." She stared into the flames.

Ian stared at her.

Usually she looked boyish, but tonight she looked pretty, with the blouse and the skirt, and those curls. *Like copper.*

He couldn't stop looking at her hair.

Jared had finished for the night. As he rowed back to shore, he heard another pair of oars dipping in and out of the water. He jumped out of the boat and pulled it up, just able to make out the other dory as it came closer. He watched it, wary.

The dory scudded up on the sand. The Legionnaire jumped out, landing light on her feet, gave the boat a jerk, pulling it up beyond the water line. She marched over to Jared's boat and, without a word, lifted a lobster out of the bin, took the pegs out, waded into the water and released it. Then she came back for another.

"What the fuck do you think you're doing?"

"I might ask you the same thing," she said coolly, taking the second lobster into the water and releasing it.

Jared grabbed her wrist when she returned for the third. He twisted it and she winced. He gripped her so that she couldn't budge without sending searing pain up her arm.

"Those are my lobsters," he said, through gritted teeth.

"I doubt it," she responded, still cool in spite of the twist he gave when she said it, hot pain radiating from her wrist up through her arm and shoulder.

"Well, they're mine now," Jared grinned, revealing a gap where he had lost an eye tooth in a fight the night before. It had been over a tart he'd nailed to the wall outside the washroom at the Legion. She'd belonged to someone else. He'd lost the fight and the broad. It had left him feeling horny and frustrated. He was ripe for some action. *This one isn't bad. A bit scrawny.*

He reached out and clamped a hand on her breast. Not much to feel, he thought, but it would do. He pulled her close. She smelled of fish. She smelled like she'd already been doing it, but she hadn't done it with him yet. He tore open her jacket and shoved a hand up under her sweater. She struggled with him. He liked that. He liked a bitch with a bit of fight to her. He slapped her. Once. Twice. He could feel himself getting hard. He hauled up for a third and she kneed him in the groin.

Then she was gone. Sheer adrenalin and sense of purpose propelled her at an astonishing speed. She grabbed the bin from his boat, heaved it into her dory, jumped in and took off, oars flashing. She rowed as fast as she could, but he did not pursue her. He was bent over, nursing the pain, the swelling that now had nothing to do with desire.

"Bitch!" He yelled after her. "Fuckin' bitch!" he repeated. "I'll fuckin' kill you!"

She kept on rowing. When she got out deep enough, she slipped the lobsters, one by one, back into the water.

Moira Toombs stopped abruptly on her way out the Hall door and her sister Madeline bumped into her stiff, unyielding back. She had a clear view of Ian's living room up the hill, the flickering of the wood stove, the pulsing glow of the iMac and two figures with heads so close together, they might have been touching. *Or kissing?* She turned her head away sharply and picked up her pace, leaving Madeline struggling to catch up.

It wasn't fair. Hyacinth didn't even want him, or else what had she been doing fooling around with that tourist last August? Moira couldn't sleep for thinking about it, jaw clenched, teeth grinding. An hour later, she got up and looked out from her window. The lights, and the fire, were still on in Ian's living room. An hour later the lights had been replaced with candles, dancing with flickering flames. It was after midnight.

Chapter Twenty-Five

"You know, maybe you're not to blame." Ian had kicked off his shoes and loosened his shirt collar. "Maybe Parker's the reason the Legion is here."

"Don't I wish…"

"He said he spent his childhood in Maine. There could be a lobster connection."

"Mutt and Jeff are from Maine."

"How do you know that?"

"They used the word 'bug.' That's what some Maine fishermen call lobsters. It said that on the blog."

"Let's say the Legionnaire does know him, and that she knows Matt and Jeff—"

"Mutt."

"Okay, Mutt and Jeff. That connects them. There must be a reason they're all here."

"And that reason is…?"

"Beats me."

"I still say it's entirely coincidental. Camilla and the Legionnaire are here because I invited them, well Camilla anyway. I have no idea why Parker came here, with his Gourmet Guggenheim-by-the-sea, but he and Guillaume are not the first weird tourists we've ever had."

"True."

They were both thinking of the New York financier who'd bought a field right across from Hy, leased back all but a small patch to the farmer he'd bought it from, and spent several weeks every Fall there—sleeping in his Cadillac while potatoes were harvested around him. One year, he had put up a shed, lived in it for a few weeks and then never came back. Now it was falling apart, door broken off, contents spilling into the fields—nothing worth having, as the thief had found out. *Jared?*

They were silent for a moment, but Ian's logical brain was seeing a pattern.

"I think we're caught in the middle of something. Think about it. Parker arrives. He builds a gourmet kitchen for his lover, who's a chef. Lobster's his specialty. Camilla brings the LLL to the Institute meeting. Pro-lobster blogs begin appearing at will on your computer. The Legionnaire shows up and trashes our lobster supper. She and Parker know each other, but they're not letting on. Two bullies chase her—and you—out of the Hall. We've had trap lines cut and interfered with and the Legion has denied doing it. If that's true, someone else must have. Don't tell me there's nothing going on."

Hy had to laugh. "When you put it that way…"

"I'm going to see what I can google tomorrow about Parker, Camilla, the LLL, *The Crustacean*…maybe even Guillaume."

"You'll be googling all day."

"I'd do it tonight, if I didn't have company."

"Do you want me to go?" She emptied her brandy snifter.

"I should have said if I didn't have such *fine* company."

The iMac screen filled, like a flower blossoming, with the image of a full moon, its glow cast across the room. It may have been just electronics, but it seemed to have some of the effect of the real thing.

She put her glass down. Stretched.

Was she leaving? He grabbed the bottle from the table.

"Another brandy?"

She had no intention of leaving. She was feeling a bit tight.

"Perhaps just one."

The fire glowed. The iMac glowed. Hyacinth glowed, as she held out her glass for what would be just the first of several refills. Ian poured, smiling a small, tight smile.

He wanted to touch her hair, but he was afraid she'd pull away.

Jared had retreated to the cookhouse, still holding on to his private parts. He was surprised to find Guillaume there, sitting in the dark, where he'd been sulking for several hours. He'd tried to rescue what he could of his cocaine stash, without success. He'd put some of the claws in the microwave, hoping the drug would dry. Instead, it had shrunk and yellowed. Guillaume snorted it anyway. He'd spent the last couple of hours knocking back a bottle of cooking sherry. He had just emptied the last drop when Jared came into the cookhouse, clutching his balls.

Guillaume raised his eyebrows.

"No lobstair?" he asked.

"No," Jared glared at him. "No fuckin' lobster. Bitch fuckin' stole them."

Guillaume frowned.

"Oh, zat girl. Yes. Zat girl."

"I'm gonna kill her ass."

Guillaume smiled. *Perhaps this Jar-aid was not so bad after all. He might be useful.* Guillaume sniffed.

Jared looked at him sharply. Guillaume put a finger to his nose. Sniffed again. Jared got the message.

"Coke. You want some coke?"

"You know where we could has some?"

Jared smiled his gap-toothed grin. "Do I? Ye -e-s." He drew out the word in the distinctive Island way, distorting the vowel sound. "You got coin?"

Guillaume frowned.

"Sorry, Bud, no money, no dope." Then an idea hit him.

"Can we take the Merc?"

Guillaume looked doubtful. He'd seen Parker come home hours ago. He'd seen the lights go out. "And I snort for free?"

"I drive—you snort for free," said Jared.

"*Eh bien. Allons-y.*"

Jared didn't understand even simple French. It was all gobbledygook to him, but it seemed that Guillaume had said yes.

"Let's go!" He'd almost completely forgotten how much his balls hurt. Soon, he hoped, his entire body would be numb to pain.

Parker had returned to an empty house. He knew that he would find Guillaume in the cookhouse, but he didn't dare go down. He was afraid of what he would find. If he did, it would mean the end. It was the end anyway, he thought, as he sat down with a bottle of scotch and a crystal glass. It was, in every real way, already over, but for the final moment, the moment he had been avoiding for over a year. More like years. Then he would be what he feared most…alone. A creature wrapped in a brittle shell of loneliness. He put out the lights and lay in the dark on the soft leather couch, drinking himself into a numb and maudlin state, nursing a thirty-year-old single malt and bemoaning a relationship that was not quite as old, nor nearly as smooth.

It had begun so well—with a jolt of desire, when his fingers first touched Guillaume's. He'd been giving him a cheque, a prize to the best chef in the restaurant chain. That handing over of money was symbolic of what their relationship would become. That he would pay the bills that gave him a right to Guillaume.

They had sex that first night under the deck of the restaurant, with Guillaume taking him roughly up against a post. It went on like that all the long summer, long as only a summer in youth can be. It was their secret, fuelling desire and short, filthy encounters that sent Parker spiraling down to a depth of depravity he never reached again, nor would want to. Then, his every thought had been of Guillaume. He could think of nothing else except those petulant lips on his body, the teeth biting, those deft fingers providing agonizing ecstasy—until he got scared.

It had started to spin out of control, Guillaume insisting on moving into territory that excited, but frightened, him. It was an erotic world he could not inhabit. He ran from Guillaume, from his own true nature, back to the woman he had left for Guillaume and into a short doomed marriage. One, two, three unsatisfactory couplings with the girl, and he had returned to Guillaume, Guillaume, who had pursued him on his honeymoon and made him pay for the desertion repeatedly, making him beg, debase himself physically in every way the distorted chef's mind could imagine. For a while, this treatment made Parker feel strangely safe—wanted, cocooned in a world of distorted desire, shameful games of slave and master, but he had finally tired of it. Guillaume had tired of him and went looking for boys, fresh meat. It was clear Guillaume didn't love him now—if he ever had. He knew that without the money, he would not possess Guillaume at all. Even with it, the ownership was tentative.

So absorbed was he in his misery that Parker neither heard nor saw the car leaving. Jared slipped it into neutral and rolled it down the lane before engaging the ignition and the lights. He did so just in time to illuminate a vehicle coming down the road in front of them. He nearly smashed into it, as he gunned the motor and took the corner, the other vehicle turning into the lane he had just left, and heading up to the house. Jared pulled off onto Wild Rose Lane, spitting lumps of wet red clay behind him, and soon was rocketing down The Island Way. It was Jared's speeding that got them to the last ferry. Guillaume's eyes were shut tight the whole time—he was scared silly at how fast the car was going.

Guillaume had no choice; he needed Jared; he needed cocaine. The need, and the memory of that last hit, were making him fidget. His tongue was darting all over his mouth, moistening it. It was dry, but everywhere else he was wet—sweat trickling down his forehead, under his arms, coating his palms. He rubbed them together rhythmically, as if trying to erase his agitation. Jared's driving heightened his discomfort and there was only a brief reprieve as the ferry chugged them across the water. Then they were heading to Winterside, Guillaume hanging on to the seat with both hands, Jared having a blast. "Let's see what this baby can do."

It could do quite a bit. The sporty Mercedes, praised by *Road and Track* for its "impressive handling, precise steering and incredible road holding," proved no match for Island roads. They'd been laid out with horses, not horsepower, in mind. Just coming into Winterside Jared missed a sharp curve.

The car veered off the road, sailed over a ditch and into a farmer's field.

Airborne.

Chapter Twenty-Six

Camilla stopped the vehicle suddenly, just where the land narrowed at one end of the "v." Not knowing the terrain, she'd almost gone over the edge. She'd seen Jared in the driver's seat of the Mercedes, Guillaume beside him. That meant Parker would be alone.

The motion light startled her as she approached the door. She knocked several times, then several more times. Someone knocked back. She knocked again. Again there was an echo. It was Jasmine. The parrot had taken up the sound and helped beat it into Parker's unconscious, waking him. Disoriented by drink and sleep, he struggled up from the couch. He didn't bother to smooth down his hair—one lock stood straight up on the top of his head, and his cashmere sweater was crumpled.

He peered through the peephole.

Time melted away at the sight of her.

It was a good thing Guillaume had made Jared put on his seat belt. They were stunned, freaked out, but otherwise okay. Jared, who thought he never got any breaks, had gotten one tonight. The car's impact was softened by a big stack of hay bales that had been sitting in the field for years. After police had completed their measurement and analysis, the accident was used for years in training exercises.

Getting down wasn't easy. They half-slid, half-fell, to the ground.

"Run!" yelled Jared. Guillaume looked at him in complete

disbelief. No one had ever said that to him before.

"It may catch fire!"

It was a distinct possibility. One spark from the car and the straw would ignite. Jared had been brought up on a diet of TV and movies in which cars were always bursting into flame, and he knew hay could spontaneously combust. He got away from it fast, with Guillaume stumbling along behind him.

Even through the peephole, he could see that she looked the same—exactly the same—the sleek honey-blonde hair, the sweater set, the pearls.

He came back to the present.

Good Lord, she still had them. A surprise after what she'd tried to do with them. Could he speak with her? She had made the first move. He should make the next. He put his hand on the deadlock.

"Okay," said Jared. "Here's what I think. I think you better stay with the car. If the cops come and find I've been drivin' it, I could be in a heap of trouble. Car theft, maybe, I don't know." He didn't add that he'd been driving without a license.

Guillaume looked as if he were about to protest, so Jared kept talking quickly.

"Here's the deal. We're not far from town. I'll hoof it into The Lazy, Eh? and make the deal. You handle the cops and, when it's all done, get them to take you there. I'll find us a ride home."

Neither questioned the idea of having the cops act as an escort to a drug deal. Jared just wanted to get away from the scene. He hoped to be in and out of the Eh before the police came to rescue Guillaume. He was so desperate, he would have said anything, and Guillaume was so drunk and drugged and panicked he swallowed it.

"What if no one comes? But I cannot stay 'ere all night." The road looked dark and forbidding. It was late. There wouldn't be much traffic. In fact, after Jared managed to hitch a ride, there wasn't any for hours.

"I'll make sure the cops know when I get into town. Even if I have to walk, it'll take me, say, twenty minutes to get there. You wait maybe a half-hour. Just don't say who was drivin', mind." He stuck a dirty finger in Guillaume's face. "Don't tell them, don't tell Parker. If you do…" He sliced a finger across his neck. "No deal."

"But I will freeze."

Jared looked over at the Mercedes.

"Get back in the car. I think it's safe now. Nothing's happened, nothing will. We could *drive* it off there." He laughed at Guillaume's look of horror. He approached it and sniffed. *No gas smell.* He hadn't imagined how Guillaume would have climbed up. Guillaume had, and it was not going to happen. Before he could say anything, Jared took off. There was a car coming down the road. Maybe he could thumb a lift.

Guillaume slumped to the ground. It was wet. He started to cry.

Parker lifted his eye from the peephole. His hand dropped down from the deadlock. *Not now.* He couldn't do it now, in this turmoil with Guillaume. *Why had she chosen now?* He turned, and with slow steps of discouragement, returned to the couch. He half-filled the glass with Scotch and knocked it back, ignoring the sound of Jasmine replicating the trickle of the liquid into the glass. It burned through his chest, bringing a false warmth to his cold heart—at least he could feel *something.* A few moments passed. He waited, body tensed, for the knocking to begin again, but it did not. Instead, he heard the sound of a car starting up. The glow of the motion light was extinguished and he was in darkness again. She was gone.

He fell into a disturbed sleep, a dream that he was a young man again and full of feeling. It was a moonlit night on the shore and his lover had shoved a rough hand between his legs. The dream turned into a nightmare with a soft caress on his cheek. It was her, wearing only the pearls. There, with him, in his shame, with Guillaume.

He woke up in a sweat and felt the house moving around him, a noise deep in the earth.

She'd failed to get through to him. Camilla realized there would be no big victory for the Legion. *Just the wearing away of stones, tiny drop by tiny drop, one lobster at a time. Maybe time to move on—to more fertile ground. This place was too small—every tremor caused an earthquake. Time to consider a change in location.* She found her way to the Legionnaire's hiding place.

Jared never did notify the police—he was stupid, but not that stupid. Guillaume spent most of the night huddled up against the haystack, alternately shivering and sniveling. No cars went by for three long hours. Finally one did, in the wrong direction, but the driver must have spotted the headlights high up on the haystack, because shortly thereafter, the police arrived.

"Whew," Murdo Black shook his head at the sight of the Mercedes perched on the haystack. Murdo was stocky, dark-haired and his fingernails were chewed down to the quick, especially since he'd been partnered with Jane Jamieson, tall, thin, raven-haired and strictly by the book. Fact was, Murdo got a lot more out of witnesses and suspects with his friendly manner than she did with all her strict adherence to the rules.

She pulled out her notebook.

"Name," she said.

"Guillaume St. Jacques." She spoke no French. He had to spell it for her.

"You the driver?"

Murdo was walking around the haystack, still shaking his head. He paced out the distance to the road, making mental notes. As usual, he'd left his notebook in the car. Constable Jamieson took enough notes for both of them.

"No…uh…yes…well…"

"Yes or no?" She snapped, unsmiling.

"Well, yes."

"License." She popped the pencil behind her ear and held out a hand.

"Well, I…uh…" He shrugged.

"No license?"

He shook his head.

"Not here? Not on you? Or not at all?"

He just kept shaking his head.

Murdo hauled himself up on the haystack. The driver's door was wide open. He reached in and turned off the lights.

"But you were driving?"

Guillaume nodded. She pulled out the pencil again and wrote *Driving without a license.*

Guillaume couldn't drive, but he couldn't think of another, better story. He was also remembering Jared's warning and still hoping he'd score. If not—well, jail might open up some new options. That's how desperate he was.

The Legionnaire was exhausted, aching from the effort of hauling up the traps and fending off the disgusting poacher. She'd be glad to clear out of here. It was under consideration anyway. She'd go wherever the LLL needed her to be. She snuggled into her sleeping bag. It was chilly. After a while, she warmed up. A glow lit her little hideaway for another hour or so, until it, too, went dark like the night.

"Your car?"

"*Oui. Mais non.* It belongs to my partnair."

Part-nair? "Your wife?"

"No. My partnair."

Murdo closed the driver's door and crawled around the vehicle to the passenger side. That door was also open.

"Business partner?"

"No, in life. *Mon mari.*"

Jamieson raised a cool eyebrow.

"Registration?"

Guillaume lifted his hands, palms upward.

"Got it here," Murdo called down. He pulled it out of the glove compartment, jumped down and handed it to Jamieson.

She looked at it. *The original. When would people learn not to keep the original in the vehicle? Registered to Hawthorne Parker. His partner?* For all she knew, the car was stolen.

"So what happened?" Murdo asked.

Guillaume tried to explain. It didn't sound like he'd been driving. Jamieson knew he was lying, but couldn't figure out why he'd say he'd been driving if he hadn't.

They took Guillaume to the police station and booked him with reckless driving and driving without a license. They were still considering a charge of driving a stolen vehicle. That would depend on what they found out when they contacted the owner. They put him in a cell with a local drug dealer.

It wasn't long before Guillaume had struck a deal for a delivery to be made to The Shores the next day. He was confident he'd be out in twenty-four hours—and high shortly after that. The thought helped calm his nerves.

Parker had been drifting in and out of sleep interspersed with memories. It was coming close to dawn and the sky was beginning to lighten. He was thinking about the pearls—and the time he'd seen her in New York—Cartier's. She came up right beside him and pulled the necklace out of her coat pocket. *Her pocket!* Parker could see the jeweller had the same thought as he did when she dumped the strand on the counter, a hard gleam in her eyes. She wanted to sell them. The jeweller touched them tentatively, reverently, hunger in his eyes.

Saltwater Japanese Akoya cultured pearls. He fingered each one, delicately. Pure white body colour, lovely rose hue, lustre off the charts. He glanced at Camilla. She nodded and he picked them up and turned them over in his hands. *Unblemished. Matching close to one hundred percent, as far as the bare eye could tell, and what other measure really mattered? Skin thickness bound to be a full millimetre, once closely examined. The clasp—unique.* He'd never seen another like it. Most pearl strands have what's called a lobster clasp, one end squeezing into the other, which grips it like a claw and holds it fast. It doesn't look anything like a lobster, but this one did—in 24 carat gold, claws and tail in two separate halves that clicked together to make the whole. It had tiny diamonds for eyes.

It was the custom clasp that gave her away. The pearls could belong to no other. Parker hadn't really looked at her until then and only the pearls would have told him it was she, wrapped as she was in a big wool scarf, with large sunglasses. He paled at the sight of her.

The jeweller put the pearls down and looked up at Parker, so well-dressed in his Burberry trench coat; she…well, the coat was out of date, vintage he supposed. Still, she was slinging this exceptional necklace around like it was a string of candy. He looked at her, doubt on his face; she read his meaning instantly and stuck her chin out, defying him to challenge her ownership. He laid the pearls down and Parker swept them off the counter. In the end, it was he who bought them. Without negotiation, Parker made out a generous cheque to her and another to the jeweller. He signed them with his convoluted scribble. Her mouth was set in a determined line throughout the whole transaction. The jeweller did the least he could for his fat commission. He placed the pearls in a black leather case lined with cream satin, perfectly proportioned to hold them. He tucked them in expertly, a finger lingering on them as if reluctant to part with something so fine so quickly. He snapped the box shut and handed it to Parker. Parker handed it to her. Her eyebrows shot up.

Parker gave one curt nod.

"They were always yours." The only words he said to her during the entire transaction.

She took the box, pocketed it, and raised the cheque to her forehead in a salute. She spoke just three words:

"For the cause," she said, and left the store.

She had spent the money on her lobster war, of course. He liked to think she'd been so hard and cold about the pearls because she felt something for them. He dismissed the thought. Their meaning was for him alone. Yet, still she had them. In the chill region of his soul, there was an icy regret forming that he had let her come and go and given her no reason to open her heart to him. *Why should she?* He hadn't even opened the door to her.

Jared had made it to the bar, where he met up with the two sisters who'd shown him such a good time a few nights before. Soon he was rubbing up against both of them in their king-size bed, but it wasn't working. For the first time ever, it wasn't working. Nothing he could do would make it work—not four boobs, not two of everything else. He couldn't even whack himself off. It was just too damn painful. *A real piss off.* They were two horny girls and they wanted some. He didn't have any to give. He pretended to pass out and then he really did. When he woke up it was morning and he was the only one in the bed. He got up, made a few calls, and soon had arranged a ride with a fisherman buddy back to The Shores.

Chapter Twenty-Seven

Hy slipped out of Ian's at first light. A thin coat of frost lay on the ground. She walked at a brisk pace down the hill straight into the red glow of the sun breaking over the shoreline, tipping the white caps of the waves with sparks of fire. At this time of morning, the sound of the ocean was a roar, even though the waves were just lightly rolling in.

There was the sweet skunky smell of foxes on the damp dawn air. She saw one as she reached the corner, on the vacant lot where the school used to be. A young fox, one of last year's litter, ginger with a black tail. She stamped her foot and it skittered off, but not far. It stopped, turned back to gaze at her, unafraid, examining her with interest and intelligence in its eyes.

As she marched down The Way, Hy tried to figure out what she could do to defuse the lobster war. She couldn't think of a thing. She picked up her pace. First, she'd get home, pull on her sneakers and go for a run. She always got her best ideas when she ran. Never mind that among those ideas had been to invite Professor Walpole and Camilla Samson to speak to Institute.

And maybe she'd be able to sort out last night.

Only friendship? Or something more?

Parker's cell phone vibrated in his pocket. It woke him, stiff and aching, on the couch where he had lain all night. He looked at his Rolex. *Six o'clock! Who'd be calling so early?* He pulled the phone out of his pocket and flipped it open.

"Parker."

Good Lord, the police.

"What?…Yes, I know him…Is any…Yes, that's my car…What?"

"What!" He repeated, in disbelief.

"Yes…yes…yes…yes…I'd be grateful for that. No. Keep him there."

When Hy got home, there was a draft blowing through the house. She felt the unusual, slightly dizzying, sensation of someone else's presence in her home. She crept into the main room and paused, listening. So still was she, she could hear her own breathing, but no one else's. *No one was here. Not downstairs.* She took a few soft steps toward the staircase, and then speeded up with strong, sure strides, straight towards the danger, she thought, if there were any. *But no—no one in any of the three rooms.* There was nowhere to hide. The upstairs rooms were tiny with no closets. There were storage containers, not criminals, under the beds. She went back downstairs, eyes sweeping the kitchen, the main room and the living room. Nothing looked wrong, but nothing seemed right.

It's that damn back window. The one in the office she never used. Years ago, when she'd been away, someone had broken the cheap plastic lock—she suspected Jared —and stolen a sewing machine. A sewing machine. How desperate was that? At the time, Hy had an ancient television and cheap radio. She'd taken her laptop with her. There was nothing else worth stealing. She had always meant to fix the window lock, but hadn't.

She opened the door to find the curtains flapping and the breeze wafting through the wide-open window.

Ian found the photo, with Camilla, the Duchess and the Prince, charming. He'd googled the Legion site and was smiling at the cheeky British tabloid headlines that accompanied the photo in paper after paper: *Two Birds in the Bush…Double Trouble on the*

Dee...One Camilla Too Many. The more sober papers had run headlines like *Lobster Lover Woos Royal Couple.*

He'd woken up to an empty house, disappointed. Why should it be any different? Whenever Hy stayed over—and she always did if they'd been drinking—she would leave when she woke, around dawn. It suited them both perfectly; both treasured their single life and their private time. *Today,* he thought, *the company might have been pleasant,* but he couldn't have slobbed around in his sweatpants, scratched various parts of his anatomy at will, put off brushing his teeth until he'd had his first coffee, and...well the list of things was rather long.

He got the coffee maker going for the second time that morning, thought he really should take a shower, but went back to the iMac. Ian had logged on to the LLL site about an hour before. He was still surfing the links. There were newspaper articles and podcasts from Europe. The media attention had begun with a campaign there about a year ago, then moved to Norway and Sweden, where the Legion had been immediately and well received. Now they'd brought their crusade to North America. Ian wondered why they'd begun at The Shores. *What publicity could they generate in this tiny, unknown community on this tiny, unknown island?* He was sure it had something to do with Hawthorne Parker.

"Yes?"

It was immediately obvious to Sheldon that Parker's usual composure had deserted him. It showed in the way he blurted out what had happened. Sheldon wasn't that surprised. Guillaume was a liability, for Parker. An asset, for Sheldon, really. *Not like that other one. That woman.*

"Jeeees-us." He drew the word out on one long breath, and then assured Parker he'd get Guillaume out. It would be no trouble. The incident actually suited Sheldon. The more chaos there was in Parker's life, the less likely he was to give even the slightest thought to the business, and what Sheldon was doing with it. He knew just what to do to hasten Guillaume's release. Even in a place he'd never been to, a place where he had no known contacts, Sheldon was confident he would find someone to whom a generous donation to a favourite charity or numbered account would unlock the power to sweep Guillaume's actions under the carpet. He would manage to ferret out just the right person and was sure that within less than twenty-four hours, the charges would be dropped, there would be no court appearance and Guillaume would go free. It was familiar terrain.

What bothered him more was the woman, and her ridiculous LLL circling around Parker. Getting closer all the time.

How far had it gone?

Before Hy could close the window, she smelled it. *God, it's awful! What a stink. Did something die in here?* It was smeared all over the walls—streaks of blood and pulverized fish flesh. Bits of scale, even a fish eye stuck to the wall, staring at her. She sniffed, and gagged. *Herring bait. Who would do this?*

It wasn't just smears. There were words—a crude message. Three words. One looked like the *c* word. Hy hated that word, even though Professor Walpole had explained that it had originally meant wise woman.

"Embrace the word," she'd said at last year's Institute meeting, raising up her arms. "Be proud. Be proud to call yourselves—"

Hy had prayed for the first time in years. Prayed that she wouldn't say it.

"Be proud to call yourselves by the word of the wise woman," she had ended, presumably knowing her audience and just how much they could be expected to put up with. Hy had thanked God, the Goddess, the whole lot of them up there in heaven or wherever it was they were.

They could have been called worse than murderers.

She tried to decipher the other two words by squinting up close and pulling back to get the long view. She couldn't make it out. *Starts with "b." Was that bitch? No, too short.*

The phone rang. She closed the window and the door. That would keep the smell out of the rest of the house.

It was Nathan—home from his annual holiday.

"Bloodsucker Lane," he said, when Hy asked him where he drove Camilla.

"Bloodsucker Lane?"

He mistook her meaning. "Or Sunshine Beach Lane, if you prefer—"

"No, I know where you're talking about. It just seems an odd place."

"That's what I thought."

She thanked him and rang off, abandoning her run and the muck coating her back room wall. She raced out the door and jumped into her beat-up half-ton pickup.

Chapter Twenty-Eight

Ian had become frustrated with his search for information about Hawthorne Parker. There were a lot of Parkers, and sticking the first name, Hawthorne, into the search wasn't helping. It was sending him to gardening and naturalist sites. He tried another route and linked Parker with lobster. And then it happened.

The Lobster Lover's Blog

There's a game they play in some restaurants and bars on the east coast. It's called Pa's Lobster Claw Game. You play it on a big red machine—like one of those arcade games where you maneuver a claw to pick up a prize inside a glass case, a tacky stuffed animal or a cheap toy. It's hard to win. The claw grabs, but doesn't hold anything. You usually drop the prize or run out of time.

Pa's Lobster Claw Game is a tank full of live lobsters swimming around in salt water. It works the same as the arcade game, only you're manipulating a mechanical lobster claw around the tank, trying to catch a live one. You lift it out of the water and drop it down a chute.

Clunk. Down comes dinner. Happily, dinner beats diner most of the time. Pa's Claw Game is a real challenge. Toys don't move around, but lobsters do. They flap and squirm as you try to catch them and two out of three times they get away.

From the retailers' point of view, it's a great gimmick.

For the customer, it's entertainment and maybe a free dinner.

For the lobster, it's like being trapped and terrorized all over again.

The sick side of it is, that Pa donates part of the sales from every game to a scholarship for Parker's Marine Camp. It's a kind of business cannibalism – feeding on itself. Kids at camp eat Pa's food—and go home with coupons for more.

They go there to learn about life in the sea—how to kill it and eat it.

The blog had come out of nowhere—just like Hy said. Ian picked up the phone and hit number one on his speed dial. No answer. *That could mean anything. She could be out in the garden. Out on the shore. Out of her mind.* Ian smiled.

Last night had been different. She hadn't pulled away.

But it hadn't been very romantic.

Hy backed down the long clamshell driveway and headed for Bloodsucker Lane. That was what it had always been called by the locals—except for a brief period when the introduction of 911 emergency service gave it a new official name, by mistake. Groups of student recruits had been sent out polling people for appropriate names for lanes that didn't have official ones. When they got to this one—the last one—they'd surprised Germain Joudry, just about to relieve himself by the side of the road. They asked him what the lane was called. "Sun Don't Shine Beach," he replied gruffly, annoyed at being disturbed. They wrote it down as "Sunshine Beach." Up the sign went—and with it a public outcry. First, from tourists, who struggled up the lane with beach towels and umbrellas, only to return battered, bruised and full of burrs when they found they couldn't get down to the shore. The villagers got the province to restore the traditional name: Bloodsucker Lane. It wasn't as romantic, but it was far more accurate.

It was as unpleasant as the name suggested, an unlikely place for anyone to be. Hy wondered what chance there was she'd find Camilla still there, if she ever had been.

Pa's. Of course, Ian thought, I should have known. *Pa Parker's.* Everyone knew the chain of restaurants that stretched down the U.S. east coast. Everyone had eaten there. He'd been there himself—with Hy. *That Thanksgiving weekend they'd spent in Bar Harbour. It had almost happened there. Almost.* Was it he—or she—who'd chickened out? He couldn't quite remember.

Pa's restaurants were family diners with predictable menus—big colourful foldouts and unending food choices with cutesy names. *Two unfortunate mascots. Ollie the Octopus looked like a happy face on drugs. Lou the Lobster had a grimace of a grin, threatening, as if he wanted to rip your heart out. Hardly Parker's style, but it would explain his money.*

Ian phoned Hy again.

Again, there was no answer.

Where the hell had she gone?

"She's following you."

Parker grunted. How did Sheldon know she was here?

"When she showed up in Paris—possible coincidence. Then Oslo, okay—say it just happened. But now? There?" He said it in a tone of utter disbelief. Sheldon couldn't figure out why *anyone* was there.

"Why would she follow me?" Parker asked, as if he didn't know. It was the lobsters. He wished it were…well, something else.

"She wants you to wash your hands of this business."

"I have."

"It's still where your money comes from."

Parker was tied to the family business by tradition, three generations of hard work and history that he couldn't let go. He owned the empire, but had nothing to do with it. He didn't want to run it, but couldn't sell it. It was his grandmother, she of the red blob painting. It was for her that he hadn't sold the whole lot off. It would have broken her heart to see it go out of the family.

She had left it all to him in spite of what she thought about his lifestyle. Family was family to a woman of her generation.

"She's never approached me." It was a lie, but not a complete lie. The closest she'd come—apart from that time in Cartier's—was last night. He'd never told Sheldon about New York, and he wasn't going to tell him about last night either. He felt oddly protective.

"Just a matter of time," said Sheldon. Here she was on his turf— just hours away from the heart of Parker's empire, and the centre of Sheldon's financial happiness.

"We've had protests. Not from the LLL, not yet, but the protests have had an impact. They're aimed at Pa's Claw."

"Pa's Claw?"

Parker didn't know what Sheldon was talking about. He didn't keep up with the business at all. Sheldon knew that, and he'd taken advantage of it—to line his pockets in a variety of undetectable ways.

"It started out great last year. A sweet little income generator."

You might think a nickel-and-dime addition like Pa's Claw Game would be beneath Sheldon's notice, but Sheldon didn't get rich by ignoring nickels and dimes. When asked the secret of his wealth, it was the little things he pointed to.

"I turn off lights," he told the surprised writer from *Fortune 500*, who'd come seeking his savvy business acumen for a front-page article he had already titled "Sheldon Coffin—King of the Lobsters."

"Turn off lights?"

"Yup. A fortune is made a penny at a time and lost the same way. The millions take care of themselves. It's the pennies you've got to watch."

That's why Sheldon was making such a big deal about what Camilla and her Legion got up to. It was only a few dollars at a time—but a few dollars times as many restaurants as there were in the chain. A few dollars times the number of lobsters bought at the wharf. A few dollars less in frozen lobster sales. Money lost to the processing plants. Fishermen feeling the pinch and cutting back on supply orders. Holding off on buying that new boat. Well, the Maine lobster industry was already in bad enough shape.

To Sheldon, a few dollars added up to millions in the end. That's why Pa's Claw Game was so important to him. As for Camilla's cause—he couldn't understand it.

Sheldon had never met a creature he didn't want to eat.

Hy got stuck behind a truck full of manure. Whenever that happened, she usually just slowed down and enjoyed the scenery, but not today. She was nosing up so close to the vehicle ahead that when it hit a bump, a load of manure dropped onto the hood of her truck. She tried to calm down. It was a long shot at best. It had been days ago that Nathan had dropped off Camilla. There was no evidence she was still around. She might have left and let that other Legionnaire take over at the supper last night. Maybe— Hy mentally crossed her fingers—that had been their parting shot and they had both left.

The manure truck pulled off into a field. Around the next curve was Bloodsucker Lane.

"What is this Claw Game?"

Sheldon had hoped Parker wouldn't ask. He told him—in as sketchy a way as he could.

"And the profits go to my endowment—the summer camp?"

"Yes." Sheldon didn't like Parker's tone. He wished he'd never mentioned The Claw.

"Odious," he said. "Pull it."

"What?" Sheldon wasn't sure what he'd heard. It was the first business decision Parker had made in ten years. There had been only two before that—when he'd endowed the marine camp upon coming into his inheritance and when he handed over control of the empire to Sheldon.

"Get rid of them. In all the restaurants. They're obviously an unnecessary irritant."

Sheldon had a feeling, a bad feeling. He'd learned to trust his feelings. He'd told the *Fortune 500* writer that too. The writer pounced on it as the kind of financial wisdom he had anticipated quoting in his article.

"It's something you can't explain. A gut feeling. An instinct," Sheldon had said. "You know what you know."

The writer quoted all of it—except that last bit. "You know what you know" didn't sound like incisive business acumen to him.

What Sheldon knew now was that Camilla must be stopped.

"Pull the Claw? I could show you some figures might change your mind."

"No figures," Parker said sharply. "Get rid of the Claw. It's offensive."

Jesus. This is her influence. Bloody bitch. What if she persuaded Parker to sell out? Where would that leave him? There'd be some explaining to do about certain business practices. Some financial "arrangements"—the kinds of things that happened when one man had a free hand and no one was looking over his shoulder.

Sheldon wasn't sure how he'd wriggle around that, and he could lose his management contract. It was a license to steal money and he'd been stealing a pile of it. Even without the management contract, he would still be a very rich man, but Parker's contract was worth millions to him.

He licked his dry lips. "Well, all right." What else could he say? Did he dare ignore Parker's command and not pull the Claw? Would Parker know—or care—tomorrow?

"On that other matter," he persisted. "Samson. Just say the word. We'll get her out of there."

There was only silence from Parker.

Did Parker have any idea who she really was? He couldn't possibly—and Sheldon wasn't about to tell him. Sheldon chose to take Parker's silence as assent. He'd already been getting at Camilla, in small ways, trying to disrupt the lobster legion's activities. Now he was going to turn up the heat.

Chapter Twenty-Nine

Hy turned onto Bloodsucker Lane. The truck bounced over ruts and dipped into puddles, splashing mucky red clay up on the windows. It might not have been quite so bad if she'd driven a little slower, but impatience was making her foot heavy on the accelerator—impatience and excitement. She was going to ferret out Camilla and the Legionnaire. Get them out of The Shores, whatever it took. Surely she could persuade them to leave, leave the village alone, if nothing else, leave her alone. She'd seen a crack in Camilla's shell after the Institute meeting. If she could direct any of the compassion she knew was in her—compassion for those ugly emotionless creatures—toward herself, maybe Camilla and the Legionnaire would relent and leave.

After he rang off with Sheldon, Parker felt buoyant. He'd surprised himself as well as Sheldon with his command about the Claw. He wondered if Sheldon would follow orders. He wondered if she was, as Sheldon obviously feared, getting to him. There followed a degree of self-questioning and self-examination about the family business that Parker had never before indulged in.

He now asked himself, as he sat back on the couch and looked out the window at the sun sparkling on the blue water: was it consistent with his love of beauty to own a business involved in killing; why didn't he just let go of it? He had severed the family ties with the life he had chosen and there would be no continuity. No one would follow him. He would not pass on the family name or the business. He might as well have Sheldon break up the empire into bite-size bits and sell it off. Something in him still resisted that final step. Like his grandmother, Parker was holding onto a slim, unrealized hope.

More tentacles than an Octopus.

That was the headline of an article Ian had googled from the business section of *The New York Times* in August of 1957. It was reproduced in a website for Pa Parker's restaurant chain which had, it claimed, been a Maine Institution for 50 years—starting with a fish and chip stand on a wharf near Ogunquit.

Not just any fish and chip shop, thought Ian.

Each generation of the Parker dynasty has to make it on his own. He gets seed money from the parent company, but has to build his own business.

Ian hadn't established yet that Hawthorne Parker was a scion of this dynasty, but he was sure of it. He just had to find the link to prove that Clayton Parker was his father, Garth his grandfather and Reinholdt his great-grandfather—men who had built business upon business, starting with a dory and a few lobster traps. The restaurant chain was only the tip of a massive financial iceberg—even larger than the one that had carved away at the Campbell causeway.

The roadbed of Bloodsucker Lane was in terrible shape, but the rest of it was beautiful—one of those forgotten roads, carved out more than a century ago by man and horsepower alone, hacked through the woods by a handful of men with picks and shovels. There were maples, spruce, birch and mountain ash growing on either side and, when in full leaf, they met in the middle, forming a canopy over the road. The leaves were nowhere near full yet, except for the poplars, shimmering in just the slightest breath of a breeze. Ferns were uncurling on the banks of the road and compact blueberry bushes were coming into leaf. The road crossed over a brook with a culvert that was caving in. Hy took it slowly, looking out through her window down a yawning hole to the water. She drove past an orchard of apple trees gone wild and lilacs spreading from an old homestead. Soon the earthy scent of the clay lane would be mixed with the sweet fragrance of their blossoms, spilling like confetti onto the red road. She came out onto the barren landscape of the high cape. Only stunted spruce and grass grew here and, in June, the wild strawberries, sweeter, redder and juicier than any Hy had tasted anywhere else.

It was on red clay lanes like this that Hy felt most at home on The Island. She felt like just another living creature embraced by it, a part of it. *Not from away.*

She didn't see it until she was almost on top of it—the camouflage jeep pulled into a stand of spruce at the side of the lane. She stopped the truck, got out and peeked in, her nose where it often was—pressed up against a window and in someone else's business.

Ian was looking at an updated graphic of the octopus from the nineteen-seventies. Each of the tentacles represented part of the Parker Empire—the bumps on the tentacles were the offshoots, encompassing every area of the fishing and seafood industry on the east coast of the United States.

Reinholdt Parker had started it all, three generations before. He was the body of the octopus. He began as a simple fisherman, but because he didn't like to spend money, started to acquire the suppliers that provided services to his companies, an idea borrowed by another east coast entrepreneur many years later. Reinholdt's boat became a fleet. He also acquired a boat repair business; a boat parts concern; a boat-building company and commercial fisheries outfitters—five of the eight tentacles.

His son Garth "Pa" Parker added tentacles six and seven, with his restaurants and wholesale seafood operation. His grandson Clayton created tentacle eight—a wildly successful retail store and catalogue business that traded in trendy fishermen's wear and related items for the growing population of summer shore-dwellers. His line of deck shoes was especially popular with the well-heeled crowd.

They were productive men—in the boardroom. In the bed-room, they didn't fare so well. They boasted a fertile business, but a relatively barren family tree. Each had managed to squeak out one requisite male heir, but no more than that. An empire that should have been peopled with many sons and daughters and nephews and nieces was left largely in the hands of others. It was an unhappy family tradition that Ian suspected Hawthorne Parker had taken to the extreme, but he still found no record of him.

He'd seen photos of the sprawling Victorian summer home near Kennebunkport, the Gothic mansion in Boston, aerial photo-graphs of a Bahamian beach compound and a Swiss ski play-ground, but he had yet to find any mention of Hawthorne Parker. There was a convincing family resemblance in the photographs—thin, aesthetic faces, steel-grey eyes and pencil-thin mustaches. If Parker was, as Ian suspected, the last of this line, the final feeble branch of a sickly family tree, he had inherited a healthy business empire and a whack of money. The Parker name was stamped all over the fishing industry in Maine and Massachusetts.

He had to tell Hy. He called her again.

'Hi. Hy here. Or not here. Please leave a message."

Was she not answering his calls?

Hy's breath was creating fog on the jeep's rear window in the chill morning air. She could just see someone curled up in the back. She rubbed the mist to see more clearly, her fingers squeak-ing against the wet glass. The Legionnaire stirred and then woke, eyes blinking in the sunlight. She stared straight into the flattened nose and wide-open eyes of Hyacinth McAllister. She sat up, looked wildly around, grabbed her cap, hunted for her bandana,

then gave up. *Surrender. Trapped—with no escape, no place to hide.*
She squeezed out of her sleeping bag, and emerged from the jeep.

Hy looked at her once.

Then again.

Chapter Thirty

Finally, Ian found the Parker he was looking for. One dogged reporter had followed his trail when he came into his inheritance ten years ago, at the age of thirty-five. He'd inherited after the death of his grandfather, of respectable old age, followed quickly by his father's demise—a massive heart attack caused by overexcitement in a threesome in a New York City penthouse. He'd been with another man and a woman. His mother had run off to Europe, married one of Italy's countless princes, and cut off all communication with the Parkers, including her son. His grandmother had outlived her mind—becoming skeletally thin and mentally thick in a Boston condominium in the care of paid personnel. The empire was in her hands, until she, too, died and passed all of it on to Parker, in spite of who and what he was.

Parker's trail had been swept clean upon inheriting the family holdings. Money could buy that kind of obscurity if you wanted it, and even the dogged reporter gave up after just one profile titled "Creature Comforts," about the aesthete who'd abandoned his lobster legacy. It was mostly pure speculation about the eclectic art collection Parker had amassed. There was no interview, no personal history—nothing more.

It may just have been that interest in Parker disappeared as he did, quietly into the background, while his henchman, Sheldon Coffin, moved into the spotlight. This Coffin guy had been running the business for him. All the articles now were about him. He'd bought the Parkers' Victorian summer home, the Boston mansion, the hideaways in the Bahamas and Switzerland. Ian felt his suffocating presence. It was as if Coffin had wrapped his own tentacles around Parker, grasping at everything that belonged to him.

The Legionnaire stood in front of Hy, ungainly feet in socks sinking into the mud. Her hair hung limp and matted. She'd slept in her camouflage clothes—with no contacts...

Her eyes were grey—not hazel.

"You," Hy said, dumbly.

"Yes."

"Just you?"

"Most of us are just..." A shrug. "Us." A grin. "Me." She pulled a foot out of the mud, looked at her white sock, coated with red clay.

"One. Not two?"

"Yup."

"Why?"

"That's a long story," said Camilla.

Metal in a Haystack." Parker was in a foul mood looking at the morning paper, his coffee gone cold on the table. The early morning sun shone on the headline over a photo of his car on top of the haystack. He'd have been even more furious to know that the photo had made the front page of every newspaper in the Atlantic region and several others on the east coast of the United States. If he'd had television, he'd have seen it on every breakfast news show in the country. It had gone national. It would soon go international when Estelle's son Lester Joudry, a student photographer and videographer, provided the hungry news media with video of the car being hoisted off the hay later in the day. It would earn him his first major league credit and enough money to take his second year of photojournalism at the local community college. The video made it onto YouTube, but that didn't mean it was just an overnight media sensation. The story had legs, as they say in the business—long ones. The photo travelled—months later—to a newspaper in La Paz and, more than a year after that, found its way in a fuzzy, pirated form into a two-page local rag in the Scottish Hebrides. Talk of North American depravity warmed cold Scot hearts throughout their long damp winter. In an exhibit of just such depravity, Parker decided he didn't want the classic Mercedes anymore. He'd have it fixed and get rid of it. He'd already arranged to have his 1960 Jag taken out of storage and delivered to The Shores.

"Helluva place to be sleeping." Hy looked over at the jeep. "Is that where you've been living?"

Camilla nodded with an easy grin, engaging and genuine. Standing there in her crumpled camouflage, sleep and a smile in her eyes, she looked an entirely different creature from the woman at the meeting. That woman—tall, in command, a bit frightening with her sweater set and pearls—disappeared into the grin. So did the rabid Legionnaire. They'd become just one girl with a cheeky look.

Hy had to grin back. Then Camilla smiled, a full smile. Her teeth were white and one front tooth was slightly askew. That was what did it. Hy knew she was looking at a friend—in spite of everything.

"You'd better come home with me."

Camilla hesitated.

"I bet you haven't had a shower or bath in days."

Another slight hesitation. She hadn't.

"Sure. That'd be great."

"You'd better leave the jeep here." Hy was willing to help Camilla, but she didn't want people to know—not with all those hard feelings over the meeting, the supper—and certainly not with that stinky and menacing message in her back room.

"Pack what you need."

The vehicle was a mess inside: clothes all over the place; plastic grocery bags filled with what appeared to be everything but groceries; coffee cups stuffed in a makeshift garbage bag hanging from the glove compartment. On the passenger seat was a map of The Island, half-open, now outdated—the causeway was still there. The only neat thing was the hanger holding the skirt and sweater set. Camilla grabbed a knapsack and a vanity case—a navy blue vintage Samsonite. She left her alter ego—the skirt and sweater set—in the car, but not the pearls. She had those looped around her neck, hidden beneath her shirt. Since New York, she'd worn them everywhere.

"The car's fine," said The Island's foreign car specialist, Carl Robertson. Parker had been surprised to find such a person on The Island, but Carl did a swift trade in fancy cars brought here as summer toys by rich American tourists. Carl Albert Robertson was his full name and the sign above his dubious garage—it looked like a big shed—highlighted the first initials of his name to spell CAR. There was a photo of the sign in the Yellow Pages ad. It had almost put Parker off, but the fellow came with a strong recommendation from his car man in the States, so he'd had the Mercedes towed there.

"Just a couple of small scratches and a dent or two," said Carl now. "Easy to fix."

"Fine," said Parker. "Fix it and get rid of it."

Carl already had a buyer.

He was going to make a nice profit on it.

The car would be fixed but the relationship would have to be scrapped. *Not so easily done.* Parker was still not ready for a final confrontation with Guillaume. What a fool he had been to think that this place might cure what was past curing—a sick connection gone rotten long ago. He should have known it was over when Guillaume had his "nervous collapse." That's how Parker still thought of it, but there had been a disturbing end to what had started out as a joke, a bit of flirtatious foreplay...

It was a Christmas present—the French rolling pin, so different from the North American kind, which is a blunt object. The French rolling pin is fat in the middle, gracefully tapering to a point at either end. This one was made by a highly-skilled artisan, of mahogany, and was a deep red colour like bull's blood.

Guillaume was thrilled with it. In his pleasure, with a wide grin and a wink, he poked Parker. Parker backed off, a smile forming on his lips. Guillaume stepped forward, wielded it as if it were a sword, backing Parker into the hall, where he picked up an umbrella.

"*En garde.*" He saluted Guillaume.

"*Touché,*" Guillaume responded as they touched the points of their weapons.

"Lunge!" They began to fence. Parker backed up the stairs, feeling like Errol Flynn until the umbrella fell open. They were both laughing and out of breath when they got to the top of the stairs.

It was a rare, playful domestic comedy. It had been a long time since they had laughed together. It was going to be a good Christmas.

Guillaume fell onto their bed, an obvious invitation. Parker went to have a shower. He felt buoyant, hopeful.

Guillaume sat up, and pulled a bag of cocaine from his pocket, to enhance the pleasure to come. He laid out a few lines on the top of Parker's dresser and snorted one after another. His eye caught the newspaper clipping, peeking out from under the kid leather box that held Parker's ivory grooming kit. The headline read: *Lobster Dinner.* The photograph was of a person of indeterminate sex, clothed in lobster camouflage, holding up a sign that pictured a lobster family: mom, dad and two crustacean kids sitting at a table, shredding human parts onto their plates. Mom and Dad were sucking on fingers, as if they were a delicacy.

That woman. Merde! He's thinking of that woman again.

Guillaume grabbed the rolling pin and stalked into the bathroom. He yanked open the door to the shower stall, and went right in, fully clothed. There was an unnatural gleam in his eyes, and for a moment, Parker thought he read a terrible intent in those eyes. He dismissed it. Overexcited, thought Parker, as he turned off the water. Too much stimulation. Guillaume began to rant—accusing Parker of "seeking out that woman." He flung accusations—that he, Guillaume, had been "bought and paid for," but he would not put up with her in their lives. He worked himself into such a state that he began to scream and wave the pin wildly. Parker tried to release it from his hand. Guillaume pulled away, slipped on the wet floor, banged his head and knocked himself out, still clinging to the rolling pin...

The paramedics had looked puzzled by the fully-clothed man passed out in the shower cubicle. They'd have been even more intrigued if Guillaume had still been holding the French pin, but Parker had removed it. It had been an ugly episode, an embarrassing public airing of dirty linen. Most of all, it had been frightening. Still, Parker clung to the term "episode"—the word the clinic psychiatrist had used. He'd called it "an isolated psychotic episode, brought on by an overconsumption of cocaine over a long period of time." "Highly treatable," he'd concluded. He could smell Parker's money and thought he could imagine the twisted tale that had brought them to the clinic. It was highly unlikely. He'd never seen a French rolling pin.

Chapter Thirty-One

"Please, call me Cam," the Legionnaire said as they drove back to Hy's. "Camilla is someone else."

"Apparently," said Hy with a frown. "So exactly who is she?"

Cam sighed. "She's the mouthpiece of the Legion. She's the front woman. She's the one who meets royalty—"

"Oh, yes. Chuck and Upchuck."

"So you saw the photograph?"

"Checked you out right after the Institute meeting. Great picture."

Cam made a face.

"Well, it was good PR, but it didn't get me very far. The Prince talks to plants and he's an organic gardener, but he's also got these really big hunting estates in Scotland. There's a valley where people have scrubbed out a living for generations—tiny stunted root crops are all that grow there. The people live on the shady side of the valley. The sunny side is his for hunting. He's never there."

"So you can't change the world. How did you get to him?"

"Him and most of the uncrowned heads of Europe. It's my talent. My special skill."

"The lobster tickling?"

"Is that what you call it? I like that. You watched the DVD then?"

"Both of them. You gave me two—both of you did."

"That's right. It was to make you think there were two of me."

Hy smiled. "Well, it worked."

"Anyway, all the privileged people want to see my work close up—at least, the green, environmentally conscious ones. The young set, mostly," she added, thinking of Prince Charles. "I feel a bit like a circus monkey performing for them, but I do it to get their support. It's why I made the DVDs. So everyone—not just the bigwigs—could see how it works."

"It's amazing to see, and hear. Where'd it come from?"

"I was on vacation—down south with a boyfriend a year-and-a-half ago. We were in a boat, over a rocky shoal. There were tons of lobsters in the water and two of them were fighting. I don't know why I did it, but I stuck my hand in the water and this sound started coming out of me.

"My friend thought I was nuts, but the lobsters stopped fighting. They all stopped moving. I touched one, then another and another. I knew then. I'd been given a gift. I had to use it."

"And the guy?"

She laughed. "Never saw him again."

"So you started the LLL."

"Yup."

"Camilla's the public persona—"

"And Cam's the Legionnaire. She does the dirty work."

"Two roles, two different people—both of them you. What's the point?"

"I'm the best one to do both and I like to keep them separate. I don't think the prince or the duchess would want to shake hands with the Legionnaire. The Legionnaire does illegal things. Camilla's the head of an organization that does illegal things, but at arm's length. It makes a difference to people."

"What about the others?"

"The others?"

"The other members of the group. Where are they? What are they doing?"

"Oh, yeah. Well, we're spread thin."

"I'd say." *Just how thin, if Camilla—Cam—was playing two roles?*
"How many, exactly, are you?"

Cam didn't reply for a long moment. "Exactly? I couldn't say."

Hy could see the Hall just ahead. "I don't mean to be rude," she said, "but could you duck down?" The last thing she wanted was Moira Toombs seeing Cam in her truck. Gus, she knew, would see her going by and wonder where she'd been and what she was up to.

The precaution came too late. They had already been seen—but not by Moira nor Gus. A pair of well-aimed binoculars, offshore, had spied them leaving the cape at Bloodsucker Cove.

Hy pulled the truck right to the door of the house, leaving deep muddy tracks across her lawn.

"Wait here." She jumped out and opened the front door, taking a quick look down the road each way. She turned and motioned Cam to come in. Cam grabbed her backpack and the vanity case and ran into the house. She dumped her baggage on the floor and looked around. The house was small and stuffed with antiques.

"Cosy." An odd look came over her face. "What's that smell?"

"Someone came in here and spread herring bait all over the wall in the back room. It says something. I haven't figured it out yet. Take a look." Hy led her through the main room. She opened the door to the back office. The smell burst out like an assault.

Cam looked inside. "Bug off cunt.'"

"What?"

Cam started laughing. "'Bug off cunt.' That's what it says."

Hy squinted at the wall. It was suddenly clear.

"You're right, that's what it says. So it must have been Mutt and Jeff."

"Who?"

"The two guys who attacked you at the Hall."

"You know them?"

Did no one get the reference?

"Mutt and Jeff. Cartoon characters. Tall and thin. Short and fat."

"Oh, yeah," said Cam, a bit vaguely. "*Those* guys." She pressed her lips together, thoughtful.

"Do *you* know them?"

"Me? I—uh—no." She lowered her head. "I don't know them." She scuffed a foot on the floor. "I don't think I know them."

Hy couldn't see her face or eyes. She couldn't see if she was telling the truth.

"We thought maybe they were here because you're here."

"Maybe, but I don't know them."

"Does 'The Crustacean' mean anything to you?"

Cam's head snapped up. She looked Hy full in the eyes. She blurted it out, without thinking.

"*The Crustacean*? Have you seen it?"

Chapter Thirty-Two

The Crustacean had been keeping well out of sight, anchored on the other side of the stretch of land that stuck far out into the water and circled around protectively inward to form Big Bay Harbour. No one laid trap lines on the far side of that land mass because there was a strong current there that would have swept the lines out to sea.

The two men had a rough ride in the Zodiac as they headed out and around the tip of the point, after they spied Cam and Hy. They hadn't decided exactly what they were going to do, but they had to do something. That was clear from Sheldon Coffin's disgruntled call earlier in the morning.

"I don't pay you to snore," Coffin barked when Bill, sleep in his voice, answered the cell after ten rings. "What progress have you made?"

Bill told Coffin what they'd done so far. Sheldon's contempt had burst down the phone line. "You'll have to do better than that. A lot better than that. Do whatever it takes. Just get her out of there. Soon. Sooner than soon. Now."

"*The Crustacean*," Hy repeated. "You know it. Is it yours?"

Cam laughed. "No. I wish it was."

"But you know it?"

"Yes." Cam responded, guarded. "I've heard of it, anyway."

"And…?"

"Oh—" She shook her head dismissively. "Just a boat that belongs to a company down in Maine."

"That where you're from?"

"Once upon a time."

This was as hard as getting information out of Harold MacLean. Cam may have confessed—under duress—to playing a double role, but she was still keeping secrets.

"Do you think those guys are on that boat? Are they here for you, to stop your activities?"

"Maybe."

Cam still wasn't telling the whole truth. Hy could tell by the way she kept her eyes on the wall, refusing to look at her.

"You're sure you don't know them?"

"Sure." Now she looked straight at Hy and crossed her heart. "I don't know them any more than you do. As for the boat, just what I told you." She looked up at the slimy message. "C'mon, let's clean this up."

"No, I'll do it," Hy said with resignation. She wouldn't mind some help. "You're a guest."

"Look, I'm no guest and I feel responsible for this mess. I'm dirty now anyway, so I might as well help clean up."

Hy didn't argue. She knew the vandalism was payback for bringing Cam to The Shores, for helping her out of the Hall the other night. An attempt to make sure she wouldn't do it again. Well, here she was, doing it again. The source of the trouble that had started at the Institute meeting, that had spread to the wharf, to Ben and Annabelle, and out onto the water, was now here, in her house. Well, thought Hy, I couldn't have left her there at the cove. It was only the decent thing to do. Hy filled buckets with hot water and detergent, grabbed some cloths and scrub brushes, and together they began to wash down the walls.

"So you said you were spread thin. How thin?" An idea had been gnawing at Hy and she was determined to find out if she was right.

"Very thin," said Cam. She kept her eyes directly on the wall in front of her, scrubbing. She seemed to withdraw into herself. Hy felt her slipping away and decided to back off. *Maybe later.* She had plenty more questions to ask. She wondered if Cam drank wine.

They had just finished and Cam had gone upstairs to the bath, when there was a loud knocking at the front door. Hy ran to open it. There, on the stoop, was a paper bag on fire. Hy knew the old trick from Mat Night, the night of fun and games before Hallowe'en, when kids played dirty tricks around the neighbourhood. She wasn't going to stamp the fire out. She whirled round to find a bowl, a vase, anything. She grabbed a hat, a tightly woven straw hat. *Better than nothing.* She turned the tap on full blast and filled it. The hat was spilling over and leaking. She tossed the water on the flames and succeeded in partly dousing them. Another hatful put the fire out.

Liquid manure dribbled down her stairs from a soft lump of steaming cow pie, with bits of blackened paper bag stuck in it. Hy looked around. *No use.* Whoever had done it would now be long gone, making a getaway while the fire had distracted her. They had probably hidden behind the trees that lined her drive, then slipped into the grove behind the house and out onto Shore Lane.

Another cleanup job, Hy steamed.

This one would require a shovel. She marched to the back shed.

Annabelle was on her way to town to meet her daughter, Rowan, when she saw Hy on her hands and knees, scrubbing up the last of the mess on the stoop. Curious, she pulled into the driveway. Hy threw the scrubbing brush into the bucket and got up.

"Phew," said Annabelle. "What's that smell? Some new cleaning product I'm not going to buy?"

"Cow shit. It was a burning bag of cow shit. Now it's diluted cow shit."

"But what…who…?"

"Beats me." Hy shrugged. "Might be some angry fishermen. Or Mutt and Jeff."

"Mutt and Jeff?"

Here we go again, thought Hy, rolling her eyes. "The two thugs. Last night."

Annabelle's eyes lit up. "Of course." She smiled. "Tall and thin. Short and fat."

That's why we're friends, thought Hy.

"It could be them." Annabelle wrinkled her brow. "It could be anyone. Our boys are pissed about what happened last night. You'd better be careful, Hy."

"I haven't done anything."

"Well, you've protected that woman."

"Annabelle…"

"I know you did what you thought you had to do, but you're not popular right now. Some here aren't happy you took her side. I'm one of them. I don't agree with that woman. You know I don't."

"I'm just not sure—"

Annabelle cut her off. "What *you* think, that's your business." There was an edge to her voice. "Did Nathan tell you where he took her? Bloodsucker Lane?"

Hy nodded.

"Did you find her?"

"No." It sounded uncertain. Hy was a poor liar.

"Maybe she did this."

"She didn't."

"How do you know?"

Hy stared down at the concrete. "I know," she mumbled.

The pump engaged, a loud sound that throbbed through the house and could be heard clearly outside.

Annabelle looked suddenly suspicious. Pumps only engage when someone's using water.

"Is she here?"

"Of course not." Hy involuntarily gulped. She always got upset like that when she was lying. Annabelle knew that about her.

"You're not still helping her?"

"Of course not."

There was the sound of running water from the bathroom window above the front door.

"There is someone here."

Hy flushed. "No. Uh…no one." Stupid answer.

"It's not her?"

"No."

Lying to Annabelle. She was lying to Annabelle. What made it worse was that it worked.

A knowing look came over her friend's face. She cocked her head and smiled.

"No one? Maybe a certain someone?"

Ian. She thinks Ian's here. Well, let her. Better than her finding out who was really in the bathroom, drawing on the pump.

"I must have left the hose running."

The hose lay, bone dry, on the lawn. Annabelle winked.

"I've gotta run. I'm picking up Rowan in Charlottetown. We're going shopping for a fancy outfit for her concert tomorrow night. We're going to stay in town and Ben and Nathan will join us for the show. Then we'll all stay the night at the Prince Charles Hotel."

"Lucky you." It was unusual for Annabelle and Ben to take time out early in the season, but Rowan was over from Halifax to give a concert in Charlottetown. Just twenty-two, she had fiddled, sung and step-danced her way to several Island and East Coast Music Awards for her CD, *Celtic Wean*. She was tiny and childlike— "must have been left under a cabbage," Gus always said—but she had a mighty voice and spirit. Annabelle and Ben never missed a local show and didn't hide their pride. They always had big smiles when they talked about Rowan or Nathan.

Hy walked with Annabelle to her car.

As she got in, Annabelle wagged a finger. "Now you behave."
She shut the door, but poked her head out the open window.
"And steer clear of that woman."

"Will do." Hy felt bad about deceiving Annabelle, but she'd had
no choice.

She went into the house and nailed two boards across the
window frame in the back room, so that it was impossible to slide
the window open. *Ugly, but effective.*

She thought of Eldon. *I should email him, apologize about the
newsletter. Get it out of the way.* She sat down at her computer.

She still hadn't noticed the message light blinking on the phone
behind her.

Guillaume had spent less than twelve hours in jail—twelve
profitable hours.

"Why? Why?" Parker berated him when he arrived home. He'd
had Guillaume taxied all the way from Winterside. Nathan had
just left with a big fat tip. Guillaume responded to Parker with a
stony silence. Later, when his conversation had advanced to the
monosyllabic, he was still sullen. Then he retreated to the loft.
Drugs, Parker suspected, but Guillaume was clean. If there had
been an attempt to score, it had not been successful. The police
had told him Guillaume was driving. He found it hard to believe,
but could get nothing out of him.

Cam was still in the bath. Hy could hear the splashing, the
water turned on again, the pump kicking in for another round.
Before writing to Eldon, she checked her email. There was one
new message. *Subject: Bitch.* She opened it.

We know she's in there. Get her out. Ditch the bitch—or else!

The smears on the wall, the use of the *c* word, the manure on
the stoop, those had made her feel fearful. Now they were spying
on her. That made her angry. *Bloody bullies. Nasty and stupid.*

Juvenile. She bashed the Reply icon.

Bug off yourself. I'm sure the police will be interested in tracking down the source of all this harassment.

She signed it: *Bitch Two.*

The helpful suggestions that popped up in the right hand column of her screen included links to dog breeding, sexual harassment in the workplace and how to dig irrigation ditches in Botswana. She sat back. *These were not ordinary fishermen. Neither local nor from away. Not with a Blackberry. If they weren't fishermen, why were they after Cam?*

The pump was silent. No more splashing. Hy hadn't heard the bathtub drain—a rude gurgling and sucking sound that traveled down a fat pipe in the main room. The plumbing had been installed long after the house was built and its workings were both visible and audible. Every time the bath drained or the toilet flushed it sounded just like Archie Bunker's "terlet."

Hy went upstairs. There was silence from the bathroom. She knocked on the door. No answer. She knocked harder. There was still no response. She panicked and tried the door. It wasn't locked. The tub was still full of water—but Cam wasn't in it.

There was a wet trail down the old boards of the hallway, leading to the bedroom. She found Cam there, wrapped in a towel, curled up in a fetal position, fast asleep on the spool bed. Hy put a duvet over her, and returned to the bathroom. Cam's clothes were lying in a lump on the floor. The knapsack was perched on top of a wicker laundry basket. She hesitated, then gingerly opened it, and felt around quickly. *There.* She felt the contours of a book. She yanked it out—a journal with a photograph stuck inside. She pulled it out.

Camilla and Hawthorne Parker.

Her left hand rested on his shoulder.

On her fourth finger was a gold Irish wedding ring.

Chapter Thirty-Three

Married to Parker? Unbelievable!

What attraction could there possibly be—on either side?

It wasn't just Parker's sexual orientation. It was everything. They made an odd match in every way. Extremely odd. Yet the photo showed them smiling, happy, leaning into each other—their body language declaring them lovers, their arms around one another.

The ring. Cam still had that ring and this old black and white photo. What more convincing evidence could there be? If she weren't looking at it, Hy would never have believed it.

In the photo Parker's face was partly shaded by a hat, but he was visibly younger. Camilla—she was definitely Camilla, not Cam, in the photo—looked the same as she did now. One of those lucky people who don't change much between eighteen and thirty-eight, mused Hy. The woman in the photo could be either age—or anywhere in between.

Hy turned the picture over, to see if there was an inscription of any kind, a date. In the bottom corner, there was something in faded pencil. She grabbed a magnifying glass she kept in the bathroom cabinet for reading the fine print on bottles. Yes, there was something. She could make out a *C* and a *P*. Nearly rubbed off: Ogunquit, with a partial date, *19—*. She flipped it back over again. The clothes were classic, so they didn't help date it. Camilla was wearing the same set of pearls she'd worn at the Institute meeting and a cotton shirtwaist dress. He was wearing casual whites with a sweater slung across his shoulders. They were standing on a wharf, a stack of lobster traps behind them. *Was it a honeymoon shot? Where did Guillaume fit into the picture?*

Hy could not have known that Guillaume had been the one taking the photograph. It might have turned out better if he hadn't been burning with rage.

Hy shook her head, puzzled. She was struggling with her conscience about looking in the journal. One quick peek, she thought, as if brevity would make it less intrusive. She thumbed the pages and they flipped by in a blur until her keen editorial eye caught two words: *The Shores*. She stopped and opened to the page dated March eighteenth. Almost a month before she had contacted Cam. It might be nothing—Hy's own agenda entries were haphazard, actual dates didn't matter to her. It might be the same for Cam—or it might be something else...

There was a thump in the hall and Hy dropped the journal as if it were on fire. She didn't move, not an inch, but stood there listening, listening for another sound, wondering where the thump had come from. Then, a cascade of sounds, and she knew immediately what had happened. The book propping open the bedroom shutter had been knocked down by a gust of wind and the shutter was banging against the wall, its slats clattering in the breeze. It might have woken Cam.

Hy quickly retrieved the journal and the photo from the damp floor. She rubbed them mostly dry on her sweater. Then came the problem of replacing them. Where did the photo go in the book? Was there a special page? She slipped it in about halfway. Her hands trembling, she shoved the book to the bottom the knapsack where she had found it. Then she picked up Cam's clothes. They had salt water and red clay stains on them but they smelled oddly sweet—of seaweed and sand and the shore. She went downstairs and put them in the wash, then tossed them in the dryer.

She snacked on crackers and cheese while she waited for Cam to wake up. The cheese was a bad idea. Nightmare food. Overcome with utter exhaustion, so tired her sight was blurring, her brain singing, her hands trembling, she went to the living room to lie down.

And she was tugged into the dream. The damn dream, punctuating her sleep with fear and foreboding, her frayed nerves and exhaustion fueling the nightmare. Down, down she went, the room hummed around her and the lights began to flash on the dark water, and something electric sizzled through her body.

Jared was experiencing a similar sensation, but of a different origin. He was buzzing with the cocaine he'd been snorting all day long, alternately fired with energy and crashing down when the hit wore off. Right now he felt euphoric, in total control. Perhaps that's why he was getting ready to go out on the water, without thinking Parker might not want him to do so after last night. In a lucid moment, when the drug was wearing off between lines, Jared did think that Parker might not have any use for him anymore, but snorted another line and dismissed it. He was willing to bet that the fat Frenchman had kept quiet. He was down to his last line when he remembered that he'd meant to save some for Guillaume. He paused for a moment. Well, there wasn't enough left anyway. He drew the whole line of powder into his nostril. Too bad for Guillaume.

Full of false energy, Jared decided to go out on the water early, as soon as it was dark, to make sure he got the lobster in before the rain came. In spite of what Parker was paying him, Jared had been spending freely and he was short of cash after last night. He grabbed a mickey of rum to warm up before he went out. When he finished it, he stuck another mickey in his pocket and jumped into his Hummer. His car payment was due in a week and he didn't have it. With an overdose of courage born of cocaine and booze, Jared was prepared to get nasty if Parker cut him out of the poaching gig. Anyway, he'd make sure he was paid for tonight.

The last person Parker was thinking of was Jared MacPherson. All he could think of was Guillaume—up there in the loft, sulking. He knew he must end it—soon, but how? There was no question now of any return to intimate relations. Guillaume hated him. It was in his every look, the sharp way in which he dodged body contact, the denial of his bed since that one night when he'd received his gift. One night in one year, Parker brooded. For all his money, fine art and furnishings, he'd been sleeping on the couch.

That's where he was sitting now, resisting the urge to drink a Scotch. He didn't want to lose control. He'd wait until five, a respectable time to open the liquor cabinet. The silence from upstairs was deafening.

Jasmine seemed to be mimicking it.

Silence was a new sound for her. There hadn't been a peep out of her since Guillaume had returned home, mute with anger, already blaming Parker for his incarceration, for the entire episode.

Parker dropped his head into his hands, rubbed his eyes, and then his whole face, trying to relax the tense muscles.

I've made all the wrong decisions in life.

He did some shoulder rotations.

Maybe I should have stayed with her…

His back cracked and creaked like an old man's.

It's possible I might have been truly loved, by one person.

He fell back against the cushions.

Instead, here he was, with that monster upstairs, weighing down his life with worry and fear and unpleasantness, more public airing of dirty laundry. When he thought of it, his cheeks flushed with displeasure and embarrassment.

Upstairs, Guillaume was tossing on the bed, craving the drug, sweating, his hands trembling. His mind was a jumble of desire, hate, sensations that made him shiver. He couldn't grab hold of a thought. Sparks were flashing around his brain, fires blazing in dark corners, illuminating them. His whole body began to shake.

Hy woke up, dry-mouthed, in the late afternoon, her nerves singing. She teetered on the edge of the nightmare—just a tremor, the aftershock of last night's full-blown nightmare at Ian's. She rolled over on the couch and sank down into a troubled but less disturbing dream in which she was unable to finish a newsletter for the Super Saver. She kept writing it and it kept disappearing from her computer screen. She received an email in the dream from Eldon that read: *Bug off bitch.* She woke with his name on her mind, but all thoughts of the Super Saver were swept from her head when she remembered the photograph and that Cam was in her house.

It was getting dark. Clouds had moved in and the wind had picked up. She could hear it rumbling against the gutters and the empty compost cart banging up against the oil tank. *I really must move that thing, but not now.* She got up and stumbled upstairs to the bedroom. It was empty. The duvet had been carelessly folded. In the bathroom, the knapsack—with that provocative photo and journal inside—was gone.

Married to Parker?

It now seemed like one of her dreams, so impossible was the thought.

She washed her face, bunched her rebellious hair into a short ponytail and sped out the door. She had no intention of letting Camilla get away on her—not without answering a whole mess of questions.

Married to Parker!

She slammed out the door.

She stared at the patch of grass in front of the house where her truck should have been.

It was gone, just like Cam.

She went back in the house and saw the note on the hutch where she always put her keys: *Sorry, I'll be back.*

Then Hy noticed the blinking message light on her phone.

There were three messages—all from Ian. She had hardly given him a thought all day.

The first was from seven that morning: "Hy. Ian. Call me."

The second at nine: "Hy. It's Ian. Where the hell are you?"

The last must have come when she was outside with Annabelle.

"Hyacinth." His use of her full name gave the message urgency. "Call the minute you get back. If you are back, pick up, for God's sake."

When she didn't pick up the third time, Ian had wondered if Hy was avoiding him. Was she perhaps upset about last night? It troubled him briefly, but he soon forgot it and headed back to the computer. After a while, he quit. He stretched his back, kinked from bending over the keyboard, eyes fixed to the screen. He wanted to find out more about Parker, but he needed a break first, a bit of fresh air before the rain came. He went up on the widow's walk. He thought he might spy *The Crustacean*, but he saw nothing on the water. Soon he was thinking of Hy again, watching her truck heading down the road. He thought she might be coming to see him, but the truck sped right past the intersection, past the Hall, past the triangle of land where Abel Mack's General Store used to be and sped off out of sight down The Way.

Where was she going? Why hadn't she called back?

Hy rang Ian's number. No answer, but she could see his lights on. She'd have to walk there. On her way out, she noticed that Cam had left the blue vanity case by the door. She inspected it. *Samsonite.* The letters *C.P.* embossed on it. She tried to open it. Locked. She put on her sneakers and left the house.

Gus had been watching the sun set on the mackerel sky, the clouds rippling like the scales of a fish, tipped with rose-red hues. For about ten minutes, The Shores lay under its neon pink canopy. Then angry black clouds moved in and choked out the sun.

Gus knew a mackerel sky always brought rain. Even weather forecasters knew that much—they were calling for rain tonight and maybe a lightning storm. She'd have to make sure to have her coat and purse by the door before she went to bed, just in case.

She was closing the curtains when she saw Hy half-walking, half-running along the road. She'd seen her go by a few times today. She'd driven down toward Big Bay and back in the morning, then headed that way again without ever calling in. *Twice today in the truck—and her so mean with gasoline.* Now here she was, on foot this time, coming from her house again. Gus wrinkled her brow. She could have sworn she hadn't taken her eyes off the intersection in the last hour.

Be there. Be there. Be there.

The chant went through Hy's head in rhythm with her feet as she rounded the corner up Shipwreck Hill. The outside light was on. *That didn't mean a thing. Glow of the iMac from the living room—ditto.* As she came closer to the house, she saw the kitchen light on and Ian at the sink.

She burst through his back door.

"Hyacinth. Where the hell have you been?"

"I've found Camilla. And—well—I've lost her."

She was rewarded by a look of astonishment on his face.

Cam, a single tear of frustration at the edge of her lashes, gazed at the wreck of her jeep. *Not a complete wreck—but it couldn't be driven.* Every one of the windows was smashed to bits—shattered spider webs of glass, hammered at repeatedly with what could only be fury and malice. *So they'd been here. Found her hiding place.* She had lied to Hy, fibbed really—she didn't know their names, but she knew who they were. Coffin's henchmen. They'd been everywhere she went for the last six months, getting in her way.

It had only made her more stubborn, more determined. One word to Parker and they'd be called off. She knew that. She had gone to talk to him, but not about that. He'd closed her out. She wouldn't try again—not even for the cause. She stuck out her chin, pressed her lips together in a firm line, and strode over to the edge of the cape, looking for *The Crustacean*. She peered across the water, but saw nothing.

She groped her way down the side of the cape and hauled out the dory from under the tangle of seaweed and sand. She'd bought it from a fisherman in Winterside and had told him to deliver it to the cove by water. The idea was to avoid setting tongues wagging, but the fisherman had been doing quite a bit of talking about the odd woman and the odd place she'd had him leave the dory. He'd been talking it up in a bar in Winterside just before Setting Day. There had been a couple of strangers in the bar—one tall and thin, the other short and fat, who were very interested in his story and had bought him a few beers over the limit. That didn't stop him from driving home anyway, though the white dividing line looked more like two after he downed the last beer in the cab of his truck.

As they drove to Bloodsucker Lane, Hy told Ian about the dual role Camilla had been playing. He told her about the Parker octopus and its tentacles.

"That's the world Parker was born into—massive wealth and privilege." He turned on the windshield wipers to clear off the few drops of rain that had begun to fall.

"Born into," she said, "but didn't fit into."

"Not entirely. He may not be getting his own hands dirty in

business, but he certainly likes sticking them into the pot of gold."

"Well, I don't like sticking mine in shit."

He looked quizzical. She told him about the mess in her back room and on her stoop. "The pump engaged when Annabelle came by and she was suspicious that it might be Cam, which of course it was, but then decided it must be you having a bath in my house."

He laughed, but they were both thinking about last night. How she had come gasping out of the dream, waking him with her cry in the night—then him holding her, comforting her. She—paralyzed with fear. He—wondering what had made her tremble so. Hy couldn't figure out what was making the dream recur so often. It hadn't been like this since she was a teenager, feeding off her raging hormones. Now it seemed to be fuelled by the trouble Camilla had brought with her to The Shores.

Hy didn't tell Ian about the photograph of Parker and Camilla. She wanted to, but didn't want to admit that she'd been snooping and still couldn't believe what she'd seen. She had a lot of questions she wanted to ask Cam first—if she got the chance. As the car neared Bloodsucker Lane, the chant began again in her head.

Be there. Be there. Be there.

Chapter Thirty-Four

Cam rowed steadily until she reached Mack's Shore. The cloud cover had brought dark on early and she set to her task, hoping to be able to return Hy's truck before she found it was missing. She felt, as she often did, that someone was watching her. She felt it more keenly tonight, knowing that the two thugs and their boat were somewhere on these waters. She thought she had heard the low hum of an engine somewhere farther offshore, but sound carries well on the water—it could easily be miles down the coast. She began hauling the traps, liberating the lobsters inside, attaching to each trap a small capsule before she lowered it into the water. It started spitting rain.

Over at MacPherson's Shore, Jared could hear her traps splashing back in the water, as she could hear his. He didn't know what she was up to—not poaching like him. Letting them go, he figured. She was pissing him off. She might draw attention to what he was doing. He'd have to stop her…soon.

So intent were both on their work—Cam for her love of the lobster and Jared for his love of filthy lucre—neither of them noticed Parker gazing out from his big window at the top of the cape, the house fully lit up so they could easily have seen him.

Nor did they see Guillaume, in the peak of those tall windows, also looking down for a different reason. He was checking impatiently for his connection, pacing back and forth across the loft, looking out the window each time he passed by, gnawing on his knuckles, rubbing his eyes, trying to erase the flashing lights and colours he was seeing in his mind. He couldn't rub the images out of his brain, or make time move faster.

Hand in his pocket, he jiggled the assorted treasures he'd pur-loined to exchange for the drug. There was his own gold necklace, with the heavy reproduction of a Roman coin, his gold chain bracelet, his gold Irish wedding ring. It meant nothing. It never had. He hadn't liked it when Parker gave it to him. He'd given her one too. For her, it had been real. For him, it was a mockery. He had never worn it. As a result, Parker had never worn his either. It was now in Guillaume's pocket, too, along with a pair of Parker's gold cufflinks and Reinholdt's gold watch. It didn't work, but that didn't matter. The gold would translate into a generous stash of cocaine.

"There it is!" Hy's truck was pulled over on the grass shoulder of the road, just at the turn onto Bloodsucker Lane. She couldn't quite figure out why it was there, but she understood when they reached Cam's jeep.

"What a mess." Ian came to a stop well clear of any possible glass fragments on the ground.

"She must have parked my truck on the road after she saw this."

"I guess so." Ian got out of the car, pulled up the hood of his jacket, and walked around the jeep. He tried a door. It opened. He came back and pulled a tarp out of the trunk of his vehicle.

"Let's put this over it. Keep the rain out."

They roped the tarp around the jeep—the wind and rain mak-ing a mockery of their efforts, billowing the whole thing up as they tried to fix it down, water streaming onto them. The rain was coming down steadily now. When they'd done the best they could, they ran back to Ian's car.

"What do you want to do about your truck?" He pulled to a stop at the end of the lane.

"Leave it here," she said. "She'll bring it back."

He raised his eyebrows and shrugged.

"I guess no one will harm it. They'll think it's a wreck anyway."
He gave her a sly smile, his eyes teasing.

She stuck out her tongue at him. Ian was always making fun of
her truck, but he was happy to use it whenever he needed to haul
something too big or dirty for his precious hybrid.

The rain was falling in thick sheets on the way back to Hy's
house. The wind was blowing it nearly horizontal and they
couldn't see—except when the lightning slashed the sky, thunder
booming down the length of the coast. They hydroplaned a
couple of times and Ian eased up on the accelerator. Hy just
wanted to get home—to her creaky, swaying old house.

Gus always swore that the best place to be in a lightning storm
was a car. Her mother had told her the rubber tires would protect
them. If she still had a car, that's where she and Abel would be.
She used to drag the whole family out in a lightning storm—all
ten of them would cram into the old Buick and a couple of farm
trucks until, as teenagers, the kids had rebelled and refused to
leave their beds. Now there was no car, so Gus would sit in the
kitchen in her purple chair, waiting, terrified, for the lightning
to stop. She counted herself lucky every time it didn't strike the
roof or the chimney or set the house on fire. In spite of her fear,
Gus refused to have lightning rods on her house—why would you
want to attract it, she always asked, and no amount of explaining
how the rods worked would change her mind.

Ian pulled up as close to Hy's front door as he could.

"Want me to come in?"

Now he offers. Hy thought it was curiosity more than concern.

"No." When Cam came back, Hy wanted her all to herself.

"Cam'll be coming back soon if she's been out on the water. I
better speak with her alone. I don't think I'll get anything out of
her with someone else around. Thanks anyway."

He looked disappointed. "You be careful."

"Bit late for that now."

She hauled her jacket over her head and got out of the car. He waited until she was inside before he pulled out.

The rain was pelting down and Jared was cursing when he came off the water. He stumbled up the beach with two plastic bins of lobsters. It took two trips. He was careless and dropped a couple of the creatures on the way to the cookhouse. When he got inside, he dumped the bins on the concrete floor beside the pond and slipped down onto it himself. He pulled out his mickey and took a swig.

Hy had a fire going in the wood stove when Cam came dripping through the door, looking shamefaced.

"Sorry. I had to go."

"I saw your jeep. What a mess."

"You followed me?"

"Well, yes. You went out on the water—after what they did?"

Cam stuck her chin out. "Yes. Especially because of that."

Hy shook her head. "You must be starving." She had a pot of hot vegetable soup on the stove. "Go dry yourself. Change your clothes. Use the room you had before."

Cam came down ten minutes later, wearing a pair of jeans and an olive green T-shirt with a photographic image of a live lobster on it and the slogan *Free a Friend*.

She was wearing the pearls around her neck.

"You look like a different person in your sweater set and skirt."

"That's the whole idea. Disguise. They're my mother's clothes. They make me look like someone else."

"So the real you—?"

"This is the real me."

The real Cam was slighter and smaller than either of her personas. As Camilla, wearing the pumps and long slim skirt, she had appeared taller, a mature woman. As the Legionnaire, in the boxy camouflage jacket and pants, she'd seemed shorter, stockier, a tomboy.

Hy wondered who the real Cam—Camilla—was, and still wasn't convinced she was seeing her now. She suspected there would be layers yet to peel away before she got to the truth. Hy put the soup, crackers, bread and cheese on the table. She'd been drinking tea to warm up. She offered some to Cam.

"Or we have this."

She held up a bottle of red wine.

"Tea first, then wine. I'd love some wine."

Later, when Cam had downed the better part of a glass of wine, Hy began asking questions. Not about the marriage. She couldn't ask about that. It was what she wanted to know about most, but then Cam would know she'd looked through her things, and would never trust her.

"What did you mean when you said, outside the Hall, that you hadn't done any of those things we thought you did?"

"I didn't."

"You didn't cut Ben's trap lines?"

Cam looked genuinely shocked.

"I swear I didn't."

"Or spell out 'Kill' on the Big Bay wharf in herring bait?"

"I've never even been there."

Was she lying? Her eyes were clear, untroubled. Not for a moment did she avert her gaze.

"Did you send out those cancellations to the lobster supper?"

"Not me. None of it was me. Everything I do, you've seen me do. That's how I operate. Not in hiding. Up front."

"The sign at the Hall? You did the sign?"

"Oh, yeah, I did the sign."

"What about freeing lobsters from Ben's traps? Poaching, he'd call it."

"Poaching?" Cam's eyes blazed. "It's not poaching. It's liberating."

"That's not up front."

"Yes it is. I don't hide what I do. If I do it, you know it's me. I can't waste any effort. I leave a calling card. I attach a small capsule to each trap line with a note in it that says lobsters have been removed from this trap by the LLL—and a paragraph of propaganda."

Hy looked thoughtful. "Ben didn't say anything about that, but he did say you're not very tidy."

Cam looked offended.

"What do you mean?"

"He told Ian that he lays the lines to the east and now he's finding them lying in the opposite direction, or all in a lump."

"That's not me."

"Then who?"

Sudden knowledge lit up Cam's eyes. "The poacher."

"Poacher?"

Cam gave Hy a description.

"Jared," she said. "I wonder what he's doing that for?"

"For Guillaume," Cam said, without thinking.

"You know Guillaume?"

Chapter Thirty-Five

Jared woke up stiff and cold, swearing on the cookhouse floor. There was an empty mickey of rum beside him. The lobster bins he had brought in from the dory two hours before were sitting by the pond in the back. Two of the lobsters had escaped and were crawling across the floor. A couple of the others were dead. He groaned and put a hand to his aching head. He struggled to his feet and dragged himself over to the bins. He tossed the lobsters— dead and alive—into the water. The live ones might soon be dead too. Lobsters don't like to be thrown. It upsets their delicate biology. Jared left the cookhouse and climbed into his Hummer.

He passed out again with his head on the wheel.

"I know Guillaume." Cam dropped her head. "At least, I met him," she said. "I saw the kitchen. I threw some of his food—all lobster—into that ridiculous pond."

"Shock theatre?"

"He was shocked." Cam grinned.

"But everything else, not you?"

"Nope."

"Then who?"

"Mutt and Jeff, I guess. Turning up the heat. Trying to make things worse for me. Pushing me out of here so I can't operate. They'll be dogging me everywhere I go now. It's going to get tougher."

"Who are they? Why do they want to stop you?"

Cam shrugged. She popped the last of the cheese and bread into her mouth.

"It seems like a crazy battle," said Hy. "How can you possibly keep it up?"

Cam finished chewing before she spoke. "It's important to me," she said. "I was given a gift. It's something I was—" she hesitated—"born with, I guess. Born to. I don't know." She fell silent.

"You're the Lobster Lover, right? The blogger."

Cam looked down at her empty plate.

"Yeah, I'm the Lobster Lover. Of course I'm the Lobster Lover."

Parker never heard Guillaume come down from the loft and was unaware of him standing behind him, boring holes in his back with the pure hate in his eyes. Guillaume knew by the set of Parker's shoulders, the stiff, tight way he held himself that he was looking for her. Parker turned away from the window, disappointed. He had seen nothing—no one—not even Jared. He caught the look of hate in Guillaume's eyes, but he didn't care anymore. *What about her?* He didn't know what to think. He didn't know whether he wanted her to come closer—or stay away. Why would he welcome her? There would be only blame, anger, recrimination—to which she had every right.

Guillaume didn't say a word. He grabbed a jacket.

"Where are you going?" *In this weather?*

"None of your beez-ness."

"I think it is."

Guillaume pulled the door open. The sound of the driving rain—and some of its moisture—entered the room.

"You do not own me."

Trite. Reduced to such trite conversation.

"I very much think that I do." *Pompous. Not helpful.*

Guillaume said nothing. He just left, slamming the door behind him.

Parker should have known that Guillaume was up to something—and maybe he did—but he was so numb and distracted he
didn't react.

"Some of it's true," said Cam. "Some of it's not."

They were into their second bottle of wine and talking about
what Hy had found on the Internet.

"I never marched into a G8 dinner in Geneva. I just threatened
to do it unless they took lobster off the menu, which they did.
That was victory enough. You don't want to alienate people all the
time."

"But you do. You did here. Yet you seem like a nice person." Hy
refilled both their glasses.

"I *am* a nice person."

"Then why such extreme tactics?"

"Like you said—it's shock theatre. I did a lot of that in a drama
group as a teenager."

Hy thought she still looked not much older than a teenager, but
the photo—the photo said differently. She wished she could have
another look at it.

"It's easy for me, because it's just acting. It's a role—and it works
to get media attention. You have to have that to get your message
across."

"You haven't had any here."

"It will come." Her voice was confident. Hy filled her glass
again.

"I'm disappointed you didn't march in on a G8 dinner. How
could the media get it so wrong? Oh well, as long as they spell
your name right." Hy thought about the Samsonite luggage and
the initials *C.P.*

"Is Samson your real name?"

Cam held her glass halfway to her mouth. She put it down.

"It is now." She pursed her lips in a way that told Hy she would get nowhere going down that road.

"To match your luggage?"

Cam's face went red—red and stubborn. Hy let it go.

"Why did you come here? It's such a small place."

"Small place. Small group. Small start."

"Just how small a group, Cam?"

No reply.

Hy persisted. "A group of say—one—or two? Just Cam and Camilla?"

Cam looked at her sharply.

"It's just you, isn't it? You're the only one."

A long silence.

"I work best on my own."

A sly grin spread across her face.

She straightened up proudly and stretched out her arms.

"Meet the team."

The headlights woke Jared from his semi-comatose state in the Hummer. He eased himself up and peeked out to see Guillaume and Winterside's most notorious drug dealer enter the cookhouse. Bernie Cusack made Guillaume look taller and plumper than he was. Bernie had been a tiny, premature baby who never caught up, never formed any convincing masculine traits. He was small and delicate and emaciated from constant drug use. His clothes hung on him. His skin was unhealthy and pimply. The whites of his eyes were usually bloodshot and yellow, the irises a sickly light brown.

Jared could see through the window as Bernie pulled out a package wrapped in plastic. He watched, with great interest, as the transaction took place. He ducked back down as Bernie left. He had to wait until Guillaume left too, a long, impatient wait.

Jared was antsy to get his hands on the cocaine he knew Guillaume was snorting right now. He knew he'd leave it somewhere in the kitchen, and that when he left, he, Jared, was going to get himself some. It was going to be a great weekend.

"I am the founding and only member of the LLL."

"But why? Couldn't you get other members?"

"Maybe, but I'm a loner."

"Like the lobster?"

"You catch on fast. I don't work well with other people. Besides, this is a personal crusade."

"Personal? Anything to do with Parker?"

Cam's eyes clouded over. "Parker?"

"Is there a connection?"

"No."

"Ian thought you knew each other."

Cam shrugged. Hy kept at it.

"His family's big in the lobster business in Maine, right? Big. Huge. He could be a target for you. Is he?"

Cam looked down at her empty plate.

Still Hy persisted. "You do know him."

"I know who he is."

"Is he why you're here?"

Cam kept her head down. "Just coincidence."

"C'mon. What's he to you?"

Cam lifted her head.

"Nothing." Her chin jutted out, defiant. "Nothing. He's nothing to me."

"If he's nothing to you, why do you hate him?"

"I never said that."

"You don't have to. It's in your eyes, whenever I say his name."

Cam looked away. Hy appeared to see right into her as if she knew the truth. She couldn't possibly. No one knew the whole story. *Not even me—or Parker.*

"I don't hate him. I don't know him well enough to hate him," she said, stubbornly. She crumpled her napkin and thrust it onto her plate.

Parker was unaware of the transaction that had just taken place at the cookhouse. He had poured himself a Scotch at five o'clock precisely and kept on drinking until he passed out just like Jared, the effect of the much more expensive liquor no different than the rotgut. Behind him, Jasmine imitated his soft snoring, so it sounded like there were two men passed out in the room.

In his gourmet kitchen, Guillaume looked like a bizarre fairy godmother, changing the mice into footmen in *Cinderella*, as he waved his lobster stunner like a wand, striking and killing lobsters. In his unbalanced mind he was performing a parody of the Disney movie, as he zapped lobster after lobster in the three-foot stainless steel sink.

Bippity bobbity boo!

Lined up in the freezer were lobster claws, stuffed, not with soft white flesh, but with cocaine. Claw, after claw, after claw, Guillaume's insurance against boredom and desire.

He was shrouded in steam, bubbling up from water boiling in big copper pots, olive oil spitting on the stove, flour flying as he put together perfect flaky pastry to surround the soft, sweet lobster meat. Not all the white powder flying around the cookhouse was flour.

Certainly not the stuff encrusted around Guillaume's nose.

Chapter Thirty-Six

Jared thought Guillaume would never leave. He dozed on and off in the cab of his Hummer. When the cookhouse lights went out, he watched Guillaume labour across the sand and up to the house. He saw more lights go off. He waited several minutes. The rain had stopped and there was light on the eastern horizon. It was nearly dawn.

He let himself into the cookhouse. He didn't notice the mess Guillaume had left behind—pots and pans scattered on the counters, a pile of utensils in the sink, the dishwasher door yawning open, dishes stuffed into it every which way. His own kitchen was worse—the floor a litter of empty beer and Coke cans, bottles of rum, China Garden cartons and Pizzarama boxes. Jared's floor mop of a dog, Newt, used to lick it clean. Not anymore. Newt had moved out the last time Jared went to jail. He was fed now, in a dish, at just about every house in the village.

Jared began opening cupboards, not bothering to close them, taking out jars and bottles and leaving them on the counter. There were all kinds of weird-looking spices and powders. *Cumin. What the hell is cumin? Somethin' like Viagra?* He tasted it and scrunched up his face. He read the other labels: Ginger, Allspice, Nutmeg—you could sometimes get high on that, they said—but no cocaine. *Where is the goddamn cocaine?* He looked in the stainless steel fridge. *Weird-lookin' stuff in there, too, but no coke.* He opened the walk-in freezer. It was lined with shelves, stacked with labelled cartons of the food Guillaume had prepared in the last few hours. *Homard St. Jacques,* his signature dish, *Homard au vin de Dents de Lion*—and some new drug-inspired dishes: *Crustacean Croutons,* in the shape of tiny lobster claws, and *Lobster à l'Anglaise,* which was lobster trifle. Jared was a plain meat and potatoes guy. When he did eat lobster, it was straight claws and tail—dipped in butter.

There were a dozen claws—cooked, red, and frozen, lining one shelf. That was more his speed. *Plain and simple.* He'd have one of those. He pulled one out and stuck it in the microwave. The microwave ended its cycle to the strains of "The William Tell Overture," an extravagant feature that was lost on Jared. He pulled out the claw and juggled it from hand to hand. *Damn near burned my fingers.* He was about to crack it open, when he felt a wave of nausea. He wasn't eating that, not on an empty stomach. *Not without a coffee. No way.* He opened the door and threw it out. A crow came by and scooped it up, just slightly ahead of a gull. Some more birds moved in, and there was a great squawking and flapping in the sky when they realized that they were too late.

Jared got in his Hummer and took off.

He'd come back later. *Tomorrow.* He knew there was cocaine in there somewhere. He drove home in a fog, ran over a fox, and nearly drove into the ditch when he turned into his own driveway.

Gus was out putting stale homemade bread on the back stoop to feed the crow she called Charlie. She claimed that when she spoke to him, he spoke back. She said she understood his every caw—although she didn't know why it was called cawing, when the sound the crow made was more like "aw." Her neighbour Estelle believed Gus understood the bird, but didn't know how she could tell a "yes" from a "no."

"Oh, I can tell," Gus had nodded sagely. "I can tell by the tilt of his head and the look in his eye." Abel insisted it must be a different eye all the time—that it couldn't be the same crow year after year. The original must be long dead, he told her. Gus didn't like to think about that. *Who was to say how long a crow might live, especially one brought up on her wholesome homemade bread?*

Charlie paid no attention to the bread this morning. He was dipping up and down with something in his beak. Ben and Annabelle's dog, Toby, was there too—also making a fuss, running in circles, worrying the crow. Toby kept jumping up to try to grab whatever the crow was clutching.

Spying Gus, the big black bird increased his cawing and swooped low. Toby managed to grab the treasure in his teeth. There was a bit of a tussle and finally Charlie let go, flying up high with a great screech. Toby ran over to Gus and dropped the trophy at her feet. It was a cooked lobster claw. *Must be from the supper at the Hall. Has a raccoon upended one of them bins?* She'd have to check—or have Abel do it. He'd got up earlier than she had this morning and was nowhere to be found—the only sign of him his empty coffee cup in the sink.

Gus hated to touch the claw. She picked it up gingerly with her thumb and forefinger and, with her arm stretched out in front of her so she wouldn't smell it, she took it to the compost bin and dropped it in. Toby and Charlie both went wild. The dog, barking and running around the bin as if chasing his own tail. The crow, squawking and swooping down at the bin. Gus tried to stop them, but couldn't. *Best leave them to it. They'll settle down.*

They didn't.

They just kept cawing and barking—all day long, and even the next.

Hy woke to a clean and bright morning, a day innocent of last night's dirty weather, a clean bolt of sunshine streaming into her bedroom window. Her first thought was of Cam. She got up and stumbled down the short hall to the guest bedroom and peeked in. Cam was scrunched into the bed as if she'd become a part of it. Hy crept downstairs, made coffee, and sat down at the computer to email Eldon. She felt the energy drain from her as soon as she opened the screen. At least there were no more ugly messages—of any kind. *Eldon can wait.* She googled Hawthorne Parker instead and became happily entangled in the tentacles of the octopus. It was nearly noon when Hy abandoned the octopus to return to the problem of Eldon.

Cam came downstairs. Hy saved what she'd started.

So far she had: *Hi Eldon, I should explain…*

She got up to make Cam some fresh coffee and the phone rang. It was Ian. He was so unable to contain his curiosity about Cam, he didn't even say hello.

"Is she there?"

"Yup."

"Would you two like to go look for *The Crustacean*?"

Parker woke up on the couch, squinting in the bright sunshine. His head was aching, his mouth dry, the thirty-year-old bottle of Scotch on the table, half gone. He dragged himself upstairs where Guillaume was snoring in the king-size bed. Guillaume looked innocent in sleep, more like the boy from Buctouche that Parker had fallen in love with—with his dark good looks, a stocky but trim physique, flashing smile, seductively shifty eyes. A boy from Buctouche, determined to make his way in the world—in a big way. He had been perfecting his Parisian-accented English and a certain sense of style. Parker had found it amusing and Guillaume utterly charming. A firecracker with a wicked smile.

Parker moved quietly across the room, thinking to wake Guillaume gently and try to have a quiet talk, but when he saw the white crust around Guillaume's nose, he stopped, blood hot in his veins. *Cocaine. Where had he gotten it? Jared. Must be. I'll soon put a stop to that.* He turned away with contempt. Guillaume was no longer a charming boy and there was more wickedness in him than a seductive smile could conceal.

"We should blow that bitch out of the water." Tom McFee was chewing tobacco. He spat a dirty orange wad of it onto the wharf.

Ben put up his hands, gesturing for restraint. He wished Annabelle were there. She brought calm to volatile situations like this one. The local fishermen were sitting outside Ben's shed on the wharf at Big Bay, the lobster catch landed and sold.

"Look, she hasn't done anything to any of you. I'm the one that's taken the heat."

He didn't like the way Scott Bergeron looked—mean as a bad dog, with the one eye always half-closed, his unruly pale ginger hair full of dandruff. Tom McFee was surly and sneering. Handsome as the devil himself, was how Gus described him. Dark hair, straight white teeth, a dimpled chin and sleepy, seductive eyes hiding a nasty streak.

"Still 'n' all..." Tom lacked imagination. He just repeated: "We should blow the bitch outta the water." His pal nodded his head up and down in agreement.

"Give over." Ben frowned. "You're on the sauce."

Scott and Tom always started drinking the minute they got off the water and sold their lobster. They'd weave home in their trucks and fall unconscious every afternoon. Then they'd go on the water again at night, still drunk, and haul up the other men's catch. Ben wasn't worried about what the other fishermen might do, but he was worried about these two. He'd wanted to get this settled before he headed for Charlottetown that night, but he could see he was getting nowhere.

"Look, let's just let it lie another day or two. She may clear out of here. If she doesn't, I promise you, I'll do something about it. She won't be allowed to hurt our season. Now, any of you seen a boat around here called *The Crustacean*?"

The men looked at one another, a few shrugged, one or two said, "Nope," and the meeting adjourned. Not very satisfactory, thought Ben as he left the wharf, but his spirits lifted as he thought about the night ahead—a restaurant meal with the family, Rowan's concert, bathing in the fey beauty and ethereal voice that he and Annabelle had somehow created, and then a king-size bed in the Prince Charles Hotel, just him and Annabelle. He was eager to get to town, but the ferry schedule gave him time to stop at Hy's to warn her that things might be getting ugly, just in case she had any more ideas about helping out that Legionnaire the way she had the night of the supper. Hy's truck was in the yard, but there was no answer when he knocked on the door. He tried the door handle. *Locked. Odd that.*

If Ben hadn't been off in a dream world, fantasizing about Annabelle in a big hotel bed, he would have noticed Ian's hybrid speeding along the road, heading for Big Bay with Hy in the passenger seat and Cam huddled down in the back. The three agreed that *The Crustacean* had to be somewhere close by if those two men had come to shore to vandalize Cam's jeep. They also all agreed that the pair had done it—and everything else—to discredit Cam and the Legion, and to get her out of The Shores.

The jeep looked the same as it had when they'd left it the evening before. Cam grabbed a few more things out of it—including a pair of silk pyjamas and some sweats.

For both of her, thought Hy, with an inner smile.

"You going to report it to police, have it towed by the CAA?" asked Ian, ever practical.

Cam shook her head. "Leave it be for now."

Ian couldn't believe Cam's casual approach. It was a good vehicle—apart from the damage.

They left the jeep and continued on down the road, past the turnoff to Big Bay Harbour. A mile or so on, The Island Way ended and turned back on itself. Just before that, there was a lane that ran up the long sheltering arm on the west side of the bay. It was impossible to drive all the way out to the end of the point—the land became sand dunes that got progressively bigger and then began to recede, until they trailed off into just a trace of shore jutting into the sea.

They got out of the car and began hiking through dunes so tall, it felt like tramping across the Sahara desert. Though the day was cool, they were sweating by the time they came around the last of the three largest dunes. There was *The Crustacean,* moored where it could not be seen—except from their perfect viewpoint.

"That's it," said Cam, Ian and Hy simultaneously. It was a small triumph. What they would do with the information, none of them knew. They might stop those two bullies before they did more damage.

They didn't know that it was already too late for that.

Chapter Thirty-Seven

"I am in ze jail—and it ees your fault." It was mid-afternoon when Guillaume finally got up. He had convinced himself that Parker was to blame for the entire episode—his journey to town with Jared, the night spent snivelling up against the haystack, the hours in jail—all Parker's fault. It was partly paranoia, and partly rationalization. If Parker hadn't brought him here…if this wasn't such a godforsaken place…if…if…if…and on and on it went, the blame becoming greater in his mind the more he thought about it.

"My fault?" Parker's eyes and mouth opened wide at the accusation. "My fault?" he repeated, unable to believe it.

"Always, your fault—from when you left me for her."

Lord, he was dragging that up again.

"I've paid for it ever since."

He looked Guillaume straight in the eyes. The glassy gleam in them should have been a beacon of warning to Parker, but he had become adept at avoiding such signs—signs that should have alerted him that Guillaume was spinning out of control and headed on a collision course that would not involve cars.

"Is Sheldon Coffin behind this?"

Cam was surprised by Ian's mention of the name. She had no quick response. They were walking back to the car, in single file, along the path through the dunes. She was ahead of him and he couldn't see her face. He persisted:

"Trying to protect his evil empire?"

"From me? I can hardly believe it."

"You do know him?"

"I know *of* him." She spoke with certainty, a ring of truth in the way she said it. He wished he could see her expression, her eyes.

"Do you know Matt and Jeff?"

"Mutt. No. No, I don't. I know only that they work for him."

"But those two have targeted you. If that boat belongs to him—"

She turned sharply, contempt in her eyes. "It doesn't belong to him."

"Well, it's in his control—like everything else."

"Everything else?"

"He's running the whole show for Parker. You must know that. That must be why you're here. To try to get to Parker."

Cam said nothing. She just kept walking. Hy, behind Ian, knew he wouldn't get Cam to open up about Parker. She'd had no luck herself—and she knew why. *That photo. This wasn't business, it was personal. It wasn't about lobsters, the industry or the cause. It was about whatever had happened between Camilla and Parker.*

They walked the rest of the way in silence, Hy anxiously wondering when—and if —she could ask Cam about the photograph. She wasn't willing to admit she'd been a snoop.

"So you write the blogs," Ian said, when they reached the car.

"I'm the Lobster Lover," said Cam.

"Why can't I link to it? Why isn't it generally available?"

"Guerrilla tactics," said Cam.

"But the whole point of a blog is to get it out there."

"Not this blog. I don't want to preach to the converted. I wouldn't get that many hits on the site other than animal rights people. This way, I make unexpected attacks on known contacts— like Hy. Pop! It shows up. Out of the blue. Out of left field."

"Why send it to me?"

"You've been getting it?" Cam climbed into the back seat. She looked surprised. "You?"

"Once."

"I don't know anything about that."

"Oh, c'mon. The claw?" Ian started up the car. "You sent it to me."

"Oh, I wrote it, but I never sent it to you."

"You must have."

"There are more things in the etherworld, Ian, than you have dreamed of in your philosophy," Hy recited, looking smug. Ian frowned at her.

"From Shakespeare's blog," she added, in a final thrust.

"It must have a mind of its own," said Cam. "I kind of like that. Anyway, you've got to admit the tactic works. Zap—out of nowhere—and suddenly you're thinking lobster rights in a way you never considered before. It gets into your head."

It had. It had been chewing away at Hy's fragile appetite for meat. It was vexing Ian's technical mind.

"So how do you do it—when you do it on purpose?"

"That would be telling."

"C'mon. Give me a hint."

"There are ways in—through the electronic labyrinth. I know a few of them."

Ian looked back at her with admiration. Hy felt a small twinge. *Jealousy?*

Guillaume was in the cookhouse with half a dozen lobsters lined up, dead, in the long, shallow steel sink. They were still that greenish-blue colour—not cooked yet. He'd killed them with the lobster stunner. It had heated up and become red hot, burning his hand. Now it lay like an oversized curling iron, cooling off. He didn't feel like cooking. He picked up a one-edged razor blade and began separating a small mound of white powder on the counter, his hands trembling. He grasped the blade so hard that he cut himself. He sucked on his bleeding finger, the rest of his body radiating with pain. He was losing control—of himself, of Parker.

He threaded thin white powdery lines across the black granite counter.

The first line disappeared. He pulled it up his nose, inhaling deeply, feeling that sharp chemical taste at the back of his throat. Then the rush began. His blood sang. He exhaled—all his senses awakened. Normal. He felt normal. He clenched his teeth, began grinding them. *More. I need more.*

Another snort, another line gone. Then another.

Ian was half-expecting to find some of Moira's muffins in his kitchen when he got home, but she hadn't come by in the last couple of days for some reason he couldn't figure out. The kitchen was a mess. He grabbed some bread and cheese and a beer, and retreated from the domestic turmoil back to the sanctity of his computer and the search for more information about Hawthorne Parker.

Guillaume was just about to snort the last line when Parker walked into the cookhouse. Parker froze at the sight of Guillaume, bent over the counter, silver straw to his nose, half a line of white powder on the black counter.

"I thought we'd done with this." Parker swept a hand across the counter.

The claw fell with a clunk to the floor. White powder spilled out of it.

Guillaume scowled.

"I am 'aving to put up with that girl, nosing around all ze time? Don't think I don't know. I know."

Parker dusted off his hands, meticulously, removing every speck of the cocaine.

"Is she to 'ave ze money? Or am I to 'ave it?"

"She doesn't want the money. She wants nothing to do with the money."

She wanted nothing from him.

"She's certainly not sticking around waiting for me to die. Unlike you." He said it because it was true. He said it because he wished it weren't and he hoped that Guillaume would deny it. Deny it in a way he could believe.

Guillaume didn't bother. He just shrugged.

"Once you were everysing to me."

It wasn't true. He had loved Parker only as much as he could love anyone, other than himself. He just liked the drama of saying it.

"Everything but this," said Parker, furiously grinding the powder on the floor with the heel of his shoe. He could not make it disappear.

Guillaume was watching, wondering if he'd be able to salvage it later. Parker saw where he was looking, knew what he was thinking. It made him furious. He gritted his teeth.

"You've lied to me, committed adultery…"

Guillaume smiled, a sarcastic smile.

"Not adultery. We were never married." It was a sore point. Parker had given him the ring, the ring he'd sold off last night, but he'd never given him the piece of paper, never given him what he'd given her.

"We couldn't be," said Parker. "When we could, I couldn't trust you anymore. It was still adultery. We might as well have been married all these years."

"Except you were married already. It is you who committed adultery."

"For God's sake, don't be ridiculous. She knew. She knew as soon as I did. It wasn't possible."

He had thought he could forget who he was in her arms. He'd been happy with her before Guillaume appeared. Then it was Guillaume he had wanted—Guillaume who had set him free—or so he thought.

He felt anything but free right now—his body taut, his fists clenched, his mouth set in one grim line. All his features pinched.

All those productive men, Ian kept thinking. *And Parker? Parker had produced nothing.* A bit more research proved him wrong. On coming into his inheritance, he had endowed the Parker Marine Camp for underprivileged kids—dedicated to C. More surfing led him to something very interesting. Following a hunch, he began jumping from genealogical to municipal, county and state records to ferret out the truth. It occupied him late into the night as he attempted to verify what was beginning to make a lot of sense. Newly energized by his discovery, Ian decided he'd go up on the walk later tonight. It would be a full moon. Maybe *The Crustacean* would come out of hiding.

Maybe they should set some bait.

"I'd like you to come on the water with me tonight."

Hy felt her blood tingle. "Why?"

"Because I'd like you to see what I do. Really see. Not in a DVD, but there, where I do my work."

Hy bit her lip and looked doubtful, fear singing through her. "No, I can't."

Disappointment dulled Cam's eyes.

"Please. Give me the chance to show you what I do. You can write about it."

The idea excited Hy, but she couldn't, could she? *I can't.*

"No one else has ever seen me, not up close, not like that. I'd like you to."

"I'm honoured," said Hy, tentatively. She was. She was scared too. Face the fear, she told herself. *The worst fear is fear itself.* As if she hadn't told herself that a thousand times before, every time she turned down Annabelle's offer of a ride in the lobster boat.

"If you do, I promise I'll leave. Just one more night. Come with me, and I promise I'll go."

The relief at that thought—of Cam going and taking all the trouble with her—overcame Hy's hesitation.

"Okay," she said. "I'll go." Cam had to leave, she must go, if things were to return to normal at The Shores. *It's too bad—just when I was getting to know her, to like her.*

"Of course I'll come," she said. "I'd love to."

As they left the house, Hy called Ian to tell him what she was up to. She was half-hoping he'd insist she not go, but there was no answer. She looked out of the kitchen window toward Shipwreck Hill. His house was dark, except for the outside light. He must be asleep, or out. She left a message, telling him she was going out on the water with Cam.

Hy's emotions swung wildly back and forth, between fear and determination. Now that they were on their way, she felt more and more that it was the right thing to do. Cam shouldn't be out there alone with those two jokers around. *No. Not jokers. Bullies. They might be dangerous.*

She was right to worry.

Chapter Thirty-Eight

"God, 'ow ugly you are." Guillaume smirked at Parker.

"You're no prize yourself. Look at you. Fat. Nose constantly running. Nails bitten to the quick. All for your love of that…" Parker pointed to the white powder on the floor.

"I 'ave to 'ave someting."

"There was me." Parker slumped, discouraged. "What was wrong with me?"

"Where do I begin? You and your sick little secrets. The things you like to do." Guillaume spat.

"I thought you liked to do them too. You did them with enough people."

"Would you like some now?" Guillaume taunted. He took a step forward, unbuttoning his trousers.

"Would you like some of this?" He came another step closer.

Parker could feel desire rise in him. He tried to erase the images that flashed through his mind. *Here. He could have him here.*

Guillaume moved another step closer, like a stalking cat.

"Which way would you like to have me? Where?"

Parker fought down the desire.

Sex had often settled their arguments, fueled by Guillaume's taking of other lovers, the young boys he'd seek out in bars, have in alleyways and then come home smelling like a tomcat. These infidelities, in some sick way, kept their own passion alive. Parker didn't think enough of himself or of sex to imagine that it could be any other way.

If he gave in now to Guillaume, it would have nothing to do with passion or love, nor even with sex, but just raw anger and hate.

Ugly.

Twisted.

Distorted.

Shameful.

With one thrust, Parker unbalanced Guillaume and sent him back against the island. He felt cold. All desire gone, replaced by disgust. For himself. For Guillaume. For what they had become.

It must end.

"But I have not started,"

Guillaume was breathing heavily. He lunged at Parker.

Time to face the fear. Face it down.

Hy looked at the sky and the water. The surf had been up that morning, following last night's storm, but it had eased off, and now the water was calm, the night clear under that bright moon, just a small smudge of dark cloud passing over its face. There was nothing foreboding. Besides, she was a good swimmer. Her grandmother had made sure of that.

"You have jackets?"

Cam looked sheepish. "Well, no."

"Can you swim?"

"No."

"You're nuts."

"Well, lobsters can't either but they live in the water."

"You're not a lobster."

This is crazy, thought Hy. Why had she thought she could do this?

She got in the dory. The sides rose up comfortingly high, the bottom reassuringly flat. At least it wasn't tippy like a canoe. Cam pushed the boat past the sandbar and into water deep enough that she could clamber in without weighting it to the bottom. The boat rocked. Hy gripped the gunwales. A shot of fear jolted her. Her blood started to sing, her heart to thump erratically. Be still, she willed it. She took a deep breath—and another.

"Don't worry, the water's calm." She said the word like her own name—Cam. The same way Gus did.

Cam took up the oars, rowing with considerable power, while Hy gritted her teeth, closed her eyes and tried to calm her beating heart. Cam threw the anchor out. It hit the water with a splash, and the coil of rope unravelled until it reached bottom. It wasn't deep here, where the lobster traps were.

The boat was bobbing on the water.

Hy kept her grip on both sides of the boat.

Cam leaned over and grabbed a lime green buoy, with the number seventeen painted on it in dark blue, and began to pull on the line. As she did, the boat tipped.

"Don't worry." Cam saw Hy biting her lip.

With one strong tug, Cam hauled the trap up onto the gunwale. It was hard work. The trap was three feet long and weighed forty pounds. The boat plunged to that side. Hy gripped so hard her knuckles went white.

Cam opened the trap's door, reached in and grabbed the flailing lobster around its middle, making soft, soothing sounds, like some exotic language—then, a high sustained note. The lobster stopped squirming, stopped moving altogether, completely under the spell of the hypnotic melody. Hy felt as if the world had stilled around them.

Cam slipped a hand under the creature's belly and gently lowered it into the water. It came rapidly to life again—thrust its tail down and disappeared.

Hy watched Cam haul traps and perform her tickling act until the Legionnaire's fingers became purple with cold.

"Your hands must be freezing."

"Yes, but the work warms me."

"What do you suppose it is that gives you that power?"

"I don't know. I just do it. I don't know anyone else who does. Male lobsters get real calm, when they smell the female's pheromone." She laughed and that great grin lit up her face. "Guess maybe I smell like a lady lobster. The males like it, and the females think I'm one of the gals."

Hy wished she had her camera. She would have liked a photograph of Cam and a lobster, head-to-head, as she lowered it into the water, her eyes intense, the lobster's antennae erect, beady eyes unseeing.

Parker had the lobster stunner in his hand. He'd grabbed it off the counter beside him. Guillaume laughed. He snatched it from him and caressed Parker's face with the cold metal of the rod.

"Would you like this?"

There was no mistaking the message in Guillaume's eyes—that strange gleam that signaled a terrible intent. He'd seen it that time before—with the rolling pin. Nothing had happened then, but it was going to happen now.

He's mad.

Guillaume traced Parker's cheek with the metal rod. He brought it down his torso, and then pushed it slowly between his legs. Parker felt vulnerable and ridiculous.

"Would you like some? Some of this?"

Parker felt no desire at all. Only fear. Something had tripped in Guillaume. *This was not a game. Not lust. This was serious.*

Guillaume shoved the rod up between his legs with a hard thrust.

Parker doubled over in pain.

"I asked you—do you want some of this?" He pulled the rod out roughly and held it to Parker's face again. Slid it down to his lips and rested it there with a light pressure.

"How will you like this in your mouth," he taunted. "It is big. Hard. But it is cold. I can warm it up for you." His thumb eased toward the power switch.

He was going to turn it on. Parker had no idea if it could hurt him, but it was clear that's what Guillaume meant to do.

He summoned all his strength and shoved him away.

Guillaume tottered backwards, one hand against the counter, one hand grasping the stunner.

Got to get that out of his hands.

Parker took a step forward.

Guillaume clicked the power switch. The rod was electrified. He took several thrusts with it in Parker's direction.

Parker took one more careful step forward.

Guillaume stepped back.

Advance. Retreat. Advance. Retreat. A few more cat and mouse moves. Like some crazy dance—with a lot at stake.

Parker would relive what happened next in slow motion for the rest of his short life. The whole world slowed down, so that he saw every detail.

Guillaume, lunging forward, holding the rod in both hands, swiping the side of Parker's face.

The implement buzzing with heat.

Red hot.

Sparking.

His nerves jangled with adrenaline—and electricity.

Chapter Thirty-Nine

Ian woke up around midnight. That was unusual. He always fell asleep within minutes of his head touching the pillow and slept enthusiastically all night long—with loud, energetic snores, appreciative grunts and groans as his body melted into the mattress and oblivion.

What woke him was the call from Hy, but he was only half-aware of it, slipping up out of sleep just as she was ringing off. He thought he'd dreamed it and rolled over to go back to sleep. He flipped around for a while, gave up, got up and saw the message light blinking on the phone.

He couldn't believe what he heard.

She's gone out on the water with Cam.

Out on the water with Cam?!

Had she forgotten her fears? Forgotten the nightmare?

If he'd known, he would have stopped her. Now it was too late. The full moon lit up the sky like a false early morning. He pulled on a pair of pants and a sweater, and went up on the walk.

The moon glowed high and bright. It washed its ghostly light across the main road, the houses and the water. Ian could see Parker's house with one outside light on. Well beyond that, out on the water, he spotted the dory, the dark forms of two people in it. *Cam and Hy?*

A dull sound disturbed the night—then a flash of light.

Bait. The word flashed into his mind.

There was a boat heading at high-speed towards the dory. It was shining a spotlight on it. Ian could now see Cam and Hy clearly outlined. *Jesus!* He stumbled down the stairs back into the house for a Thermos filled with hot water. *A blanket. Couple of jackets. Pair of pants. Flare gun? No time.*

The sound of a motor cut through the night, and a spotlight blinded them.

A Zodiac was aimed straight at them, Cam and Hy in the little dory, beside the lime green and blue lobster buoy.

It was a Futura Commando, more than twice the size of their six-foot boat. It was speeding toward them. It was almost on top of them, when it veered off and whipped by within inches of them. The dory began to roll from side to side. The Zodiac was capable of exceptional maneuvering. It made a tight turn, and returned on the other side, again passing within inches.

The dory was rocking violently.

Hy froze.

Cam jumped to her feet. The boat tipped and she went flying into the water. The Zodiac made another tight turn and began to come back.

Hy was disoriented. The light blazed into her eyes, blinding her.

"Help me up." Cam was clinging to the side of the dory.
Hy grabbed onto her hands and tried to haul her up. Cam kicked at the water. It was no use.

The Zodiac was on them again.

Cam lost her grip and the churning water pushed her away from the dory. She went under. She came up, sputtering and gasping for breath.

"Swim." Hy called.

"I can't."

Oh God. That's right.

As the Zodiac made another turn, Hy jumped into the cold sea. Head under the water. Swallowing it down. Harsh salt scratching at her throat, making her retch. Surfacing, she could hear the sound of the motor coming closer again.

Sirens. She could hear sirens in her head. But there were no sirens in this night—only the relentless throbbing of a motor as the black boat sliced through the water toward them again.

The water was freezing and she was numb. Her brain was buzzing with a chilling fear. This was no dream—no nightmare. This was real. Hy struggled to control the waves of terror pulsing in her blood, her heart beating a rapid rhythm, her mouth dry.

She looked around. *Cam? Where was Cam?*

One strong push, aided mightily by Guillaume's drug-induced disorientation, had sent him tripping backwards over the power cord. Parker watched, aware as he did of its motion picture quality—how it seemed to happen in slow motion, frame by frame, every movement of Guillaume's arms rising as he was upended.

Frame by frame, he fell back into the pond. The water splashed up. The power coursed through him. His arms jerked, muscles contracted, hands locked onto the implement that was killing him. He gripped it against his will, could not let go. Shock animated his eyes. His whole body convulsed.

Snap. Crackle. Pop.

The long metal rod fell off the handle and dropped to the floor.

Bang.

The fuse blew, but not soon enough.

Guillaume's cold heart stopped.

He had been fried along with several lobsters. *Boiled?*

He lay there like an ingredient in a surf and turf supper, a Pa Parker's meal gone wrong. The lobster didn't seem to mind. One, just one, had survived the electric jolt that surged through the water. It had butted at its dead tank mates, then crawled up onto Guillaume's chest. It began to claw at his cheek. Parker fell to his knees and buried his face in his hands. He rocked back and forth, moaning.

Guillaume.

If he could have, he would have screamed, but he had no breath. After a bit, he let out one long faltering moan. It went up into the high tones and became a weak cry for all that was lost to him.

Guillaume. Gone.

He was silent for a moment. Silent and rocking, back and forth, the enormity of his loss crept into his consciousness.

Guillaume dead.

He let out another long, low moan, until the breath was squeezed right out of him.

An accident?

A silent scream that only he could hear.

No, I killed him.

Utter despair.

I have killed Guillaume.

The lobster was now investigating Guillaume's eyes. They stared, frozen open, straight into the light that illuminated the grotto.

I wanted him dead.

The sound of the motor was growing louder.

Cam had surfaced, and Hy swam to her and grabbed her.

"Hold onto me," she ordered.

Every nerve was alive, so alive, so hot with fear that Hy never noticed how cold she was.

The Zodiac was slicing through the water, not five feet away, the spotlight blinding.

"Duck," yelled Hy. They went under the water, hand in hand, as far as they could go—down, down into the cold, dark fear. The Zodiac passed above them, churning the water, sending them spinning down. Hy struggled to pull them both back up.

They burst through the surface, gasping for air. The boat had begun to turn toward them again. One deep intake of air and Hy pulled on Cam and forced her under. The Zodiac circled back.

Down, down they went, into the black cold, Hy's grip on Cam tight with possession. She opened her eyes. The murky glow of moonlight filtered through the water and cast an eerie sheen on Cam's blonde hair floating like seaweed in brine. Cam was floating too. *A natural swimmer.* There was surprise in Cam's eyes, but there was fear, too.

Her lungs bursting, Hy hauled them both up to the surface again. No time to gather strength. The boat had already turned one more time and was bearing down on them relentlessly.

Down they went again, down into the swirling waters, Hy exhausted, ready to give up. *Sudden flashing lights. Wailing. Real, or am I in the dream?* She was dizzy with disorientation. Darkness beckoned her. She could go down into the darkness, find the dream, find sleep. *So compelling…so seductive. Into the warm, welcoming womb of the water. The first place.* It could reclaim her now, as it had not before.

Cam began to panic. The violent yanking on her limbs pulled Hy down farther into the nightmare. Now she began to panic, struggling to unlock Cam's grip with her free hand, trying to pry Cam's fingers loose, to be free of her.

She looked into Cam's startled eyes and wrenched herself back to reality. *This was not the dream. This was real.* She must have one thought. One thought only.

Survival.

She had not lived then to die now.

She had not survived in that place to die in this one.

She dragged Cam up to the surface again.

She had fought for life once and she must do it again—for herself—and for Cam.

Ian gunned the motor and squealed out of his driveway. He skidded on the road, moist from the night dew. He corrected and sped off toward the shore. He'd seen the boat circling the dory. He checked his tidal watch. *Coming on high tide.* He'd have to take the long way round to Mack's cove. Otherwise he'd be wading through water around Vanishing Point.

Incapable of speech, Hy's eyes bored into Cam's—pleading for her to understand what they had to do to survive.

Cam nodded. They both took deep breaths and plunged under the water again. They stayed still, the throb of the power motor sending the waters into a swirl above them. Hy's lungs were bursting. Cam began to struggle to rise to the surface, but Hy held her tight. Kept their eyes locked to calm her, to keep her with her, to communicate her purpose to her, to make her strong. *If we can just stay down long enough...*

Their only chance was to swim under the dory, over to the other side of it, and perhaps not be seen. She couldn't stay under much longer. She began to swim, one arm around Cam. After that one panicked, disoriented lapse, she held on to Cam like a part of herself. There was no thought now of letting her go. If they were to survive, they would survive together. Or both die.

A few more strokes.

Just a few more strokes.

She looked up at the underside of the dory. She had to get past it.

The water was churning on the far side, where the Zodiac was circling.

One more stroke. Now one more. One stroke at a time, she propelled them forward, until she could do no more. If her lungs hadn't already exploded, they were about to do so. She powered to the surface, one arm around Cam, bringing her along with her, slowing, painful as it was. She came up, up, using all her willpower to break through the water's surface silently, hoping not to be detected. Her head was hammering, blood pulsing, lungs gasping for air as she broke through.

She watched the Zodiac pass by on the other side of the dory. It circled a couple of times, and then took off into the night.

Free.

Hy put Cam's hands, first one, then the other, onto the gunwale of the dory.

"Gonna… boost you…count of three." Labouring for breath, she gave the count. Cam was light and lifted easily—she got her belly up onto the side of the boat and slid in. Then Hy hauled herself up. It wasn't easy. She was exhausted, freezing, gasping for air, but she made it. Cam was slumped in the bottom of the boat. Hy grabbed the oars and began to row back to shore. Cam's teeth were chattering and her body shaking. Rowing was difficult. Hy's breathing was quick and shallow. Her lungs were burning. *How long had they been in the water? It felt like forever.*

She wouldn't remember later how she managed to haul the dory up onto the shore. She just remembered sensations. Cold. Dampness. Darkness. She felt dizzy. Fainted. Slumped half-in and half-out of the boat. The waves moved in and out.

The tide was edging into shore, freeing up the dory and taking it back into the water.

Ian veered from side to side as he drove down Cottage Lane. He couldn't see the dory in the water any longer. The Zodiac, too, had disappeared. He was leaning over, trying to open the glove compartment to get the flashlight. It stuck, then fell open suddenly. The momentum jerked him forward, and the car veered to the wrong side of the road again. He kept feeling around in the glove box; the car manual slid out, along with some driving gloves, a present from Hy he'd never worn.

He kept driving furiously, fumbling around the passenger seat to see if the flashlight was there in the pile of junk that had accumulated. *Maps. Camera. Shoe. Shoe?*

Hy came to. The dory had floated free of the shore, but was knocking up against the sandbar. She got up. Her legs were like lead, her feet frozen, and she was unable to take a good, deep breath. She hated going back in the water. Knee-deep, she moved behind the boat and pushed it forward. Keep going. Keep going. She had to keep moving. She felt so weak, so tired, so cold. She would not give in. Cam would not, she knew. If things were reversed and she was lying in the bottom of that dory, Cam would bring her in. You could tell that about her.

Hy shoved the boat solidly up on shore with the last of her strength. A large cloud had passed across the moon and she could suddenly see nothing, not even the body, lying so still in the bottom of the boat.

"Cam," she called

No reply.

"Cam!" There was a stirring and a groan. She was alive, at least. Hy slumped onto the sand. *Had it been an attempt to kill them, or was it just a warning? Was it those two again? Someone else?*

Her eyes closed and she blacked out.

Ian was groping on the floor as he made the turn that would take him to Mack's Shore. *There!* He felt it. It had rolled under the passenger seat just…out of…his…grasp.

The car nearly went into the ditch. Ian sat up abruptly. He wasn't thinking clearly. *Just get there. Park. Get the flashlight then, but get there, for God's sake, get there. Let it not be too late.*

Hy had no idea how much time had passed. *Minutes? Hours?* She slowly raised herself up, and breathed in deeply a few times.

"Cam?" she called.

No answer.

She stood up. Took a tentative step forward. Leaned over to look in the boat.

Cam was gone.

Chapter Forty

Parker ground his fists into his eyes, trying to erase what they'd seen. He huddled on the floor, head cradled in his hands, crouching in a fetal position.

Horrible. Horrible. This cannot be happening.

The thing was done and could not be undone. He couldn't look up. He couldn't breathe. His chest was heaving, jerking as he gasped for air and could not get it. The scene played out in his mind, repeatedly. It had happened so quickly—and so slowly. The film in his head rewound, sudden, irreversible, then time held in suspension like watching a movie in slow motion. Every motion exaggerated—the arms raising, first one foot and then the next leaving the floor, Guillaime's body poised over the water, then falling into it in a staccato series of movements.

He would always see—until his own death—the look of shock frozen on Guillaume's face. He would see him tumbling back, back into the pond. The splash, drenching Parker's clothes, droplets falling from his hair like blood—translucent blood dripping down his face. Blood on his hands too, as surely as if he himself had waved the weapon.

He could still hear the spit and crackle of the current, the bang of the fuse popping too late; he could see the stunner break apart and the steel rod go flying through the air, with its deathly surge of electricity. He could smell acrid smoke from the fuse box and the faint whiff of plastic burned into human flesh. And he could not erase from his mind the sight of Guillaume's body jerking, jerking, and then still. The image was seared onto his brain, fixed there as firmly as the plastic to the dead hand.

It was the *click, click, click* of a lobster claw against teeth that made him look up. The creature was exploring inside Guillaume's mouth. Parker was paralyzed with horror, as still as the corpse. *Stay still. So still. Still still.* The stupid words caught hold of him, and throbbed in repetitive sequence in his mind, so numb that nonsense was all it could accommodate. He squeezed his eyes shut again, the permanent knot in his gut throbbing with guilt, his face etched with sorrow, distorted with pain—*the pain of the whole world, the useless, senseless pain of living at all, of loving anyone.* He felt himself collapsing under the impossible burden of this feeling. His face contorted in so many ways that he would have been unrecognizable even to himself.

It began as a very small, high-pitched sound, but soon Hawthorne Parker's grief for his lost love and hope, the emptiness of his life, filled this strange room on the shore of this odd little village where he had come hoping for a reconciliation, a new start. It was a high, keening sound that the lobster seemed to like. It raised its head and its antennae moved back and forth, in rhythm with that awful empty sound and its profound desolation.

Cam couldn't remember how she got here. She was very tired. She was following a sound, a sound that carried on the wind and over the water and around the point. She could only just hear shards of it—high-pitched in one moment, low and terrible the next.

She felt compelled to follow it.

Ian had clambered down to Mack's Shore. He was stumbling across the sand, his urgency making him clumsy. He could see the dory down by the water and he heard Hy:

"Cam! Cam!" Her voice was edged with fear.

"Hyacinth!"

She didn't hear him at first. The wind and her own shouting drowned him out.

"Hy!" Finally, she saw him.

Her legs were like lead, but she moved toward him as fast as she could. She thrust herself into his arms, shivering and sobbing. He held her tightly, tightly, and felt an electric jolt of desire. He thrust it aside. Not now.

She pulled away from him.

"Cam—disappeared! Have to find her!" Her speech was a bit slurred. She sounded drunk—a symptom of hypothermia, like the shivering and shallow breathing. He drew her to him again. She was going to have to get out of those wet clothes.

Cam was wandering dreamily down the shore on the other side of Vanishing Point. She'd kicked off her boots and socks and waded through the water, knee-deep, around the point. She wasn't quite sure where she was—or why. It was dark. Clouds had moved in and covered the moon. She was alone. *What am I doing here?*

Ian held up a blanket for modesty while Hy stripped off her wet clothes. His dry ones were baggy on her. He took the blanket and wrapped it around both of them. He pulled her down onto the sand with him and held her close.

"We really should look for Cam," she protested.

"I know, I know," he said, "and we will, but we have to take care of you first. You can't do anything right now. You have to warm up. Maybe I should look for Cam myself."

He poured her some of the hot water from the Thermos. She took the cup, sipped, choked on it, and spat it out.

"What's wrong? It's only water."

"I know that now," she laughed. Some of the water had gone up her nose. "I thought it was tea." She wiped her nose on her sleeve. She sipped again. The hot liquid felt good. Ian felt good, too. She melted into the warm cocoon of him, breathed in the comfort of his masculine scent, but she was worried about Cam.

Cam had no cocoon. There was no blanket around her, but she felt warm—with each moment, warmer still, until it was oppressive. She removed her jacket, flung it down into the water, where it bobbed, gathered up sand and got stuck, the colour of it making it look like a strange piece of seaweed, with long snaking arms that came and went with the lapping water.

The heat was unbearable. It rose inside her, spreading to every cell and making her want to burst out of her skin. She pulled off her turtleneck in one quick, desperate movement. It, too, went down into the water.

The heat pulsing in waves inside her, her brain bursting with it, she unbuttoned her pants and dropped them. One leg stuck around her ankle and she kicked it off—and kicked again. Her leg was heavy, clumsy. Just as she reached the door of the cookhouse, she yanked off her bra and pulled off her panties. Only the pearls remained around her neck.

Droplets of water slid down small, perfectly formed breasts, the nipples tight like rosebuds reacting to the cold her brain could not feel, to which her body was quickly surrendering, dying, dying all the while she felt warm life surging through her.

She went inside the building—stark naked and burning with fever—in reality, freezing to death.

Heading for the freezer—not a cocoon. A coffin.

Chapter Forty-One

Hy's legs felt like a new colt's standing up for the first time. They buckled under her. Ian supported her with his arm.

"You okay?" He extended a hand to steady her.

"I'm fine," she said with a weak smile, all she could muster. There were flashing multi-coloured zigzags in the corners of her vision.

"Just fine," she added. Her head throbbed. "We have to find Cam."

"If you're sure."

"Let's see if we can find any footprints in the sand."

He aimed the flashlight at the ground behind them.

"None leading up towards the dunes, except mine."

"You can't go around the cape at that end, even at low tide. She must have gone the other way."

He shone the light in front of them, sweeping it back and forth across the sand. "A duck—a large one, seagulls, a fox." *No human prints.*

"So she must have gone along the edge of the water and the tide's washed out her prints."

They headed in the direction of Vanishing Point. Parker's house was eerily illuminated by its one outside light and the moon, intermittently casting silver light over The A, shadowing it when clouds flitted across its face. Ian looked up at the thickening cloud. The breeze was picking up from the northeast.

The tide was so high around the cape that they had to take off their shoes and socks and roll up their pants.

"You shouldn't come," he said. "You just got warmed up."

"I don't care. I'm coming. We've got to find her—soon." Cam had been in worse shape than she and had wandered off. *Not a good sign.*

They waded in water up to their knees, the rocks underneath slimy with seaweed.

Ian held out a hand to help Hy navigate the slippery surface.

"I think we should get you out of here fast, out of danger."

"Danger?"

"That boat came at the two of you. Not just Cam. She may have been the target, but you were in that dory as well. Whoever did this—those two guys, I guess—wanted to scare you off or to kill you, one or both of you. They'll find out that you're alive. If not tonight—soon. That makes you a witness. Maybe—" he hated to say this—"to a murder."

What he was suggesting was chilling.

"Cam's not dead," she said stubbornly, "She can't be," as if that would make it so.

"If they were trying to kill, they could try again."

There was someone out there who might want her dead. She shoved the thought aside. It didn't matter now. What mattered was Cam, with her strange whispering language and high-pitched song—Cam, who wouldn't hurt a fly, the champion of those ugly sea insects. *Where is she?*

Parker punched his fists into his eyes, grinding at his tears, as if he could wipe them away and, with them, the certainty of death. So concentrated was he on not seeing, on fighting all sensation, that he had no idea when she crossed the room and passed by him.

He was still huddled on the floor, his head pounding. His throat ached. He could not make another sound. Nor could he take in any, his mind blocking out everything but his despair.

He sensed her not at all, neither heard her nor saw her. At another time, he would have been deeply moved by the sight of her, he who so loved things of beauty, she of a perfection so far removed from this room and its obscenities. He would have reached out to touch her, to convince himself that she was real and that she belonged to him.

He didn't see her. He saw nothing but the imprint on the inside of his eyelids, a photographic image—the apron, the face, the blue hand all a blinding white; the dark recesses of the grotto, black as the sins he had committed against life, against love, come to this.

She was naked, except for the pearls around her neck. Her skin was damp, her lips blue like the dead man's hand. Her body was slight with slim hips, a smooth curved belly, small breasts tipping upward, nipples taut in the cold. Her hair was wet and slicked back, giving her the stark profile of a blonde Nefertiti, without the pharaoh's crown. Her stumbling feet were the one ungainly feature. From sleek head to those odd feet—her legacy—she looked like a sea creature, unused to walking on land, just emerged from a deep ocean cave.

She didn't notice the live man or the dead man as she stopped for a moment and gazed around the room. She didn't register the lobster exploring the cook's mouth, seeking food. If she saw anything, she didn't respond to any of it. Her eyes were riveted on one thing: the walk-in freezer. *My only chance for survival.*

She moved forward, compelled by the blistering fever, seeking release from the pounding in her head, toward the image shimmering in the steel-grey door of the freezer, an androgynous apparition; it was her own distorted, ghost-like reflection.

She was dying, dying of cold, but suffocating with heat, an overpowering heat that had made her shed her clothes. Tiny pearls of liquid glowed on her skin in the fluorescent light. They were either droplets of water or beads of perspiration: she wasn't capable of distinguishing which. Her hot body told her they were sweat. It was a mistake.

Forcing her hand to reach out and grip, she opened the freezer door, and fell inside.

It was cool. *So cool.* She felt her eyes close, her body surrender. *Safe.*

"Look." Hy fished Cam's jacket out of the water. She found her pants floating a little farther up shore. She held them up, smiling. Ian looked puzzled at the smile. He didn't understand that Hy was soaring with the sure knowledge that Cam was alive. She grabbed Ian's arm so tightly he winced.

"She's alive!"

"But—"

"Paradoxical undressing," she said.

"What?"

"A false sense of warmth." In better circumstances, it would have pleased Hy to be the one giving scientific information to Ian, rather than the other way around.

"A deadly stage of hypothermia," she said, speeding up and pulling him along. "It means she was still alive when she dropped these clothes here, but in bad shape. I hope we're not too late."

On the sand in front of her Hy spotted a bra and panties—lacy and pink. *Who would have thought?*

No!

Bright light burst in and Cam's eyes flew open with the door.

Grabbing hands. Dragging.

No! Safe here. No!

Leave me in the cool place.

Her eyes shut tight against the harsh light and she began to shiver.

The lobster had slid off Guillaume's body and landed with a

clunk on the concrete floor. Parker had looked up in time to see the small female hand pulling the door closed, the Irish wedding ring on her finger. He jumped up, dragged her out, and now she was here, in his arms, naked, except for the pearls, the pearls he would have known anywhere, around her neck.

Why is she here—like this? What is she doing? Trying to kill herself? Why does she not respond?

He fell to his knees, holding her, her body half on him and half on the cold tile floor. He struggled out of his jacket and wrapped it around her.

She's perfect.

Except for her feet.

It was then that he knew she was his, had always been his. He clutched her to him, forcing her to face him. Her eyelids flickered open and all of his doubt dissolved, chased out by her grey eyes.

A rush of joy suffused him. He knew now what he had never dared believe.

She belongs to me.

The tears came then. He was crying for his loss of Guillaume— and of her. She cried too. She didn't know who he was. She didn't know where she was. She had no idea she was naked. Right now she felt cold again. *So cold.*

He squeezed her, not just to warm her, but to possess her—this woman that he had rejected, because he thought she couldn't love him, because he couldn't bear her contempt and hate.

"There. I bet she's in there." Hy was clinging to Cam's clothes, with the lacy panties and bra wrapped around her wrist.

The cookhouse door was banging open and closed in the gathering wind. When they walked in, neither registered what they saw. There was too much to take in at first glance. Second and third and fourth gave them a series of images they could barely comprehend, but there was Guillaume lying splayed out in the grotto, a lobster examining his mouth.

Parker was on the floor, his arms around Cam's naked body. Rocking, he was rocking her, and holding her hard as if she might escape him—but she was not moving.

Hy wanted to rip his face off. Then a few of his other body parts.

"You bastard!" she shouted. She had thought Parker was a jerk, but not a deviant. *Taking advantage of Cam in this state?* She lunged forward. Ian grabbed her by the wrists to stop her. She struggled with him, tried to beat at his chest with hands he held tightly in his grip.

"She's his daughter," he said.

It was an electric moment, flashing with images—*the ring, the vintage clothing, the photograph, yes, even the photograph.* It all came rushing at her, not a clear, linear process of thinking, but a jumble that fell together like the pieces of a puzzle being put together in fast motion—a jumble that suddenly, clearly made sense. *The photograph. Not Parker and Cam. Parker and the mother. Like mother, like daughter. Mother and daughter. Why didn't I see it? Cam was not eighteen. Not thirty-eight. She was somewhere in between—and somehow Parker's daughter.*

There were tears streaming out of Parker's eyes. Cam's—grey like his—were wide open, as unseeing as Guillaume's. There she was, her body exposed under the harsh light of the room, only partly covered by Parker's jacket, a young woman, perfectly formed—all but the feet.

Hy had written about them, but never seen them.

Webbed feet.

Chapter Forty-Two

"The large duck." Ian spoke softly. He'd never seen anything like them. Hy had, but only in photographs. *Webbed feet. Unusual, but not particularly rare.* She knew because she'd written about them for the Department of Fisheries and Oceans website—in a sidebar of facts about the ocean. By the time she got to people with webbed feet, she was running thin on material.

"I've seen pictures," she said, "Nothing like this." Usually the webbing was between the second and third toe. Cam had webbing between each toe. Most people still had the web between the thumb and forefinger—a leftover gene from our sea creature ancestors. Cam just happened to have the webbing on her feet.

Parker saw them looking at Cam's feet. It was her curious feet—just like his—that had told him she was his daughter.

"The Parker feet. Why didn't she tell me? Then I would have known. Why? Why?" *From those pathetic few efforts with her mother had come this beautiful child. His...his daughter. Now she was gone—surely. Hopelessly gone.*

Hy's hands were shaking. Every part of her was shaking. She was still suffering from her struggle in the water and now vibrating with this new knowledge.

"Ian, find her pulse. I'm no good at that."

He kneeled down, but he didn't bother with her pulse.

"She's dead, Hy."

Parker began to heave, a dry silent sobbing.

"No." Hy shook her head vigorously. "She is not dead. I won't let her be dead."

"Hy. Be real."

"No. You don't know Ian. I do."

"She's cold. Dead as dead. Dead cold."

"There's no such thing," she said, "until they're dead and warm." A chilling thought gripped her. *Warm. She must have been warm, to take off her clothing. Maybe it was too late.*

"How do you know so much about hypothermia?'

"I've known it all my life."

"But how?"

His question irritated her. *At a time like this?*

"Google me, if you want to know." Her words had a hard edge— a dig at his obsession. She was furious that he had known what she should have known, wondering how long he'd known it.

"How did you know she was his daughter?"

"I'll tell you some other time." His word were clipped, his tone terse.

"Look, this is no time for us to argue," said Hy. "Find her pulse."

Ian took Cam's hand and felt at her wrist for a pulse. If any, it was very weak. He began to rub her arm, to bring some life back into the body.

"No," Hy cried out. "Don't do that."

"Why not?"

"I forget why not. You're not supposed to massage them, that's all I know. I think maybe it might cause cardiac arrest."

"I think that may already have happened."

"What do you mean?"

"I think she's dead, Hyacinth. She's cold. Her lips are blue."

"No!" There was desperation in Hy's voice. "No! Don't give up. You're not supposed to give up. She could come back anytime. We'll do CPR! Now! Now!"

They pried Cam out of Parker's reluctant arms, removed the blanket and laid it on the floor and her on top of it. Ian tried to push life into her and Hy to breathe it into her, in a pattern so rhythmical you might have thought they were accustomed to doing it. Hy had never used the CPR skills she'd learned in the countless courses her grandmother had made her take. Ian had only just learned from a course several villagers took after the Big Ice.

Parker watched helplessly. Hy became aware of him again.

"For God's sake," she said to him between breaths, "go get help."

Parker's eyes were unblinking. He was frozen.

Push. Breathe. Push. Breathe.

"Call 911," Hy urged.

Still Parker didn't budge.

Push. Breathe. Push. Breathe.

"Go man."

Just as Parker was leaving, Ian added:

"Call Nathan. Call Nathan too."

"Nathan's in town," said Hy. "At Rowan's concert."

"Damn."

Push. Breathe.

"Call anyway. Ben's voice mail gives out all their numbers. Call 911 and Ben Mack 8336." You didn't have to give the telephone prefix in The Shores. Everyone had the same one.

Parker got up, mouthing: "911...8336...911...8336."

Hy hoped he'd get it right.

Push. Breathe. Push. Breathe. Over and over—for how long Ian didn't know. Every time he tried to stop, Hy made him go on.

"No, no, keep going. Don't stop. I know how this goes. She's not lost, she's not..."

Finally, he couldn't go on anymore.

"That's it," he said. "She's dead, Hyacinth, she's dead."

"If you won't do it, I will."

"Oh, c'mon Hy. I can't stop if you won't stop."

A small triumph gleamed in her shattered eyes. She was exhausted and tears were running down her face, blotting her vision, but she knew everything there was to know about hypothermia. She wasn't going to let Cam go without a fight.

"There's been a…a…an accident. No—two." Parker's voice cracked down the phone line. His clothes were damp with sweat. *An accident—and a murder.* That's what it was, he knew in his heart, but he couldn't confess it.

"Yes. Two accidents. An electrocution…and…and…well, a case of hypothermia…I'm not sure…no…they're trying to…"

Parker felt helpless. Those two, the writer and the scientist—in no way related to him—held the life of his daughter in their hands, trying to bring life back into her body, and here, he couldn't even tell the police what had happened.

"What? How long? My God. I know…I know…yes, try that. Thank you."

He didn't feel thankful at all.

Hours. It would be hours. They would have to come by boat. The Mounties kept two Boston Whalers on The Island—one for each end, but one was out of service and the other over east, searching for the body of a man who'd got caught up in the riptide after the big wind a few days back. They were about to abandon the search, but it would be hours before the boat could be brought by trailer across the island and slipped in the water this far up the North Shore. The ferry would be running by then.

Parker looked at his Rolex. *That wasn't for four hours. If she wasn't dead now, she surely would be then. What was that other number?* He began the ritual chant. *911…8663….911….8663…* yes, that was it.

"Damn." Bill kicked the motor of the Zodiac. He couldn't get it going again. They had motored as far as Big Bay before the engine had cut out. They were drifting far into the wide-open mouth of the harbour, the tide and the wind pushing them where they did not want to go, toward the sandbar. Bill grabbed the oars and shoved them at Wendell.

"Row," he barked, and got on the cell phone.

8663...

Parker had got the wrong number but the right person. It wasn't Nathan's house, but he was there. He never got to Charlottetown, because he was called out on an emergency. Not much of one, as it turned out. Ida Arsenault had a bit of a heart condition. She lived alone and called 911 whenever she had an angina attack. Nathan always took it seriously, because she was old, her heart wasn't good—and his was. The drill was always the same. He'd calm her down, check her pills and do an ECG. He'd spend a little time with her and then leave. That's exactly what he was about to do when Parker's call came through. He would have been out of luck otherwise, because Nathan wasn't planning on going home. He was going to his girlfriend Chrystal's house, and turning his cell phone off.

"Lord tunderin' Jesus." Nathan used any excuse to utter the phrase he'd learned from an uncle in Newfoundland. He used it now, when Parker blurted out what had happened, in a nearly incomprehensible jumble of words. Nathan understood enough to know it was serious.

"Don't wet your pants. I'll be right there."

Parker hurried back to the cookhouse to see the child, his child, the child he had found and lost in what seemed like just one sharp intake of breath.

Any hope he had was shredded when he saw her still unmoving, Hy and Ian trying to force breath and life into a body that had given up both. He looked at his daughter. She was her mother in every way, except the eyes and feet. Those belonged to him. Apart from newspaper photographs, he'd seen his daughter only three times in her life—in Cartier's in the big scarf; here at the Hall, in that ridiculous lobster camouflage; the third time, through the peephole in his door; and now. A crack in his shell burst open, revealing new flesh underneath, raw and tender.

His daughter—conceived from those few pitiful nights. Those lacklustre attempts to be—or appear to be—what he thought was normal. He knew now that no one was normal.

"He's coming."

Hy looked up. "Who?"

"Your Nathan. He never went to town."

"Thank God." Her muscles had become stiff from crouching. Parker looked, an appeal, at Hy. She shook her head.

Lights flashed in through the open door and bounced up into the air, as Nathan came over the rise at the top of Wild Rose Lane in his old camper van, the makeshift ambulance.

Parker squinted into the light, defeat on his face. Ian's efforts had become rote, unconvincing. Suddenly angry, Hy shoved him aside and took over.

"Get out. Give Nathan a hand."

Cam. Cam. C'mon Cam. Maybe the power of thought would bring her back. Nothing else seemed to be working.

Nathan came in with the stretcher and stopped to stare, shocked at the scene in front of him. He wondered which body he was meant to transport and where—hospital or morgue? They both looked dead to him—but not to Hy.

"I think her lips aren't blue anymore." She wondered if it was just a trick of the light. "I think she might be breathing." Excitement welled up inside her. She bit her lip. Dare she hope?

Nathan took Cam's pulse. "It's faint, but it's there."

Gently, Ian took Hy's arm and helped her up. Then he and Nathan lifted Cam onto the stretcher. Parker unclasped the pearls from around Cam's neck.

He needed them more than she did—a talisman.

He stared at her for a moment, thinking he might be looking at his daughter for the last time. He was.

"What about him?" Nathan asked, jerking his head in the direction of Guillaume.

"Forget him," said Parker. "If he isn't dead, he should be."

Chapter Forty-Three

"You idiots!"

Sheldon Coffin was knocking back a brandy in the book-lined study of the former Parker summer home. The books had come with the house. He'd never read any of them—except the special "gentlemen's" volumes, Victorian pornography that had belonged to Reinholdt. Naughty, as only the Victorians could be. Lifted dresses, dropped trousers, bare buttocks blushed red with strokes from flashing whips and rods. Naughty, naughty men and women astride benches, beds and each other, begging for punishment and for mercy with exclamation marks jumping off the text. *Dirty. Stimulating.* Sheldon would read them and go searching for Stella. He'd pin her roughly to the bed, wishing she had more flesh on her.

"I didn't say kill her…I know I said get rid of her…but you know perfectly well what I meant."

But once he was over the first shock of it, his brain shifted gears.

"Are you sure she's dead?" He never meant for her to die. *By God, I'm not a murderer. But now, if she's out of the way, well…all the better.*

He called the police and reported *The Crustacean* stolen. He said he suspected two former employees he'd recently fired. Yes, they both had records.

Though she was light, all four of them carried her—like pall-bearers, Hy and Ian at the head, Parker and Nathan at the foot. It was tougher-going across the sand, carrying the dead weight of her. No. Not dead, thought Hy. *She could not be dead.*

"Will she live?" she asked Nathan, when he had done his best to stabilize Cam. He didn't answer. He'd rarely seen worse—and what he had seen, in this shape, had never survived. He just bowed his head, and tucked blankets around Cam's prone form. He turned to Hy. "You coming too?"

"I'll stay with her."

He nodded and jumped down, closing the door behind him.

"How will you get over?" Ian had just remembered the ferry.

"Taken care of." Nathan jumped in the cab and sped off.

Constable Jane Jamieson was on her way to coerce the ferry operator into putting the vessel into service early that Sunday morning. Chester Gallant was a religious man who'd had to make peace with his Maker on the point of working on the holy day. The double-time-and-a-half pay had helped convince him of the right thing to do, but he was not a happy man to be awakened at nearly three in the morning and pressed back to work.

Jamieson hadn't phoned him. She had simply found out where he lived, drove straight there with her partner Murdo, walked, heavy-booted, along the wooden porch and rung the bell with an urgency that struck terror into Chester when it woke him up.

A short, squat man, he had the body of a wrestler gone to seed. He pulled on a pair of pants over thick, hairy legs and stumbled through the dark house, feeling along surfaces he knew by heart to get to the door without switching on lights. Even in a crisis, he was a thrifty man.

There were two police officers. Chester had never done any-thing wrong in his thoroughly Christian life. It could only be bad news. His brother Alf had a poor heart.

Constable Jamieson flashed her I.D.

"You run the ferry over Campbell Causeway?"

He nodded. *Was something wrong with the boat?*

Parker was standing in the middle of the room, staring blankly into the dark night. The full moon was shrouded in the dark clouds building up along the coast.

"Storm coming." Ian was standing beside Parker—and the Egyptian god of death—the dog of death. Parker went over to the bar. He grabbed a bottle of Scotch, and two glasses. He set them down on the coffee table, sat down, and splashed the drink into the tumblers as if it were water. They clinked glasses—a grim toast. The look that passed between them was sombre.

Ian took a sip and raised his eyebrows. He rolled the Scotch around his mouth. It slipped down smoothly, the heat of it flowing through his chest. He picked up the bottle. Thirty-year-old single malt. It was just what the label claimed—"seductive."

"What happened?" Parker seemed stunned. "What happened to her?"

Ian told as much as he knew about the boat buzzing the dory—and a bit more about whom he suspected—Coffin's thugs—and about the presence of *The Crustacean* on the coast.

Parker looked as if he had been struck.

"My fault." He collapsed back on the couch. "I've killed her. I killed him and I've killed her. My own daughter."

Ian didn't know what had happened between Guillaume and Parker. For all he knew, he was sitting beside a murderer. If so, he knew he wasn't in any danger.

"You didn't know she was yours?"

"No, but I should have known. I had no reason to suspect Claire was lying—but I didn't think she could be mine. I couldn't, not really, not the whole way, with a woman, you know."

"Why'd you even try?"

"Well, it's complicated."

"It seems we have time for complicated."

The emotional events of the evening had the effect of letting down Parker's natural reserve. He was thinking of the past anyway, because of Camilla.

"Her name was Claire. She was fourteen. I was sixteen. Local girl. Foster child. One of my grandmother's protégés. She came to help in the restaurant kitchen for a summer job. She was beautiful, honey-blonde, delicate features…"

"Like Cam."

"Like Camilla." Parker nodded, remembering.

"Four years. We clung to each other. Two misfits. A foster child in a world of wealth—and me." He rolled the glass around in his hands. Ian kept silent.

"I had no love at home. My mother was a socialite. She simply produced me because that was the unspoken bargain she made when she married. I don't remember her ever hugging me. My father hardly paid any attention to me at all. In Claire's arms was warmth—and love."

"Puppy love."

"Precisely. I didn't know who—what—I was then. We kissed. I touched her breasts. They were perfect, and her skin—like a pearl. She might have let me do more, but I didn't want to. I just liked to fondle her breasts because they were beautiful, and stroke her naked skin, I suppose, because it was forbidden."

"Like any teenager."

"Yes—if you forget about the desire that should have been there. I loved the heat and the warmth of close physical contact, but I had no desire."

"Did you love her?"

"I did—in my way. Before I knew who I was, we swore to each other we'd marry. We did marry. Guillaume thinks I jilted him for her, but it was the other way around really. The sex—the act—it was awful. A disaster. She was hurt, so hurt. That was the end… the end…the absolute end."

Parker fell back into the couch, silent, closing his eyes, remembering what he didn't want to remember. Ian remembered Jasmine—and that she had not uttered a sound. She was blanketed in her cage. He was tempted to get up and go to her, but he resisted. It wouldn't be fair to get that bird squawking now.

Parker sat up again.

"When I met Guillaume, it was then that I knew who…what…I was. I was obsessed with him. For one whole summer I ignored Claire, hurt her with my mental and physical absence. She had always been afraid I would grow away from her, because of my family, but it was Guillaume, Guillaume who took me. All that summer, the secret meetings, the sex, even then, twisted, distorted. My need for him frightened me and I lashed out. At him. At my family. At myself. I thought it was the only way I could save myself. I thought I could escape who I was. I don't really know what I thought. I was young, stupid. Claire and I went to a Justice of the Peace."

He pulled the pearls from his pocket and laid them on the table.

"My grandmother knew who I was. She encouraged the elopement. She gave me these pearls for Claire, with her blessing. She hoped it would change me. Claire wasn't suitable in many ways, but at least she was a woman. We had three nights. Three nights before we both knew it was hopeless. Guillaume had followed us on our honeymoon, so the marriage never really had a chance. He was charming at first, won her over. She didn't know what he was to me, and when he told her, she was shattered. I went crawling back to Guillaume and clung to him like a life raft."

More like a rubber dinghy full of holes, thought Ian.

"But Cam—"

"Yes, Camilla. Claire wrote me, later, that I had a daughter. Guillaume found the letter and raised a holy stink. I couldn't believe the child was mine anyway. I gave her money—and kept her at arm's length. That was the end of it—I never spoke to her

again. I heard she'd died—just last year. Then Camilla showed up
for the first time…"

He caressed the pearls and slipped them back in his pocket—his
talisman, part of his deal with the god of death. If he held them,
he held her.

When he found out that Jamieson wanted him to get the ferry
running, Chester protested—about the Lord's Day, his much-
needed sleep; he even had the temerity to talk about setting bad
precedents. In the end, Jamieson won out. She generally got what
she wanted.

But when she, Murdo and Chester finally got to the ferry
landing, the boat was already on the water, its lights headed for
the opposite shore.

Parker had recounted the entire tale of his life with Guillaume
and finally retreated into silence and what Ian thought looked like
sleep. It was four in the morning. The police had still not come.
Jasmine was fussing in her cage, and he peeked under the cover,
and saw that her water container was empty. He filled it and
brought it back. She allowed him to stroke her without pecking
him before he replaced the cover. In spite of the dark mood in the
room, he felt a thrill.

Ian let himself out, looking down at the cookhouse where
Guillaume's body lay.

He wondered if Guillaume had been searching for love too—or
trying to escape it. Ian's research into drugs had taught him that a
CAT scan of the brain of someone on cocaine looks just like the
brain of someone in love. 'Just say no,' he thought, might apply
to romance as well as to drug abuse. The thought was somewhat
close to home.

He got in his car and headed home. He expected the police
would be knocking at his door soon, and he should get some rest,

but his brain refused to shut down. He wondered how Hy and Cam were getting on. Hy had known an unusual amount about hypothermia. She did have odd pockets of knowledge because of her work, but this was different, deeper, more intense. What had she said?

Google me.

She'd been irritated, but it was permission, of a kind.

Ian had never googled Hy. Now he did.

Chapter Forty-Four

Nathan's "ambulance" rolled onto the ferry. He jumped out of the vehicle and gave a high-five to his pal Shaun Dooley, Hal's son. Shaun did an occasional shift operating the boat and didn't hesitate when Nathan called and asked him to get it running. The Dooleys owed a lot to the Macks for helping them out after they had lost their boat and fishing gear in the storm surge. Besides, Shaun and Nathan had known each other all of their lives, eyed girls on the beach in summer—fought over one of them—buzzed around in snowmobiles in winter, and graduated high school together. They were so alike to look at, you might have thought they were brothers. Only Shaun was even taller than Nathan, and skinnier. He went into the engine house and started the ferry. Nathan opened the back door of the van. "Everything okay in here?"

"I guess so." Hy hadn't moved. She was still crouched beside Cam, in spite of the shooting pains up her legs and her numb feet. She was holding Cam's hand. She had begun to lose sensation in her arm as well.

"Any change?" He got up into the van, felt for a pulse, fussed a bit, and jumped down again.

"Just keep praying."

Hy was praying for the first time in her life—not to God, but to the wind, blowing down the bay, across the half-finished causeway and straight at the brave little ferry, rocking it on its line.

She called the wind on Mutt and Jeff.

She looked at Cam's pale face.

Take them.

She held Cam's hand.

Take them.

She listened for Cam's faint breathing.

Let them die on the wind, she thought bitterly.

It became her mantra.

Let them die on the wind. No mercy.

The makeshift ambulance bobbed on the ferry. Nathan was feeling a bit seasick, but, for the first time, the motion didn't bother Hy. All she could think of was Cam. Cam, lying there, looking like a ghost.

All he had to do was key in Hy's name and more than a dozen sites popped up—medical, magazine, newspaper and book publishing sites. It was a story that had made national and medical news nearly forty years ago. A one-year-old child stuffed into a life jacket, tied to the body of her dead grandfather, bobbing on the water beside a bush plane in a not-quite-frozen lake. Hy's grandfather, an experienced bush pilot, had inexplicably done a nose-dive into the lake while evacuating his daughter and her child from a log cabin deep in the woods. Hy's mother was presumed drowned—her body never found. As a last act, she had tied her child to the grandfather's dead body to increase her chance of survival.

Ian jumped to the CBC archive link and found a recent documentary series, "Back to the Landers." One of the episodes was about Hy's rescue.

"We were worried about them." Hy's grandmother, Mimi McAllister, appeared in archival footage, in her front yard—tight pin curls, white apron, clapboard house, picket fence. "We didn't know Ray, my son-in-law, was dead—he was caught in one of his own traps and died of exposure. We hadn't heard from them, so Hugh flew in to see what was up. I don't know what went wrong."

A photograph of the downed pane flashed on the screen, followed by one of Hy, being removed from her grandfather's body, her tiny face blank of all expression. She, too, looked dead.

The site for a medical journal outlined the details of Hy, the miracle child, in an article titled "Hy-pothermia." She was rescued, hypothermic, believed dead, but revived. Later, her grandmother would make sure she knew everything about hypothermia, swimming and survival in the woods. So she wouldn't have another loved one die on her.

Hy had outlived her grandmother—and lived on the legacy her mother had tucked into her tiny life jacket—a manuscript titled *A Life on the Land*, written on paper she'd made from birch bark with textured leaf impressions. It was acid-free, and could last thousands of years, like Egyptian papyrus. She had used homemade quill pens and ink made from plants. The drawings were in charcoal from the embers of the woodstove. The book was an instant classic in the back to the land movement and sold copies steadily for more than a decade. Every now and then it had a resurgence of interest and went into another edition. Its early fans thought the most recent was an abomination, but they'd all bought it—a coffee table book, in simulated birch bark, her mother's neat hand replicated by digital technology. Hy inherited, not only the manuscript and its proceeds from her mother, but her doggedness and writing skills as well.

Ian passed a hand across his head, several times. It explained a lot. He decided to have something to eat, then head into town with the first ferry, whether the police had come to question him or not. They'd find him soon enough.

Parker hadn't moved from the couch since Ian had left. He lay sunk in a pool of sorrow, thinking the same thing over and over.

Guillaume is dead. Camilla is dead.

He kept repeating it to himself. Partly, he was torturing himself.

Partly, he was forcing himself to believe the unbelievable.

Guillaume is dead. Camilla is dead. I have killed them.

On it went. When would it stop? When would he accept what he had done? For he had killed them both, as surely as if he had held a gun to their heads and pulled the trigger.

He poured another Scotch.

In sickness and in health. No. In sickness. Guillaume's. His own.

It had brought him to murder. He had said it was an accident, but Parker knew that in the moment before Guillaume fell backward into the pond, he had wanted him dead. He had wanted to kill him. If murder was intent to kill, he'd had murder on his mind.

The moon was now fully obscured by clouds and the wind was blowing hard and steady from the northeast. The Zodiac was floundering on the sandbar at the mouth of Big Bay, and Bill and Wendell were struggling to get the craft off the sandspit and out of the bay to the safety of *The Crustacean*. The wind and the tide kept shoving them back and their efforts to paddle out did little to move them, only left them forever in the same place, battling against the storm and the big lump of sand that stretched across the bay.

"She walked up one side of us, down the other, and then did it a few more times, she liked it so much," was how Nathan later described Constable Jamieson's reaction to their commandeering of the ferry. After flinging about phrases like "obstruction of justice," "aiding and abetting" and a number of others that would and would not hold up in court, she was on her way. Having taken down their names and details, she realized they had no more time to waste than she did.

"Don't go anywhere," was her parting salvo. "I'll be speaking to you."

Nathan had them at the hospital in Winterside in half the time it should have taken. The roads were empty and clear and he took advantage of his semi-official status to exceed the speed limit—and then some.

The intensive care doctor, Dr. Fabio Diamante, was diminutive, dark and foreign. He looked out of mournful brown eyes—like a cow's eyes.

"It's time to call the family."

On The Island, that meant the patient was dying.

Hy thought for just a second. *Parker was family, but he was worse than useless right now. Was there any other family? Cam had never spoken of any.*

"I'm her sister," she blurted out. She looked away. "Her...our father...he can't come right now. There's been a—" she almost said 'another'—"death." Too much information, she thought. *When you're lying, keep it simple.*

Dr. Diamante and Ed, the huge intensive care nurse with a blonde crew cut and an earring in his left ear, looked at her doubtfully. *Sister? They didn't look anything alike. But they were both clearly from away, so it was anyone's guess.*

"She's not in a living state." The doctor coughed, looking at Hy with those big bovine eyes.

He didn't say dead.

"She's in a coma. If her heart had stopped—we are not sure of that—her cells may have begun to shut down. They could continue to die for days. The cold may have protected the brain, lungs and immune system, but—"

"You don't know."

"No. She seems stable," he said, "but she could be digesting herself."

"Digesting herself? What do you mean?"

"The body could be breaking down, slowly being eaten away, by itself, from inside."

Was this real medical opinion—or just his inability to explain himself clearly in English?

His next words were plain enough:

"Be hopeful, but prepare for the worst."

Chapter Forty-Five

It was four in the morning when Jamieson and Murdo finally arrived at Parker's. He took a while to answer the door. He was still collapsed on the couch, drifting in and out of a tortured twilight—sleep, cut with periods of unconsciousness. The banging on the door took a while to get through to him. He sat up, polished off the Scotch in the glass, and walked to the door like an old man.

"Responding to a 911 call. Report of one, possibly two, deaths. This the house?" Jamieson asked curtly.

He thought she might have been pretty if she didn't have her hair so severely drawn back. Her skin was immaculate. An odd thing to notice at such a time, but how could you not notice it? Pale, unblemished, smooth as silk. Odd that it could contain such a hard creature.

"Constable Jane Jamieson." She appeared to be the one in charge.

"Squawk! It's the law! Run!" Jasmine had woken up, her cage still covered. She startled the two Mounties.

"My bird," said Parker.

"Murdo Black," said the constable behind Jamieson.

"Hawthorne Parker." He should be reluctant to let them in. Not all of his treasures would have passed a customs inspection. He wished this were just a customs inspection.

"Please, come in." He opened the door wide.

Jamieson didn't move right away. Her eyes swept the room. She was a tall woman—six foot, and she bent out of habit as she entered the door. The older Island houses made it necessary. Not this one though. Murdo, shorter, rounder, friendlier, came in behind her—always a step behind her, mentally and physically.

Neither of them had been in a room—a house—that looked anything like this before. They gazed around them. Jamieson registered the dozens of *objets d'art* that she knew must be worth a small fortune. She looked, puzzled, at the huge canvas with the red blotch. She was sure that was worth something too, but she couldn't see why.

"You the owner of this residence?"

Parker nodded.

She flipped open her notebook.

"The 911 call came from here?"

Parker nodded again.

She walked farther into the room.

"I have a report of a death. Where's the body?"

Parker said nothing.

Jamieson looked at her notes. "There *is* a body?"

"Yes," said Parker.

"Where?"

"Down at the cookhouse. In the pond."

"In the cookhouse—or the pond?"

"Both. There's a pond in the cookhouse."

"Who found the body?"

"I did," said Parker. "No—I didn't find it. It happened while I was there."

"What happened?"

"Well, it was an accident." He was becoming adept at lying. "We—"

"We?"

"Guillaume—"

"Guillaume!" Jasmine shrieked. She sniffed…sniffed again. "Guillaume!" Sniff. Sniff. She laughed hysterically.

"Who is Guillaume?" Jamieson had heard that name before, just recently.

Parker looked down at the floor.

"My chef."

Jamieson looked at Murdo. He was biting his nails. He shrugged. No one said anything for a moment or two. She considered silence a valuable detection tool. People began blurting things out, just to fill the void. Parker was no different, in spite of his apparent sophistication.

"Guillaume is—was—a friend."

"…and the victim?"

"Yes. The…victim."

She waited.

"He is—was—also my partner."

"Business?"

"Yes."

"Your chef, your friend, your business partner, the victim." This sounded familiar. "Anything else?"

He bit his lip. It was known in the village anyway.

"My life partner as well."

Guillaume. Life partner. This was the owner of the car.

"So, what happened, and what does—" Jamieson rifled through her notes—"this other incident, the boat, the hypothermia, have to do with it?"

"Nothing. It has nothing to do with it. That is a separate incident."

Jamieson sighed. *It was going to be a long night.*

"Okay. What happened in the cookhouse?"

"Guillaume and I were having an argument. Things got out of hand. He tripped over an electric cord and fell backwards into the pond. He was electrocuted."

"I think you better walk me through it. At the scene." Jamieson flipped her notebook shut.

Two words popped into her mind. *Domestic dispute.*

Jamieson was too well-trained to show surprise when she entered the cookhouse, but she was surprised—more by the gourmet kitchen and the lobster grotto than by the corpse itself—though that was a bit of a surprise too. A lobster was clawing at the corpse's face. Her instinct was to grab it and throw it off, but she couldn't disturb the scene. It may turn out to have been an accident, but with no actual witnesses and only Parker's word, the Major Crime Investigation Unit would have to be brought in.

"You're sure he's dead?" She strode across the room.

"It's been several hours."

Jamieson looked at the open eyes. *Lifeless.*

"Tell me exactly what happened. Start at the beginning please, and try to be precise."

When he had finished, she asked him to tell her again—partly to check the facts, partly to see if the story was the same the second time around. Checking to see if it sounded like he'd memorized it and was repeating by rote, or if it had really happened the way he said it had and he was simply telling the same story again, required excellent listening skills.

One of Jamieson's strengths was that she was a good listener—not caring or supportive, mind. She heard exactly what was said, unfiltered, and could parrot it back verbatim. She could also tell the difference between truth and lies. She listened to every nuance in Parker's voice and his choice of words. His anguish, as far as she could tell, was not faked—nor was the anger that had precipitated the event—anger that still burned in him and which he did not try to conceal. *It had the ring of truth. His guilt? That had yet to be determined.*

"You'll have to come down to police headquarters to make an official statement."

Jamieson and Parker drove off—she in the RCMP vehicle and

he in his rental car. Murdo stayed at the cookhouse to secure the scene and wait for forensics. He tried to wrap yellow police tape around the building, but it blew away on a gust of wind. He went inside and spent several unpleasant and cold hours guarding the dead man, until the forensics team arrived, investigated the scene and took the body away. During the long wait, Murdo had looked in the freezer, tempted to grab one of the lobster claws and heat it up, but he lost his appetite when he saw the beast clawing at the corpse's eyes.

Cam was out on the water—the only place she ever felt truly at peace. The lapping of the waves was soothing.

The sense of calm ripped apart with the image of a body, splayed out in a pond, his eyes staring wide open, full of shock, a lobster clawing at them.

She grabbed the creature and threw it across the room.

I should not have treated the lobster that way.

She felt bad about the lobster, really bad.

"Ms. Samson? Ms. Samson?"

Ed shook his head—still no response. Hy thought it might have helped if he'd used the right name, but no one knew what that was. *Samson? Parker? What name would she answer to, if she were able to?*

Parker drove by the hospital after making his statement. The police had cautioned him to remain in the area. He had assured them that he wasn't going anywhere. Except, now, in circles. He drove by the hospital several times. He went as far, once, as the parking lot. He sat there for…he didn't know how long. Then started the car again and left, regret following him all the way home. If she were alive, she wouldn't welcome him.

A child is not meant to die before its parents.

Perhaps this one would not.

The parent might die before her.

The thought, at first, surprised him.

By the time he got home, it had taken hold of him.

Chapter Forty-Six

"Why'd you never tell me?" Ian had arrived at the hospital shortly before seven that morning. He was sitting with Hy in the small waiting room across from Intensive Care, probing her about her past.

"Because it scared the shit out of me. I couldn't talk about it. It would make it real. I thought if I talked about it, the nightmares would get worse."

"Or maybe better," he said. "Did you think of that?"

"Well, no."

"How did you ever go out on that boat with Cam and then get back to shore?"

Hy smiled, a soft reflective smile. "Don't ask me. Adrenalin. Maybe it was the catharsis I needed."

"I don't think you needed that."

She thought he was wrong. *I feel different now. Different about the dream.*

Parker stood up, shaky on his feet, grabbed the bottle of Scotch and began to stumble around the room, looking at his treasures, one by one. He picked up a Greco-Roman statuette. *Things. My life has been about things—beautiful but inanimate things. Cam was—had been?—as fine and beautiful as any of it. She should have been my treasure, not these things that could not love me back.*

He put the statue down carelessly. It slipped off the pedestal and smashed on the floor. *Broken. Irretrievable, just like she will be—if she lives. Hopelessly broken.* It was his fault. He should have made it clear to Sheldon that she was not to be bothered.

He hadn't—a sin of omission.

The only real beauty in my life and I have failed to care for her. But I can take care of this.

She, not he, would be the last of their line. He would make a bargain with the jackal.

Jamieson had caught up with Hy and Ian at the hospital.

"Can you describe this boat you say bore down on you? What kind was it?"

You say. Hy heard doubt. *Was Jamieson doubting the story?*

She wasn't, particularly. She just liked to put people on an uneven footing.

"Boat? What kind of boat? A fast one. A big rubber one."

Probably this cop could reel off boat makes and models. She looked highly trained and well-turned-out, not a wrinkle in her outfit, not a hair out of place—a perfect specimen of Mountie training. Hy knew how hard it was to get in. It took years. They often rejected you several times first. She'd done a web profile of ten candidates once—five successful, five unsuccessful. You had to be the brightest and the best. Then you got posted to some backwater like this. You didn't get to be a Mountie by just lacing your boots correctly—it was a tough job. Constable Jamieson's boots were laced perfectly, of course, but, to Hy's satisfaction, they were also covered in red clay.

"Surely you have some idea of a type?"

"No." Hyacinth drew out the word in exasperation.

"Calm down, Hy. She's just trying to help." Ian liked the look of Constable Jamieson—sexy in a severe sort of way. Hair he'd like to get his hands on—mess it up. *Beautiful alabaster skin. Full rose lips.*

Hy didn't like the way he was looking at Jamieson. "Yeah, yeah, I know."

"Is the dory still down at the shore?"

"I guess so. We pulled it up high so the tide wouldn't get it."

"We'll have a look at it later. I don't suppose there's much it will tell us. They didn't come in contact with it?"

"I don't believe so."

"It appeared to you to be intentional?"

"Appeared! They came around repeatedly—and only took off after we ducked under until my lungs burst. Damn right it was intentional."

"Intent to kill?"

"I don't know. Intent to frighten, for sure."

"Aimed at you? Her? Both of you?"

"Her, certainly. Me, maybe."

"Do you know why?"

"Because Cam had been stirring up trouble around here."

"Ian!"

"Well, she was. People didn't like what she said—or did."

"Who were these people? Who had a reason to dislike her?"

Hy and Ian looked at each other. They weren't going to name names...except for two they didn't know. Hy told Jamieson about Mutt and Jeff, the threats, and the attacks on her house.

"What did she do that people didn't like?"

"Terrorize by day. Liberate by night." Ian regretted his flippancy immediately. He was punch-drunk tired.

"Terrorize?"

Hy told her about Cam's performance at the W.I. meeting, and about the disruption of the lobster supper.

"She's a lobster tickler."

"Lobster tickler?"

"You know, like a horse whisperer. She's a guerilla fighter for animal rights."

Jane Jamieson felt as if she'd slipped into an alternate reality. *These people were odd.* She couldn't wait until she was posted somewhere more civilized. She didn't realize there is no such place in law enforcement.

"She was freeing lobsters from their traps. That's what she was doing last night."

Jamieson looked up sharply from her notes.

"That's poaching," she said.

"What? Even if you throw the lobster back in the water?"

"Still poaching. Theft. You can consider yourself an accessory."

"But I'm a writer. I was doing research."

"Writers commit crimes, and you may have done so by being a party to your lobster *tickler's* illegal activities."

"It was no party," Hy muttered.

"Excuse me?"

A parent is not meant to outlive a child.

This parent would not. It seemed to him that he had always been gnawing at the bone of regret. He'd lost the taste for life. Fear had made him live in this small, bitter way. *Fear of not being good enough, not good enough to be loved—and with good reason.*

What had he ever done to deserve love?

He could not smooth out all the dark coils of his misunderstanding, could not untwist them far enough, long enough to see that love is not deserved, it is simply given.

I can do nothing right.

Only one thing.

One thing.

This one thing right.

He pulled himself up from the couch, full of resolve. He slid out a sheet of paper from a roll-top desk that had once belonged to Thomas Jefferson. The paper promised to resist fire and water damage and last four hundred years, but this document did not need to last that long. It only needed to outlive him, and that would not be long at all. He pulled out his Aurora solid gold and burgundy fountain pen and the gold tip scratched across the paper.

I, Hawthorne Parker, being of sound mind and body…

He wondered if what he was about to do would negate that statement.

Chapter Forty-Seven

Ian had gone home with instructions from Hy:

"Bring back her knapsack—in the guest room—vanity case by the door, laptop. Bring it all."

No one had yet asked for a Medicare card, which Hy was sure Cam didn't have. She'd have to look through her stuff to see what documents there were.

Ian had tried to get Hy to come with him, but she refused to go. She wouldn't leave the hospital. She felt as long as she was there, Cam would stay alive. The nurses and doctors were used to people feeling that way and were businesslike in ushering friends and family out when they got in the way—but they found it unusual that Cam's vital signs grew steady and rhythmic when Hy was in the room. Those signs flickered when she left. So they let her sit by Cam's bedside, a human link in the technological tangle of wires and tubes and monitors keeping Cam alive. She was hanging onto a thread that may have been more firmly attached to Hy than to the respirator or the IV—an invisible filament of friendship, linking her to life.

Hy talked non-stop. "Look at me," she'd say. It was the same calming technique she had used with Cam in the water. It had saved her once, it might again. Never mind that Cam's eyes were closed. That didn't stop Hy from repeating, "Look at me," as she held her hand through the long day into the night.

She was swimming. Really swimming. She felt gloriously free, and she wondered why she'd never tried it. It seemed as if she had always

been able to do it, never had to learn it. But she was underwater.
How was she able to breathe?

Dr. Diamante looked down at Cam, lying unmoving in the bed.

"It won't be long now," he said to Hy on the way out. For a moment she felt a trill of hope. Then his words and eyes came into focus—sad cow eyes. *Cam is dying.* Soon Parker would have to make a decision about what would happen to his daughter. If he'd been asked, in his despair he might have told them to pull the plug. Hy began to pray again—not for life, but death, thinking of the killers who had put Cam here.

Let them die on the wind.

She began the mantra again.

When he finished writing, Parker went upstairs. From the armoire he pulled out a red leather case. He opened it and put his hand on the ivory handle of a woman's gun patterned after the "tiny little gun" made famous by Nancy Reagan. His grandmother followed the First Lady in fashion, including accessories, and had commissioned this gun to be custom-made. There was only one silver bullet remaining. The others had landed up in the wall of her bedroom when his grandfather had come home late one night. She'd said she'd thought he was an intruder. In a way, he was. They'd rarely shared a bed. The bullets had made sure they never did again, as surely as if they'd hit their target.

Parker loaded the single remaining bullet. Downstairs, Jasmine started shrieking. She'd been stuck under the cover since the night before. The wind had been howling around the house and she had taken up its sound—moaning and flapping her wings, biting at her cage, squawking: "Help! Help!" To quiet her, Parker uncovered and unlocked the cage and she flapped past him, frenzied, flying around and around the room. It was lucky he was saving the last bullet for himself, or he might have shot her.

The Zodiac had lodged on the sandspit overnight. Bill and Wendell had sheltered under a tarp that kept flapping in the wind and letting the rain in. They were soaking, limp with lack of strength, unable, when the crashing surf loosened the boat from its perch, to prevent it from being sucked out to sea. It rounded the end of the spit—in full view of *The Crustacean*, but was swept along on a current that carried it well offshore as the peak of the storm hit.

It did so with a fury few had experienced before. Harold MacLean had predicted it.

"'Spect it'll rain hard," he said when he'd looked out of his window that morning. For once, he was right. It rained and rained.

"The heavens have opened," said Gus, looking out later on the black day. The wind and the rain reached a pitch, in perfect harmony, producing what would forever after be known as the May Gale, the term generally reserved for nasty storms in August.

Gus took to her purple chair, handbag and coat at the ready as the gale blasted the tiny island. The houses creaked and swayed. The surf swept across the causeway. The waves whipped halfway up the cape and the cathedral windows of Parker's house were soon coated in salt spray. On the shore, the sand scoured the beach and rolled up in a cloud of stinging particles, the rain slicing sideways.

Furiously, the wind beat around The A. It sounded like a train thundering through the house, or a 747 landing on the roof. The cathedral windows rattled and it would not take much imagination to see them shatter at the next big blast. The earth groaned in agony beneath Parker.

"O sole mio..."

Pavarotti's voice, emanating at peak volume from Parker's Bang and Olufson stereo system, dueled with the forces of nature, rose above the wind, then dipped down below it, and then rose again with such power it was, at times, difficult to tell which was the storm and which was the tenor.

Hawthorne Parker was dancing. Something he had only ever done with a partner, the odd sedate waltz. *Never this kind of dancing.* His wide grin looked crazed on a face that rarely smiled. The gleam in his eyes spoke, not of joy, but of despair. It was molting season—and he had shed his carapace—all his raw emotions and regrets drove him to dance, all his desire riding on the mounting music.

He whirled around in circles until he was dizzy. He faltered, fell back, and dashed the Ming dynasty porcelain cat off its pedestal. It smashed in hundreds of tiny pieces, skittering across the floor. Feeling only a small stab of pain at the loss of this most precious artifact, Parker stepped on a piece and crushed it. He kept on dancing, as if he'd accidentally smashed an ashtray.

"*O sole mio...*"

There was a deafening creak, like someone taking a giant crowbar to the roof. He looked up at the beams that didn't quite fit. Let it go, he thought. *Bring it down. Let it collapse and crush me, and everything in it. There is nothing precious here.*

Hy was cocooned from the weather in the shelter of the modern hospital, her attention focused on Cam. As Parker danced his dance of death, Cam fought for her life. Hy had become better at lying. When a new overnight security guard—*Tom* his badge read—had questioned Hy's right to be there, she'd said with conviction: "She's my sister." That's what it felt like. When Tom didn't budge, she stared him down. "She's dying." The word caught in her throat, but it made Tom back off. Another lie, she told herself.

Please, let it be a lie.

The hospital lights had dimmed along with the daytime bustle and the halls outside the room had that peculiar hushed sound, layered by artificial hospital silence, the buzz of fluorescent lights, accompanied by various machines punctuating the night with their life-sustaining beeps and hisses. She fell asleep sitting in the chair, still holding onto Cam's hand as the storm raged outside and Cam waged her battle inside.

Parker launched an attack on his treasures. It started with small things—the crystal glasses in the cabinet Harold MacLean had made out of vintage doors and new pine wood. One by one by one, he picked them up and smashed them to the floor in rhythm with the music, their shattering lost on the rising crescendo.

He danced around the couch, slapped the penis-shaped sculpture to the floor.

Nothing.

Picked up an Aztec water jug and smashed it to the ground.

Nothing.

He swept three primitive hand-built African bowls off the shelf.

Nothing.

They meant nothing to him.

It was over.

She was gone and had never been his.

He was gone—the worst mistake of his life.

"*O sole...o sole mio...*"

He became someone else. *I'm the conductor.* He commanded the music with bold strokes of his arms, small flicking gestures of his hands and fingers. He became Pavarotti. He sang out loud with his thin, reedy, untrained voice, as insignificant as the shattering glasses. It could not be heard, even in his own ears, above the crashing sound coming from the speakers and the thundering storm.

Jasmine, thrilled by the sounds, but unable to compete, had flown up to the very peak of the A-frame, where rain was coming through the fault in the beams.

He became the storm. As wild as it was, so was he. With each streak of lightning, his arms raised to heaven; with each crash of thunder they came down, down, slicing through the air; he glided on the whistle of the wind, around and around the room.

Free. He was free—for the first and last time.

He smacked an Indonesian fertility god off its pedestal.

Then a Sevres porcelain plate.

A Limoges jardiniere.

A Fabergé egg.

Venus.

She broke in two, head and torso split, when she hit the floor.

Hy was down in the dream again. The child, bobbing on the water, the dark, the flashing light—the images were all the same, but the fear was gone. No longer sizzling through her, vibrating her awake into paralyzing terror. *She was floating over the fear, sheltered in a warm, safe place that allowed her to come softly awake.*

Saved.

The word was on her mind as she came up out of the dream. *Saved.*

She had, after all, been saved. *Twice now. Saved.*

She woke, not to terror, but to aching bones, joints and muscles. She hurt everywhere. Every part of her body was stiff or cramped or hot with the pain of sleeping in a hard hospital chair. She let go of Cam's hand and stood up like an old lady, unfolding herself slowly. She heard a low moan. She thought it came from herself, but she had made no sound. It had come from the bed. She buzzed for the nurse, and grabbed Cam's hand again.

He was heedless of the movement of the earth below him, the shifting of the house. The first sounds were lost in the fury of the storm. One creak was concealed in the crash of lightning—another, hidden by the thunder. As the sounds of the earth and the house breaking apart built up, so, too, did the storm, until one was no longer distinguishable from the other, until it was all a whole: the storm, the lightning and the thunder, the howling wind and the rain slapping on the shuddering glass of the great windows; the creaking of the house, the moaning of the earth; the full, deep, rich, resonant voice of Pavarotti hitting the crescendo, then descending. In the final lingering strains of the ballad, Parker, too, was twirling and descending, slowing down, fading with the song.

A smashing bolt of lightning, a blinding white explosion, the house illuminated in one burst of sight and sound, and then—

Darkness.

Chapter Forty-Eight

Ed hustled Hy out of the room and called Doctor Diamante. He came quickly. Hy tried to follow him back into the room, but Ed stopped her with a firm hand on her shoulder—and good news.

"She's awake."

"Out of the coma?"

Ed nodded, once. "Awake," he repeated, "but not out of the woods. We don't know what she'll be like. We don't know if—" Doctor Diamante came out, beaming. "A miracle," he pronounced, crossing himself.

"Can I—?"

He shook his head. "Give her time. She's weak, very weak. She needs to sleep."

Wasn't that what she'd been doing all this time?

Gus had sat through the storm in the big purple chair. She would later say she hadn't slept a wink, but she had slept through most of the night, only waking to see if Abel had come into the kitchen to join her. He had not, and she had no idea where he was now. She woke up feeling stiff, hardly able to move. She looked out of the window. The sky was clearing, the wind pushing out the last gloomy clouds, threads of wispy grey reluctance trailing behind them, the sun laying delicate fingers of light on the day. The provincial flag flapped crisply on the pole outside the Hall, showing tatters already and up only a month. She looked at the clock.

My Godfrey! It was gone eight. She had slept in—in this awful chair.

The phone rang. It was Estelle, crowing. "Have you looked out your back window, Gus?"

To her chagrin, Gus had not.

When she did look, she was shocked, not so much by what she saw, as what she didn't see. Hawthorne Parker's A-Frame had disappeared. Gone. With the wind, she couldn't help thinking. A stream of cars was bumping up the corduroy road to the cape. The villagers were stopping their cars well back from the newly carved edge, nodding "I told you so," as they looked alternately at each other and down at the damage. The v-shaped piece of land had separated from the rest of the cape and Parker's house had gone sliding down into the yawning hole created by its collapse. It lay, pulverized—a scene of devastation everyone had long expected, but that was even more spectacular than they could have imagined.

One whole section of the roof seemed to be clinging to the raw exposed cape, the bottom of it buckled into the debris of the house below it. The other major section of the roof was propped up, in part, by the frame of the once majestic cathedral windows, their glass shattered and jagged, thrusting up into the sky out of the skeleton of the house, a jumble of smashed drywall, broken pieces of plywood, beams and joists full of nails, the ugly under-pinnings of what had once been a thing of beauty.

A ruin.

Like all ruins, it contained treasures—cracked, broken and buried, some of them soon unearthed, others hidden for years, even centuries, under the shattered dreams—Parker's dreams. The dreams of the people who'd built the house in this precarious place, on land that had never been lucky for anyone—not the settlers who had brutalized their bodies to clear it nor the unsuc-cessful farmers who followed. All built on sand where Harold MacLean, he of few words, said: "A rabbit would have starved."

The toilet, couch and coffee table had been tossed out onto the beach, where they made an unusual three-piece suite, all three having landed completely upright, as if carefully placed there. The king-size box spring had been tossed out of the collapsing house as well and came down, upended, leaning on part of the roof. Underneath the tent-like shelter was Jasmine's cage. She was in it. She had flown through the aperture at the peak of the house, just as it had shattered in two. She'd found her cage when the debris settled, squeezed into it and stayed there, her head tucked into a wing, hiding.

"Bound to happen." She'd heard it said so many times she began to memorize its cadence, and to mentally mimic the sombre tone in which it was stated. The villagers would have been gleeful if it hadn't been tragic. Few doubted that Hawthorne Parker would be found alive under the rubble.

A search and rescue team was just setting out. Jane Jamieson was off-duty but preparing to return to The Shores. She felt a kind of ownership of the sequence of events there. She told herself her interest was strictly professional.

"You can see why I thought it was her, why I assumed they were married." Hy was pointing at the black and white photo, the honeymoon picture of Parker and Cam's mother that Ian held in his hands.

"She looks exactly like Cam," he said.

"Exactly. Just the eyes, a bit different in the eyes." *A different colour? With black and white, it was hard to tell.*

He handed the photo back to her. "Her name was Claire."

"How did you find out about her? About Cam? Why didn't you tell me?"

"Various genealogical sites. I was just poking around when, there it was. Camilla was registered as Parker's daughter. I never got a chance to tell you. You were out on the water."

Ian had returned to the hospital with Cam's things late the previous evening and had been stranded there by the storm. The ferry was off its run.

Hy had not been allowed to see Cam after she had showed signs of life, but medical personnel had been in and out of the room all night. She didn't know whether that was good or bad. Someone from admissions—a Moira Toombs look-alike, scrawny, tight-faced and impeccably groomed, had just been to ask for Cam's Medicare card. Hy had stalled her, saying she needed to look through her belongings, and had begun to root around, guilt-free, in Cam's knapsack. She'd pulled out the photo and showed it to Ian. She found a key to the vanity and opened it. A pile of DVDs, laptop battery and a wallet containing a social security card, driver's license and credit cards—issued to Camilla Golightly. *Another name.*

And a birth certificate. Mother: Claire Golightly. Father: Hawthorne Parker.

"There you go." Hy passed it to Ian.

Near the bottom of the case was a brown manila envelope. Inside were several pieces of paper, folded together—two letters. One, a typewritten carbon, the old ink smudged by fingerprints, from Cam's mother, Claire, to Parker:

This is to let you know that your daughter was born today. Since you haven't answered any of my letters to you, I guess you no longer want to speak to me or see me. I bet Guillaume is behind that. I hope you will acknowledge Camilla as your daughter for her sake. You will know why I chose the name." It was signed: *"Love, Claire."*

The other letter was a response, from Parker to Claire.

I do not believe that anything that happened between us could possibly have created a child. I cannot believe she is mine. Not wishing to get into a long protracted argument on this point, I will, however, supply you with more than adequate funds for your child's support, in addition to what you already receive from me. Please do

not—either of you—communicate with me in future." It was signed,
"*Parker.*"

"What a prick," said Hy, handing the letter to Ian.

"Apparently not." Ian raised his eyebrows. "He claims they didn't really do it, or rather he tried but couldn't go all the way."

"Then how'd Cam happen?"

"Leakage, I guess. It only takes one plucky sperm."

Hy looked across the corridor to Cam's room.

"Well, she's sure a plucky one."

She pulled the last item out of the case. A diary. She flipped it open. The first entry read: *Haight Ashbury May 3, 1967. Astral gave birth to a baby girl today. We named her Claire, for the clarity of the moon and the stars and the sun....*

Hy kept her nose stuck in the journal for the next hour and Ian read along with her, living through the Summer of Love and the hippy lives of Camilla's maternal grandparents, Astral and Luther—a California beach babe turned mother earth and sky goddess and a white farm boy from Illinois, who'd renamed himself after his hero, Martin Luther King. They'd taken the surname of Golightly to signify their tread, softly, on the earth. Both Astral and Luther had written in the journal, including a litany of hallucinogenic drug experiences that stopped as suddenly as the Summer of Love, with a terse entry—"the Light of our Lives" had been taken from them by "The Man." Another document showed that it had been a woman from Child Protection who took baby Claire from their litter-filled home. Astral may have been an earth mother and sky goddess, but neither she nor Luther were homemakers. Their wall-to-wall floor covering was pizza boxes.

Slipped into the diary was a yellowed newspaper clipping from December 1967. Astral, Luther and two of their friends had died on a drugged-out road trip on a California freeway. Luther was the driver. The one survivor of the crash, a pleasant long-haired fellow called Speedboy, claimed Luther's last words were either:

"Beam me up, Scotty," or "Pass me that smoothie." He wasn't quite sure which, explaining he'd been "a bit out of it" at the time.

When they finished reading, Hy and Ian had a better idea of who Cam was. The fisherman blood of her Parker great-grand-father flowed in her veins and made it boil at the presence of a poacher. The blood of her love child mother, Claire, made her an idealist. Trace chemicals of the mind-altering substances Astral and Luther had ingested had been a time bomb inside Claire, the seed of the cancer that had killed her. In Cam, those same traces may have accounted for her extreme and offbeat dedication to her peculiar cause.

Ian had no idea, as he lost himself in Astral and Luther's alter-nate reality, that he was missing out on a drug bust in his own backyard.

Chapter Forty-Nine

Gus thought her old legs would never take her down to the shore and no one had offered her a lift. She said later that she hadn't wanted to gape, mouth wide open like a fish. She had done some of that privately, from her back stoop, staring at the empty sky where the A-frame had been for the past five years. She'd soon get used to seeing nothing there and be happy for it.

She went back inside to fetch the kitchen compost. It was pick-up day. For the first time in a week, she spotted the patchwork lobster square on the floor of the kitchen. *Too late to send it now. Was cotton compost? Must be.* She went out to the bin to see Toby lying on the ground in front of the green compost cart and Charlie, sitting on top of it. She threw the lobster square into the bin, the white quilt batting sticking out of the rip in the middle.

When she tried to move the bin, Toby growled, actually growled, at her. Charlie pecked at her hands and flew up onto the edge of the bin. He stuck his beak under the lid. Gus opened it. Charlie snapped up the lobster claw and dropped it to the ground. Gus picked it up. Toby grinned and wagged his tail. The crow's caw sounded, strangely, calm and satisfied. Gus examined the claw. There was something inside. *Not lobster meat.* She looked at the quilt block, the stuffing coming out of it, then back at the claw. She snapped it open. It was full of white powder.

Gus's experience was not vast, but she wasn't completely out of touch—she watched crime shows and soaps on TV. Drugs, she thought immediately. What kind of drugs, she didn't know, but they were drugs, no doubt about it. She forgot all about the compost cart. She left the lid open and Charlie had a feast. Not to be outdone, Toby jumped up onto the cart and flipped it over. He had a feast as well.

As Gus walked back to the house, she sniffed at the powder and got some up her nose. It was unpleasant. She wet a finger, stuck it into the powder and took a taste. *Well, it's not soda. Or salt. Or flour.* Her mouth and nose began to feel numb. She hoped she hadn't poisoned herself. She was sure of one thing—Charlie had brought her this claw "apurpose." That's why he and Toby had been kicking up such a fuss around the bin. She bet it came from Jared's cookhouse. Ian would know what it was.

Hy was standing at the open door of Cam's room. She still wasn't officially allowed in, but all night she'd been sneaking closer and closer to the door, watching Cam sleep. Now she was awake.

Cam tried to sit up, but Ed gently restrained her. Slowly, Cam's eyes focused on Hy and she smiled. Hy's knees buckled and Ian had to hold her up.

Hy grabbed him and held him tight. He could feel the full length of her up against him, every piece of her. His body came alive with the force of her embrace and the impact of what it might mean. He was about to kiss her, really kiss her, when—

"You can come in."

They broke apart. Ed beamed at them. Ian could have throttled him.

Cam's lips moved.

No sound came out.

They moved again. Hy could hear a light whisper. Ed put his ear to Cam's mouth, to catch what she said.

Then he laughed. "Hi to you, too."

But what Cam had said—her first word after waking from her long nightmare—was "Hy."

Ian put his arms around Hy again. She leaned back against him, smiling. It felt good, but the moment had passed.

Gus wasn't surprised when Ian didn't answer the phone. *Probably down at the cape.* She didn't leave a message. She never knew what to say to a machine. When she hung up the receiver, Gus was surprised to find she was holding a pencil, two paper clips, assorted elastic bands and a baby's comforter. For some reason she'd been absently organizing the kitchen junk drawer. There was stuff all over the counter, in piles—old cracker Jack prizes from the fifties, elastic bands, expired coupons, pennies. She didn't know why she'd started cleaning the drawer. She felt quite agitated, gritting her teeth and biting her lip. *My Godfrey, I've been drugged!* She didn't need Ian to tell her what that white powder was.

Ian left the hospital when he heard the morning news. The storm and the house going over the cape were the lead stories on every radio station in the Maritimes.

"*...Locals have long claimed that too many cottages are being built too close to the edge of the cape along The Island's North Shore. Today's tragedy may result in the setting up of a special commission to investigate proper placement of properties along the fragile cape system. Geologists say that the cape collapse should not have happened on The Island and scientists are keen to study the area. They claim the fabric of The Shores differs from the make-up of the rest of The Island.*"

Ian sniffed with contempt. He could've told them that.

Jared seized his first chance to get back into the cookhouse. He'd been partying and hungover since the night Guillaume died and had missed everything that had happened there. If he'd seen the police going in and out, he might have been a free man today. Instead, when The A came sliding down the cape and all attention was focused there, he slipped into the cookhouse to see what he could find—cocaine, if he was lucky—or unlucky, as it turned out.

Jared looked everywhere and, finally, in frustration, opened the freezer door and looked at the lobster claws and the specialty frozen foods. The police had ignored them, not of interest in what they'd decided was not a murder—just a nasty accident.

That gourmet food would bring a few bucks in Charlottetown, where they liked that kind of stuff. He grabbed a packing box from the storage area and loaded it up with Guillaume's culinary legacy—tails and claws and *Homard au Crack Farci*.

Jared's ignorance of what was in the claws would prove no defense.

Gus had seen Jared's truck heading for the shore. She knew where he was going, and she bet she knew what for. She invoked the Women's Institute phone chain. Gus phoned Estelle. Estelle phoned Moira. Moira phoned Olive—and on through the women of the Institute. All of them, except Hy, were soon huffing and puffing their way to the top of the Shore Lane. They came from every direction—from their houses, from the cape, from the Hall itself, where they were preparing for the Frasers' fiftieth anniversary lunch that day. The village children later said that they'd never seen old ladies move so fast.

They gathered just as, down by the cookhouse, Jared was tossing the box of illegal goods into the back of his Hummer.

"This is important," said Gus. " I don't have time to explain. Just follow me."

To their credit, they did precisely that. They walked in the mud and splashed through the puddles all the way down the Shore Lane just as Jared was starting up his engine. They made quite a sight. Most were already dressed in their Sunday best for the Frasers' party. It's just as well they were. Not because they were charged with conspiracy to intimidate a roadway—as they very nearly were—but because they, and their photo, became front-page news.

The Institute women stood en masse in front of the Hummer racing up Wild Rose Lane. Gladys led the pack. Her heft and weight attached her firmly to the ground. She thrust out her chin and clenched her fists. Her eyes burned with determination. If looks could stop a truck, hers would.

April Dewey was huddled in the back. It wasn't because she was shy, but because she was mortified at having left her apron on. She'd rushed out in the middle of making her blueberry muffins.

There they stood, twelve of the thirteen ladies of the Institute, dressed in their Sunday best. They didn't move, they didn't flinch, as the truck came bearing down on them, so sure were they of the righteousness of their cause and that the Lord was with them—so Gus told Hy later. It was the approach she'd used with Abel when he took her to church, the only place she'd drive with him, before he'd been relieved of his driver's license. She'd known before the authorities did that he was too old to be at the wheel.

Jared was not a murderer—in spite of what Gus might think—and he certainly wasn't a mass murderer. Just shy of tiny Madeline Toombs, with Annabelle towering behind her, Jared hit the brakes, did a one-eighty and then slid off the road. It was one of the few things to his credit—that he did not mow the women down.

Farmers, itching to get on the land, wouldn't allow their tractors in the saturated fields yet. But in Jared's truck went. Even though it was an off-road vehicle of near military capabilities, the local mud proved too much for the Hummer. It stalled in the thick sludge of Island clay.

Jared jumped out and tried to run, but the red mud sucked both shoes off.

By now every dog in The Shores was, for a change, earning its keep. Led by the valiant Toby, the dogs had circled the field, blocking off all possible escape routes, doing such a fine job of growling and making menacing movements you'd never have guessed that they spent most of their time sprawled out and semi-comatose. Even Newt was there, all twelve pounds of him, snarling in the direction of the man who used to be his master.

Lester Joudry couldn't believe his luck, following hard on the heels of what would become his award-winning photo of the Mercedes on the haystack. He'd been heading down to the shore to take pictures of the mess that had yesterday been a home, when he recorded another journalistic coup: the ladies, Jared, the truck and the dogs—the whole thing on video camera, which he sold to the local CBC TV news and with which he insisted on regaling the whole community at the local Christmas concert several years in a row.

Lester got some great shots on digital camera, too, including the group photo that was his third professional sale. *The Winterside Weekly* ran the photo on the front page under the headline: "Institute Women Sew Up Drug Case." Toby was front and centre, nearly obscuring tiny Madeline Toombs. You could barely make out a blueberry smudge on April Dewey's apron. The dogs hammed it up for the camera, baring their teeth. They looked threatening, but they were actually grinning.

Toby had the biggest grin of all.

Most of the women didn't know whether to smile for the photo or not, looking tense—as people do when they're told to pose in a group. There's no chance everyone will look good, but they could hope, at least, to look respectable. As it turned out, all of them, except April Dewey, looked as neat as a pin in her Sunday best.

They were glad of that.

It was all over by the time Ian boarded the ferry. Ben had been called in to restrain Jared until the Mounties got there. Constable Jamieson arrived and made the arrest. The police vehicle was waiting to get on the ferry when Ian got off. He waved at Jamieson as she drove on, never suspecting that Jared was slumped down in the back seat, handcuffed, sulking about the fact that he never got any breaks. Nor could Ian have guessed that the trunk of the police vehicle contained evidence for the drug charges Jared would face. When he did find out, it put him in a bad mood for days.

Ian drove along The Island Way, up and down the rolling landscape, until he topped the highest point of The Shores, the ocean spread out before him, as if, in that instant, it had been newly born. It happened every time at the top of this hill, the sudden display of breathtaking beauty, always beautiful, no matter the light, the weather or season. Today, its splendour was marred by devastation. As if on cue, the radio announcer described the sight in front of Ian's eyes, as he threaded his car down the curving incline toward home.

"The lobster fishery is in disarray. Thousands of traps have been thrown onto the shore by last night's wind and wave action. Fishermen will have to work hard—recovering, repairing, replacing and resetting the damaged traps. The Department of Fisheries and Oceans is considering extending the season to allow fishermen to recoup time and money lost as a result of this devastating storm."

There were at least a hundred lobster traps littering MacPherson's Shore.

There was a hole where The A should have been, a missing tooth on the horizon.

Ian sped up, drove down into the village and onto the cape. He parked at the top and looked down on the shore and the ruin below. Search and rescue volunteers were making slow progress. Unable to bring any heavy equipment over the delicate dune system, they were using muscle strength alone to work through the debris.

Would they find Parker dead—or alive?

Chapter Fifty

Cam was looking at the photograph of Parker and her mother, Claire. Her eyes were wistful. So were Hy's. She was nursing a sense of emptiness and regret. For Cam, there were so many emotions wrapped up in the photograph—love for her mother—maybe hate for her father, and longing for what might have been. When Hy looked at her own family photos—the bearded father and braless long-haired mother, the babe in arms, she felt nothing.

Nothing at all. She had no idea what parents are. Her only relationship with her parents had been one of absence. Their absence. She supposed she was meant to love them, but how could she love someone she didn't remember? Not like Cam.

"She does look exactly like you. Except for the eyes. Were they a different colour?"

Cam nodded. "Hazel. I've got Parker's eyes—and feet." Cam wiggled a set of webbed toes out from under the sheets.

Hy took the photo from Cam. Even though she knew it wasn't Cam, it still looked exactly like her.

"You can see how I was mistaken. And the ring. You wear the ring."

"Only as the Legionnaire."

"Oh yeah."

"She always wore it. I don't know why. I wear it to remind me of her."

Maybe, thought Hy. *Or maybe they both wore it for what might have been.*

Cam's hand grasped at her neck. Her eyes and mouth flew open.

"My pearls."

"Parker took them off you. I'll get them back." She couldn't tell Cam about Parker now. She didn't know anything anyway, aside from the news reports that the house had collapsed off the cape.

"Why would he do that?"

"Something to hold on to? To keep you alive? "

Cam looked perplexed, then shrugged.

"I took them to Cartier's in New York last year to sell them. Well, not really. It was more shock theatre. I'd been tailing him, planning how and when and if I would approach him. I saw him go into Cartier's. I was wearing them—I have since the day my mother died—but I took them off and shoved them in my pocket as if I didn't care about them. I came right up beside him. He did a double take. He knew that she was dead, but there I was, just like her—and the pearls confirmed who I was."

"But not that you were his?"

"Looking like my mother was no proof he was my father. All it would have taken were three little words to convince him."

"I love you?"

"No. Has your feet."

They laughed.

"Maybe it wouldn't have made a difference. Guillaume made sure Parker had nothing to do with me. He had this hold on him, right from the beginning. He pursued them on their honeymoon. He took this photograph. That's his shadow on Parker's face. Guillaume was always in the way."

"Not anymore."

"He's dead then? I didn't just dream it?"

Hy nodded.

"What happened?"

"Electrocution—by lobster stunner."

Cam smiled, a slow, satisfied smile.

"Good," she said. Her brow furrowed. "But it's too late. Without

Guillaume—who knows what might have happened? They might have had a marriage no better and no worse than the rest of the Parkers. They were only able to pump out one heir apiece. Ever think about that? Hawthorne may have been the only genuine one among them. He, at least, came out of the closet."

"I read the letters—your mother's and Parker's."

"What a prick he was. I never knew until I saw that letter. When she died, I read it, and began the LLL. I wanted to get to him, to get at the empire."

"The octopus."

"Yeah, the octopus. So you've been to the sites. You know what a big deal it is. If the Legion could infiltrate that—well, you can imagine."

"One lonely little Legionnaire could have major clout."

"Maybe. Maybe still."

If Parker were alive.

Hy thought about Claire's letter to him. "Where does the name Camilla come from?"

"My great grandmother's name. Camilla. Mother was grateful to her, in a way. The old lady was only serving her own purposes, but she encouraged the elopement. Neither of my parents told her about me, or that I'd been named after her. My mother was a free spirit, an independent spirit. She took the money from him, because she thought she'd earned it. But otherwise she didn't want anything to do with him—him or his family."

"But you? You did. You wanted something from Parker."

"I wanted him to see me, to know who I was."

Hy wondered how Cam would feel if Parker was dead—as he surely must be.

Ian turned off the ignition and got out of the car. The shore was a mess. There were easily a hundred traps on the beach. He counted twenty-three smashed up against the sea rock. Then there was The A. He trudged over and came within about fifteen feet of the rubble.

"Bound to happen. Bound to happen. Search and rescue. Search and rescue. Call 911. R-r-r-ring. Squawk. Hello? Hello? All aboard?"

Jasmine!—running through a whole repertoire of her latest hits. Her call for help came just in time. The workers were about to pull the box spring off the top of the debris. It might have collapsed and crushed her. Ian held up his hands and shook them frantically in a "no" gesture. The workers stopped, box spring perched on their shoulders.

The villagers peered down from above. *Parker? Had he found Parker?* The men watched, holding the bed still aloft, as Ian scrambled over the debris, exposed nails slashing his hands and knees. He hardly noticed. His body was vibrating relief. Jasmine didn't hesitate when he poked his finger forward. She jumped on it and stuck her claws right in. He winced and smiled at the same time. When he drew her out, she flew up on his shoulder—his new companion for life.

The rescue workers dropped the box spring, disappointed, but bemused.

A parrot? Here?

When Hy got home, the message light on her phone was blinking. Before she had a chance to check, the phone rang.

"Hy. Playing hard to get?" *Eldon.* She steeled herself for an unpleasant conversation, but it turned out to be a pleasant surprise.

"Look, I'm calling to say we'd like more of the same."

"What?"

"Brilliant, the cockroach and spider bits. Lots of response. Lots of great response. Thousands of hits. And customers have been coming in to buy lobster in defence of your attack on the industry.

Great stuff. Great stuff. Keep it up."

A slow smile spread across Hy's face. *What a jerk.* He was sounding just like the big boss himself, parroting Stewart Montgomery, right down to his repetitive manner of speaking. What did she care? She was off the hook. She promised plenty more of the same and rang off.

She put out her compost bin and her recycling bags and jumped in the truck to meet Ian down at the shore. As she reached the intersection of the Shore Lane, she saw that Moira's recycling bag had split open and papers were blowing out of it. She stopped her truck and picked one up.

It was a copy of the notice cancelling the lobster supper. There were a few more papers swirling on the wind around her. She picked up another and another. They were all the same. She left her truck running, burning up valuable fuel, as she followed the paper trail to Moira's house. The recycling bag contained several different versions of the invitation canceling the lobster supper.

Moira.

Moira had made them. To make me look bad. She'd never suspected because Moira didn't know how to use a computer—at least not until now. She had once asked Hy if she used "one of those things" to write. Moira disliked Hy so much, she'd learned to use one to get at her. Hy wondered if she should confront Moira.

No.

She simply stuffed a fistful of the papers in Moira's mailbox to let her know she'd been found out. Then she returned to her truck and drove down to the shore.

Jamieson was back, overseeing the rescue operation, unwilling to admit to herself her unprofessional fascination. It took some digging to find Parker's body. Hy and Ian watched silently as the workers lifted out his grandmother's painting. They had to pull it off Parker's body. They had to pry him off the jackal. He had been impaled to the painting by the pointy ears of the Egyptian dog of death. An aesthete killed by a lapse in taste.

Jamieson examined the body when they brought it out on the stretcher. In his pocket, she found the acid free paper, the pearls and the tiny gun, with the silver bullet still in its chamber. He'd never had a chance to pull the trigger. Climate change had gotten him first.

Looking at him, Jamieson did not feel much pity. She'd been wronged by him, she was sure, over the car incident. He'd used his power and wealth to make the charges go away. In her secret heart, she suspected a corrupt superior. Someday, she'd be in a position to prevent that sort of thing happening.

She was a very ambitious woman, but she wasn't without compassion. Jamieson looked at the paper, front and back, then beckoned to Hy and gave it to her, with the pearls.

"You'll know what to do with these." She didn't see any point in getting personal articles all tangled up in red tape. It was unlikely that there would be an inquiry into this…incident—or the chef's death. An initial forensic report showed the implement that had killed Guillaume St. Jacques was not equipped with an immersion protection plug to prevent electrocution, and the wiring of the cookhouse was not up to code—it was amateurish and dangerous. Add the saltwater pond and a concrete floor and it was a recipe for death. *A recipe for murder? Well, not premeditated.*

Hy took the paper and the pearls, thanked Jamieson and stood beside her as paramedics pulled a sheet over Parker's body. All his wealth had not protected him. She was safer in her little house and modest life than he had been with all his money.

Maybe there was justice on the wind.

They watched the paramedics carry Parker away.

"It's always about love," said Jamieson, with unusual feeling. "There's either too much of it. Or not enough."

She turned away to follow the body up to the lane and Hy

watched her with a grudging respect. Maybe Jamieson wasn't the cold fish she appeared to be.

Hy slipped the pearls into her pocket and looked at the paper. On one side it was Parker's handwritten will and testament, leaving everything to "my daughter Camilla," should she survive. If she did not, he had left it to her anyway—to the Lobster Liberation Legion, in her name. He never knew, thought Hy, that the LLL was only Cam.

On the other side, in his spidery scrawl:

To fear love is to fear life, and those who fear life are already three parts dead.

A suicide message? She knew that Jamieson had read it too. It didn't take anything away from the police woman's insight, but Hy did puzzle over what she'd said. *What exactly did she mean?*

Was it death—or life—that was always about love?

The storm that had levelled Parker's house had also capsized the Zodiac carrying Bill and Wendell into the cold waters of the Atlantic. They were officially recorded as missing. Sheldon found it very convenient—it avoided the inevitable difficulties he would face if they'd been arrested for stealing *The Crustacean*. Now if she would just die too, he was working on a way he could absorb the Parker holdings.

But she didn't die.

Hy brought the will, the pearls and the news of Parker's death to Cam. She strung the pearls around her neck and stroked them. She said nothing at first, then:

"I'm sorry for him."

Hy could still see Parker, his arms wrapped around Cam, rocking his daughter, and his grief, on the floor of the cookhouse. She felt sorry for him too.

"That's all?"

Anger flashed in Cam's eyes.

"That's a lot. How could I feel anything more? What did he ever do for me?"

"Well, he gave you life."

"An accident. Smart sperm, that's all."

"He felt bad at the end, Cam. Devastated."

"What about me? I had this hole in me all my life. I wanted a father." Tears welled in her eyes. "I found a pathetic little man wasting his love on that disgusting creature. How could I love him? The best I can do is feel sorry for him."

"And yourself."

Cam looked down, biting her lower lip, chewing on it. She was silent a moment, unable to speak.

"I hated him. Hated that I couldn't love him. Hated to be so full of hate."

Hy, helplessly: "It wasn't your fault."

"I know. I know that, but knowledge couldn't fill the hole. Neither could he."

"That's what you were after—with all this lobster stuff?"

Cam looked up.

"Maybe—partly."

"I'd say more than partly." Hy thought Cam's cause was clearly a public cry for private attention. *Attention from the father who had rejected her.*

When Hy left, Cam picked up the Halifax daily paper—another coup for Lester Joudry, who would never need to return to journalism school. Photographs of lobster traps smashed up and overturned under the headline: *Bottoms Up.*

"My work is done," she said, to no one in particular. She could keep her promise to Hy and leave The Shores. She had a few other plans, too, as the heir to two legacies: the Parker fortune and the Golightly tradition of treading softly on the earth.

It was wind—or a lack of it—that brought justice to Sheldon Coffin's door.

He was eating a breakfast of lobster crêpes, thinking about what a very, very rich man he was going to be, as soon as that annoying girl gave up and died. He was just considering a couple of clever, undetectable ways to have the company buy the company for him, when the butler brought in the newspaper.

The headline: *Lobster Heiress Cheats Death and the Taxman.*

There were two front-page pictures of Camilla—one in her lobster gear, the other, smiling from her hospital bed, the string of pearls around her neck. The cutline read:

"Camilla Golightly inherits entire estate—and lives to tell the 'tail.'"

Sheldon scanned the article quickly. It relayed why Camilla had gone by the name Samson, a name she told the press she had chosen from a set of suitcases belonging to her mother. Now she took on her hippie grandparents' assumed name and mission to tread lightly on the earth. Except for the vanity case and the pearls, Camilla planned to divest herself of the family baggage, including her massive inheritance. She would sell off the octopus and use the money for the renamed ALL—the Anthropodia Liberation Legion, dedicated to lobster and tarantula rights.

Sheldon began to choke.

He stood up, gasping, his eyes bulging from his head, staring at his wife in shock and pointing to his throat. He sputtered, gagged, coughed weakly, bent over and shook his head.

A vision of herself as a wealthy, unencumbered widow flashed before Stella's eyes. She could not have performed the Heimlich maneuver had she known it, she protested later to paramedics, then friends, then anyone who would listen, because she could never have got her arms around his barrel chest.

Many years later, when her widowhood, by distance of time, could no longer be considered tragic, she would paint an amusing picture of her helplessness in this scenario, asking dinner companions what she should have done. She couldn't have butted her head into his belly, surely. "Well, it might have worked," said one potential paramour dryly.

But she didn't even try.

It was left to Sheldon to attempt to deliver himself of the food lodged so securely in his throat. In a macabre joust with death, he grabbed hold of the high back of his chair and slammed his chest into it repeatedly to try to dislodge the offending comestible, fast robbing him of breath and life.

Stella waited a moment before she rang the bell.

If she didn't ring it, would that be murder?

She tinkled it lightly to summon assistance.

It didn't come in time.

Sheldon fell to the floor in a great lump—felled by a large piece of lobster meat. He was dead by the time the butler, who did know the Heimlich maneuver, arrived.

Revenge is sweet—and sometimes savoury.

Epilogue

The sun rose in splendour at The Shores all through the hot dry summer that followed. It blazed through the day, and set in triumph every night—shooting rays of colour across the big sky and endless water.

People were saying that they needed rain.

They were also saying that Hy was a hero, honking at her when they passed by her house, waving when they saw her walking in the village. They had embraced her as one of their own—once they saw the media coverage and heard talk of a medal of bravery, she became "our Hy." Gus and Ben and Annabelle organized a dinner in her honour at the Hall. The villagers didn't approve of the woman she'd saved, but she had gone—and wouldn't be bothering them again.

Cam had given up her laptop, her jeep, her cell phone—all modern devices. She'd sailed away on *The Crustacean* to an obscure island in the Indian Ocean, where she had finally learned to swim. She turned out to be a great little swimmer. All the Parkers were. Experts say webbed feet don't enhance swimming performance, but Cam knew better. They gave her thrust, like a lobster's tail. She'd had that confirmed by an Olympic coach who was first drawn to her feet—and then the rest of her. They were now living together in their tropical paradise. Hy received the odd letter or postcard, hopelessly outdated by the time it reached her, but it didn't matter. Just knowing that Cam was alive in the world was enough.

Hy, to her horror, had become an authority on lobster and

animal rights in the minds of the editors of various nature and geographical magazines after she published an article on Cam's lobster tickling. She was inundated with requests to write lengthy articles on that subject and others. It meant actual work.

She was also secretly writing *The Lobster Lover's Blog*. It was a deal with Cam to keep the ALL out of The Shores. She hadn't even told Ian.

Ian had tinkered endlessly with his computer to find out how Cam's blog had hacked in. He would never find out, even though he worked away at it for months when he wasn't working on his other projects: the Nightview Webcam and the GPS units now stationed at what was left of Vanishing Point.

Construction on the causeway was delayed and Ian had begun a petition demanding a "fixed link," but he wasn't getting many signatures. The villagers really didn't mind being isolated. It was the glue that kept them together as a community—and the tourists seemed to find the car ferry "charming" and "quaint." Ian got more exercise than signatures that summer, walking around town with his petition—his parrot on his shoulder almost everywhere he went. People smiled. He was well-liked and from away, which explained a lot.

Gus was starting a new quilt. She'd tried one of those fancy modern ones that are like a painting with fabric and texture. She took Canada's birthday as a theme. All she'd come up with was a red blob on a white background. She had tossed it aside. It lay on the floor for months, while she finished another nine-patch.

Jane Jamieson worked like a terrier chewing on a bone in her pursuit of the boat that had buzzed Cam and Hy. She did it on her own time. Her superiors had refused to allow her to follow a trail that wasn't there. She was vindicated when a Zodiac washed up on the Gaspé shoreline, minus Bill and Wendell.

In the process of her investigations, she managed to book Scott Bergeron and Tom McFee for poaching. They met up with Jared in jail and spent many hours talking about what they might do when they got out.

While Jared was locked up, The Byrds were using his cookhouse to incubate their nestlings—and their seedlings.

Everyone in the village went back to eating lobster without feeling guilty about it. Everyone, that is, except Hy. The rest of them boiled it as long as they wanted, threw it in head or tail first, as they wished, baked it or barbecued it, and gave only a passing thought to That Woman, who'd tried to change their ways.

Toby and Newt were in dog heaven through the long, beautiful days of summer, dashing along the shore with kids whose names they knew and who all knew theirs. Charlie got fat on the leftovers in the fast food packages he found tossed in ditches along the road. The villagers were busy from dusk to dawn, and beyond—bed and breakfasting tourists, fishing the waters, farming the land and mowing their lawns. Mostly, mowing their lawns.

Every morning through that long hot summer, and all the years of April Dewey's long life, the village air was scented, not just with the sweet grasses and tang of the ocean, but with the heavenly aroma of her blueberry muffins.

Her recipe remained her secret.

As for whatever was going on between Hy and Ian, speculation and gossip continued. So did the intimate dinners and the occasional overnights. They happened more frequently in the inflamed mind of Moira Toombs. Not even Hy's closest confidants, Gus and Annabelle, could figure it out. If anything was going on, the two remained firmly in the closet—together —doing Lord knows what—but they had not come out as a couple, even in their own minds.

Moira watched and waited through slanted, spiteful eyes.

Was it only friendship, or was it love?

Annabelle watched as well, her eyes soft and warm.

What is friendship, if not love?

Acknowledgements:

Thanks to all the friends who read early drafts and supported my efforts. Great gratitude to Janet Campbell, whose sincere interest and enthusiasm kept me going.

Thanks to Kirsten MacLeod for providing tireless and excellent advice on the manuscript, queries and synopses.

I'm deeply grateful to publishers Terrilee Bulger and Laurie Brinklow of The Acorn Press for liking "Lobster" and making the book happen, and to my editor Sherie Hodds, the italics and active verb wizard.

Thanks to coastal geoscientist Gavin Manson for informing me that cliffs in PEI don't act the way I wanted them to, and then telling me to go ahead anyway – considering that The Island of the book is a slightly altered PEI.

Thanks to lobster fishers Stan and Margo Pickering for filling me in on what they do, and to all the fisherman of the North Shore for providing, year after year, that evocative sight of the boats heading out on Setting Day – and the lobsters they come back with.